The Shadow Saga

Of Saints and Shadows
Angel Souls and Devil Hearts
Of Masques and Martyrs
The Gathering Dark
Waking Nightmares

ABOUT THE AUTHOR

CHRISTOPHER GOLDEN is the award-winning, *New York Times* bestselling author of such novels as *Of Saints and Shadows, The Myth Hunters, The Boys Are Back in Town,* and *Strangewood*. He has also written books for teens and young adults, including *Soulless, Poison Ink,* and the *Body of Evidence* series of teen thrillers. His current work-in-progress is a graphic novel trilogy collaboration with Charlaine Harris.

A lifelong fan of the 'team-up,' Golden frequently collaborates with other writers on books, comics, and scripts. He has co-written three illustrated novels with Mike Mignola, the first of which, *Baltimore, or, The Steadfast Tin Soldier and the Vampire*, was the launching pad for the Eisner Award-nominated comic book series, *Baltimore*. With Amber Benson, he co-created and co-wrote the BBC online animated series *Ghosts of Albion*.

As an editor, he has worked on the short story anthologies *The New Dead, The Monster's Corner,* and *21st Century Dead*, among others, and has also written and co-written comic books, video games, screenplays, and a network television pilot. The author is also known for his many media tie-in works, including novels, comics, and video games, in the worlds of *Buffy the Vampire Slayer, Hellboy*, and *X-Men*, among others.

Golden was born and raised in Massachusetts, where he still lives with his family. His original novels have been published in more than fourteen languages in countries around the world. Please visit him at www.christophergolden.com

THE GRAVES OF SAINTS

A Peter Octavian novel

CHRISTOPHER GOLDEN

**SIMON &
SCHUSTER**

London · New York · Sydney · Toronto · New Delhi

A CBS COMPANY

First published in Great Britain by Simon & Schuster UK Ltd, 2013
A CBS COMPANY

The right of Christopher Golden to be identified as the author of
this work has been asserted by him in accordance with sections 77
and 78 of the Copyright, Designs and Patents Act, 1988

1 3 5 7 9 10 8 6 4 2

Simon & Schuster UK Ltd
1st Floor
222 Gray's Inn Road
London WC1X 8HB

www.simonandschuster.co.uk

Simon & Schuster Australia, Sydney
Simon & Schuster India, New Delhi

A CIP catalogue record for this book is available from the British Library

ISBN: 978-0-85720-964-1
Ebook: 978-0-85720-965-8

This book is a work of fiction. Names, characters, places and incidents are either
a product of the author's imagination or are used fictitiously. Any resemblance
to actual people living or dead, events or locales, is entirely coincidental.

Typeset by Hewer Text UK Ltd, Edinburgh

Printed and bound by CPI Group UK (Ltd), Croydon CR0 4YY

IN MEMORY OF DR GEORGE J. MARCOPOULOS
Gentleman, teacher, scholar, and friend

ACKNOWLEDGEMENTS

Much gratitude and appreciation to my editors, Maxine Hitchcock and Sally Partington, and my agents, Howard Morhaim and Caspian Dennis, for all of their work on my behalf. Thanks also to all of the folks at S&S UK, in particular the art department for the sweet covers. As always, love and thanks to my wife, Connie, and our children, Nicholas, Daniel, and Lily, as well as to the friends and family who keep me sane. You know who you are. Finally, an extra special thanks to Nancy Danos for her keen eye and input. After all this time she knows these books better than I do.

1

September 21

Brattleboro, Vermont

The witches gathered in a circle, as sleek and somber as a conspiracy of ravens. Outside that ring was another, made up of friends and employees of Summerfields Orchard, but they kept their distance and observed a respectful silence, all of them watching the witches. Peter Octavian stood perhaps furthest of all from the circle, practically at the edge of the hillside clearing, at the center of which stood a single apple tree, remarkable for the leaves and fruit which blossomed from the branches as if summer were still in full swing instead of coming quickly to a close.

The witches began a ceremonial chant that seemed half incantation and half prayer, and Octavian studied them closely. They had come from all over New England to participate in a joyous occasion – the autumnal equinox – and the various rituals that went along with it for people of their beliefs. Those rituals were still to come but today they were attending to a different sort of ceremony: the funeral of one of their own.

Several of the witches wore robes, preferring perhaps to keep to the old traditions, but most were dressed in ordinary clothing, snug in sweaters and wool coats. When the breeze shifted just right, the wind carried the scent of cinnamon and cider up the hill from the shop in the barn, where bakers were making donuts for visitors. But no visitors were being allowed up onto the hillside this morning. Not just yet.

The chanting witches held their hands out in front of them, fingers stretched toward the soil. The stance gave them a stiff, formal pose, and Octavian was reminded again of black birds. Once upon a time, a cluster of ravens had been called an *unkindness*, and the word felt appropriate. Though the witches had convened this gray morning for only the most generous and blessed of purposes, it was fate's unkindness that they should have to be here at all.

No rain fell, but clouds hung low above the orchard, dark and pregnant with storm. Octavian would have preferred it if the rain and wind had come already, nourishing and cleansing this small valley on the outskirts of Brattleboro, Vermont, and sweeping away the ominous aura that filled the air with the threat of menace. Keomany Shaw had died to keep chaos and entropy from enveloping the world. The battle had been won, the casualties counted, and order restored. So why did it feel like the storm had yet to break? It was more than the clouds, Octavian knew that. As much as he grieved for Keomany, his skin prickled with the certainty that there was worse yet to come.

The earthwitches raised their hands to the sky as if to part the clouds, but the heavens were indifferent. Together the women intoned a new prayer, commending the spirit of their sister to the earth and the sky. There were seventeen of them in the circle, including Cat Hein and Tori Osborne, the married couple who owned Summerfields, and who had been Keomany's closest friends. The others had arrived in a steady trickle over the past couple of days, in preparation for the equinox ceremonies that the earthwitches would be hosting at the orchard.

'Never saw this coming,' the man standing beside Octavian said in a low voice.

Octavian studied the thin, sixtyish man with the round glasses and the wispy white beard, trying to recall his name. *Patrick*. Tori had introduced him as the husband of one of the earthwitches, which Octavian had thought interesting. A couple of the others had arrived with companions who were not witches, but for the most part they had come alone or in the company of other witches. Either they were single, or they'd left their non-witch partners at home.

'You knew Keomany?' Octavian asked quietly, glancing at the circle of witches to be sure the whispered exchange would not disturb them. There were perhaps twenty other people outside the ritual circle, and they were all observing in silence.

Patrick smiled sadly. 'We all knew her and loved her. If any of us ever needed proof that Gaea loved us, that the earth mother was still with us, all we had to do was look at Keomany. She'd been chosen, you know? It just radiated from her.'

If he hadn't known better, Octavian would have scoffed at the suggestion that the ancient sentience of the earth itself paid any attention to the human world, or that it had touched Keomany Shaw, given her elemental gifts not bestowed upon others. But he had seen those gifts himself, and he knew the bond that Keomany had forged with the elements. With the earth.

'No doubt about it,' Octavian said, and this seemed to satisfy Patrick, who nodded and said no more.

In the midst of the witches, Cat stepped forward. Tall and curvy, she reminded Octavian of the Rubenesque representations of fertility goddesses in classical art, though her stylish burgundy sweater and black jeans belied the comparison. Cat's face was lined with tears as she reached for the wine bottle in Tori's hands – the wine bottle Octavian had brought back from Massachusetts with him. The wine bottle that contained all that he had managed to collect of Keomany's ashes.

As if she could sense his attention – and perhaps she could – she shot Octavian a withering glance. Though he had once saved her from a very painful death, she had no affection for him. Now, in the wake of Keomany's death, dislike had turned to venom.

Tori handed the wine to her wife, bringing Cat back into the moment. She accepted the bottle and the couple shared a lingering look of sadness. Tori wiped away her own tears and then pressed both hands to her chest as though to quiet her thundering heart. Cat gave Tori a small, sorrowful smile and uncorked the bottle.

Octavian had been surprised when the witches had told him they were going to scatter Keomany's ashes this morning. He had assumed that with the equinox so close, and given the renewal it represented, they would want to wait until then to perform this ceremony. But Keomany had purified the soil in this clearing and had planted the seed of this lone, remarkable apple tree herself, using her earth magic to grow it from seedling to maturity in a matter of minutes. They wanted Keomany to be a part of this soil before the equinox so that she could be purified with it, and grow and have her spirit renewed, joined with Gaea forever.

Who was Octavian to argue?

After all, in the eyes of the witches, he was the man who'd gotten Keomany killed.

It had begun, if Octavian understood correctly, right here in this clearing. Keomany had been using her earthcraft to purify the soil, but when she had reached down into the world and tapped into nature, she had been struck by a wrongness so profound that it had shocked her into unconsciousness. Chaos had infected the world and begun to spread, and Keomany had been able to pinpoint ground zero of the blossoming infection. Several times in the past, Octavian had drawn her into danger in order to combat some supernatural threat, but she had always come back alive. With the crisis in Hawthorne, Massachusetts – the waking of an ancient Chaldean chaos deity called Navalica – it had been Keomany who had sounded the alarm, and who led the charge. The moment she had returned to consciousness, she had called Octavian.

But the witches still blamed him. He had argued the point, but now, as he watched Cat sprinkle Keomany's ashes into the soil amidst the circle of witches, he admitted to himself that he bore at least some of the blame. The first time Keomany had faced real evil, Octavian had been drawn into the fight because she was an old friend of the woman he loved. But after that crisis had passed, Octavian could have kept Keomany out of it. He had enough magic of his own; surely there had been no need to keep putting Keomany in danger.

He frowned and dropped his gaze to the prickly grass underfoot, his own sorrow beginning to break down the defenses he'd erected to hold it back.

No, he thought. *It was her fight, too. With her connection to the earth, she wanted to be a part of it.*

And that was true, as far as it went. After all, Keomany had called him, this last time. But there had once been measures in place to prevent things like the awakening of Navalica, and Octavian was partly to blame for the fact that those measures were no longer functioning. He had helped to tear down the church's magical hierarchy in order to save the Shadows – the beings most people called vampires. But only in the past couple of years had he begun to fully appreciate the consequences. There were many Hells, and within them lived unimaginable creatures who would have loved to bring the human world to ruin, or make a feast of them, if only there weren't barriers keeping them out.

Without the magic to refresh those barriers – magic no one alive knew how to perform – this dimension's defenses were failing, and humankind was entirely unaware of it. Fortunately, for quite some time, nor had the denizens of the thousand Hells that bordered the human world. But when Navalica woke, it had been like a beacon shining out across the dimensions. Octavian and his allies had captured and imprisoned her, cutting off that beacon. But he knew that some of the demons and monsters would realize what it had meant, or would shamble vaguely in its direction and find that walls which had once kept them out had now fallen.

Keomany was dead. As awful as that was, and as good a friend as she had been, she would not be the last casualty. Things had been set in motion now that he would not be able to stop without a great deal of help. But his first duty had been to Keomany, to take her ashes home so that the people who loved her could mourn her properly. He owed her that, at least.

As for the rest, he decided it would be best not to mention any of it to the witches. Cat and Tori and their friends, though they practiced earthcraft and had some small skill with such magic, had only a fraction of the elemental power that had come so naturally to Keomany. Even if they hadn't disliked him, and blamed him for Keomany's death, Cat and Tori wouldn't have been able to help him.

He had done all he could for Keomany, and for the witches
of Summerfields. The time had come for him to be reunited
with the woman he loved. Nikki Wydra was a musician and had
achieved a certain amount of success. She had seen her share of
impossibilities become real, had faced darkness and horror
with courage, but she wanted a simpler, more ordinary life.
Octavian did not look forward to having to explain to her what
had happened with Navalica . . . and what it meant. But after
the events of the past few days, he longed to have her in his
arms again.

Soon enough, he thought, for it appeared that the witches
were nearly done with their ceremony. A light breeze began to
eddy some of Keomany's ashes across the clearing, but they
blew toward the base of the apple tree at its center, and that
seemed only right.

Distant thunder rolled across the sky, the storm getting
closer. It seemed the ritual had been timed perfectly, for the
clouds were darkening overhead as if it were dusk rather than
morning. The witches came together around Cat and Tori, all
talking amongst themselves, embracing and wiping away tears.
After a few moments, several of them broke away from the
group and began to talk with some of the other mourners who
had gathered there. A young hipster couple who worked at
Summerfields made their way into the circle to join Cat and
Tori, the guy gesturing first to make sure they were welcome.
Tori hugged them, but Cat only smiled sadly and turned to gaze
at the apple tree, with its fruit hanging heavy and ripe with
promise.

Octavian turned away. There was nothing more for him here.
He hadn't been able to reach Nikki since leaving Hawthorne the
previous day. Tonight she was due to perform in Philadelphia, so
he knew that she might be too busy with rehearsal and sound

check or a dozen other things to respond to the two messages he'd left. But he had also sent her a text asking her to let him know she was all right, and her lack of response had him worried. He imagined it was something trifling – that she'd lost her phone or dropped it in the toilet – but as soon as he was back in his rental car and on the way to the airport, he intended to ring her hotel in Philly. She would be grief-stricken to learn of Keomany's death, and heartbroken that she'd missed this ceremony, the only sort of funeral her old friend would have. But there were other things Octavian and Nikki needed to discuss, like how to make sure the rest of the world didn't end up in ashes, like Keomany.

'You taking off?'

Octavian looked up to see Patrick studying him through those round spectacles.

'I've got a plane to catch.'

'Without saying goodbye to your friends?' Patrick said, nodding back up toward the witches in the clearing.

Octavian glanced at them, saw Cat and Tori holding hands and talking to a small cluster of people.

'Keomany was my friend,' he said, surprising himself with his honesty. 'Trust me, they'll be happier when I'm gone.'

Even as he spoke, Cat seemed to sense the weight of his regard. Wiping a tear from her cheek, she glanced over at him. Her eyes narrowed and her lip curled up in a snarl. Without a word to the others, she broke away and started down the slope toward him. Patrick wisely retreated.

'You son of a bitch,' Cat said, jaw so tight she seemed to bite on the end of each word.

Octavian cocked his head slightly, not sure how to proceed. Past Cat, he saw Tori making swift excuses to their friends and hurrying after her wife. But not even she was going to be able to put out the fire he saw in the earthwitch's eyes.

'Something I can do for you, Cat?' he asked.

He saw the punch coming. It would have been easy to dodge the blow, or simply to stop her. With a gesture, he could have frozen her in place or knocked her backward. But he could feel the fury and grief pouring out of her and he knew that if he let her connect, it would at least give her a moment's catharsis. And in the back of his mind, he figured he deserved it.

Cat hit him so hard that his neck snapped to the side and he turned, staggering a few steps before he was sure he wasn't going to fall down. He'd heard and felt one of her fingers break on impact, but these witches were capable of healing that quickly enough.

'What the hell do you think you're doing?' Tori shouted, grabbing Cat by the arm to keep her from further violence.

'That it?' Octavian asked. 'Or is there more?'

Fuming, Cat tried to pull away but Tori held her tight.

'That's enough,' she said.

'Keomany's dead because of him!' Cat said, never taking her eyes off of Octavian.

'Baby, listen to me,' Tori pleaded, reaching up to touch Cat's face, turning her so that they were eye to eye. 'You were there. Keomany called him. She knew what the stakes were every time she walked into one of these situations with him. You want to hit someone, you want to scream. I know, 'cause I feel the same way. But Peter loved her, too. He lost her, too.'

Cat began to sob and Tori pulled her into an embrace. It should have looked awkward, with Cat so tall and Tori so petite, but they fit together perfectly, as lovers always do. Octavian wanted to walk away, but whatever Cat needed to help her grieve right now, hating him was part of it, and he wanted to make sure she'd said what she needed to say.

As Cat held her and wept, Tori whispered in her ear, but not so quietly that Octavian couldn't hear.

'Think of how long he's been alive, and how many people he's lost. Almost everyone he's ever loved is gone. Some of them died right in front of him. You want to punish him, baby, but there's no way you can make him suffer any more than he has already, just by surviving this long.'

Octavian flinched and took a step back. Noticing the movement, Tori glanced up at him. Her copper eyes held no apology, only pity.

'You should go.'

There were things he wanted to say, small comforts and reassurances, but he knew if he spoke now it would be to ease his own heavy heart. Instead, he glanced once at the others gathered around the clearing on the hill – most of them studiously minding their own business – then he nodded to Tori, turned, and started back down toward the barn and the parking lot beyond.

At the bottom of the hill, people were buying apples and early-season pumpkins while their children were drinking cider and eating fresh-baked donuts at picnic benches and begging for a hay ride. But as Octavian passed amongst them, the first raindrops began to fall, and the sky rumbled with thunder, still distant but coming closer.

The storm had arrived.

The rain drove the mourners indoors. Most of them abandoned the orchard quickly, though the witches were not so intimidated by the storm. The elements were the glory of nature, and the earthwitches both worshipped and took their magic from them. But still they were only human, and on a day of gray sorrow, none of them had any desire to be drenched in cold September rain.

Tori and Cat were the last to leave the clearing, the last to stroll down through the apple trees toward the barn below. Their earth-craft was nothing compared to Keomany's, but they had magic enough to keep the rain from touching them for a few minutes. With the storm coming in so quickly and so unexpectedly, most of their customers would be leaving, and so would their friends. Tomorrow they would all gather to celebrate the equinox together, but today Tori and Cat wanted only to return to their home in the grounds of the orchard, make strong coffee, and wrap themselves in a warm blanket, trying to forget that Keomany would never return to the bedroom they had given her in their own house.

Back on the hill, rain pattered the leaves of the trees and the wind picked up, shaking their branches. Overripe apples came loose and fell to the ground, rolling before being caught in the ragged grass or in ruts in the earth. Lightning flashed, turning the sky white, and the thunder that followed it shook the hills and echoed along the small valley.

A large, perfect apple fell from the new tree in the clearing the witches had left. It did not roll. Strange winds worked against the gusts of the storm, swirling along the newly rejuve-nated soil of the clearing, picking up dirt and grass and stones and all of the ashes that the earthwitches had sprinkled onto the ground during their ceremony. Small shoots worked their way up through the earth, roots that seemed to clutch at the apple, plunging through its skin and flesh in search of the seeds within, inspiring them to send out shoots of their own. Impossibly.

The ash and soil and other detritus of the autumn harvest spun about in that unusual wind, collecting around apple and root, growing and taking shape, sculpting and building something new.

For Gaea was threatened, and she would not weep for her daughter.

*

New York City, New York

Charlotte still hadn't quite gotten used to waking up in daylight. It shouldn't have been that difficult; only seven months had passed since the sadist who called himself Cortez had turned her into a vampire. She remembered life before death very well. But in the time she had spent with Cortez's coven before running away, he had gotten into her head in a way that no one ever had before.

Really, there were no such things as vampires – at least not in the way the movies had always portrayed them. They were blood-drinkers, yes, and they had evil in them, but their true nature was much more complex than that. Vampires were human beings who had been afflicted with a kind of supernatural infection before being killed, a taint that altered them on every level. They were both demonic and divine. 'Angel souls and devil hearts' was the phrase that had been popularized to explain their origins. When one such creature made another, they were resurrected from death as something entirely new, beings capable of shifting their flesh on a molecular level, becoming virtually anything they desired.

For centuries, calling them Shadows, the church had attempted to eradicate them. When that did not work, the Vatican sorcerers responsible for hunting them began to capture the Shadows instead, using magic and torture to alter their thoughts and memories. Many of the vulnerabilities that popular lore attributed to vampires had been invented to weaken them, lies implanted in these Shadows to be released into the world, and soon enough, the Shadows believed that if they went about in daylight the sun would burn them to ash. They began to fear the cross, and to accept themselves as the creatures of evil the church portrayed. These fabricated limitations made them easier to hunt and kill, and soon, their numbers dwindled and they retreated to the darkness for safety, becoming what the church had named them.

Vampires.

With a handful of allies, Peter Octavian had changed that. He had led them to an understanding of their true nature, to realize that they were not simply monsters. The Vatican sorcerers had tried to exterminate them once and for all in a single, climactic battle in Venice, but the Shadows had defeated and destroyed them, the entirety of the truth revealed to the world through a live camera feed from the site. The church had collapsed as a result, and from that day forward, the Shadows had been trying to live side by side with humanity.

Most of them.

Some had no interest in coming out of the darkness. They were unwilling to give up the blood and violence and the hunting of humans. These creatures embraced the name 'vampire' and all that it entailed. They wanted to be the soulless leeches portrayed in folklore, to sleep in grave dirt and kill and feed indiscriminately. But now that the existence of vampires was public knowledge, preying on humanity was more difficult than it had been in earlier ages. International laws were in place. The United Nations not only had Shadows advising them, they established a global Shadow Justice System that required all Shadows to sign their names to a Covenant outlining a code of behavior they swore to follow. Those who refused to sign were labeled rogues, and could be imprisoned for their refusal. The worst of them, the ones who still called themselves vampires, were hunted by a special unit called Task Force Victor.

Charlotte didn't want to be hunted. She had never wanted to be a Shadow or a vampire or anything other than what she had been, a San Diego beach bum who dreamed of being an actress someday. Then her nineteenth birthday had rolled around, and she had found herself dragged into the back of a van by two men who had beaten and raped her, and who had liked the way she fought them enough to bring her home to their master. Cortez had nursed her back to health and then he had turned her and indoctrinated her into the life of a predator. If she closed her eyes now, she could still remember the way her first taste of human blood had made her feel, the rush of pleasure and power and primal celebration. She could practically still taste it on her tongue, and it made her shiver every time she thought of it.

She had run away from Cortez, thinking every moment that he would find her and kill her, that she would awake with him standing over her bed, or turn a corner on the street in Manhattan and see him standing on the sidewalk, still as a statue while the crush of pedestrians flowed around him. His brown eyes and his long, proud nose and thin goatee should have combined to make him handsome, but Cortez only looked cruel. Her fear of him prevented her from ever going home or trying to get in touch with any of her friends from San Diego, so she had started over in New York, hiding from Cortez but also hiding from the rest of the world. Since she had not signed the Covenant, she was a fugitive. A rogue vampire. One of the reasons that she had come to New York in the first place had been to register with the UN, but days had passed, and then weeks, and then months, and she had never gotten up the courage. They would want to know where she came from – who had made her – and that would mean she would be questioned by Task Force Victor.

Meeting Peter Octavian had changed everything.

Charlotte had found herself inexplicably drawn to a small town on the north shore of Massachusetts, a place tainted by chaos which had been growing exponentially. Octavian could have killed her the moment he found out what she was, but he had heard her out – he had trusted her – and she had helped him to take down the ancient chaos queen, Navalica. But Octavian had made it clear that stopping Navalica hadn't put an end to the danger the world was in. The chaos bitch had metaphorically planted a flag and tried to claim the world, and Octavian said that other things – demons and the like – would know it. They'd feel it. And they would come to try to finish the job that she had started.

As a young girl, Charlotte had had dreams. Now, for the first time in her life, she had a purpose. But if she was going to help Octavian, she had to make sure Task Force Victor wasn't going to kill her on sight.

'Shit,' she rasped, holding up a hand to block the wan morning light seeping through her blinds.

A glance at the clock on the nightstand told her it was going on ten a.m. She hadn't been so completely brainwashed by Cortez that she had actually believed the sun would burn her to cinders. The whole world knew the history of Shadows, so when he turned her into a vampire, he couldn't make her afraid of the daylight. The closest he could come was making her afraid of him. Still, four months of sleeping during the day and shying away from the sun had taken its toll. She stayed up well into the night and dozed through most mornings.

Not today. Charlotte wouldn't be going back to her job at the theatre, but she had an appointment to keep.

She threw back the covers and slid to the edge of her bed, sitting up and burying her face in her hands.

'Oh, shit,' she mumbled again into her cupped palms.

Crazy powerful as she was – and there were times when, despite the horror of how she had become like this, she reveled in it – the idea of walking up to the UN Shadow Registry Office scared the hell out of her. The typical person off the street would have no idea how to even hurt her, never mind kill her, but those guys had to have figured out half a dozen ways to obliterate vampires by now.

She felt sick just thinking about it, but Octavian had promised her that she would be all right. He had coached her on what to say and how to approach them, and had asked her to call him as soon as it was done so that he could tell her where he wanted her next. In her human life, Charlotte had never liked authority, always bristling when anyone tried to tell her what to do. But she was joining Octavian's fight and she wanted to help him. He would know best how to use her.

A tiny smile ticked up the edges of her mouth. Then she shook her head, chuckling softly. *No naughty thoughts*, she chided herself. She had always liked older men, and Octavian looked maybe thirty-six or so, but the guy had been hundreds of years old even before he'd been to Hell. No, there'd be none of that. *Not that he'd even try*, she thought. *To him, you're a kid*.

She stood and stretched. Glancing at herself in the mirror above her bureau, she wrinkled her nose in distaste. *Looking like this, even dirty old men aren't gonna give you a second glance.*

Charlotte shot her reflection the middle finger and laughed as she headed for the bathroom. She turned the water up as hot as she could stand it, soaped and shampooed, then spent another ten minutes just letting the heat get into her flesh and down to her bones. When she stepped out, she toweled off, blew dry her wavy, fox-red hair, and brushed her teeth. Padding back into her bedroom, she put on a pair of gray skinny jeans and a red, long-sleeved top with pencil stripes. She pulled on her beat-up Timberland boots and slipped into a wool jacket that she only wore for special occasions. She didn't feel clean; since the first time Cortez had made her kill a human being for blood, she had never felt clean. But the clothes were laundered and warm and comfortable and this time when she glanced in the mirror, she thought she looked damn good.

If she was about to be arrested or killed, at least she'd look pretty.

The thought made her laugh as she turned and went to the door, making sure she had her keys, even though she couldn't be sure she'd ever come back.

When Charlotte opened the door, the vampires were waiting for her in the hall.

2

New York City, New York

Charlotte knew what they were on sight. Two men in long black coats with the collars turned up, wearing black gloves and wide-brimmed black hats and mirrored sunglasses on a cloudy late September morning? It stunned her that they'd been able to move around New York City without arousing suspicion, but here they were in her apartment building, on her doorstep, and she had no doubt that Cortez had sent them.

Skittish, one hand still on the knob of her open apartment door, she glanced from one to the other, seeing nothing in their mirrored sunglasses, not even herself.

'I'm not going back,' she said, mustering up enough courage to raise her chin and stare boldly at them.

One of the vampires smiled, showing pearlescent fangs. 'He doesn't want you back.'

The two reached into their jackets, hands vanishing into folds of fabric with inhuman quickness and reappearing with guns. Before the first glint of the metal gun barrels showed in the dim light of the overhead fixture, Charlotte moved. She pushed back into her apartment and swung the door closed behind her with all her strength, not bothering to slow down to attempt to bar their entry. Their entrance was not in question. Cortez might bow to vampiric traditions, encourage his coven to return to the monstrous predators of legend, but he wasn't a fool – his children did not need an invitation to come through the door.

Bullets came first, splintering wood and plunking into walls and furniture and shattering glass. Charlotte dived to the floor as the first of the shots seared the air above her, transforming even as she landed on the carpet. She had adapted to the true abilities of the Shadows, but it was still easiest for her to metamorphose into one of the standard forms, and by instinct she chose mist. Her flesh and bone and clothing dissipated in an instant, as if the impact of her body on the floor caused her to turn to smoke.

Mist would be best, because she had a feeling Cortez's killers weren't firing ordinary bullets at her. They wouldn't be that foolish. A bullet would do nothing to a vampire or Shadow but irritate them. But from everything she'd been taught, Task Force Victor had another sort of bullet, one infused with a toxin that inhibited the molecular alteration that allowed Shadows to shapeshift. That was how they caught rogue vampires . . . how her kind could be killed. Now, somehow, Cortez had gotten his hands on some of the UN's ammo.

The door split in two as the first vampire crashed through it, and the black-clad figure glanced around the apartment, those mirrored sunglasses making him look even less human than he was. As mist, Charlotte churned toward the window above the breakfast table in her tiny kitchen, knowing he would notice her any moment. The second vampire slid fluidly into the apartment, distracting the first for just an instant, giving Charlotte a fraction of a second to solve a problem.

As mist she had no mass, and the window was closed up tightly.

A ripple went through the white mist and she drew herself together, resculpting flesh and bone at the speed of thought. Copper-red hair, wool coat, beat-up Timberlands, she crashed through the glass five stories above 2nd Avenue. One of the vampires shouted and both guns coughed again, but by the time the bullets reached her she was mist again, slipping downward toward the street. She was half a block from 50th Street, maybe half a dozen from the UN. The Shadow Registry Office was on 46th, even closer, if she could just get there.

The gunfire stopped. They knew she'd run for it and that meant they had to get down to the street, but Cortez had trained them too well to be nocturnal creatures. These fools were so dedicated to ancient legend, to being the nightmares that had terrified humanity for eons, that they had themselves *believing*, just like old times. Without the cover of their creepy black ensembles, they'd burn, which meant they had to be damned careful.

Charlotte couldn't afford to be careful.

Transforming into a crow, she let out a caw and stretched out her wings, wheeling into the narrow alley that separated her building from the one next door. With a quick glance to make sure she wouldn't be observed, she shifted again, alighting upon the ground as herself and shuddering slightly, getting used to her own form. Shifting so much in such a short time always made her true body feel a little foreign at first. She had never liked shapeshifting; it made her feel less human, reminded her she was a monster.

A service door clanged open in the alley and she spun toward the sound, mind whirling. No way they'd gotten down from her floor this quickly. Charlotte blinked when she saw the vampire emerge into the alley. She was tall and thin, with long blond hair beneath the same black hat the others wore, and Charlotte recognized her right off. Annabel, one of Cortez's wives.

Idiot, she thought. She'd never considered there might be a third.

In her frustration, she didn't move quickly enough. The gun was already in Annabel's hand. Charlotte felt the pain sear her chest as the bullet struck, even before she heard the shot. A wave of nausea swept her immediately and she knew that her guess had been correct – Cortez had the toxin. She didn't know what the UN had officially named it, but vampires called it Medusa, because it effectively turned them to stone.

Stone.

She wasn't a statue. She could move. She couldn't shapeshift but she could run, and though the sky was white with thin clouds, the sun was strong behind them. Staggering backward, she practically spilled out onto the sidewalk, cursing herself for her foolishness. If she had just stayed a crow she could have flown the distance to the Shadow Registry in a couple of minutes, but she preferred to be herself, to stay on two feet, and she'd thought she had left the vampires behind.

'Charlotte, you won't get far like that!' Annabel called after her.

More shots rang out. One of them struck the back of her shoulder, spinning her halfway around. She flashed Annabel the finger and let her momentum carry her into the street. Brakes screamed as cars skidded to a halt, two of them colliding with a crunch. Then she was across the street, racing down 2nd Avenue. Medusa had taken away her shifting, but she was still a Shadow, stronger and faster by far than a human being.

Annabel shouted something she couldn't hear over the bleating car horns and the angry shouts of drivers. Charlotte glanced back at her building and saw the other two vampires emerge, and then all three of Cortez's assassins were giving chase. The wind blew the hat off of the taller male and his face began to burn instantly, blackening and smoking. Screaming, he raced after his hat and the others ignored him, running on, but now they clutched their own hats to their heads, making sure the wide brims blocked most of the sun. They looked so utterly ridiculous that any other day Charlotte would have taken the time to laugh, but there was nothing funny about being hunted, and that was exactly where she found herself – hunted on the streets of New York.

Just blocks away, she thought. And she ran.

Fear drove her to abandon any pretense at being ordinary. People shouted in surprise as she sprinted past them so fast that there was no disguising what she was. A woman screamed and dragged her curly-haired daughter out of the way. On the corner of 49th Street a falafel vendor ducked down behind his cart and crossed himself. She darted between cars, not waiting for a break in traffic. The driver of a UPS truck had his eyes on her instead of the road and struck a double-parked cab. A Lexus skidded to a halt to avoid crashing into the truck and Charlotte dodged between the vehicles.

More screams pursued her down the street, but she knew that these were not because of her. She glanced back over her shoulder and saw Annabel and the two males crossing the street. A police car was among those jammed up by the first collision Charlotte had caused, and as the cop climbed out, gun drawn, one of the males punched a hole in his chest. The gun went off, shattering glass, but the vampires kept coming as if nothing at all had happened. Annabel vaulted onto the police car's roof and began leaping from car to car while the males dashed between them. Then they were on the sidewalk and people were shrieking and jumping aside.

If it had been night, Charlotte knew they would have caught her already. She'd be dead by now. It made her wonder what they'd been thinking, attacking during the day. The only way it made sense was if they had been watching her place for a while, waiting for her to come back. She'd been gone for nearly a week. Somehow she'd managed to get into her apartment last night without them noticing, but when she'd gotten up this morning, they had spotted her, maybe through a window, and had come after her in daylight because they were afraid she might leave town again before they could take her down.

Charlotte raced past the Manchester Pub. A dog started barking and she dodged left to avoid tripping over its leash. There were too many people on the sidewalk ahead and she shouted for them to move, keeping close to the building, sliding along with that uncanny speed, knocking over a diplomat with a briefcase.

She saw the baby stroller just in time to avoid colliding with it or with the woman pushing it, but as she passed them – the woman recoiling from her as if Charlotte were on fire – she crashed into an old man exiting the corner market with a sack of groceries. The bag tore as the two of them fell in a tangle of limbs, spilling cans and fresh produce to the ground. The man cried out as his head struck the sidewalk.

No! Charlotte thought, reaching for him, anguished over the thought that she might have killed him. But though he must have been eighty at least, the old man groaned and started to prop himself up, staring at her as if she were insane.

'What is wrong with –' he began.

'Ohmygod I'm so, so sorry!' she said, extricating herself from him and climbing to her feet. Shaking her head, she backed away from his anger and confusion. 'I'm sorry. I've gotta go. I've gotta –'

The look in the old man's eyes turned to fear and she knew he wasn't looking at her anymore. Charlotte spun just as the male caught up to her. He grabbed her by the throat, his fingers digging into her flesh, cutting off the flow of air she didn't need. In the shadow of his hat brim, he grinned widely, his fangs extending to demonic proportion, and she knew then that the time for guns and bullets was over. This leech intended to tear her apart.

Charlotte struck in a blink, plucking out his left eye. The vampire screamed and released her, staggering back a step, and she was on him. She stripped off his hat and his flesh began to smoke and ignite. Snarling, she tore at his clothes, ripping the long black jacket off of him and then the shirt beneath. In seconds his whole upper body began to char and burn and he ran toward the front door of the corner grocery to get out of the sun.

'What the fuck did you think was going to happen?' she screamed at him. 'Did Cortez pick the stupidest assholes he could find?'

The other male plowed into her from behind, lifting her off the ground and carrying her into the plate glass front window of the grocery. The glass shattered, raining huge shards onto the floor as they careened off of a checkout counter and knocked over a candy rack. As Charlotte scrambled to her feet, the vamp grabbed her ankle. His eyes burned red as his claws dug into her, down to the bone.

She picked up the cash register and brought it down on his skull with all her strength. The wet crunch satisfied a deep gnawing hatred inside her, but already he was turning to mist, so she leaped over the fallen candy rack and raced for the shattered window. The half-naked, scorched vamp tried to catch her before she reached it, but she hurled herself out onto the sidewalk and he skidded to a halt, not wanting to burn again.

It had all taken only seconds. Outside the grocery, Annabel strode across 2nd Avenue toward her. Charlotte turned south and began to sprint, but Annabel bolted after her on a course to intercept. Running, the human world seemed to slow down around her, but even so the taxicab seemed to come out of nowhere. It shot out of 48th Street and struck Annabel, dragging her under even as it screeched to a halt.

The driver's door flew open and a handsome, dreadlocked black guy stepped out. 'Get in, girl. She won't be down but a second.'

Charlotte's eyes went wide. The cabbie had hit Annabel on purpose. He must've seen it all unfolding, realized that it was vampires who were after her. He thought he'd be her knight in shining armor, help her make her getaway. The fool.

She didn't even have time to shout a warning to him before he was dragged screaming under the taxi.

But he'd bought her a few seconds' head start, and Charlotte wasn't going to waste it. All she needed was two blocks, and she'd be damned if she'd let them catch up to her again. She took off running, swerving into the street to get around a cluster of gawkers trying to see who was screaming. Her wool coat flew behind her, bits of broken glass shedding from it, tinkling as they struck the ground. Even with all the noise of the city around her, the scuff of her boots on the asphalt seemed loud in her ears.

Crossing 47th Street, she wondered how long the toxin lasted. She didn't like shifting much; it made her feel less human. But frozen in one form by Medusa, it felt like someone had put shackles on her.

A delivery man came out from behind a parked truck with a loaded dolly, and she barely avoided another collision. *Focus*! she thought. Another fall, and she might not be as lucky as she'd been the first time. Legs pumping, hair flying, she increased her already impossible speed, and in moments she saw 46th Street ahead.

'Stop there, bitch!' Annabel shouted after her. 'You speak, you die!'

Charlotte wanted to laugh as she turned the corner and spotted the gated entry to the Registry diagonally across 46th. They were already trying to kill her. It was too late for threats.

The wind blew. She could smell the East River not far off. The Registry had a broad façade of thick glass and guards at the heavy double doors. A garage entrance had a guard posted as well, with a thick metal wall that jutted from the ground, blocking the way in. She'd seen such things once on a class trip to Washington DC, but never since. But she didn't have a car. It was the front door for her, or right through the glass wall if that's what it came to.

Annabel shouted again, and one of the males roared something, still in pursuit and still, no doubt, holding onto their hats and looking foolish. Charlotte couldn't believe they hadn't given up the chase.

The gunshots came from nowhere, echoing off the buildings. Charlotte flinched with each pop and stared at the guards, who were all just now drawing their weapons, ready to defend the Registry entrance. So where the hell had shooting come from?

She spun, even as more gunfire echoed along 46th Street, and saw bullets punching through Annabel and the male vamp still with her. They both staggered and the male went down on his knees. The sun didn't matter to them now; burning in daylight was just another form of shapeshifting. It wouldn't be able to kill them.

'Down!' a voice called from high above, like God himself finally making an appearance. 'Get on the ground!'

Charlotte obeyed, hands behind her head like she'd seen on so many cop shows on TV. On her knees, she glanced frantically around. Traffic had stopped flowing; some kind of blockade in the street, a metal barrier like the one in front of the garage. She looked up toward where the voice had come from, and saw that the bullets had come from there as well. Bullets loaded with Medusa. Windows had slid open in the façade of the building, three stories up, and snipers were leaning out with their weapons trained on Charlotte and her pursuers.

'Don't shoot!' Charlotte called. 'Please, help me! Peter Octavian –'

With a clatter, metal plates opened in the sidewalk on both sides of the street. Shouting men and women in UN-emblazoned combat gear emerged, some with guns and others with flame-throwers. Charlotte stared at them, terror racing through her like the deadliest poison.

'No, please!' she shouted, but then she saw that they weren't focused on her.

She twisted around and watched as the male tried to flee, staggering to his feet. He made it half a dozen steps before the flame-throwers burned him down, so that he collapsed in a screaming ball of fire. Annabel lunged at one of them, trying to murder her way onto a path to freedom, and the flame-throwers roared. When Annabel's hair went up in a cloud of fire, Charlotte looked away . . .

Into the barrels of half a dozen guns and two flame-throwers.

A terrible sorrow clutched her heart. She looked into the eyes of the nearest soldier.

'No,' she said softly. 'I just wanted to sign the Covenant.'

One of the soldiers, an Asian man with grim features, took a step nearer. 'On your feet, Miss McManus.'

Charlotte stared at him. He knew her name.

'Come on,' he said, lowering his weapon and reaching for her arm to help her rise. 'Up.'

Confused, she staggered to her feet. 'How . . . ?' she asked.

The soldier glanced at one of the others, an African woman she took to be his superior officer. The officer nodded and the soldier looked at Charlotte, dead serious.

'Mr Octavian told us to expect you.'

The officer laughed softly, then spoke in a heavy accent.

'He didn't tell us you would be bringing friends.'

With that, they marched her through the front doors under heavy guard. But they didn't burn her to death in the street, so Charlotte decided to count that as a win.

Philadelphia, Pennsylvania

Dark thoughts were nesting in Octavian's brain. He sat in the back of the cab, silently urging it forward and feeling powerless in the face of his frustration. His hands were fisted in his lap, a warm static energy bristling around them. The turmoil of his emotions had stirred up the magic in him so much that it was all he could do to rein it in. There were things he could have done to speed the taxi along its route from the Philadelphia International Airport to the hotel where Nikki was staying, hex magic that would have affected the flow of traffic or spells to compel the driver to ignore the law, common sense, and safety concerns. But Octavian told himself not to be reckless, that he was overreacting.

Nikki's fine, he reassured himself, or tried to. It wasn't working.

This morning he had been only vaguely concerned. It was unlike her not to call him back, but there were so many possible explanations. The fastest way for him to get from Brattleboro to Philadelphia had been to drive the ninety minutes to Bradley Airport in Hartford, Connecticut and hop a flight from there. During that hour and a half in the car, he had resisted the urge to call Nikki, telling himself that the messages he had left were enough, that he didn't want to seem like a mother hen or, worse, a jealous lover. It wasn't that he was jealous; he didn't think Nikki had found someone else. But a tight ball of worry had settled into his gut and would not disperse, so when he had reached the airport, turned in his rental and seen that he had nearly two hours to wait for the next flight to Philly, he couldn't help himself.

Her line rang and rang and then went straight to voicemail, but now he couldn't even leave a message because her mailbox was full. Which meant that other people were leaving her messages as well – leaving her messages and not getting a reply. Nikki had a sold-out gig tonight at the Union Transfer and there would be no way she would let down the people who had bought tickets to come and see her.

During the flight, he told himself that by the time he landed she would have sorted out whatever the problem was with her phone. Or perhaps, he thought, she'd been feeling ill and been trying to rest in order to recover in time for the show. Though he didn't like the idea of Nikki being sick, he tried to persuade himself it was possible. He ignored as best he could the little voice that whispered in the back of his head that she would at least have sent him a text.

He realized he should have checked her social media sites to see if she'd posted any messages for her fans. His phone was in the front right pocket of his jeans and he kept touching it through the denim. Flight regulations required that it be turned off and he wanted to crawl out of his skin, wishing he could check those sites, and thinking that she might even now be calling him back. The idea quickly began to make him feel a bit better and he promised himself that there would be a message from her when he landed.

There were no messages. Worse, a quick search proved she had not posted any messages to fans. As far as he could tell, the show at the Union Transfer was still on. The moment he'd gotten into the taxi and told the driver to get him to the Hotel Sofitel, he tried ringing Nikki again with the same results. No answer. Mailbox full.

She's fine, he told himself again as the cab slid along 17th Street toward the hotel. All those messages, someone would've checked on her. The club promoter. Her agent or manager, getting no answer, would've sent someone, maybe even asked the hotel's front desk to send someone up.

But you didn't. It's only been a day, so you didn't. Octavian knew it was the truth. He hadn't called hotel management because it was only a day and wasn't it just possible that Nikki was pissed at him, or pissed at the world, and hibernating? Of course it was. Perhaps she'd learned about Keomany's death somehow, or had some other emotional crisis that had caused her to retreat from the world for a while. Anyone might decide to hide from the world for a single night and day.

Except she wouldn't. The thought turned that anxious knot in his gut to lead. After all they had been through together, all of the horrors they'd faced and the dangers they'd survived, Nikki would have known what her radio silence would do to him. Even if he'd somehow pissed her off so badly that she never wanted to speak to him again, she'd make one last exception to tell him that.

The taxi drew up in front of the Sofitel. Peter shoved two twenties through the hole in the partition and didn't wait for change. He jumped out of the cab before the doorman could reach it and raced for the hotel's revolving door. A young, perfumed couple in Euro fashion were speaking to the concierge and all three shot him a disapproving glance as he stormed past them, glancing quickly around for the elevator and then hurrying toward it.

'Sir?' called a front desk clerk. 'Is there something I can . . .'

Octavian ignored him. His haste and demeanor had raised some concern in the lobby – he could hear two employees talking worriedly as he hit the "up" button and waited impatiently – but he didn't mind if they wanted to send security after him. If there was a rational explanation for Nikki's silence, he could simply apologize.

He prayed that he would have to apologize.

The elevator dinged, the doors slid open and he stepped in. For half a second he frowned and stared at the bank of buttons, trying to remember Nikki's room number. It had been in his mind just a moment before and now he couldn't recall it and wanted to scream and shatter the rows of buttons, wanted to lash out with a wave of destructive magic that would obliterate the elevator and the shaft above, wanted to tear his way up the stairs and wreck everything he passed along the way.

Seven-two-seven. That was it.

He exhaled and pressed the button for the seventh floor.

When the doors slid open on five to reveal a middle-aged man in a suit holding an ice bucket, the urge toward violence rose again. Then he noticed that the man's shirt was untucked and that he wore no shoes – only black socks with a hole at the left big toe – and his frustration dissipated. The businessman had had a long day and wanted to put something on ice for tonight. Octavian couldn't blame him.

The guy flinched when he saw Octavian's glare.

'Going up?' Octavian said.

With a wary nod, the businessman stepped in to the elevator. He said nothing as they rode up two more stories, but when the doors opened again and Octavian stepped off, the businessman wished him a good night. Could it be night, already? Not quite, but the day was coming to an end.

'You, too,' Octavian replied, the sentiment sounding emptier than any words he'd ever heard himself say.

As he rushed along the corridor, his phone began to vibrate in his pocket. He slipped it out, thinking it must be Nikki, but the screen said *unknown caller*. If her phone was broken it might be her, calling from another line. He touched the screen to answer.

'Nikki?'

'Peter, it's Leon Metzger. I think you and I need to have a chat.'

Octavian grimaced. Metzger was commander of Task Force Victor. A call today could only be related to Charlotte showing up at the Shadow Registry to sign the Covenant and telling them about Cortez. Octavian had called ahead to tell them she was coming and not to make it difficult for her, promising to explain himself in greater detail soon. But not today.

'Leon, I can't do this right now. I'll get back to you.'

Commander Metzger started to argue, but Octavian ended the call. He held his phone as if it were something alien, staring at the hotel room door in front of him.

727.

He knocked, calling out her name. Several seconds ticked by and he lifted his hand to knock again, but faltered. A faint odor emanated from behind the door, and the moment he'd caught the scent it became stronger. For a second, he refused to accept it, but he knew that smell all too well, and always had.

Octavian splayed the fingers of his right hand against the door and slumped forward, deflating so badly that he nearly sank to his knees. Ice seemed to flow through his veins and he shuddered as the sick knot in his gut twisted harder. For a moment he feared he would be sick.

He found himself staring down at his phone, which he still clutched in his left hand. It remained defiantly still and silent.

There would be no call from Nikki. Not ever.

He stuffed the phone into his pocket and took a deep breath. With a thought, he sent magic flowing up his arm. A crackle of dark green fire glowed around his right hand as he grabbed the door knob and released a focused burst of concussive sorcery that blew the knob inward, tearing out the locking mechanism. He pushed on the door and other bits of the lock and the wood around it gave way before he strode across the threshold and into the room. There were other scents within, the sorts of perfumed soaps and air freshener spritzes that one would expect to find in a French-owned hotel.

Nikki lay in bed, curled beneath the covers in a picture of peaceful repose that would have been adorable, if not for the dreadful paleness of her skin, and the utter stillness of her form. And the spatter of blood on the carpet, and the light spray of it across the bedspread.

Octavian breathed her name. His chest ached with the suffocating weight of grief and tears began to slide down his face. In his long, long life he had lost so many that he had loved, and had seen so much death and suffering that he often thought himself immune to it. But as he watched her lying there in the false comfort of the twisted tableau her killer had created with her corpse, he could hear her singing still, not just the songs that she had written but those that had been her favorites by other artists, the ones who had inspired her and spoken to her heart and given her the faith in herself to allow her to speak to the hearts of others. He could see the crinkle of her nose when she smiled and hear the lilt of her laugh. He could recall the curve of her body when he pressed himself against her in bed after a long day and the smell of her hair when he buried his face in it.

He felt small and broken as he walked over and knelt beside the bed. Growing numb, he drew back the bedclothes. Nikki was naked. Her skin was alabaster pale and there was not a drop of blood under the sheets. Her killer had carefully arranged this picture of her for him to find.

Octavian stroked her hair, pushed it back behind her ear, then bent and kissed her cold lips. Rigor had long since set in and showed little sign of dissipating, which meant she had been dead at least twelve hours, though he knew it was longer than that . . . probably shortly before he'd left Massachusetts for Vermont, or soon thereafter.

With both hands, he rolled her slightly to get a look at the underside of her neck. The wound there was ragged and gaping, a chalky pinkness of torn flesh flecked with brownish dried blood. Other than what had splashed onto the carpet and sprinkled the bedspread, it was all that remained of her blood.

All the rest had been drained from her.

It hadn't been blood he had smelled from outside the door, though that odor was also much too familiar to him.

No, the scent had been that of death. The death of his love.

He kissed Nikki's forehead as he returned her to the illusion of sleep and drew the bedclothes up to cover her again. Tears were drying on his cheeks. Eyes narrowed, he stood and glanced about the room, cold, murderous rage building inside of him. He had been a warrior and a vampire and a sorcerer, had faced demons and madmen and true monsters, but he had never wanted to kill more than he did in that moment.

Octavian took a breath, and then another. In a few minutes, he would use his phone to call Leon Metzger back. The police would have to know about Nikki's murder, but Task Force Victor would want to be on top of it as well. No Shadow had done this; it had to be a rogue vampire. And Nikki hadn't been chosen at random. Someone had wanted to hurt him or to send him a message or both. Octavian had problems with the way Task Force Victor went about their work, but he would provide them with whatever information he could.

As long as they stayed out of his way. As long as they understood that whoever had done this would die by Octavian's hand.

Moving around the room, he began to study everything more closely – the walls, the windows, the carpet, the pattern in the bloodstains. For decades while he was still a vampire, after he had abandoned the coven to which he had belonged for centuries, Octavian had lived amongst humans without killing for blood. He had taken only what was freely given, or what could be gotten through other means. During that time he had blended into human society by crafting an identity for himself in which he could interact with people. Influenced by films and novels and television, he had become a private detective, and found that he learned a great deal from his clients and from his enemies. And he helped them, trying in some small way to begin to atone for the horrors he had committed over the ages.

There would come a time, quite soon, when he would need to rely upon the savagery of the warrior and the vampire. But first he had to figure out who had done this thing and then he had to find them. The crisis in Hawthorne, Massachusetts would lead to others, and soon. Evil must already have been tearing at the crumbling barriers that kept it from the world.

None of that mattered.

The world would have to wait. The only thing that mattered now was blood – the blood that had been shed and the blood that he would spill in return.

'I love you,' he whispered, knowing even as he spoke that Nikki's spirit would be long gone. Wherever she was, she could no longer hear him.

So he spoke to the person who had been in the room with her when she died. The monster who had killed her.

'I'm coming,' he said.

3

Brattleboro, Vermont

The doorbell rang while Tori was scrubbing pots. She almost called for Cat to see who it was, but then she recalled that her wife was in the shower. It had been a long day, full of tears and hard work, of grief and hopeful preparation. Tori found it difficult to look forward to the equinox with the pain of Keomany's death so fresh. She had become like a sister both to her and to Cat, a constant reassuring presence, and her absence would leave a dreadful void.

'Damn it,' she whispered, wiping the back of her hand across her eyes.

It had been like this ever since Octavian had shown up with the news, and with Keomany's ashes ... *in a damned wine bottle*. She'd be fine, and then the tears would start.

Frustrated with herself, even though she knew that her grief was entirely to be expected, she rinsed her hands and shut off the tap. The doorbell rang again as she dried her hands with a dishtowel and she tossed it onto the counter as she hurried out of the kitchen. She and Cat had an agreement; at dinner time, one of them cooked and the other one cleaned up afterward. Since Cat's culinary achievements rarely went further than sautéed vegetables or tofu stir fry, Tori tended to be the one making the meals. Tonight, one of their sisters in the craft had brought fresh swordfish, and Cat had gleefully prepared it blackened Cajun style, with dirty rice on the side, the one dish she really felt confident in making. If they'd had time, Tori would have made a light gumbo to go along with it, but today hadn't been the day for such things. A quiet night of reflection with the woman she loved, a nice meal, a glass of wine . . . these were all she required to find contentment tonight.

And perhaps there would be more to look forward to, tonight. Cat had a strange reaction to death, and always had. It made her angry and it made her want to seize life with both hands and squeeze. It made her want to scream and to laugh, but especially it made her want to lose herself in love and in mind-shattering orgasms – both giving and receiving. This had gone unspoken between them, but Tori knew her pattern. For herself, she would rather have mourned quietly, shared memories of Keomany, and left it until the equinox to make love, as they always did at the turns of the year. But she knew what Cat needed, and she would open her heart and her body to provide that solace.

That plan, however, did not allow for unexpected visitors.

It was strange, getting a knock on the door. Most of the employees had gone home by now, and the earthwitches who had arrived from out of town for the equinox had all pursued their own plans for the evening. Several of them, those Cat and Tori knew best, had originally been invited to stay here at the orchard house, but as if by mutual agreement – and perhaps that was the case – they had all retreated to hotels upon learning of Keomany's death, giving their hosts time to mourn.

Tori cocked her head, trying to see through the tempered glass panels in the front door. She flicked on the outside light, turned the lock, and pulled the door open.

'Ed? What's wrong?'

The orchard foreman stood on the front steps, breathing hard and looking at her with wide eyes. Ed Rushton had been with them for three years, overseeing all of the harvesting at Summerfields. Fifty-one years old, tall and powerfully built, he always wore a baseball cap to protect his balding pate from the sun. Night had fallen, and now he clutched his cap tightly in both hands.

'Best you just see for yourself,' he said, nodding, and he started down the steps. The ATV he used to motor around the orchard sat on the dirt road, fifty feet from the front door.

Tori moved out onto the stoop. A strong breeze blew past her, bringing the rich smells of earth and plants and apples.

'Ed?'

He shot her a look that spoke of fear and wonder in equal measure. 'Tori, please. I've seen a lot of things since coming to work here, and I can't complain. You and Cat gave me the rundown before I started. Elemental magic, naked witchy rituals, loving the earth . . . to be honest, I like it. And not just the naked part. I don't understand witchcraft – earthcraft, or whatever – but I know you're good people and that there's only love in what you do. But this is . . . Hell, I don't know what.'

'*What* is going on?'

Despite his farmer's tan, the foreman looked pale.

'You've gotta just come with me,' he said. 'If I try to explain, it'll sound crazy or stupid or both.'

'All right.' She glanced back into the house, thought of Cat in the shower, and then pulled the door shut behind her. Whatever this was, she'd be back soon. And she had her cell phone; Cat would call or text her if she was worried.

Ed climbed onto the ATV and Tori got on behind him, holding tightly to him as she straddled the machine. Growing up, she'd always ridden like this on the back of her brother Johnny's dirtbike, and the memory rose up and lingered in her head as Ed drove her down the road and turned up into the orchard. Johnny had died when she was fifteen, and memories of him were always bittersweet. She loved her life, loved Cat and what they'd built here at Summerfields, but she'd have given almost anything to have another day with Johnny. Unfortunately, there were some things even magic could not do.

The ATV jounced through a pothole in the path leading up into the orchard. They passed pumpkin beds and entered the thick of the orchard, with rows of apple trees stretching across the hill for acres in either direction.

When she realized where Ed must be taking her, she clutched him even tighter.

'What the hell *is* this?' she called over the guttural growl of the ATV's motor.

He turned his head and raised his voice to be heard. 'You're going to have to tell me.'

Then they were pulling into the clearing where they had said their goodbyes to Keomany that morning, and where they would be conducting their equinox ceremony. In the center of the clearing stood the new tree that Keomany had nurtured from seed to maturity in moments. It was the most robust tree in the orchard, now, with the finest apples.

Something else had grown in the clearing.

Ed killed the ATV's engine, its growl echoing in Tori's ears for several seconds. The silence that followed, broken only by the rustle of the breeze in the trees, felt like the world holding its breath.

She climbed off the back of the ATV. Ed stayed where he was, staring at the new thing that had sprouted from the soil. He had obviously come across it while traversing the orchard and now, having seen it once, had no interest in getting near to it again.

'Goddess,' Tori whispered as she walked toward it, unsure even as she spoke if it was a prayer or a cry for help. The smell of earth and apples filled the air, swirling on the breeze.

Her heart thrummed in her chest, a captive hummingbird. Her face felt flushed and her breath came in short, shallow sips as she knelt in the dirt and stared at the new growth, which looked like no tree or bush she had ever seen. Perhaps fourteen inches high, it had skin like an apple, and thick roots that went deep into the ground, covered in bark. It had the shape – the figure – of a woman, though it did not move except for the stirring caused by the wind, and though it had no expression, it did indeed have a face.

Keomany's face.

Goddess.

Tori began to weep. Though she felt a shiver of fear, most of what she felt – what made her hands shake and caused the grin that broke out on her face – was the joy of miracles.

'Ed,' she said, her voice cracking with emotion. 'Get a fence up around this right away. Tonight.' She stood and looked at him. 'And don't breathe a word.'

Airborne

The deep, bass chop of the helicopter's rotors felt like an assault on Charlotte's ears, a thumping on her chest, as if she sat inside a quickening heart that beat from without instead of within. Normally she would not have been quite as nervous. A vampire could easily survive a helicopter crash – even an explosion. But she still had traces of the Medusa toxin in her blood and she didn't like her chances if the chopper went down.

Five people shared the rear compartment of the helicopter with her. Three of them were rank-and-file members of Task Force Victor, soldiers-turned-vampire-hunters who clearly had a very dim view of her. The youngest, a buzzcut Chinese guy named Song, no more than twenty, kept stealing glances at her that seemed to say he thought it was a shame that a cute girl who looked near his own age was a bloodsucking freak. Song kept getting disgusted scowls from the only other woman on the chopper, a Brazilian named Galleti who had a quartet of scars on the left side of her throat that could only have been clawmarks. The two of them took orders from Sergeant Omondi, a New Yorker by way of Kenya. He was maybe thirty, six and a half feet tall and built like a tank, though the intellect sparkling in his eyes belied that great size. Omondi was no brute.

As much as they intrigued her, these armed soldiers who had dedicated their lives to exterminating her kind, she was far more interested in the other two people riding in the back of the chopper. The rumpled, goateed Barbieri carried a few too many pounds, especially as he looked to be nearing fifty, but he had kind eyes. He certainly didn't match any image her mind would have conjured of a forensics expert specializing in tracking vampires.

Of all of them, it was Commander Leon Metzger who scared her the most. When she'd been taken into custody in front of the Shadow Registry building, it had been Metzger's order that kept her from being burned alive with the assassins Cortez had sent. Charlotte had been bustled indoors and into a room that was the equivalent of an iron box and seated in a steel chair bolted to the floor, where she had waited alone for hours while someone – she was sure – tried to persuade Leon Metzger to burn her and be done with it.

Peter Octavian was the only reason they hadn't killed her on the spot, and the reason that instead of burning her, Metzger had come into the iron box with two cups of coffee and sat down across from her.

'I know, it's a TV show cop cliché. But it's here if you want it. Actually, the coffee around here's pretty good,' he said, taking a sip as he slouched back in his chair.

Charlotte hadn't hesitated. She'd taken the coffee and swigged it, wishing for more sugar but relishing it just the same. A little bit of civilization in the midst of madness. And she hadn't spent a moment worrying about what kind of signal it might send that she was so willing to drink . . . to accept what he offered. Either he was playing some kind of head game with her or he wasn't; she couldn't bring herself to care.

'Thank you,' she had said, and she thought he'd known she'd meant it as gratitude for both the coffee and her life.

'I'm not going to drag this out,' Metzger had said. 'Octavian says you can be trusted, and that's good enough for me. Whatever issues my predecessor had with him, I don't share them. So in a few minutes I'm going to have someone come in and explain the Covenant to you and then you're going to sign it, both because you say you want to and also because if you don't, you won't leave here alive.'

The strangest part of that bit of interaction had been that when he'd said it, Metzger had smiled in such an amiable way that Charlotte had smiled in return. She'd found herself somewhat charmed by a man who had just threatened to kill her, and so she had told him that she had come there specifically to sign the Covenant and nearly been killed already by assassins who wanted to make sure that never happened. Metzger had turned thoughtful, then.

Two soldiers – Song and Galleti, though she hadn't known their names at the time – had come in with a pen and a copy of the Covenant. Charlotte had only skimmed it, but she got enough of the gist. It wasn't hard to imagine what humans would want by way of promises from vampires. *I won't hunt humans. I won't take blood without permission. I'll be a good little Shadow.*

Then the interrogation had begun, about Cortez and the killers who had been hunting her, about Octavian and how she'd come to meet him, about what she'd done while she'd been answering to Cortez, and after. It had gone on for so long that she'd lost track of time, until Sergeant Omondi had come in to interrupt his commander with news that he was needed on the phone. Metzger had been irritated, right up until Omondi told him it was Peter Octavian calling and that he'd said it was urgent.

Less than thirty minutes later, they'd been boarding a helicopter, Charlotte and a handful of people who made their living hunting down vampires. Now here she was riding in the back of a chopper with them like she was somehow part of the team, and it felt like one of those dreams about going to school in your underwear. Charlotte had been vulnerable most of her life, and she didn't like it. She had been drugged and raped and murdered and transformed into a monster, and the only upside of all that horror was that people couldn't physically hurt her anymore. Medusa had taken that away and now Charlotte felt haunted and uneasy, acutely aware of every possible threat to her well-being.

The thrum of the chopper pounding at her ears, she glanced out the small window beside her. The pilot had said the trip would take about forty minutes, so she figured the sprawling lights below must be the city of Philadelphia. That was good; it meant they would be landing soon. Thus far today her luck had been for shit – sort of par for the course of her life – but if it turned in her favor at all, she would never have to get on a helicopter again.

'You don't look good,' a voice called.

Charlotte glanced up to see Metzger watching her with ice blue eyes. He arched a wiry gray eyebrow as if punctuating the comment, turning it into a query.

'I'm fine,' she said.

Metzger cocked his head to indicate he hadn't heard. With the roar of the rotors it was necessary for her to speak up.

'I said I'm fine!'

He nodded, though he looked doubtful. 'Not hungry? When was the last time you fed?'

Charlotte winced at the question. *Fed*, not *ate*. Like an animal. A beast on the prowl. It shouldn't have surprised her to get this peek into the way Metzger saw her kind, but thus far he had treated her fairly humanely, so it did shock her a little. And how was she supposed to answer that, anyway? Yes, it had been a while since the last time she had had human blood to drink, but she would survive. She figured the most fundamental difference between the Shadows who lived in peace with humanity and those who chose to embrace the word 'vampire' was self-control. She chose to ignore Metzger's question, turning again to look out the window.

She didn't hear him unsnap the rig that belted him into his seat, but she caught sight of the motion in the corner of her eye and turned back just as he grabbed hold of her wrist and crouched beside her seat. Charlotte glanced at the others. Barbieri had nodded off, but the three soldiers were alert with tension, watching their CO closely.

'Let's be clear,' Metzger said, squeezing her wrist for emphasis, gazing at her with those ice blue eyes. 'I'm not just being hospitable. If you need blood, I will see that you get it, not because I'm just that nice a guy but because I don't want you losing control and trying to drain one of my people. You might hurt somebody, and then we'd have to kill you. Octavian would be pissed and nobody wants that. I don't want the guy turning me into a newt, right?'

He grinned as if this was a joke, but Charlotte could hear the truth in it.

'You still haven't told me why we're doing this,' she said. 'Octavian sent me to you and now you're bringing me back to him?'

Metzger gave a small shrug. 'It's Octavian's business. You'll learn soon enough. But I brought you along because he asked for you, and because I trust him. If I didn't trust him, I'd have to kill him, and I'm not quite sure how to go about it. So I don't really have a choice – I have to trust him. Don't get to thinking that extends to you, though. The last time the commander of Task Force Victor trusted a vampire, it didn't turn out too well.'

Charlotte scowled. Allison Vigeant had been a Bloodhound for Task Force Victor until its previous commander, Ray Henning, had gone kill-crazy and tried to take down every Shadow he saw, ally or enemy. Allison had put him down like a rabid dog, which was fairly close to the truth.

'What was it you were saying about blood?' she asked, raising her voice over the chopper noise. She smiled and her fangs slid out.

Metzger hesitated, staring at her teeth. 'I see the Medusa toxin is starting to wear off.'

Charlotte ran her tongue over the sharp tips of her fangs. 'Sure looks like it.'

Metzger nodded slowly. 'When we're on the ground, I'll make a call to local law enforcement and set up a volunteer. There's always some freak who's willing to share.'

She didn't rise to the bait of his disdain. After a second, Metzger slid back into his seat and buckled himself into his restraints. The chopper began to yaw and pitch a little, in addition to the usual shuddering, and she glanced out the window to see the lights of the airport below, with trucks darting to and fro and the large H of a helipad looming closer.

They were landing. Octavian would be waiting with answers, but for the first time, Charlotte wasn't sure she wanted them.

There were cops in the hotel lobby, keeping an eye on everyone who came and went. Two uniformed officers stood near the elevator bank and checked the identification of everyone who went up or came down, keeping a log. Charlotte saw a pair of men in dark suits talking to a cop who looked like he must be a captain or a lieutenant or something, and figured the suits for FBI. Whatever had happened here, Octavian was right in the middle of it, and it had been significant enough to warrant this kind of attention. The nineteen-year-old girl in her wanted to make a run for it, but all of these grim-faced investigators with their guns and handcuffs weren't there looking for her. Besides that, she could feel the Medusa toxin wearing off, her ability to alter her flesh returning almost like an injured muscle regaining its limberness.

Soon, if she wanted to get away from Metzger and his team, she'd at least have a shot at making it before they hit her with another dose of the toxin. But before she took any action, she wanted to see Octavian and find out what this was all about.

'She has no ID,' Sergeant Omondi told the cops barring access to the elevators.

'Then she stays down here,' the older of the two cops said, lifting his chin in pride and defiance, wanting to make sure they knew who had jurisdiction.

Galleti smirked, closing her eyes a moment.

'Something funny, Miss?' the older cop asked.

Metzger shot Galleti a dark look. She stood up a bit straighter, no smile on her face now, chocolate brown eyes very serious. Omondi and Song followed suit, perfectly grim, but Barbieri shook his head in open pity for the uniformed policeman.

'This should be –'

'Barbieri,' Metzger said, the warning clear in his tone.

Then he turned back to the cops, who had already seen the identification of each member of the team from Task Force Victor.

'Officer, maybe you're not aware that Task Force Victor is charged with its duties under the United Nations amended charter, and has been given jurisdictional authority over all vampire-related incidents,' Metzger explained, feigning patience.

The cop sniffed, shot a can-you-believe-this glance at his partner, and then cocked his head to look at Metzger as if he were an unusual animal on display at the zoo.

'Given I haven't been in a coma or on the moon, yeah, I'm aware. But let me tell you what we've got upstairs. A murder victim and a *magic*-man,' the cop said, waggling his fingers at the end, mocking the idea of magic. 'There's no vampire here.'

A chill went through Charlotte. Octavian had come to Philadelphia to reconnect with his girlfriend, now he was in a swanky hotel room with a corpse.

'Shit,' she whispered, 'it's not Nikki, is it?'

The cops both glanced at her, as did Barbieri. The soldiers did not.

'Your victim was killed by a vampire. The investigation is yours; that's not what we do. But you're bound by your own government's laws to cooperate with us. If you impede us – '

'Didn't say you couldn't go through, Van Helsing,' the cop said, then pointed at Charlotte. 'But she's got no ID, and my orders are clear. You want to cross swords over jurisdiction, that's fine, but until someone changes my orders—'

'She's our new Bloodhound, you idiot,' Barbieri growled. 'She's a vampire!'

The cop laughed. 'Hell, that's not going to win you any points. You want her with you, go through channels. Get my lieutenant on the line and have him order me to let her pass. Until then, no go.'

'Points?' Metzger said, his patience frayed.

His nostrils flared with anger. He cast a sidelong glance at Sergeant Omondi and gave a curt nod. With a clatter, Omondi, Song, and Galleti put their hands on the butts of their weapons but did not draw them. The younger cop, who looked like he might piss his pants, started to reach for his gun, but the older one shouted at him and grabbed his wrist to keep him from doing so.

'You're wasting my time,' Metzger said. 'Both of you step aside. One of you call your lieutenant. If he has a problem with us being here, he can damn well come up and tell us himself. He can tell Octavian. I have a feeling he won't want to do that. Now, cooperate or I take you into custody and we let the city of Philadelphia fight it out with the UN, if you think they'll even bother.'

Charlotte shuddered in disgust. 'Enough with the dick-waving contest,' she said, turning to the cop. 'You lose. Right now you're just trying to find a way to save face. Well there isn't one. Fucking get over it.'

The cop glared at her for a second, and then laughed. It wasn't a derisive laugh, more an appreciative chuckle. He put his hands up in surrender.

'All right, Commander. You and your team can take your ferocious vampire upstairs.'

The cops made way, letting them through, and aside from a cold bit of courtesy from Metzger, they were all silent as they waited for the elevator. Charlotte kept glancing around at their faces, but none of them looked back at her until they were on board, ascending toward the seventh floor.

'What the hell was that?' she said.

Metzger watched the numbers light up. The others ignored her as the elevator passed the fifth floor with a ding. Finally she turned to Barbieri.

'They didn't believe you were a vampire,' he said. 'Young, pretty, mouth like a street kid.'

'I should eat his face,' Charlotte said, knitting her brow.

'You should,' Galleti muttered.

Metzger shot her a withering glance that caused Galleti to stare straight ahead at the elevator doors.

'Sorry, sir,' Galleti said. 'I didn't mean literally.'

Charlotte threw up her hands. 'For fuck's sake, neither did I!'

Both Song and Galleti smiled at that. Sergeant Omondi remained stoic as ever. When the elevator dinged to a stop on Seven and the doors slid open, Metzger was the first one off and the others all followed in his wake. Barbieri made a flourishing bow and gestured for Charlotte to precede him.

'It's going to be an interesting day,' he said.

Half a dozen other cops were in the corridor, either carrying crime scene equipment, taking statements at the doors of other guests' rooms, or standing guard at the entrance of one room. When Metzger and his team approached, the sentries just muttered a greeting and waved him through, and Charlotte figured the asshole downstairs had radioed up with a warning.

The minute she walked into the hotel room, all of the trivial politics and posturing of the authorities was forgotten. She had smelled the blood as soon as they got off the elevator, but now the smell filled up her head, rich and powerful. Metzger had called ahead for a volunteer – someone to give her blood – but nobody had shown up for the job as yet. The Philadelphia police would have some on hand, as would any hospital, but she didn't think she was going to get any handouts here in the City of Brotherly Love. The hungry animal inside of her stirred in its sleep and she licked her lips and swallowed drily. This was a problem that needed solving, but not yet.

A couple of plainclothes detectives stood inside the hotel room, which seemed crowded to Charlotte even before she heard Barbieri start bitching.

'What the hell is this?' the forensics expert asked, pushing ahead so he was just behind Metzger. 'You've had the Macy's parade in here. How am I supposed to –'

'Whoa, hold up,' one of the detectives said. 'The job is done, pal. CSU has been here and gone already. They just took away the last of their equipment. The scene's already been processed. Only thing still here that shouldn't be is the . . .'

He was about to say 'victim'. They all knew it, could feel it, but he faltered and just let the sentence hang there unfinished. When the detectives turned to glance awkwardly back into the room, they could all see why.

Peter Octavian lay on the bed, fully clothed, beside the body of Nikki Wydra, the woman he loved. He had stripped the sheet from the bed and swaddled her in it, wrapped her as if he'd been preparing some Egyptian pharaoh for burial. He lay there beside her cocoon, studying her face with a longing that broke

Charlotte's heart, unconcerned by the knowledge that there were witnesses to his anguish. Charlotte studied Nikki's face, the only part of her that was exposed. Even her lips were so pale they seemed made from alabaster.

The awkwardness of the moment expanded until it filled the room. Charlotte lowered her gaze and half-turned away, wishing they would all have given Octavian his privacy. The mage looked terrible, his eyes rimmed with red, his hair mussed and his clothes rumpled.

'Goodbye, love,' Charlotte heard him say, and she glanced back in time to glimpse him brushing his lips against her forehead.

Octavian climbed to his feet, cast a final look at Nikki's corpse, and then turned to the detectives. 'Finish your work. Let me know if you have any further questions and I'll do the same. Task Force Victor will need to be kept informed of your progress.'

These detectives weren't likely to appreciate being told what to do any more than the uniformed cops downstairs, but they weren't going to argue with this man.

Octavian slid past the detectives, glanced once at Metzger, and then went to Charlotte. He took her hands and kissed her cheek, peering at her with those dark eyes.

'Thank you for coming,' he said, as if she'd had a choice.

Then he looked at the other members of Task Force Victor gathered there and nodded once in greeting before turning again to Metzger.

'I've secured us a room down the hall where we can talk,' Octavian said. 'Do what you need to do and let's get to it. The balance of things is shifting, and we need to act before it's shifted so far that it can't be righted again.'

Metzger ordered Barbieri to examine the crime scene, regardless of the fact that the Crime Scene Unit had already been and gone and many people had trampled through the room since then. The forensics man got to work immediately, putting the detectives on notice that he'd want someone to take him to the police labs as soon as he was done there. Song stayed behind to assist him and to look out for him in the event that something went violently wrong. Where Shadows and the supernatural were concerned, it was always best to be careful.

Octavian gestured for Charlotte to walk with him and she complied, the two of them leading Metzger, Sergeant Omondi, and Galleti down the corridor to the second to last door on the seventh floor. Charlotte expected him to produce a key card but instead he rapped lightly on the door in a certain rhythm, a signal knock, letting whoever was inside know it was him. She glanced at Metzger and saw him frowning in confusion.

They heard the deadbolt click open and the chain on the door slide back, and then the door swung inward.

The woman who stood there holding the door open looked incredibly familiar. Something was different about her, though, and it took Charlotte a second to realize that it was her hair. Once upon a time it had been a dark red and now it was a light brown, long and lush and veiling part of her face. But she knew the face.

So, after a moment, did the soldiers from Task Force Victor.

'Holy –' Galleti began, drawing her gun.

Metzger snatched up his own weapon, quick as a gunslinger, and in his eyes Charlotte saw death. She understood it, too. The woman was Allison Vigeant, who had murdered his predecessor – torn his throat out with her teeth. She had been Task Force Victor's most wanted for years.

With a flick of his wrist, Octavian froze them where they stood. Their hands and weapons crackled with a silver, electric mist. He looked at them with a ferocity that would brook no argument.

'We're going to talk. *All* of us,' he said. 'Which means you're going to put your weapons away and you're going to listen. Do not make the mistake of thinking you have a choice.'

'Fine,' Metzger said, staring at Allison before he flicked his gaze toward Octavian. 'But whatever you've got to say, it better be good.'

4

Philadelphia, Pennsylvania

The hotel room unsettled them all, not because there was anything unusual about it but because it was so ordinary. Octavian had counted on them being inhibited by the mundane setting, enough so that the soldiers would hesitate before they opened fire. Thus far, he was not disappointed.

Allison stood by the sliding glass door that led onto the balcony. The door was open perhaps eighteen inches but all she needed was a crack. If Commander Metzger or either of his soldiers tried to shoot her with Medusa-treated bullets, she'd shift to mist and be gone. Octavian didn't think it would come to that, but the situation was volatile and unpredictable.

Not just the situation, he thought. A cruel smile touched his lips but there was no humor in it. Instead, he felt a trace of madness tickling at his brain. In the hours since he had found Nikki dead, his mind and body had undergone a strange, invisible metamorphosis. His grief had split in two, one part a terrible numbness that made him feel hollow and light – as if he were a ghost haunting his own life – and the other a burning, seething rage.

'What the hell is this?' Commander Metzger asked, in the clipped tones of a man used to giving orders.

He looked awkward as hell, standing there by the bureau with its flatscreen TV. They all did – him, Sergeant Omondi, whom Peter knew, and the woman on his team, who was unfamiliar. The hotel room was nothing special, but large enough to fit two double beds, which meant that nearly anywhere they stood, there would be furniture separating them from their potential enemies. Furniture wouldn't stop bullets, but it made maneuvering difficult, whether to attack or retreat. These were tight quarters to be in for any hostilities that might unfold.

'What's your name?' he asked the woman from Task Force Victor.

'Galleti.' Last name only. A soldier, through and through.

Octavian nodded, then turned to Charlotte. Poor Charlotte, thrown into the midst of something she had never asked for, first by Cortez and now by Octavian himself. The vampire girl stood in the middle of the room, in the no man's land between the two beds, caught in the crossfire of mutual distrust.

'Charlotte, come sit down,' he said quietly, gesturing to the two comfortable chairs that flanked the floor lamp, blocking the immobile side of the slider.

The vampire girl did as she was told. With her copper hair and delicate features, she had always been lovely, but she was even more beautiful in distress. As she sat down in the chair, Octavian noted that she did not sink back into it, instead sitting just on the edge. She could taste the possibility of violence and wanted to be ready for it.

Octavian took the other chair, so that he sat with Charlotte on one side and Allison – in front of the open slider – on the other.

To his credit, Commander Metzger had not asked his question a second time, letting it hang in the air as his distrust and wariness grew. Galleti looked anxious, and of the three of them she was the one who worried Octavian the most. They had already drawn their weapons once before he had forced them to put the guns away, but Galleti seemed like she wanted to give it another try.

'I'd invite you all to have a seat,' Octavian said, nodding toward the beds, 'but I can see that you're not in the mood to get comfortable.'

Metzger took a long breath and let it out, calming himself. He glanced at Allison only once, otherwise choosing to pretend – at least for the moment – that she was not in the room.

'Peter, listen, I'm sorry for your loss, but –'

'But *what*?' Octavian asked, feeling the sneer coming but unable to prevent it. His skin crackled with angry magic, and he could feel it bristling all over his body, purple-black light sizzling around his hands and in front of his eyes.

Galleti put her hand on her gun, but Omondi stopped her from taking it further.

Metzger flinched, Allison's presence entirely forgotten as he recognized the more immediate threat in the room.

'You can't possibly blame us for what happened to her,' Metzger said.

'I don't blame you,' Octavian said, his anger still crackling in the air around him. 'A vampire who calls himself Cortez did this. I assume Charlotte's told you something about him, or maybe not. Maybe she hasn't had the chance yet. Cortez, you see, is flying under your radar. He's not just a rogue vampire, he's a new leader for them, building something that might be just a coven, or that could be an army. And he's an arrogant son of a bitch, too. You see, he considers me the only real threat to whatever he's got planned, so he decided to . . . hurt me.'

Octavian ground his teeth together, trying to contain his rage and his grief and the hatred he now aimed at himself.

'Nikki died because she loved me,' he said, jaw tight. He looked up at Metzger. 'I have to live with that. This Cortez wants me off balance. He figures it'll make me more vulnerable. And for that, he killed her.'

Octavian stood, barely feeling the ripple of magical energy that flowed from him, a silent assault on everything around him. The floor lamp rocked but didn't fall. The glass in the sliding door cracked, as did the television screen. The three ordinary humans in the room were all knocked back a step, but none of them made any move to defend themselves. Octavian saw the realization in their eyes, the cold fear at the knowledge that if he wanted to kill them, there would be nothing they could do to stop them.

'Cortez did this,' Octavian said, walking toward Metzger. 'But there is plenty of blame to go around. Part of it's on me, because I couldn't protect her. And part of it is on Task Force Victor.'

'But you said—' Metzger began.

'I said I didn't blame you, personally, Leon.' Octavian glanced over his shoulder at Allison for a moment. 'But Task Force Victor? The UN? Part of the blame is on all of you. See, the guy who had the job before you, Ray Henning, was a good soldier who snapped. He couldn't see that human beings and Shadows aren't very different from one another, that there are angels and devils in all of us. He wanted to exterminate all Shadows, even though he had one of the finest people I've ever known, human or otherwise, working for him. Henning snapped, stopped caring how many innocents were killed in collateral damage from his war. Allison Vigeant did what had to be done in that moment. She took him out of the fight.'

Octavian poked Metzger in the chest. Where his fingertip had touched, the commander's shirt smoked and blackened.

'You bastards should have pinned a medal on her. Instead she had a target painted on her back. Task Force Victor took their best vampire hunter and made her their primary target. They diverted their attention – and consequently, Allison Vigeant's attention – from their main objective, which was to stop rogues like Cortez from building up a coven, so the kinds of wars we've seen between Shadows and vampires or between humans and Shadows, would never happen again.'

Octavian leaned in so that he was eye to eye with Metzger, their noses only inches away.

'And now Nikki's dead.'

To his credit, Metzger didn't flinch this time. 'I didn't witness Henning's death with my own eyes. If what you're saying about Vigeant is true, then I agree with the rest. Let's proceed from that assumption, at least for the moment. What do you propose we do about it? You called us, remember? Why are we here?'

Octavian nodded, stepping back from him. He glanced at Charlotte and Allison and then at the soldiers.

'I called because that's the protocol, Commander. A vampire did this. Task Force Victor is supposed to be my first phone call. I called because your people are partly to blame for this, and I expect you – and them – to step up and do whatever it takes to help me find Cortez and his nest and put them all down.'

'Of course—' Metzger said.

'And,' Octavian interrupted, 'I called because there's a crisis looming that's going to require your attention. The

UN's attention. The world's attention. It would have been my number one priority, but now . . . now I have something to do that's more important to me than saving this godforsaken world.'

As swiftly as he could, he laid out what had happened in Hawthorne, Massachusetts, ending with the death of Keomany Shaw and the defeat of the chaos queen, Navalica. He explained that before they were able to take her down, Navalica had unleashed such a wave of chaos magic that it must have been like sending up a flare to let other supernatural entities know that the path to Earth lay open.

'Open,' Allison interrupted, speaking up for the first time. 'But not undefended.'

Octavian gave her a nod. 'No. Never that.'

When he was done, even stoic Sergeant Omondi looked frightened. Galleti's gaze was far away, as if she were thinking about all of the people she loved and needed to see before demons tore the world apart.

'How quickly is this going to happen? This . . . invasion?' Metzger asked.

Octavian batted the question away. 'It isn't like that. We're talking about potentially infinite parallel dimensions. Some of them are nothing but scorched ground and dead civilizations, while others are just . . . stillness, never having had a spark of life. Yes, there are all sorts of horrors out there, but it isn't as if they're organized. They're not plotting against us. And the barriers have deteriorated dramatically, but they're not gone entirely. That will slow things down a little. There won't be any coordinated invasion, but there might be a hundred small ones. You're going to need to be able to react at a moment's notice and shut these incursions down as quickly as possible. You may need to respond to more than one at a time, and that's going to require Task Force Victor being able to mobilize regular UN troops, as well as those of allied nations if necessary.'

Commander Metzger lowered his gaze. 'Christ.'

'Yeah, he's not going to show up like the cavalry,' Allison said.

'That's not helping,' Charlotte said.

Allison arched an eyebrow, clearly amused that the younger Shadow had thought to correct her, but she didn't argue.

'Peter,' Metzger said, his tone wary. 'I understand that you want to go after this Cortez yourself, but you know that our mandate means that we're going to be hunting him, too.'

'I'm counting on it,' Octavian said, locking eyes with Metzger. 'That's why you're here, Leon. You and I, we're going to sit down with Charlotte together and she's going to tell us every detail she remembers. You'll go after him your way and I'll go after him mine. Anything you learn, you'll pass on to me –'

'You know I can't do that.'

'You *will*,' Octavian said. 'You will. I'll speak to the Secretary General myself, and it will all be okay. We're all on the same side. Some people wish that wasn't true, but it is. That includes Allison, and you, Commander, are going to square that with the Secretary General yourself. That's your end of this.

'You'll pass along any information you find about Cortez. If you locate him, you will not go after him. You will tell me where he is, and you will stay the hell out of my way.'

Metzger looked like he wanted to argue, but he held his tongue. Octavian glanced at Sergeant Omondi and Galleti, but they were both too overwhelmed to do anything now except watch their CO for a cue.

'Once upon a time,' Octavian said, 'I had a coven of my own. Not a vampire coven, but one made up of both Shadows and humans . . . people I trusted. When a supernatural crisis occurred, we did whatever we had to do to resolve it. A lot of my friends died along the way, but it worked.

'That's the way it's going to be again, Leon, starting with Allison and Charlotte, if she's willing. As soon as we're done here, I'm going to make some calls. I have a funeral to plan. My old friends are going to want to be there, but it's going to have to happen fast. Once Nikki is laid to rest, my friends and I will be going after Cortez, starting with whatever intelligence you can gather in the meantime.

'When Cortez is dead, I'll worry about the rest of the world.'

* * *

September 22

Saint-Denis, France

Hannah Barclay leaned back in the passenger seat of the battered blue Renault, relishing the view as they wended their way out of Paris and north to the small commune of Saint-Denis. It was a picturesque suburb famous for the presence of the country's national stadium, and for the Cathedral Basilica of Saint-Denis. Hannah loved soccer – or football, as Europeans called it, always with enough emphasis so Americans knew they were being corrected – and she wished she were on the way to the stadium for a game. Spending the day doing research at the Basilica was not her idea of a good time, but she only had one semester to study at the Sorbonne and if she wanted to make the best of it, screwing up a research paper before September had even ended would be a terrible idea. Already she had spent too much time drinking wine in cafés along the Seine. She needed focus.

'. . . you even awake, yet?' Charlie was saying from behind the wheel.

Hannah frowned and turned to look at him. Twenty-one, perpetual two-day stubble, hipster glasses, not bad in bed. They were both students at Columbia University in New York and had spent much of the fall semester of their sophomore year fucking each other's brains out. It had been gloriously uncomplicated, or so she had told herself. When Charlie had found himself interested in someone else and drifted off in that direction, Hannah had responded with the same combination of aloofness and sarcasm that she brought to everything she did. She was just self-deprecating enough that her friends didn't complain about her snark. Not much, anyway.

But she missed him. Maybe it wasn't love, but she liked Charlie a lot more than she had ever let on. Now here they were, both juniors doing a semester abroad at the Sorbonne. His girlfriend, Brittany, was back in New York. But instead of taking the opportunity to get closer to Charlie, maybe tell him how she really felt about him or at the very least seduce him, all she had to offer was snark. Sarcasm was the only arrow in her quiver, and that sucked.

You're such a coward, she thought.

And accepted it.

'What are you saying?' she asked.

Charlie said to her, 'You didn't look like you were sleeping, but your brain certainly isn't awake.'

'Must be the oh-so-stimulating company,' Hannah replied. 'I was ruminating. It's something intelligent people do when trapped in the car with drooling morons.'

He laughed and shook his head. 'Isn't it too early for you to be such a bitch?'

'I don't have to be awake to be a bitch.'

Charlie smirked. 'I remember.'

'Oh, please, my friend the scintillating conversationalist. What was it you wished to discuss this fine French morning?'

'I was just bitching about having to get up so early to come out here. I wish I hadn't put my research off so long.'

'You'll be fine,' Hannah said, more warmly. 'You do better under pressure and you know it. That's why you wait until the last minute. I have no idea what my excuse is—'

'Too much wine and too many cute Parisian guys.'

Hannah smiled. 'And one girl.'

'You're such a tease. I know you did not make out with that girl. You're just toying with my helpless male brain.'

'Maybe. Anyway, it doesn't matter. We'll both be fine. Me more than you, of course, because I picked something easy and you decided to get all philosophical.'

'Picking a dead king and doing research with no room for conjecture about the future would have bored the shit out of me. Besides, this way I get to spin theories that will eat up some of the assignment's word length. Trust me, fifteen pages on Marie Antoinette losing her head would have ended with me throwing myself from the top of Notre Dame.'

Hannah laughed.

'My suicide is funny to you?'

'No. But I'm calling you Quasimodo for the rest of the day.'

They both smiled, but then lapsed into the silence of old friends, long-ago lovers, and other people who no longer have anything to prove to one another. Charlie drove around for a while trying to figure out where he was supposed to park in order for them to explore the Basilica. When he finally had it sorted out, they found themselves right in front of a café and couldn't resist going in for a coffee. A few minutes later, coffee in hand, they strode down the street and paused to gaze up at the building's façade.

The Basilica of Saint-Denis was a huge, sprawling, Gothic cathedral that had served as the prototype for an entire wave of architecture. It had been founded in the seventh century by Dagobert, one of the Merovingian kings, who had chosen the site because it held the tomb of Saint Denis. Hannah couldn't deny that all of the stories that had their endings at the basilica were interesting. The place became an abbey, the center of a Roman Catholic monastic society, and over the course of many centuries, myths and stories had sprung up about its various architectural advancements. More importantly to her and to pretty much the whole world, the Basilica of Saint-Denis was known as the necropolis of France – eight hundred years' worth of kings and queens and other royals were buried there. What had started as a tomb for Saint Denis had become the crypt for Charles Martel, Pepin the Younger, and a whole host of kings called Henry and Louis.

To most tourists, the main attraction at the basilica was likely the tomb of Louis XVI and his wife, Marie Antoinette. Hannah had never been inside the place, but as she and Charlie walked along the street toward it, she glanced around for a cake shop, certain that someone must have taken advantage of the opportunity. When she didn't find one, she wasn't sure if she was disenchanted or pleased; home in the US, she felt sure there would have been a shop called Let Them Eat Cake right outside the cathedral doors.

Hannah hadn't come to research Marie Antoinette or Louis XVI, however. She was much more interested in Catherine de'Medici, who had been ignored by her husband during his reign as king, but then gone on to hold the reins of power for three decades after his death. She'd seen her three sons each become king in succession, but all the while she had been in control. Catherine had a reputation for brutality, but other than that, she was Hannah's sort of woman. As she tipped back her coffee and drained the last bitter dregs, she gazed up at the cathedral. It was both beautiful and formidable, but what really struck her was how much money must have been involved in its upkeep.

'Who pays for all of this?' she asked.

Charlie gave her a sidelong glance. 'So now you're interested?'

For a moment she wasn't sure what he meant, and then realized he thought she was asking about his own research paper.

'Not in what you're working on. I'm just wondering. There's no way Rome has the budget for it.'

Charlie nodded. 'You wouldn't think so, but you'd be wrong. When the Vatican fell apart after the revelation, the church treasury was frozen. Payments weren't being made because they were trying to protect church wealth from lawsuits. Yeah, the Papal hierarchy completely collapsed, but not for long. It was only, like, two years before the College of Cardinals were able to agree on a new Pope.'

The revelation. The day, many years ago, now, when the world first learned of the existence of the Shadows, and of the clandestine arm of the Vatican that had consisted of sorcerers and killers. Faced with incontrovertible evidence that the church had been involved with black magic, people had turned their backs on Rome. Had the revelation not coincided horribly with the murder of the then-current Pope, someone might have been able to get the disaster under control. But after decades of conspiracies and scandals that had eroded the public's trust in the church, the revelation had been the last straw. The power of the Vatican had been largely dismantled. Or so she'd thought.

Hannah frowned, glancing around for a trash can where she could dispose of her coffee cup.

'That makes no sense,' she said. 'The Third Ecumenical Council was only four or five years ago. And the American clergy didn't even attend that one. No way was there a new Pope that soon after the shit hit the fan.'

Charlie rolled his eyes. 'How do you not know any of this? No wonder you're only interested in dead queens. Look, I'm talking about the internal restructuring that happened long before Vatican III. The church was embarrassed, yeah, and a huge percentage of money just stopped coming in. The American Catholic Church broke off from Rome and a lot of people in other parts of the world either didn't want to fund the Vatican after the secrets that had come out, or they didn't think there was anything left to fund.

'But there was. A skeleton crew, yes. But a Pope, absolutely – Pope Paul the Seventh – and a new College of Cardinals. They started quietly rebuilding the Roman church only a couple of years after the revelation, putting the pieces together, getting control back of their most valuable properties. A lot of European governments, including the French, financed the maintenance and security of the church's landmarks for a lot of years. Now the church is starting to take over managing the properties for themselves again, and those governments want to collect. The French government and the Vatican are in the middle of a huge legal battle to decide who actually now owns the Basilica of Saint-Denis.'

Hannah hung her head a little, smiling at her own self-absorption.

'Y'know,' she said, 'I'm going to do something I almost never do.' She looked up at him, searching the blue eyes behind those hipster glasses, and tried to forget all the times he had kissed her. 'I'm going to apologize.'

Charlie clapped a hand over his chest and dropped his coffee cup, its remnants spilling onto the broad sidewalk in front of the basilica. He staggered and grunted as if rocked by a heart attack.

Hannah punched him in the shoulder. He let out a girly sort of 'ow', but his grin remained.

'I'm serious,' she said. 'That's almost verging on interesting.'

Charlie linked arms with her. 'I'll take that as a compliment before you ruin it. Now, come on. I want to interview a few visitors, some staff, and at least one clergy member if I can find one, and I don't want to be here all damn day.'

Nearly two hours later, Hannah had filled many pages in her notebook with observations about the life and death of Catherine de'Medici and the resting place of her remains. Most of what she needed to include in her paper she had already known before visiting the basilica, but the on-site research had been required and, truth be told, she hadn't minded at all. Every inch of the place was beautiful, its history fascinated her, and as she explored its naves and tombs, she felt as if she were breathing ancient air. Now, though, with her stomach grumbling she had tracked Charlie down and had been attempting to hurry him toward the completion of his own research.

They were at the bottom of a curved stone stairwell that had been accessed by a small, carved wooden door at the rear of the abbey, away from most of the tombs. A narrow corridor ran off to the left, beneath the abbey church, lit only by an occasional dimly burning bulb. In front of them was a black, wrought-iron gate, beyond which she could only see more stone.

'Please, Charlie, I'm hungry,' Hannah said. 'What the hell are we doing here?'

'Waiting for the priest,' he said, as if she might be too simple to understand.

Hannah sighed. She knew very well they were waiting for the priest to come back with a key. During the French Revolution, a lot of the tombs of the royals up in the abbey had been opened and the remains of monarchs had been dumped into a pit and dissolved with quicklime. She had sort of assumed that anything that might have been left of Saint Denis would have been destroyed, but according to Father Laurent, the grimly handsome abbot of the basilica, that was not true.

According to legend, upon his execution by beheading, Saint Denis had picked up his own severed head and walked the six miles from the site of his execution to the place where he would eventually be buried. These days nothing remained of his body, but Father Laurent insisted that the head of Saint Denis remained entombed in the crypt beneath the abbey church.

'So, what's the tomb upstairs for?' Hannah demanded.

'That's where he was buried until the revolution. It's mainly for tourists.'

'And, what, Father Laurent's going to show you the real tomb because you're doing a research paper?' she scoffed.

Charlie smiled. 'He's going to show *us* because I asked. It's not a big secret or anything.'

Her stomach rumbled hungrily. 'Come on, Charlie. What does this have to do with your research? Remember you were all obnoxious about how easy your paper was going to be because it was all going to be theories about the future of the church instead of its past?'

'Well, yeah,' Charlie said. 'But it's the severed head of a saint. It's cool, right?'

She threw up her hands. 'It's not like we're going to be able to *see* it!'

He shushed her, glancing down the corridor, and when she turned she saw Father Laurent making his way toward them, passing from pools of dim light into shadow and then back into the light again. For a priest, he wasn't bad looking. It had occurred to Hannah that if the new Vatican could draw young, intelligent yet formidable looking guys like Laurent into the priesthood, maybe they would someday re-establish their former power and influence.

The priest carried an ornate key on an iron ring.

'The church is more concerned with tradition than security,' he said in fluent but accented English, shaking his head as he slipped the big key into the lock. 'I am constantly amazed by how much we rely upon our assumptions of what will never happen . . . until it does.'

'Is this really it?' Hannah asked. 'What about the doors upstairs? They must be alarmed.'

Father Laurent nodded. 'Yes, and there are cameras, of course. But a single, determined individual could get in and out easily enough, if they had a plan.'

The hinges squealed as he swung the gate inward. He turned to glance at them. 'Neither of you is planning a heist, I hope?'

'Well, actually . . .' Charlie replied.

Hannah laughed. 'You've seen too many movies, Father.'

The priest smiled and then stepped through the gate, gesturing for them to follow. With his graying hair and square jaw, he had a hard look about him, but the smile gave him a warmth that made Hannah feel safe in his presence. She found herself wondering how his life had led him here, and thought she might ask him a few questions for her own research when Charlie had finished.

'It's incredibly nice of you to do this,' Charlie said as he and Hannah followed the priest into the narrow corridor beyond the gate.

'It is my pleasure,' Father Laurent said. 'It is a nice break from performing services for a tiny congregation while noisy, rude tourists wander around the abbey as if they are children at the zoo.'

He turned and reached into the shadows for a switch that brought to life a sequence of caged light bulbs along the ceiling of the corridor. The bulbs offered only splashes of light to navigate the darkness.

'As you can see, our power is almost as archaic as our security,' Father Laurent said.

He set off down the corridor, moving from one pool of light to the next, and they followed.

'If you don't mind me asking, Father,' Hannah began, 'I was wondering how long you've been a priest.'

They both knew the unspoken remainder of the question: had it been before or after the revelation?

'Only three years,' he said without turning. 'I found my calling later than most, but the church needed—'

The whole corridor shook around them, the stone floor seeming to rise and shift beneath their feet. Hannah cried out and caught herself against the wall. The caged lights flickered, one of them popping and going dark. Father Laurent stumbled and fell to his knees as the floor bucked under them. Hannah caught a glimpse of Charlie's face, saw that his lips were moving, but she couldn't hear him over the deep rumble of the world around them and the grinding of stone. Dust sifted down from the ceiling and then two more bulbs popped in quick succession, so that very little light remained.

Ohmygod ohmygod ohmygod.

A fucking earthquake.

Only seconds had passed but already it felt like it had been going on forever. With a horrible crack, a fissure appeared in the wall to her left and she knew she had to get the hell out of there. Back in the archway, at the gate . . . that was what they said about earthquakes, wasn't it? Get into a doorway. Or was that for hurricanes? She couldn't remember and suddenly all she could hear was the thunder of her own heart in her ears. It beat against the inside of her chest so hard that she put one hand over her breastbone and reminded herself that she was too young for a heart attack, too young to die, too young to be killed in a fucking earthquake.

It kept going.

And then she was screaming for it to stop, fear swallowing her, enveloping her. Charlie grabbed her outstretched hand and tugged her toward him, or drew himself toward her – it was hard to tell. He pulled her into his arms even as they tried to keep their balance and he kissed the top of her head.

Hannah slapped his hands away, frantic with terror, just wanting to reach the gateway. She saw the hurt in his eyes and wanted to scream at him for being so sensitive when thousands of tons of stone were about to come down on their heads. Instead she grabbed his wrist and dragged him back the way they'd come. How long had it been going on now? Twenty or thirty seconds. It had to stop soon, didn't it?

As if in answer there came a bang and crash behind them, down at the darkened end of the corridor, so loud that for that one moment it muffled the grinding roar of the earth's distress. The ground shifted violently and threw them into the wall. Hannah stumbled and fell, then immediately began to regain her feet. She looked up to see Father Laurent coming toward them, a cloud of dust roiling behind him in the corridor. He looked more anguished than afraid, and she realized that something had just happened to the tomb of Saint Denis. The ceiling must have given way and caved in on top of it, or the floor beneath it had split.

She wiped dust from her eyes, blinked and looked at her hand to discover that the dust was mixed with blood. She had banged her head.

'Come on!' Charlie said, squeezing her hand and getting her to focus.

It took her a moment before she realized that she had heard him, and then to understand why. The quake had quieted to a tremble.

And then it ceased.

Father Laurent caught up to them. 'Please,' he said. 'We must not remain here. It may not be safe.'

Hannah nodded. The priest passed by them, taking the lead again. Hannah held Charlie's hand, grateful for his touch, her heart still pounding in her chest and thumping in her ears as she wondered if the stairs would be blocked. She'd had panic attacks before, and suddenly her thoughts raced with claustrophobic terror at the baseless idea that they might be trapped down there.

'We're okay,' Charlie said, sensing her terror. 'It's over. We just have to get outside and we'll be—'

An electrical crackle filled the air, followed by a loud pop as the rest of the caged bulbs went dark, sparks falling from the shorted fixtures. If not for the light of the stairwell coming through the open gate up ahead, they would have been in total darkness. Hannah still feared being trapped, but the light acted as a beacon, speeding her forward.

'I must hurry,' Father Laurent said. 'I can't imagine the damage in the village, or in the city. I fear for Paris. There will be people who need my help.'

Last rites, Hannah thought. *He's not talking about digging through rubble. He's talking about taking away their sin before they go to God.*

Somehow that made her panic worse, but she swallowed it down and just nodded, squeezing Charlie's hand as they approached the light spilling in from the stairwell on the right. The ceiling had buckled slightly above the gate, so that it could not be moved. If Father Laurent had closed it behind them, they really would have been trapped there. Her heart leaped as she glanced at the stairs and saw that although some debris had fallen, their way out remained open.

The stink of something rotten filled her nostrils. Flinching in revulsion, she turned to look at Charlie. For a moment, her mind could not make sense of the thing she saw looming in the darkness behind him, could not take in the multitude of sickly green eyes or the rotten, oozing splits in its flesh or the glistening red shards of bone or horn that protruded through its skin all over.

It wasn't until it opened its mouth and revealed rows of teeth like hundreds of black needles that she truly *saw* it, and felt something inside her die . . . something that might have been hope.

The demon wrapped long talons around Charlie, lurched forward, and bit off his head. Blood jetted from the stump of his neck, bathing the demon's face and filling the air with the acrid copper stink of it. Hannah knew she was screaming, felt her throat go ragged from her shrieks, but she couldn't hear her own voice. All she could hear were Father Laurent's prayers behind her, as if he were whispering in her ear.

In front of her, the demon dropped Charlie's twitching corpse, dragged itself over him, and reached out one long, black-taloned hand.

5

Charlestown, Nevis, West Indies

The breeze off the ocean was warm, as always. Kuromaku stood on the rough-hewn deck of the thatched-roof hut and breathed it in. A few light clouds lingered above the island of Nevis, but otherwise the sky stretched on forever, a vivid, unbroken blue. On the horizon, it met the water of the Caribbean and the two merged into one. Every day he woke to find himself in this place, his heart soared with the joy of life.

Every day but today.

The call had come during the night; Octavian, more anguished than Kuromaku had ever heard him. They had been friends for long centuries, had fought side by side, joining in savage wars and regional skirmishes for no other reason than that there were oppressed people who needed something to help turn the tide. Sometimes that had meant fighting for lost causes, but Octavian and Kuromaku – and a handful of other Shadows who had seen the world in the same way – had gone to war regardless. They were warriors, after all. In combat, they had managed to feel alive long after their human lives had ended.

Over the course of those many years, they had each made human friends and taken human lovers, and even fallen in love. But entropy was the great curse of immortality. Things fell apart. Lives and loves ended, and eternal warriors were forced to watch those who mattered the most to them grow old and pass from the world forever. Kuromaku had offered the gift of immortality – the life of the Shadow – to more than twenty-five people since he had first become immortal, and all but four of them had chosen to age and wither and die, to follow the natural order of things. Of those four, three now hated him, and one had given himself to the fires of the sun back in the days when Shadows still believed that it would burn them.

The longer he lived, the more he grieved, just as he did this morning. He had not spent a great deal of time with Nikki Wydra, but they had fought side by side more than once and she, being only human, had proven herself brave and loyal. And Peter had loved her, and now he grieved for her, and Kuromaku grieved along with his brother.

'Fly, spirit. You are free,' he whispered to the warm tropical breeze.

A small smile touched his lips. He grieved, yes, but no matter how much pain and loss he had endured in his long life, he had found more joy than loss, more laughter than heartache. He still embraced life. With his partner, Sophie, he still owned and ran a vineyard in Bordeaux, France, and when they felt they had worked long enough, they turned the management of the vineyard over to his assistant and retreated to this simple hut on Nevis, a stone's throw from St Kitt's.

'If you don't get going, you'll miss your flight.'

Kuromaku turned at the sound of Sophie's voice and his heart filled with adoration. Once upon a time, her father had been his attorney, and Sophie had inherited the role from him. Kuromaku had watched her grow from infant to gangly teen to beautiful, confident woman. It had been difficult for him to separate the girl from the woman at first, but they had been thrown together to face otherworldly horrors that would have driven many people mad or caused them to curl up and weep in surrender. Sophie had proven herself not only a woman, but a formidable one, and during that time he had realized that he loved her.

'I don't want to go,' Kuromaku said.

'Of course you don't,' Sophie said, arching a suggestive eyebrow. 'Look at me.'

He did. Her light, silken robe hung to mid-calf and was tied loosely enough that her breasts were only partly covered. Her blond hair shone in the sun and her blue eyes sparkled with invitation.

'How could you want to leave this?' she said.

But the playfulness drained from her tone before she had even finished the sentence and she faltered, swallowing hard and swiping at the moisture welling in her eyes. Kuromaku went to her and held her, whispering love in both of their languages.

'You know I don't want to go.'

'Part of you does,' Sophie said. 'Part of you can't wait to draw your swords.'

He could have argued that he didn't have his swords with him, but she knew all of his secrets, knew that his swords were no different from the clothes he wore when it came to the shapeshifting abilities of a Shadow. They changed on a

77

molecular level, and that extended to whatever they wanted it to, except for living flesh. He couldn't shift and forcibly merge another person into himself, but he could make his katana and wakizashi seem to vanish and reappear at will.

If he'd said he hadn't brought them to the Caribbean with him, he'd have been lying.

'I'm a warrior,' he said.

'And I'm her friend. We haven't seen Nikki much, but I was her friend just as much as you were. I should be at her funeral.'

Kuromaku caressed the line of her jaw and lifted her chin so that she was forced to meet his gaze.

'You should be, my love,' he said, and kissed her softly. 'But you cannot be. This Cortez that Peter spoke of . . . he killed Nikki because Peter loved her. It's possible that anyone who comes to mourn for Nikki will also be a target. We can't be sure the funeral is safe.'

She put her palm on his chest and gave him a gentle shove, putting a bit of distance between them.

'I can take care of myself,' she said.

'As much as any mortal can.'

'And when I can't, I have you.'

'Yes. You do.' He kissed her forehead. 'But when the funeral is over, we are going hunting. And when we find the creatures we hunt, we are going to battle. It isn't safe for you to be with me, and it wouldn't be safe for me if you were. Worrying about you could get me killed. Is that what you want?'

Sophie kept her hand flat on his chest, but she dropped her gaze. After a moment, she sighed deeply, and when she lifted her eyes again, he saw the tears streaming down her face.

'I want this to have never happened. I want us to be here, warm and safe. I want to drink wine and make love on the beach. I want paradise.'

Kuromaku let her words hang in the air as he glanced around at their little piece of the island. Over the thatched roof of the cottage hut he could see the green hills at the center of the island rising toward the perfect blue sky. To his right, their small dock jutted out into the water, the sailboat tethered at the end, bobbing in the water with the sail tightly furled.

'This is as close to paradise as this world has to offer,' he said, stroking her face, brushing her tears away.

Sophie slapped his hand away. Then, angry with herself, she wrapped her arms around him and laid her head upon his chest.

'Not today it isn't,' she said through her tears. 'Until you come back to me, this place is going to be Hell. Come back to me, you understand?'

'I do, and I will.'

'Promise!'

He promised, hoping that time would not prove him a liar.

Carlsbad, California

Santiago didn't know how long he'd been staring into the glass. A final sip of whiskey remained but somehow he hesitated to tip it back. It had been long enough that the sweet burn of the liquor had gone from his throat. His thoughts drifted into numb meditation, only partly brought on by the alcohol.

Twenty-four years. That was how long it had been since he had last heard from Peter Octavian, but the hard son of a bitch had apparently kept tabs on him. Enough so that when the time came that he needed to reach out to Santiago, all it had taken Octavian was a phone call. The old warrior would have chalked it up to him having signed the Covenant, but he hadn't given the damned UN his correct address or telephone number. He was practical enough to know when the winds of change were blowing, so signing up had been a no-brainer, but he wasn't stupid.

Octavian, he thought.

The name brought a cascade of sounds and images into his head, gunshots and screams and flashing swords, hopeless causes and tight corners, their backs to the wall. Until the one time in Namibia when they had found themselves on opposite sides of a fight. Things had never been the same after that.

Tonight, just before ten a.m. local time, his cell phone had rung. The conversation had been brief and Santiago had considered hanging up, fighting the urge to feel sympathy for his old friend's grief. But then Octavian had said the magic words.

There will be combat. Maybe war. And, if something isn't done, maybe the last *war.*

Octavian had been at the center of so many conflicts in recent years and he had never called before. Santiago had resented it. There were times when he knew he could have helped, especially in killing Hannibal, but the call had never come. He could think of only two reasons why Octavian had reached out to him at last; either the situation truly was that dire, or the bastard son of the last emperor of Byzantium had finally run out of allies.

Either way, Santiago knew what his decision had to be. He'd known it the moment he'd picked up the phone and heard Octavian's voice, but still, here he was, sitting on his usual stool in Luna's, a dive bar on Tamarack Avenue, on the southern end of the Barrio, staring into the last wet inch of whiskey in his glass.

'Tio,' a soft voice said.

It wasn't the first time he'd heard the voice, but the first time it had registered. Then he felt the gentle touch on his arm and he blinked, waking from a daze, and glanced up from his glass.

Anita with the storm-gray eyes stood beside him looking tired and worn – much too worn for a girl of only twenty.

'Tio, please,' she said.

He frowned, not understanding, and she glanced away worriedly, as if she might fear his reaction. This puzzled him. Santiago had been coming into Luna's for years; they all knew him here. Tio was both a play on his name and the Spanish word for 'uncle', indicating the protective fondness he felt for the owner, Ana Moon, and the people who worked there. His appearance could be intimidating; he knew that. Though only five foot six, he was powerfully built, with ancient tattoos over corded muscles, and his bald head and long, pointed goatee spoke of menace and violence, even when he didn't want them to.

But these people knew him. The idea that Anita might be nervous around him would have made him laugh if not for the pang of hurt and disappointment he felt.

'Did I do something wrong?' he asked.

Anita smiled, but he could see that it was forced. 'Tio. It's three o'clock in the morning. We just want to go home.'

Santiago knitted his brow, trying to process that. He glanced around and saw that the bar was empty except for Anita and himself, and for Miguelito the cook, who sat slumped in a booth with an empty beer glass in front of him. Even the bartender, Rubio, had gone home. The chairs had been put up onto the tables and the wooden floor was damp with ammonia-scented mop water. The music had been turned off. He had no idea how long he had been sitting in near silence.

He shook his head, trying to clear his mind, and knocked back the final swallow of whiskey, setting down the glass. Then he slipped two twenties from his wallet and left them on the bar. When he slid off the stool and moved toward Anita, she flinched back. It hurt him all over again.

'No, no. Now, come on,' he said. 'A man just gets a little lost sometimes.'

Perhaps she saw the hurt in his eyes, for she stood still and let him kiss her cheek. He had to stretch a little to do it; Anita was two inches taller.

'My apologies to you both,' he said. 'You won't see me for a while.'

'Don't be that way, Tio,' Anita said quickly. 'It's only that we're tired.'

Santiago glanced at Miguelito, who looked so tired he didn't even feel any of the anxiety that had been troubling the waitress.

'I know, *bonita*. I'm sorry about that, but I didn't mean I wouldn't come into the bar. I'm just going away for a while, that's all. Go home and get some sleep. I'll see you when I come back.'

Santiago headed for the door. His flight to Philadelphia was at 7:10, which gave him plenty of time to go home, shower, change, and pack a bag, and still make it to San Diego in plenty of time. He could've flown out of McClellan, but changing planes would mean a layover, and he wanted the fastest route east.

'Where are you going?' Anita asked as he opened the door.

'To a funeral,' Santiago said. 'After that, maybe to war.'

Philadelphia, Pennsylvania

Charlotte's eyes fluttered open. She was surprised to find that she had been dozing, her head nested between pillows and the bedclothes pulled up to her neck. The drone of voices from CNN came from the television in the hotel room that Octavian had secured for her. She had been watching numbly and had had no intention of sleeping. Shadows had the capacity for sleep but not the human necessity; yet she had apparently drifted off.

Drifted? she thought with bleary amusement. *More like plummeted.*

She sat up and propped herself on a couple of pillows, staring at the television and trying to make sense of the images there. Football players in action, some kind of sports report. Then the reassuring smile of a news anchor before cutting to a Middle Eastern city street scene, black smoke rising as a crush of people fled from uniformed men wielding batons. Children, covered in blood, being treated in a makeshift hospital.

The world we've made, she thought. Whenever she pondered such things, she had to wonder if immortality held any real allure.

There came a brisk knock at the door, the sort that implied it hadn't been the first. Had that been what had woken her?

Frowning, she whipped back the covers and padded to the door in her underpants and a fitted black tee. She would need clothes, especially something for the funeral. Charlotte had gone days wearing the same outfit in the past, but never on purpose. If anything, she had grown more concerned about hygiene and clean clothes since leaving humanity behind.

She stood on her toes and looked through the peephole in the door, spying Allison Vigeant standing in the hall. As Charlotte reached for the deadbolt, the other vampire knocked again.

'All right, hang on!' Charlotte said.

She removed the safety latch and opened the door. 'What's up?'

Allison arched an eyebrow. 'You were sleeping?'

'I crashed,' Charlotte replied. 'Weird, right?'

'Sometimes we need to go dormant, like hibernating,' Allison said. 'Other times it's just reflex. Conditioned behavior from human life.' She looked Charlotte up and down, surveying her many intricate tattoos. 'Can I come in a minute?'

'Sure. Sorry,' Charlotte replied, backing up to let her pass. 'What can I do for you?'

'I just thought we should get to know each other a little,' Allison said. 'You being the new girl and all.'

Charlotte closed the door and followed Allison back into the room. She glanced at the nightstand and saw the clock.

'Sort of a strange time for a get-to-know-you, isn't it?' Charlotte asked. 'Quarter past six in the morning?'

Allison slid into a chair and gazed at her, once again seeming to take her measure. In another life, Charlotte would have felt self-conscious about being in her underpants and t-shirt in front of this woman she barely knew, but modesty had mostly died with her humanity.

'I didn't expect you to be sleeping,' Allison said.

Charlotte nodded, then crawled back into bed, sitting up against the propped pillows. She crossed her hands in her lap.

'What do you want to know? Octavian and Metzger spent about two hours interrogating me last night. I figure you've probably already heard about it from them.'

'From Peter, yes,' Allison said. 'Metzger is afraid to come near me in case I decide to rip his throat out.'

'That's going to make for an interesting alliance.'

'Yeah. It is,' Allison replied. 'What do you know about me?'

Charlotte shrugged. 'Only what Octavian's told me. One of his best friends. Badass vamp hunter. Fugitive. UN figured you for a traitor. Now Octavian's going to shove you down their throats.'

'How does that strike you?'

'If Octavian vouches for you, that's good enough for me. It's not like I have a lot of choices. He's pretty much the only reason I'm alive right now. He could have killed me when we met, and he's had opportunities to let me die.'

'But he's taken you under his wing,' Allison said.

'I guess, yeah.'

'And that's enough for you to be willing to go to war for him?'

Charlotte bristled, cocking her head. 'Cortez and his coven raped and murdered me and turned me into this. If I go to war, it's not for Octavian.'

'What if he wants you elsewhere?' Allison asked. 'The chaos you helped stop in Massachusetts is going to have repercussions. The world is going to start unraveling.'

'That's my fight too, isn't it? I have to live here.' Charlotte slid to the edge of the bed and stared at her. 'What exactly do you want from me? You want me to leave?'

Allison settled back into the chair, steepling her fingers on her chest. 'Not at all. I'm like you. If Peter vouches for you, that's good enough for me. But that doesn't mean I don't get to be curious and to wonder about you and your allegiances.'

Charlotte threw up her hands. 'Look, I told those guys everything I know about Cortez. I told them every safe house I ever visited and the names of every member of the coven I knew. It's a hell of a head start, I think. There's nothing else I can offer. And if I was out to kill Octavian, I'm sure I had an opportunity or two when we were fighting Navalica. You want to know whose side I'm on? Don't be stupid. I'm on my own side first. But I'm smart enough to know that Octavian's on my side, too. He wants to keep me alive and to take Cortez down. Seeing as how those are my two top priorities, yeah . . . I'll fight for him. Wherever he wants me, that's where I'll go.'

Allison nodded thoughtfully, turning to glance out the slider at the gray sky lightening over the city.

'He's a sort of mentor to you, now, I suppose,' Allison said, turning her attention back to Charlotte. 'He's good at it, you know. Being the "vampire godfather", taking ordinary Shadows under his wing and making heroes out of them. He did it for me and a lot of people I loved. But you'd better be very sure that's what you want.'

'I'm sure,' Charlotte insisted.

'See,' Allison went on, 'there were a lot of us, once upon a time. What Peter was talking about last night, the group he mentioned? Most of us are dead. Old friends and old lovers. We won the battles that mattered, yeah. But not without a cost. Not without a price that you have to be willing to pay if you're going to get into this. Most of us never got the chance to decide, to know what we were getting ourselves into. So maybe I'm coming off as a cold bitch. I'm sure I am, actually; I haven't had a lot to laugh about, or anybody to laugh with, for a long time. Might be I don't remember how to be pleasant. But I wanted to give you the opportunity to really think about what you're getting into, and to run like hell if you want.'

Charlotte blinked in surprise. She had thought that this visit was about suspicion, and that was certainly part of it. But what Allison had brought her this morning was an unexpected kindness.

'I . . .' she began, faltering. 'Look, I appreciate it. Honestly. But whatever happens from here on in, I'm choosing it. After I got away from Cortez I just wanted to have a life, but now that I know all of this is happening, I can't just do nothing about it. Besides . . . even if I wanted to run, I've got nowhere else to go.'

Allison sat forward, pushing her hair away from her face. 'All right, then. You're in. But Peter's going to have a lot on his mind, so if he's your godfather, from now on I'm your fairy godmother. You have questions, you need combat training, you're trying to deal with the life you left behind, come to me. I'll do what I can to help you get through it.'

Charlotte smiled, touched by her words and slightly taken aback. Allison stood to leave and Charlotte scrambled out of the bed to follow her.

'Thank you,' Charlotte said. 'Really. Thanks so much.'

She didn't expect to find a friend in this grim hunter. She didn't express the sentiment out loud, however. It seemed clear that there would be no hugs and late-night girl talk between them. Perhaps 'friend' was too strong a word, but 'ally' would do.

'My pleasure,' Allison said, reaching the door. She pulled it open and then turned, standing silhouetted against the corridor beyond. 'Let's be clear, though. If it turns out you're bullshitting and that you're still taking orders from Cortez, I'll spend hours killing you.'

Charlotte could only stare, wide-eyed, as Allison left, shutting the door behind her. She'd believed every word.

It seemed that perhaps even 'ally' was too strong a word.

Saint-Denis, France

Hannah woke in seething pain. Her skull felt like it might split and her belly and ribs ached so much that she couldn't breathe. Tears sprang to her eyes and she cried out, head back, venting her pain to a God she feared must be deaf. *Where the hell am I?* she thought. *Charlie?*

And then she remembered the demon, and that it had killed Charlie, whom she had never really stopped loving.

The pain turned her mournful sob into a moan. 'God!' she cried out, reaching down to put one hand on her belly – her rounded, distended belly. Something moved beneath the skin and she screamed, eyes widening as she propped herself up.

On the stairs.

Leading up from the sepulcher in the basement of the cathedral.

At the bottom of the stairs, the demon lay upon Charlie's corpse, stripping flesh and muscle from the bones, which jerked and twitched obscenely. Her eyelids fluttered and the edges of her vision dimmed, but she forced herself not to pass out again, searching her mind for the last traces of memory from before she had fallen unconscious. The demon had killed him, then come past him, reaching for her.

Why did it let me go? she wondered.

Another spasm clutched at her gut and she cried out in pain and put both hands on her stomach. Eyes wide, she felt a fullness descend inside her, stretching her open, searing her vagina with pain, and then she knew and felt stupid for not understanding immediately.

The demon had not let her go at all.

Her heart raced and her breath came in desperate hitches of denial. She propped herself higher on an elbow, the hard edges of the stone stairs biting into her back, and she looked down and saw the blood soaking through the crotch of her pants.

'Oh, God,' she whispered, tears springing to her eyes. *What is happening to me?*

Horror swept through her, her gorge rising in disgust even as the pain and fullness grew worse. Something inside her, growing and twisting and trying to come out . . . trying to be born.

Shrieking, tears streaming down her cheeks, unmindful of anyone who might bear witness, Hannah reached down and tore at the button and zipper of her pants. Even as she shrugged them down, fighting the pain and weakness that had left her stranded there on the stairs, she felt the surge from inside her, the stretching of her vagina as something wriggled inside her, struggling to be free. Pushing her pants down, she caught sight of herself . . . opening . . . and the blood- and mucous-smeared thing that was emerging, its skin a chitinous, insectoid armor.

As it pushed free, pain wrenched a scream from her throat and she threw her head back, slamming her skull against the stairs. Her thoughts blurred and her legs began to spasm and kick of their own accord, splayed wide. For a moment she thought the grotesque birth had already taken place, her lower half numbed by trauma, and then she felt it push again and slide from within her.

She couldn't look at it, could only close her eyes tightly and feel it slither over her, leaving a wet, stinking trail. It mewled beside her, fetid, brimstone breath on her cheek, and then she heard it on the stairs, clicking and then clattering as it slid up into the cathedral, where people would still be recovering from an earthquake, unable to imagine what the earth had shaken loose.

For several minutes, sickness roiling in her gut, she lay weeping on the stairs and listened for the screams she knew must come from above any minute now. Below her came wet, grinding, snapping noises and she wondered if the demon had begun to gnaw on Charlie's bones. Sobbing, she pushed all thoughts of Charlie away. She couldn't think of him, now, couldn't allow herself to wonder what might have happened if she could have just stopped with her sarcasm and little cruelties and opened her heart to him, told him how she really felt. That she still loved him.

Shaking, eyes burning with tears, pants around her ankles, she turned on her side and began to consider modesty. *So weak*, she thought. In all her life she had never felt so fragile and tentative. Grief felt like an iron shroud upon her, crushing her, suffocating her so that she did not even want to rise from her defilement.

But she had to. If she stayed here, when the demon had finished consuming Charlie, it would crawl up the stairs and come for her. Again.

Hannah forced herself to reach a trembling hand down and begin to drag her pants upward. Then she halted, brows knitted. *How?* she asked herself. The last thing she remembered was the demon reaching for her, touching her, and then a cold fire racing through her and pain shooting through her belly that sent her reeling toward the stairs. She had fallen on the stone steps and unconsciousness had claimed her. But when she'd come around, her clothes had not been torn. She'd had to remove her own pants for that . . . *Stop. Don't think about it.*

The demon had impregnated her with nothing but a touch.

A spasm wracked her body, bile burned its way up the back of her throat and she twisted to one side, spraying vomit onto the wall and stairs. Disgusted, she inched away, wrinkling her nose at the smell and at this humiliation added to all the rest.

'Come. You've got to hurry,' a voice said.

Recoiling from the gentle kindness, she fought for modesty, trying to drag her pants up the rest of the way even as she lolled her head back and looked to see who had come upon her in her ruin. Light from above silhouetted him, but when she blinked she saw that she knew him, and her humiliation was complete.

Father Laurent. She had entirely forgotten about the priest.

Hannah opened her mouth to speak but could only sob again, throwing a hand across her face to hide her shame.

'Ssshh,' he said. 'You are in shock. But we must get you out of here. There is another upstairs. It just passed me, but who can say how many more there might be?'

No, she thought, wanting to explain to him. This new demon, this thing with its chitinous armor, had not come from the tomb of Saint Denis like the other. It had come from—

Hannah cried out, contorting with the pain of fresh cramps in her belly. Her first thought was to wonder what damage the thing had done, growing inside of her. And then she felt the swelling and the squirming and the hideous pressure from within, and her legs widened instinctively, preparing once again for birth.

Eyes wide, breath catching in her throat, she began to shake her head furiously, even as Father Laurent's words echoed in her mind. *Who can say how many more there might be?*

And oh, how she screamed.

6

Philadelphia, Pennsylvania

The morning passed in slow motion. Octavian had made the necessary phone calls the night before and then slept for several hours, plagued by dark dreams he could not recall upon waking, but which nevertheless seemed to haunt him from the corners of the room. He'd risen before five a.m., showered and dressed, and then spent hours sitting in a chair by the window, looking out at the gray skies and the rain that pattered the glass. Allison had brought him a bouquet of yellow roses, though he had no idea where she had gotten them in the middle of the night. From time to time he stared at the flowers, reaching out to feel the softness of their petals and to marvel at the fragility of the world.

Nikki had grown up in Philadelphia. Most of their friends didn't know that, or had learned it once and promptly forgotten. His love had been a troubadour from the moment her mother, Etta, had died. Etta had taught her daughter to love the blues and to sing from her soul, as if she had known that Nikki would need an outlet for her grief. Nikki had been sixteen when her mother died. She had never met her father and though her mother had a sister in Baltimore, the women were estranged. When Etta had passed away, Nikki had been on her own, and she had hit the road with her guitar and a few changes of clothes.

When Nikki left Philadelphia behind, she had truly left it behind. There were a few childhood friends she still heard from now and again, but with Keomany dead, the only people she had been close to had been friends she and Octavian shared and those who came from her life as a musician. Word of her death had already hit the media, and this troubled him. Nikki hadn't been a huge celebrity, but she had achieved a modicum of fame – certainly enough that strangers and past acquaintances and photographers would show up at any public funeral service, and he didn't want that.

He'd called her manager and asked him to spread the word to Nikki's old bandmates, and he suspected some of them would show up for the funeral. The details of the service were being kept secret, but anyone willing to do a little digging would be able to figure out that Nikki would be laid to rest with her mother. She would have wanted that, Octavian knew – to share eternity with the woman who had taught her about love and compassion and music.

Eternity, he thought, staring out at the rain. He didn't know how long he would live. Once he had evolved beyond vampirism and become human again, he ought to have lived out the balance of an ordinary lifespan, but with the magic that coursed through him, he had suspected for some time that he was not aging. Nikki had broached the subject more than once, wondering whether they would be able to grow old together, and Octavian had insisted that he didn't know.

Now he had the answer.

Numb and hollow except for the hot ember of fury in his gut that helped to burn away the grief, he sat in the chair and let hours tick past. Metzger and his team were doing their jobs, hunting down leads and trying to locate Cortez, mostly thanks to information they'd gleaned from the interview with Charlotte last night.

Sergeant Omondi had taken Charlotte back to New York with him this morning to trace one of her contacts. Octavian wanted to join them, wanted the cathartic passion of the hunt to ease his sorrow. In the time he'd spent working as a private detective, trying to get to know the modern human mind better and to help where he could, he had taught himself to be perceptive and to make leaps of deductive logic. He wanted to put those skills to use tracking down Nikki's killer, but not until after the funeral. He wouldn't leave her until she was finally at rest.

Afterward, there'd be hell to pay.

A knock at the door interrupted his ruminations. Octavian frowned, this visitation unwelcome. Reluctantly, he raised a hand, contorted his fingers – which crackled momentarily with an icy blue light – and the door unlocked and swung inward.

'Hello?' Commander Metzger said, with as close to uncertainty in his voice as there might ever be. He was not a man prone to self-doubt or uneasiness.

'Come in, Commander,' Octavian said, not rising from the chair.

Metzger stepped into the room, frowning and wary as he glanced around to figure out who had opened the door. But the mystery didn't hold the man's attention for long. Octavian could see by the set of his shoulders and the grim steel in his eyes that this was no mere condolence call.

'The press is looking for you,' Metzger said. 'The hotel is under strict orders not to reveal that you've taken a room here, but don't be surprised if one of them finds you sooner or later.'

'They'll find me only if I want to be found. But you didn't come here to warn me about the media, Commander. Tell me you've located Cortez.'

'Not yet, but we've identified the San Diego safe house that Charlotte described and the FBI have the building under surveillance right now. They're cooperating fully, searching for emergency exits that might not be on the architect's original plans. I've got a squad on the way there. We're searching Los Angeles for the home base Charlotte claims Cortez and his coven were using, but no luck so far.'

'All right,' Octavian said, already moving beyond the conversation, drifting back into the darkness of his ruminations, thinking about eternity and vengeance. 'Keep me posted.'

'That's what I'm doing,' Metzger said. Then, instead of retreating, the commander came further into the room, taking up a position five feet from Octavian, standing over him expectantly. 'But we have other problems, now. Trouble that requires your attention.'

Octavian tore his focus away from the rain on the window-pane to study Metzger's features.

'Whatever it is can wait.'

'Tell that to the people who are dying,' Metzger said.

Octavian shot Metzger a withering look.

'I've been fighting to keep the wolves from the door for years,' he said. 'And I'll do it again. But this is my time – mine and Nikki's – and I'm not letting anything tear me away from that. If I'd known my days with her were numbered, there are a lot of things I'd have done differently, but I can't get those days back.'

Metzger regarded him carefully. He seemed about to leave, but then came nearer instead and sat on the end of the bed, barely out of arm's reach. Not that Octavian needed to touch the man to hurt him; they both knew that.

'All our days are numbered,' Metzger said, with a combination of steel and sympathy. 'But these people who are dying in France . . . they're down to minutes, or maybe seconds. They're dying right now, and every single one of them has people who are going to wish they could have back the days they squandered on less important things.'

Octavian tried to ignore the words, but he could not prevent them from echoing in his head. Nikki was dead and no amount of mourning would bring her back, so what good could he do here in Philadelphia? If a crisis had broken out in Europe, could he simply ignore it?

He ran his hands over his face, chin stubble rough on his palms.

'Tell me,' he said, without looking up.

'There was a localized earthquake just north of Paris. The Cathedral of Saint-Denis was damaged and there are—'

'That's for the Red Cross to—'

'—*things* coming out of it. Demons. No one's seen anything like them since the thing with the Tatterdemalion years ago. They're not wraiths, though. Serpentine bodies covered in some kind of exoskeleton, arms on an upper torso, and lots of teeth. We should have images shortly, but I'm told they're not clear. Power is disrupted, along with all satellite and broadcast signals. Not gone, but rife with interference.'

Metzger leaned forward, making sure Octavian met his gaze.

'The French are marshalling a military response, but you and I both know that when an incursion like this takes place, it's usually more than conventional weapons can handle.'

Octavian looked out the window again. The rain seemed to be coming down harder, battering the window so hard that the glass vibrated with its punishment. He thought of Keomany, who had felt the chaos growing in Massachusetts early enough to warn him, to make sure he was there to help set things right. Without Keomany to sense it, he had not seen this coming at all, and he couldn't help but wonder what other horrors were even now stirring beyond the barriers between worlds.

He studied the vase of yellow roses, brow knitting. Rather than wilting, they had blossomed further, growing and blooming with remarkable health, though they had surely been cut many hours before. And had the thorns been so prominent before? He wasn't certain, but the vigor of cut flowers seemed a poor thing to focus on at the moment, a way for him to distract himself from the truth. Every death in France left a little more blood on his hands. He had acted from pure motives, but he shared responsibility for the dreadful state of the world's magical defenses. With the fall of the Roman church and the loss of the Gospel of Shadows – the spellbook that contained all of the magic accumulated by Vatican sorcerers since the founding of the church – the safeguards had vanished. Whatever happened now would be partly his fault, and he couldn't live with himself if he pretended to ignore that. Still . . .

Exhaling sharply, he glanced at Metzger.

'I'll advise you,' he said. 'There are mystics and occultists who can help, at least temporarily, to try to contain the demons. But until the funeral tomorrow morning, I'm not going anywhere.'

'Octavian,' Metzger prodded.

'She loved me. I'm staying with her until the last shovelful of dirt is thrown over her coffin. By then, we'll have more than enough help on hand to deal with whatever these demons are.'

Metzger sighed, but he nodded. 'All right. I'll be back with an update in an hour or two.'

'If you confirm Cortez's location—'

'You'll be the first to know, as agreed,' Metzger said. 'You get the kill.'

Octavian nodded and turned again to study the uncannily healthy roses. With a gesture, he caused the hotel room door to unlock and swing inward. If Metzger felt intimidated by this display of magic, he left the room without commenting.

'I know I should go,' he said, whispering to the rain against the glass. 'But I can't leave you. Not yet.'

I'd never forgive myself, he thought.

A ripple of nausea went through him as he realized that he had already passed that point. On the night when Nikki had needed him most, he had not been here for her. He hadn't been able to protect her.

Some things could simply never be forgiven.

Brattleboro, Vermont

'It's so wonderful to see you.'

Cat smiled. 'You too, Heather.'

The pretty young earthwitch, who had driven all the way from South Carolina, gave her a firm hug, smiling warmly. With her big blue eyes and fairy-smile, Heather had an almost ethereal presence that Cat had always found very soothing. Of all their friends, Heather was the only one Tori ever seemed to be jealous of, which was funny because the younger witch hadn't the slightest interest in women. Not that Tori would have had anything to worry about, regardless. Cat adored Heather, but she loved Tori with all her heart.

Heather sighed, her expression turning sad.

'I'm sorry I couldn't make it here in time for Keomany's memorial.'

'I know you'd have been here if you could,' Cat assured her. 'And we'll say goodbye to her again tonight, say a prayer, and raise a glass.'

Heather smiled, satisfied with this reply.

'You heard about Nikki Wydra, I assume?' she asked.

Cat nodded, a dark weight settling on her heart. 'How could I not? With all the media coverage, she's going to be more famous for having died than she ever was for her music. It's a sin.'

'Did you hear from Octavian? You guys are close, right? Are you going to the funeral?'

Cat frowned. 'Keomany was close to them. We haven't heard from him. I feel for the guy, but I also can't help thinking he's to blame.'

Heather's big blue eyes grew even bigger. 'You think he killed her?'

'No, no,' Cat said quickly. 'But look at what happened to Keomany. Octavian's reckless. So many of his friends have been killed as collateral damage in these battles he's had. I know he's doing the right thing, saving lives, all of that . . . but I can't help thinking that he isn't careful enough, that people like Keomany and Nikki die because they love him.'

Heather nodded gravely. 'I never thought about it that way.'

'Anyway, it doesn't matter. Tonight, we celebrate,' Cat said. 'Go on into the house. You're sharing the attic room on the left with Jaleesa. She's down at the barn getting cider and donuts, I think. You can head on down there or just rest a bit. I know it's been a long journey for you. I have to check on some things in the orchard and then I'll be back and we can catch up.'

'Excellent,' Heather said. 'I *am* tired, but . . . donuts!'

She picked up her duffel bag, gave Cat a kiss on the cheek, and then headed into the house. Watching her go, Cat couldn't help feeling guilty. She didn't like to deceive anyone, even if she had only committed sins of omission, but she couldn't very well tell the other witches what was going on in the orchard – at least not until they knew for certain themselves.

Cat set off on foot. It was a ten-minute walk from her house on the property to the clearing in the orchard, but she relished the time she spent amongst the trees, the air sweet with the scent of apples and rich with the smell of earth and growing things. She felt cradled in the embrace of the goddess here, and never wanted to be anywhere else for very long.

When she arrived at the clearing, she saw that Ed, the orchard foreman, had put a mesh covering over the enclosure he'd cobbled together around what Cat and Tori and Ed himself had been hopefully referring to as 'the new growth'. There were customers wandering through the rows, picking apples, and as Cat approached the clearing she saw a couple with two precious little boys pause to try to look over the enclosure, through the mesh. The father had one son on his shoulders.

'What do you see, Kyle?' the father asked.

'A tree, I think,' the little boy said. 'But it's moving.'

'Dad, come on!' the older son whined, and then the family headed off into the rows. The mother and father exchanged a smile and Cat thought she heard the mother say 'moving trees', with the amused indulgence particular to mothers.

Cat turned right and worked her way around the enclosure. She heard Tori and Ed speaking before she saw them emerging from a gate that the foreman had included as part of the enclosure. It was a crude thing, just hinges and plywood, but it did its job and had a hoop for a padlock.

'What's going on in there?' Cat asked.

Tori looked up, a bit startled, but her troubled expression relaxed and she went to give her wife a quick hug and kiss. Ed had been uneasy with their displays of affection once upon a time, but he'd grown used to it.

'Everything under control for tonight?' Tori asked.

'Yeah, yeah. We're good,' Cat said, waving the question away. 'Except, y'know, for this incredible, impossible thing that we have no idea how to address with our guests. So . . . talk to me.'

Tori exhaled and smiled at Ed before turning back to Cat. She shrugged.

'It's growing. Gotta be two and a half feet high by now,' she said.

Cat nodded. 'That little boy said it was moving.'

'Nah,' Ed put in. 'Just the breeze in her hair.'

Tori and Cat both shifted awkwardly. They had been trying to avoid calling the new growth *she* or *her*. It seemed too hopeful, somehow, particularly since they were not at all certain what they were dealing with. The new growth might have a human shape, but it also had bark in some places and skin like an apple in others, and its features were stiff and unmoving. Roots thrust deeply into the ground, long thin branches that gave the illusion of hair, there was no doubt that this thing was a plant of some kind.

Yet, loath as they were to say it out loud, the new growth was also somehow Keomany.

'All right,' Cat said. 'What do we do tonight? Do we tell them all what's going on, and if not, how do we hide this from them?'

'We can't tell them. Not yet,' Tori said. 'Anything could happen. The new growth could be damaged. We have to protect it.'

'There's that space at the end of row forty-six, on the west side of the hill,' Ed suggested. 'It ain't as big as this clearing, but it'd be big enough if you wanted to do your ceremony there.'

'I hate hiding this from them,' Cat said, sighing as she went to the enclosure and peered over the top, looking down through the mesh thanks to her great height. 'They're our sisters, after all . . . tonight more than any other. It just seems wrong.'

Tori edged up beside her and took her hand, squeezing it. 'I love them, too. Well, most of them. Heather, Vicky, Ella, Jaleesa . . . I want to share this with them. It's a miracle, Cat. But I just don't want to take any risks yet.'

Cat nodded. 'I know. Me neither.' She turned to Ed. 'Row forty-six it is. Can you get the staff to set up some chairs there? Tori and I are going to have to start preparing the ground for the ceremony.'

She hesitated, then turned to her wife, taking both of Tori's hands in her own. 'But we're going to check in an hour before sunset. It could be that by then she . . . it . . . will have grown enough that there will be no question about the miracle that's happening here, and then we can share it with all of them.'

Tori smiled. 'Deal.'

They started back down the hill together, hand in hand, both of them wearing enormous grins. The earth magic that had blossomed in their orchard was unlike anything either of them had ever encountered or even heard about.

If – *no, when!* – the new growth reached maturity, would it open its eyes and speak? And if it did, would it speak with Keomany's voice, or was the thing rooted in their orchard some new creature entirely, given life by the goddess?

Cat couldn't wait to find out.

*

Philadelphia, Pennsylvania

Kuromaku stood in the hotel lobby, letting the ebb and flow of human life wash over him. The colors of their garments might be vivid or drab, but he saw beyond such outward expressions, felt the heat of their blood and the vibrancy of their aspirations. There were times he thought he could even see the ties that bound them to one another. Octavian had undergone a metamorphosis years ago that had split his Shadow nature into three parts. Kuromaku had not lived long enough yet for that transition, but he did believe himself to have undergone a slow evolution over the years, a series of small epiphanies that led to what he considered the beginning of wisdom.

He was still a warrior, of course, and he had always had honor, even when others would have called him a monster. But he had lived long enough first to grow to disdain human fragility and whimsy, and then to cherish it.

The lobby of the hotel where Nikki Wydra had been murdered held interest for Kuromaku. There had been dozens of so-called journalists outside, along with more than one hundred spectators, many of whom he surmised were fans of Nikki's music. The local police were keeping them out, allying themselves with hotel security to determine who were legitimate guests and visitors. Kuromaku presumed it must be creating havoc for hotel guests, who would undoubtedly want some sort of compensation for the inconvenience.

Nikki's death, an inconvenience. He closed his eyes a moment. As much as he had come to find humanity beautiful, he was far from immune to frustration, and other emotions.

When he opened his eyes he saw the police officer who had let him in to the lobby coming toward him, moving around a furious-looking woman who tugged a tow-headed little boy by the hand, even as a bellhop followed with her luggage. She headed for the front desk, having begun her tirade even before she reached the counter, preparing to check out.

'Mom? Mom? Mom?' the boy intoned, yanking her arm to try to get her attention. 'Are there really vampires in the hotel?'

The boy glanced around, eyes wide with a combination of fear and fascination, as if a vampire might pop out from behind the giant potted fern he had just passed. Kuromaku smiled at the boy's expression. *If you only knew*. The mother, however, only hushed him.

'Excuse me, sir,' the young cop said, approaching Kuromaku. 'Can you come this way, please?'

Kuromaku glanced once more at the boy and his angry mother and then nodded to the officer, gesturing for him to lead the way. In the chaos of noise and confusion in the lobby, a more polite reply would have been lost. Even now, as he followed the officer past two dark-suited security guards, a man near the concierge desk began to shout about the rights of the press, clutching a camera as he was hustled toward the doors.

'This is a total mess,' the cop said, glancing back at Kuromaku. 'Bad enough you got a celebrity murder case, but throw vamps in and everybody goes bugfuck crazy. It's only gonna get worse as word spreads about how she died.'

Kuromaku silently agreed as the officer led him past the entrance to the hotel's restaurant and toward the opening into a grotto of elevator banks.

Concerned, the officer slowed and looked at him. 'I didn't mean any disrespect, y'know? About the victim?'

Now that they were away from the epicenter of the chaos and it was quieter, Kuromaku nodded.

'Of course. A day like today, I imagine your job becomes difficult.'

'Exactly!' the cop said, nodding grimly. 'It's a nuthouse in here.'

They entered the elevator grotto to find two people seemingly awaiting their arrival. One was a Chinese man who carried himself like a soldier, while the other was an old friend.

Kuromaku smiled and opened his arms as he went to her. 'Allison. I'm very happy to see you.'

Allison Vigeant embraced him firmly. 'And I'm glad you're here, 'Maku. I just wish it were under different circumstances.'

With a sigh, he released her and stepped back, though he kept one hand on her arm as he met her gaze. In that moment, they had forgotten the other people standing in the grotto with them.

'So do I. How is he?'

Eyes haunted, Allison lowered her gaze for just a moment before looking up at him again. 'About how you'd expect. But he'll be glad you're here. There's all kinds of nasty shit hitting the fan. He's going to need us, and more besides.'

Kuromaku nodded once, unsmiling, and stood a little straighter. 'Take me to him.'

When the knock came at his hotel room door, Octavian tore his gaze away from the window. He had been watching the silent tumult of the clouds, his thoughts everywhere and nowhere, his grief lying in wait for him to begin to think again.

'Who is it?' he called from the sturdy, cushioned chair.

'An old friend.'

Octavian froze halfway through a deep breath, then rose and strode purposefully across the room to open the door.

One of Metzger's people was there with Allison – *Song*, Octavian reminded himself – but his focus was on the third visitor, the one who had spoken, although now he stood behind the others. It had been months since they had seen one another, perhaps more than a year, but most days that seemed like no time at all for men such as they were. Today, it seemed far too long.

'My brother,' Octavian said.

Kuromaku smiled. Allison did as well, as she stood aside so that the old friends might be reunited. Kuromaku might not truly be Octavian's brother – they didn't share the same father or mother or the same vampiric progenitor – but they were comrades in arms and had been friends for centuries, and to Octavian's mind, they were closer than any brothers who shared the same blood. Their bond had been forged in blood and in bloodshed, their own and that of their enemies.

Octavian pulled him close and clapped him on the back.

'Thank you for coming,' he said.

'It is where I belong today,' Kuromaku said.

They shared a quiet moment of understanding. Octavian could have said more, but they would have been words he had spoken too many times before. They stood together today and all days, whatever might come.

He nodded and turned to Allison. 'Come with me, both of you. Now that Kuromaku's here, there's something we all need to see.'

Octavian pulled his door shut behind him and started down the corridor. All three of them made to follow him, but he paused and glanced at Song.

'Not you.'

'Commander Metzger instructed me to—'

Octavian held up a hand. 'Stop. This isn't an argument, kid. And no offense meant. But these people here? They're my family, and what happens next is family business. You go and explain that to Metzger if you want, but if you try to force your way into family business, there'll be blood, and none of it ours.'

He said it as kindly as he could, though he watched Song's eyes to make sure the soldier understood he meant it. From Song's irritation, and the sliver of fear in his gaze, it was clear he had gotten the message.

'As you say,' Song replied, his words clipped, and colored by his accent. 'I will deliver the message.'

'You do that,' Allison said, and she gave him a little wave. 'Buh-bye.'

Octavian led the way down the corridor, past hotel rooms that were either empty or were occupied by members of Task Force Victor. Metzger had turned this level into a temporary command center for his team and for the investigation into Nikki's murder. Allison had a room and there was one waiting for Kuromaku as well. Given the killing that had taken place here, the hotel had willingly accommodated the request to clear the floor of guests and reinstall them in other rooms. They might not have been happy about it, but Octavian suspected most of the guests were only too pleased to be away from the police, FBI, and TFV foot traffic.

'You don't seem to like Corporal Song,' Kuromaku said.

Allison sniffed. 'He's Task Force Victor. Our disdain is mutual.'

Octavian knew that Kuromaku would want a longer conversation with him. His old friend would want to offer his condolences more formally. But they had stood side by side or back to back in enough battles and lost enough loved ones down through the years that Kuromaku's sympathy was understood. To soldiers such as they were, the aftermath of tragedy was nearly always the time for action.

107

'Here,' Octavian said, stopping in front of Nikki's hotel room. He was surprised no guard was on duty.

A rap on the door brought a swift reply. With a click, the door swung inward to reveal a thin, fortyish woman in an FBI jacket. The room was a mini-suite, with a little sitting room sort of foyer and the main bedroom area beyond. Beyond the FBI agent, Octavian could see Barbieri – the TFV forensics specialist – along with a couple of FBI crime scene techs.

'Can I help you?' the woman asked, frowning as she gazed at the three of them.

Octavian ignored her, looking at Barbieri. 'I need the room.'

The FBI woman scowled. 'Who the hell are you?'

Barbieri had the good sense to look uncomfortable. 'Agent Kline, this is Peter Octavian.'

The woman's face went blank and she drew back slightly. 'I see.'

'I need—' Octavian began again.

'I'm sorry for your loss, Mr Octavian,' Agent Kline said, 'but I'm sure you understand that the crime scene is still being processed.'

Octavian felt a flare of anger that caused him to clench his fist and make his hand crackle with the dark purple light of deadly spellcraft. It was happening more and more, his emotions stirring the magic within him, and he knew he had to be cautious. There was danger here.

'Bullshit,' he said evenly. 'Philadelphia PD was in here. Barbieri and his UN vampire hunters have been over the room, top to bottom. Your own people have been in here for hours. You're done. It's my turn, now.'

Agent Kline glanced beyond him at Allison and Kuromaku, then focused on Octavian again.

'For what?' she asked.

Octavian stared at her, then shifted his gaze purposefully back to Barbieri.

'To do it my way. Get them out of here, Barbieri. I won't ask again.'

He didn't need to. Agent Kline continued to protest, but mostly in muttered asides. Octavian was certain that Barbieri – like Song – would report back to Metzger, but none of that mattered. Metzger needed him far more than he needed Task Force Victor.

'This is the place, then?' Kuromaku asked, when the others were all gone.

Octavian glanced around the bedroom, his eyes lingering on the bed where he had found Nikki displayed in a macabre tableau. Kuromaku knew the answer. He had asked only to give Octavian a chance to speak, to explain.

'This . . . yes,' Octavian replied. He gestured to the bed and then around at the markings and little numbered plastic tents that the forensics people had left behind. 'Most of it you can imagine for yourself. I've tried not to imagine it, but I've failed. It's in me, now . . . this thing. Every breath I take, it haunts me.'

'We're going to kill him and his whole coven,' Allison said.

'We will,' Kuromaku agreed, but he reached out and put a strong hand on the back of Octavian's neck. 'But it won't help the pain.'

'Maybe not,' Octavian said, 'but we'll kill them just the same.'

He took a deep breath, steadying his heartbeat and narrowing his eyes. Reaching down within himself, he summoned up the magic there and extended his hands. During the millennium he had spent in Hell, he had learned thousands upon thousands of spells and hexes and enchantments and glamours, but at a certain point his understanding of magic had outstripped what

109

could be studied and entered the world of intuition. Sorcery was a combination of elements that included the extant supernatural energies woven into the fabric of reality, as well as a facility to wield and weave those energies. Nikki had once compared his abilities to a nuclear scientist being able to manipulate atoms merely by thinking of them. She hadn't been far off, though magic was more involved than that.

It took focus and discipline, knowledge and purpose . . . And it took passion. Love worked, as did anger. Or grief.

'I could have done this before you arrived, but I wanted you both to see it,' he said.

'What are we seeing?' Allison asked warily, her usual bravado gone.

Octavian contorted his hands and dragged them through the air, which had become warm and malleable around him. It flowed sluggishly around his fingers like paint and slow ripples spread outward, reality shuddering and changing.

The room grew darker, and the curtains that had been open a moment before were now closed. The time here in Philadelphia, on the twelfth floor of the Loews Hotel, was late afternoon, but a sliver of early morning sunlight shone in through the gap in the curtains.

'Just in case,' Octavian said softly. 'I'm worried that I'll miss something important . . . some detail that we'll need.'

'Peter?' Kuromaku said warily.

'Hush,' Octavian said. 'Just watch.'

He kept his back to them. He didn't want to see their expressions, or his own reflected in their eyes.

Out in the foyer of the mini-suite, there came two clicks, one soft and one slightly louder. The door swung inward and Nikki entered the room. Octavian felt a surge of love and longing that quickly turned to ice inside him. He could smell a citrus odor that he realized came from the maid's cleaning products, a scent that had been lacking when the crime scene people had finished their work.

'Peter, you don't have to do this,' Allison said. 'We know what happened.'

'Just in case,' he said again, steeling himself.

Octavian, Allison, and Kuromaku stood like ghosts in the room as Nikki put the key card for her room on the small coffee table by the loveseat out in the mini-suite's foyer. She walked into the bedroom and stripped off her black shirt, glancing around until she spotted the discarded pajamas laid across a chair by the heavily draped windows. Looking tired and grateful to be able to exhale, she unhooked her bra and removed it.

Shadows swirled like liquid blackness in the corner of the room, coalescing into a lean, sculpted figure.

'You *are* lovely,' the figure rasped.

Cortez had arrived to murder her, to tear out her throat and nail her to the wall, and Octavian could only watch, for these events had already unfolded.

Revenge seemed such a small thing to him, now.

But it was all he had.

7

Siena, Italy

Gabriel Baleeiro felt more relaxed than he had in years. Arm in arm with his wife, Jessica, he strolled through the square in front of the Basilica San Domenico and breathed in the cool, clean night air of Tuscany. He had never thought of churches as romantic, but with the lights strung throughout the square and the late-night lovers wandering together, the façade of the fortress-like basilica made him feel like he had stepped back in time.

'Penny for your thoughts,' Jessica said, bumping against him playfully.

Gabe smiled and swung her in front of him, playing at the image of a dashing leading man from some 1940s film.

'After twenty-five years, you need me to tell you what I'm thinking?'

She grinned, shyly dropping her gaze. 'You're thinking you can't wait to get back to the hotel.'

'I can wait,' he said. 'It's a beautiful night. But I am looking forward to what happens when we return to our room.'

'Me falling asleep?'

He laughed. 'Not tonight.'

She gazed up at him, searching his eyes with the kind of adoration and yearning he hadn't seen in her in ages. Music drifted from the open door of a trattoria across the square.

'No,' she agreed. 'Not tonight.'

The Baleeiros were doctors, Gabe the senior surgeon at St George's in London, and Jessica the head of the pediatric oncology unit there. She was British born and bred, while Gabe hailed from Brazil. They'd met in medical school and fallen in love during all-night study sessions, but twenty-five years had passed in a blur of patients and surgeries and they'd had to steal romance in the tiniest sips. Aside from the occasional week-long sunny holiday with their two sons, who were now twelve and fourteen and staying with their grandmother in Milton Keynes, they had rarely been away from their work. This sabbatical – two weeks together in Tuscany, no kids – was something of a second honeymoon, and Gabe had spent the past week falling in love with his wife all over again.

'You know what this reminds me of?' Jessica asked as they walked along the cobblestones in the shadow of the church. 'With all the lights?'

'Sao Paolo,' Gabe said. 'The festival, that night you first met my parents.'

Jessica slid her arm through his again and leaned against him as they walked. 'You know me well.'

'I know *us* well. Sometimes I forget, but this trip has reminded me.'

'Aren't you a bloody romantic?'

He smiled. 'Well, I *am* Brazilian.'

Jessica tugged him toward her and gave him a quick kiss. It felt to Gabe like he'd won a prize of some kind, but he knew that his life with Jessica was the prize. For the second time they stopped where they were, right in the middle of the square, and gazed at each other. He knew he had aged well – the white streak in his hair the one thing that put the lie to his boyish face – but Jessica had aged even better. Not that she had been untouched by the years; instead, the lines at the corners of her eyes and the edges of her lips had given her an austere, digni-fied beauty that youth could never achieve.

'I don't want to go home,' he said.

'How long, do you think, before the boys noticed our absence?'

'With your mum spoiling them, at least a couple of months.'

She laughed, and then grew serious again, reaching up to touch his face. 'We need to do this more often, love. Take some time for ourselves.'

'I don't know,' he said, shaking his head. 'It's unbecoming in doctors, you know. All this soppy affection. And very un-British of you, too. You're meant to be wry and jaded and hold love at arm's length.'

Jessica gave him a playful shove. 'Bugger that.'

Then she pulled him to her and Gabe went along willingly. He didn't wait for her to kiss him, wrapping his arms around her and bending to meet her lips. The late-night revelers and strolling couples around them were forgotten. The moment belonged only to them.

And then the night exploded.

The air ruptured as the front of the church blew out, glass and rubble erupting and crumbling down onto the cobblestones. The blast threw the Baleeiros off their feet, still locked in an embrace, and they hit the street in a tangle of limbs, rolling and sliding to a stop. Gabe struck his head and blacked out, coming to moments later with his ears ringing and the echo of the explosion still resounding off of the façades of the buildings in the square.

Jessica was kneeling by him, blood dripping down her cheek from a laceration at her left temple. Her eyes were glassy but she seemed otherwise unharmed. It took him a moment to realize that she was talking to him, calling his name, shaking him.

'I think I'm okay,' he said, and realized he'd spoken in Portuguese.

Not that it mattered. She'd barely have heard him over the screams of the other people in the square. Some were cries of fear and others of pain or grief – as a doctor and a surgeon he had come to be familiar with so many different types of human anguish.

The cobblestones shook beneath him and he heard the rumble of more of the church collapsing. His chest rose and fell with shallow, ragged breaths and he glanced around, blinking at the realization that he might be slightly in shock.

'I'm all right,' he said, this time in English. 'Just shaken up. Come on.'

He sat up, wavered a bit, and then stood and stared at the church. Most of its face had collapsed and its interior yawed vast and dark, the glow of the festive lights in the square barely reaching within.

'Are you sure you're all right?'

'We've got to help.'

She hesitated, her concern for him etched on her face, but then it vanished and was replaced by the determined mask of the doctor.

'Where do we start?' she asked.

'Follow the loudest screams.'

They scanned the square, ignoring the people only now streaming out of the trattoria and a wine bar, as well as the busker who was on his knees weeping over his broken guitar.

'This way,' Jessica said, grabbing his hand.

They ran toward the church. A sixtyish woman stood over a man who'd been struck by stone debris. He looked shattered, his chest misshapen and his jaw askew as blood bubbled from his mouth. Gabe and Jessica exchanged a dark look, and he knew they were thinking the same thing. *Triage.*

This guy wasn't going to make it.

Not far away, a pair of college girls was crying, trying to move a chunk of wall off a third. It took all of Gabe's will to turn his back on the dying old man and run to them.

'Wait!' he said. 'Let me look at her first.'

They looked confused and he realized they didn't understand English. He started to gesture to himself, saying 'doctor,' but then Jessica was there, rattling off something in simple, passable Italian and they took a step back. The two girls stared in shock at their fallen friend, whose legs and pelvis were trapped beneath an enormous slab of wall. The trapped girl was blessedly unconscious.

Gabe dropped to his knees beside her, checking her pulse as he lowered his head and listened for breath sounds. Her pulse was weak but steady and she was still breathing. If paramedics arrived with their gear in time, and the rubble could be shifted off of her, she might live, but it was going to be a near thing.

'Honey,' Jessica said. 'Have a look at this.'

He turned and saw the two college girls staring at him hopefully. One of them, a tall, olive-skinned girl, had blood soaking through the fabric of her long, stylish sweater in a dozen places or more. Small pieces of jagged glass jutted from the left side of her face and from slices in the thin sweater. She cradled her left arm against her chest, and he knew something other than glass had struck her, but it was the glass that concerned him most. The girl blinked, studying him, and then she spoke to him in Italian, gesturing at her fallen friend.

She staggered a little, weak from loss of blood already. In minutes, or less, she would be unconscious. She would die unless he could staunch the flow of blood, but there were so many wounds.

'Jess, help me with her. Get her to lie down. Christ, we've got to figure out how to get these—'

'Gabe,' his wife said, and her tone brought him up short.

He glanced at her and saw that she had never moved. She stood staring at the ruin of the church with wide eyes, her mouth slightly open, a kind of sickly fear etched upon her features. Only then did he realize that she had never meant for him to look at the bleeding girl, never been worried about the college girls at all. Not once she had seen this.

There were things emerging from the blasted husk of Basilica San Domenico.

Gabe blinked to clear his vision, thinking that he must still be in shock and that something must be wrong with his head, for the winged figures rising coming from within the church faded in and out of sight as if they were there one moment and gone the next. They seemed to be made of charcoal smoke, phantom harpies who beat their wings as they darted from the black void of the church and into the sky above the square. He cocked his head back to watch their ascent, blinking again as they shimmered in and out, vanishing and reappearing. Demons made of smoke.

'*Meu Deus*,' he prayed in a whisper.

But as he watched more and more of the smoke demons emerge, he knew that God had turned his gaze away from Siena tonight.

*

Saint-Denis, France

The helicopter set down a quarter mile from the Saint-Denis cathedral. Even from the air, Beril Demirci had been able to see the cracks in the street from the earthquake that had struck just before noon, now twelve hours ago, but nobody was worrying about the earthquake now. Somewhere in Saint-Denis, she imagined structural engineers were trying to figure out whether there were buildings in danger of collapse, but she doubted many of them would be doing much firsthand evaluation. Not if they valued their lives.

'This is as far as I go!' the helicopter pilot shouted, wanting to make himself heard over the chop of the rotors.

Beril gave him the thumbs up, trying to seem competent and knowledgeable but secretly almost as terrified of the helicopter as she was of the horror unfolding in Saint-Denis right now. She had never been in a helicopter before, and now that she had she hoped never to do it again.

'Thank you!' she called, trying to figure out how to turn the latch that would open the door.

As she fumbled with it, someone did it for her from the outside and the door rattled as it slid on its tracks. With only a small satchel as her travel case, she jumped down from the chopper – could she call it a chopper, or was that silly? – and turned to face the soldier who had opened the door.

'Miss Demirci?' he shouted over the noise.

She nodded and he turned away, gesturing for her to follow. The soldier moved at a trot and she kept pace with him, slipping the strap of her bag over her head so that it hung behind her as she ran. The roar of the chopper increased and then quickly began to diminish and she glanced back to see that the pilot had already taken off, headed away from here as fast as his aircraft could carry him.

Smart man, she thought.

Which makes me what?

With the helicopter gone, the sound of artillery shelling grew even louder. It thumped the air and she felt every shot and every impact in her chest, shaking her heart. The soldier led her toward a cluster of military trucks and smaller vehicles, where a group of other people in uniform was clustered around a folding table. Though her Turkish homeland had its share of military activity, Beril had rarely seen soldiers up close and knew next to nothing about the way such things were organized. Only by their bearing could she identify these people as officers of some kind, so she followed her escort and relied upon him.

Her soldier brought her not to the table but to a tall, dark-eyed woman in full military gear. Beril thought her bulky helmet made her head look enormous and out of proportion to her body, but she bit her tongue. She had a tendency to speak her thoughts unfiltered; it frequently got her into trouble at home and she didn't want the same thing to happen here. She had been called into the midst of an unfolding crisis, and knew the focus needed to remain on the horrors at hand. It was simply that she sometimes couldn't stop her thoughts from racing off on tangents and her tongue from following.

'Major Rojas,' the soldier said. 'This is the woman you've been waiting for.'

The dark-eyed major frowned. 'Beril Demirci?'

'That's me,' Beril said, her small voice likely getting lost in the roar of nearby battle. She looked around, hoping for some kind of shelter, but the major seemed in no hurry to take cover.

'Major Paola Rojas, UN Security Forces. You've heard of Task Force Victor?'

Beril nodded.

'Good,' Major Rojas said. 'Come with me.'

She nodded to the soldier, who turned and ran off to wherever he was meant to be next. The major led her past the table where other officers were barking orders into phones and radios, though they seemed to be having trouble with communications and having to repeat themselves. Runners came up to the table, received orders and raced away. One of the officers poked furiously at a blueprint or something spread out on the table and tried to make a point the others were ignoring.

'In here,' Major Rojas said, and Beril looked up to discover that they were outside a long trailer and the major was holding the door for her.

Not much by way of shelter, but at least it would muffle the noise of war. Beril went up the few steps and found herself inside some kind of communications center. Video screens showed flashes of explosions and glimpses of horrible things, all in some kind of night vision she had only ever seen in movies, but each image was fuzzed with static and slashed with jagged lines that reminded her of lightning.

There were four people already in the trailer. Two were technicians who were cursing and trying to get their equipment to function more effectively. The other two were an odd pair, a young male soldier clad in what she now recognized as UN fatigues and a very old man whose hair and beard were a frost of tight white curls and whose skin was the color of cinnamon. The old man wore a kind of tunic, beige and faded, a pair of loose brown trousers, and conspicuously expensive but well-worn hiking shoes that were startlingly discordant with the rest of his appearance.

'Beril Demirci, this is Sergeant Ponticello, also Task Force Victor,' Major Rojas said. 'And maybe you already know Mr Chakroun.'

'Not Yousef Chakroun?' she asked, catching her breath a little.

The old man's eyes crinkled and he nodded in greeting. He and Sergeant Ponticello had been sitting in office chairs that seemed bolted to the floor around a small table, but now both men began to stand. Chakroun looked exhausted and somewhat bedraggled, but she presumed a man of his age must always have an air of weariness about him. The Moroccan mystic was rumored to be at least ninety-six.

'No, please. Don't get up,' Beril said.

'Miss Demirci,' Chakroun said. 'Octavian speaks highly of you.'

Beril shook her head. This was too much. It had been startling enough for her to get a phone call from Peter Octavian, a more powerful mage than any she had ever encountered – or heard reputable stories about – but the idea that Chakroun and Octavian had discussed her made her feel slightly faint.

She found herself smiling. 'I don't know what to say.'

'Don't say,' Major Rojas cut in. 'Sit down and help us figure out what the hell we're supposed to do.'

Chastened, Beril nodded and slid into a seat at the small table. Break table? Lunch table? Or was this tiny, round surface efficient for whatever official business took place in this –

Stop. No tangents.

'Tell me,' was all she said.

Major Rojas remained standing. It was clear that she wanted action, not words, that it upset her to be here while not far away demons were attacking Italian and UN troops and trying to get past the military blockade to kill more civilians. Many hundreds were already dead, some killed in the earthquake but most slain by the creatures emerging from the bowels of the basilica – Beril knew that much – and some must be getting past the guns and soldiers.

'Mr Chakroun arrived nearly seven hours ago. He's been able to pinpoint the breed of demon—'

At the mention of the word, the two techs glanced at the little meeting table nervously.

'—but we haven't managed to identify the source.'

Chakroun leaned toward her across the table. A faint scent of spice wafted from his clothes, or perhaps from his body itself. 'We don't know where the little ones are coming from.'

'Little ones?'

'Oh, there is a big one. No doubt about it,' Chakroun said.

'We haven't seen it yet,' Sergeant Ponticello added. 'Mr Chakroun tells us—'

'Tells them,' Chakroun said with a sniff.

He passed his hand over the table in a swift, circular motion, and a kind of mist rose up from the surface, shifting and drifting and then coalescing into something horrible. For the first time, real fear raced along her spine, a cascade of icy shivers. The demon had an insectoid body, but fat as a slug, with long upper arms that ended in sharp talons. Its mouth was a maw full of rows of black teeth like long needles, and there were eyes all over its upper half.

Beril felt sick to her stomach.

'Is it . . .' she began. 'I mean, I've seen woodcuts of it, I think. Is it a Tatzelwurm?'

'Think of it as a cousin of the Tatzelwurm,' Chakroun said. 'The Akkadians called these creatures *utukki*.'

'Akkadians?' Beril said. 'But why would a demon of Middle Eastern origin appear in France?'

Major Rojas sighed in frustration. 'It found a way in. That's all. It's here, and now we deal with it, and its offspring – if that's what the others are.'

'They must be,' Chakroun said. 'Otherwise we would have seen other adult utukki.'

The ancient mystic waved his hand over the mist-figures and they dissipated. Beril stared at the place where they had been for a moment and then leaned back in the chair, wondering what Octavian was thinking, calling her to come here. Yes, she knew a great deal of magic and could wield it with some confidence, but this was war. She had never been a warrior.

'Hey,' Sergeant Ponticello said, snapping his fingers in front of her face.

They had been talking to her but her mind had been elsewhere. She glanced at the techs, catching them staring, and the two men turned around quickly. The many screens continued to fuzz and distort, the images becoming worse instead of better.

'I'm sorry,' Beril said. 'I just don't know why I'm here. What can I do that Yousef Chakroun cannot?'

Chakroun reached out and put his hand over hers. 'Beril, listen. I have befuddled them, clouded their primitive instincts to keep them from straying far from here, to give the soldiers a chance to destroy them. But I am an old man. I haven't the power to destroy them or even to fight them properly. Octavian tells me that you have spent your life studying the occult, that you have the knowledge and the skill and most importantly the heart to fight the utukki.

She shook her head. 'No. I really do not. Octavian is the true mage. I can fight them, perhaps even destroy some of them, but there are so many. Even if I could kill them all, I have never faced a creature as powerful as whatever brought them into our world.'

'People are dying out there,' Major Rojas said. 'Soldiers and civilians. Husbands and wives, mothers and children. We're doing the best we can at holding them, but no matter how many of them we kill, more just keep coming. We might be able to hold them like this for days if we have to, but if there's no end to them, at some point they're going to get through. I don't like sorcery. I'm not going to lie. But magic's the only thing short of bombing the hell out of Saint-Denis that's going to put a stop to this.'

'We don't know if bombs would do it, Major,' Sergeant Ponticello said, his Sicilian accent strong. 'However the utukki got into our world, if there's a passage, bombs could just rip it wider.'

'Exactly,' Major Rojas said. 'We need you. Help us hold the line. Help us destroy these things.'

A loud rap came on the door and then it was yanked open. The same soldier who had been Beril's escort poked his head into the trailer.

'Major, you're going to want to talk to this guy. We've got a priest out here who says he's seen the demon that's causing all of this.'

Chakroun said something in his own language, nodding in anticipation.

'Well, bring him in.'

The soldier ducked out and then the door opened wider. Her first impression of the priest was of bruised wisdom. Thin and drawn, face battered and his arm in a sling, he looked defeated. But then he raised his eyes and surveyed the people in the trailer, and she saw the courage and anger in him. His gaze rested a moment on Major Rojas, likely sensing her command status, but then the priest focused on Chakroun.

'My name is Laurent,' the clergyman said. 'I woke in a tent

hours ago, being treated by a nurse. I'd have come right away but they wouldn't let me out and then no one would listen.'

'We are listening, Father Laurent,' Chakroun said softly.

'You saw the demon?' Major Rojas added.

'I believe I was there the moment it broke through,' Father Laurent said.

'And the others, the offspring?' Chakroun asked. 'You know where they come from?'

A look of horror passed across the priest's features.

'I do,' Father Laurent said, visibly shuddering. 'God help me, I do.'

Hannah had lost track of the hour, and even the day. She had lost track of the number of times she had fallen unconscious and woken again. She had lost count of the demons that had slid from inside of her. Every time her eyes fluttered open into bleary awareness of her surroundings she would begin to cry. Tears had dried on her cheeks and she could taste their salt on her lips.

Then her breathing would quicken again and she would feel new convulsions in her belly and realize it was this that had woken her from blessed oblivion. Another monster was about to be born. She lay on the stairs with rubble strewn around her, half-naked and bruised and violated, and she wondered how many times she could give birth before the blood and fluid that slid from her would be too much.

I should be dead by now, she thought, more than once. More than a dozen times.

Whatever infection or curse the thing from the crypt had afflicted her with, it must also be keeping her alive. In a moment of clarity, her thoughts coalescing for a moment out of pain and anguish and disgust, she realized that it was only logical – if

125

the creature in the bowels of the cathedral meant for her to be the host for its children, whatever sickening magic made that possible must also keep her alive. She was less mother than she was doorway.

The thought made her twist around and vomit onto the stone steps.

Shaking, sobbing, she unleashed a wordless scream for mercy, for help, for an ending. Down below her, just outside the iron gate that led into the subterranean crypt, the demon shifted. Its body made a crunch and clack on the stone floor and the debris shaken loose from the ceiling by the chaos going on outside. The basilica shook with each explosion and echoed with the screams of nightmare things that had no place in this world.

It's wrong, she thought, catching her breath to scream again. *This is a holy place. A house of saints.*

The demon could have slithered up the stairs after her, could have gutted her with those dagger fingers or burrowed its shark teeth into her chest and eaten her heart. She had tried to rise, tried to run after Father Laurent – had that been today or yesterday? How many hours had passed? – but before she managed two steps she would be wracked with contractions again, another monster forcing its way out of her, chittering and gnashing its jaws. But Hannah understood now that the demon did not climb up to her because it had no desire to kill her.

It wanted her alive, and breeding.

She didn't look down at the demon anymore. The last time, she had nearly stopped breathing when she caught a glimpse of its eyes – so many eyes – looking right back at her, and a feeling of approval had washed over her. The thing had chosen her to bring its spawn into the world, and it was proud of her sorrow and her screams. Hannah could sense it, somehow, as if the long hours of agony and desperate humiliation had created a link between them.

Or maybe they *can sense it, and I can feel what they feel.*

In the near darkness, with only the flickering orange emergency lights casting their wan illumination in the stairwell, she felt another contraction coming and let out a terrible sob. Closing her eyes, she prayed for an attack that would bring the ceiling crashing down on top of her, putting an end to this.

A gush came from between her legs and she felt the wriggling begin again, the pressure and the pain as a new monster twisted and slipped and slithered its way out, stretching her vagina to obscene extent. Her breath came in hitching gasps and she grunted, fighting the pain, until a wail of despair erupted from her lips, wrenched from some hopeless place inside of her.

Please, she thought, praying again for the church to fall down upon her.

Then she was beyond conscious thought, her scream so loud that it drowned out the chittering of the newborn and the thunder of combat outside.

Her mind shut down and for a time she would be lost in saving darkness.

Until the next one came.

8

New York, New York

Charlotte felt breathless and off-balance, like the earth was shifting underfoot. Her life had been nothing but upheaval since the night that Cortez's lackeys had dragged her from that California parking lot. Cortez had killed her and brought her back, and then tried to mold her into his own monster, as he had done with so many others. She had escaped his influence and tried to start life over, persuading herself that her dreams were still possible. And then the dark influence of Navalica had lured her to Massachusetts and she'd met Octavian. The changes she'd undergone since then had been just as drastic as those thrust upon her by Cortez, but this time, nobody was forcing her to do anything.

Her life had become a tornado, but even though it twisted her around and threw her about so quickly that her thoughts blurred, Charlotte embraced it all. She had been fooling herself into thinking she could live an ordinary life after all that had happened to her. The things that had been done to her were haunting. They had taken root inside of her and would never let her be at ease. She understood, now, that her only path to peace of mind . . . was war.

When Cortez had been destroyed, perhaps then she would no longer feel so haunted. And if it didn't work – if her ghosts remained – at least the son of a bitch would be dead.

A static-fuzzed voice crackled in her ear. 'Charlotte, are you all right?'

She blinked and glanced around the alley, wondering where the TFV soldiers were hidden. Not that she expected to see them. This sort of thing might seem surreal to her, but to them it was just another day's work. If her heart still beat like a human's, it would have quickened. Still, ordinary heartbeat or no, she felt something inside her tighten in anticipation.

It was just after nine p.m. People milled in the alley, most just arriving but some already departing, turned away from the metal security door in the side of the building that housed the dance club. Once upon a time it had been a bank. According to a TFV background search, it had metamorphosed over the years first into a bookstore and then a restaurant, both called The Vault, after which – for six years – it had been nothing but a crumbling vacancy. Now it was a dance club with no sign either at the front of the building or in the side alley, but the barely legal crowd of aloof well-financed club kids knew just where to find it.

The place was called Faux, and as far as Charlotte knew it had earned the name without irony. One online writeup of the club called it the place 'where nobody is who they seem'. To Charlotte it sounded like the perfect cover for a vampire bar, or some other kind of occult operation, but apparently the people who ran the club were just that – people.

129

With or without the owners' knowledge, though, Faux was the perfect hunting ground. Bored, disaffected, rich kids with plenty of money and nobody looking out for them . . . when they vanished, it took days for people to start looking for them, and if they showed up dead in a bathtub with drugs in their system, bled out from slashes on their wrists, vampires were far from the first suspected cause of death. It wouldn't be hard to find an inhuman predator at Faux, but she was looking for one in particular.

'Charlotte?' Omondi prodded.

She flinched and looked around again, checking out the corners of building roofs and the sleek yellow sports car gliding down the alley. All she knew was that she had backup, but they might have been in dumpsters or darkened windows or already inside the club, for all she knew.

'Going in,' she muttered.

A trio of girls looked up from their chattering and their cell phones to shoot her a wary glance, then gave identical lazy sneers before looking back down to their phones. She suspected they were texting friends, trying to figure out who they knew who could get them in the door. They clustered like birds on a wire, together but hardly aware of one another, tugging down the hems of their dresses but failing to avoid giving the peeks of ass and crotch that they hoped would get them in if none of their friends came through.

This was Faux.

Charlotte crossed the alley, aware of eyes on her. Some were the hidden gazes of TFV soldiers, while others belonged to club kids who stood in line, wondering who the hell she thought she was, walking right up to the door as if there weren't two dozen people behind an invisible velvet rope, waiting for a chance to be judged. Charlotte knew she looked good, knew the red dress and her red hair and her intricate, ornate tattoos would earn her a second look. But that was only to get her to the door, to make sure nobody noticed anything out of the ordinary.

The tall, powerfully built black man who stood beside the metal door watched her approach with an impassive gaze. His head was shaved bald and he had a golden ring in each ear; Charlotte found him deliciously handsome, and it surprised her as she drew nearer to see that he had kind, intelligent eyes. This wasn't just some bruiser. Doorman at Faux couldn't be his only occupation, but tonight it was the only one that mattered – the one that could cost him his life.

He stood at attention, giving away his military background. Several people bitched loudly as she strode up to him. The doorman didn't speak, but regarded her curiously enough that it amounted to a question: who are you? Or, more accurately, who do you think you are? It was, after all, Faux.

'Hi,' she said brightly, cocking her head. Wetting her lips. Lifting one corner of her mouth in a suggestive smile. 'I'm Charlotte.'

Despite himself, the doorman smiled. 'And?'

'I'm looking for Danny Rouge.'

The delicious, kind-eyed doorman gave her a disappointed look. 'Huh. Didn't figure you for one of them.'

'Donors?' she asked. Men and women who willfully offered themselves to vampires, some out of some bizarre sense of noble generosity and others out of fetishistic sexual interest, had earned a dozen nicknames in the years since the Venice Jihad, the battle during which the Vatican sorcerers had attempted – and failed – to exterminate all Shadows, only to be destroyed themselves.

'That's one word,' the doorman said, studying her.

'Send the bitch packin',' someone called from the line.

'Back of the line!' shouted another.

The huge, handsome man ignored them. His enormous hands were still crossed in front of him; he remained at attention. But despite what he thought Charlotte was there for, he remained curious about her, apparently sensing something was different about her. She liked him.

'What's your name?' she asked, dropping the coquettish act.

'Marcus.'

Charlotte licked her lips, letting her fangs slide out. She smiled sweetly to give him a good look.

'I don't want to kill you, Marcus. I just need Danny Rouge.'

Marcus nodded appreciatively. Fearlessly. 'We're on the same page, honey. I don't want to die. You want Rouge, check the vault.'

He stood aside to let her pass, provoking a flurry of angry and envious shouts. One guy broke away from the line, rushing toward the metal door even as Charlotte opened it.

'You gotta be fuckin' kidding me!' the guy sneered, reaching for Charlotte, trying to snatch the back of her dress to pull her back. 'This bitch waits in line like every—'

Marcus grabbed him by the throat, lifted him and hurled him backward, where he sprawled at the feet of the three peekaboo girls with their cell phones. Charlotte had paused to watch, but she hadn't come here for the entertainment. She let the door slam behind her and ventured into the wall of sound inside Faux.

Music thumped so loud it felt like a physical assault, felt like she had waded into a rushing stream of drums and guitars and vocals, all fed through a computer to be smoothed into synthetic, soulless music. Charlotte hadn't known Nikki Wydra, but she had heard her music, and she had a feeling this was the sort of thing that would have made Nikki want to throw up. Though she was only nineteen, Charlotte didn't much care for this synth-pop dance crap either.

People swarmed around her, some dancing, some texting, some drinking and some even trying to hold a conversation, which was next to impossible here. She slid through the crowd, avoiding arrogant and desperate men who tried to touch her or draw her onto the dance floor. She saw two waitresses but they weren't what she wanted. Searching the crowd, she focused on a woman near the bar who had a pale, hungry, hopeful expression – one she had seen before.

Human, but wanting so desperately to feel fangs in her throat.

Riding the wave of sound and flashing lights, Charlotte glided toward the woman. A hand touched her arm and she turned to see a too-handsome, spike-haired guy wearing a hyena's grin. He started to speak but faltered and backed up a step. Perhaps he'd seen the brutality in her eyes, her familiarity with blood and shadows. Either way, he glanced away, head hung like an admonished child, and she left him there. No one else tried to touch her.

The woman at the bar saw her coming and searched Charlotte's eyes, maybe trying to figure out if her prayers had been answered. Maybe twenty-four, she had a killer body and a lovely face, with high cheekbones and full lips, but even with the gold eyeshadow, the desperation in her eyes would have driven most people away. Anyone could have seen there was something off about her.

'Hi!' Charlotte said brightly. 'What's your name?'

'Velvet,' the woman replied, wary but hopeful.

Charlotte wasn't sure if it was a stripper stage name or the product of cruel parents, but either way she had to fight not to roll her eyes.

'You know where the vault is, Velvet?' she asked. 'This is my first time and it's a friggin' madhouse in here.'

'I know where it is,' Velvet replied. 'They don't just let anyone in, though. It's like a club inside the club, y'know?'

'They'll let me in. Maybe you want to come with?'

Velvet lit up, color flushing her cheeks so much it was detectable even with the lights and the makeup. She wetted her lips with her tongue as she nodded and led the way, mumbling something that was lost in the crashing dance beat. When they reached the thick of the crowd, Velvet reached back and took her hand. Many eyes tracked their progress toward the rear of the club, past grinding dancers and bar counters packed six deep. Two pretty girls wearing an air of urgency, hand in hand – the men were going to watch and the women were going to watch the men watching, to monitor just how much attention was being diverted.

The vault still had a door, a huge, heavy thing that Charlotte figured was mostly for ornamentation, and she had to admit that it looked cool. It hung open, and it made her think of the rock that had been rolled away from Christ's tomb. A buzzcut, tattooed bouncer sat on a stool, half-blocking the entrance into the vault. He wore a paisley vest over a cream colored shirt with the cuffs rolled up. Though not the handsomest man she had ever seen, his features were pleasing enough, but his huge hands were knobby and ugly. Undamaged face, damaged hands; the combination suggested a life of violence delivered but very little received. A dangerous man.

'Hey!' Charlotte said, tossing her hair and cocking her hip as she looked at him.

Velvet hung back. The bouncer gave her a disapproving look, but that came as no surprise. Charlotte figured the blood-slut had been turned away from the vault before. As a Shadow,

Charlotte had no fear of the sun, but Cortez's vampires shunned the daylight. They believed in the old ways enough to burn, so they hid from the sun. It might be dark outside now, but rogue vampires liked caves and hidden places. The vault was perfect.

Charlotte took Velvet's hand and started through the vault door.

The bouncer reacted instantly, reaching out to grab Velvet by the arm. Charlotte shook her loose and kept going as the bouncer swore and Velvet called her a bitch. The two of them tussled for a moment, giving her precious seconds to take in the layout of the vault. The small room had been done over in racks of expensive wine and plush burgundy booths and loveseats. A private bar at the far end served only expensive tastes. There were fewer than thirty people in the space, but the air felt heavy and the music still thumped – though muffled – from small speakers in the corners. The place smelled of sweat and perfume, of old booze and desire.

Charlotte scanned faces, searching for Rouge. Several guys had their backs to her, but one of them must be him.

A scarred, crushing hand slammed down on her shoulder.

'Where the fuck do you think you're—' the bouncer began.

Charlotte turned, backhanding him hard enough to crack his cheekbone, then took his hand, pivoted and hurled him into a wine rack. Bottles shattered and red wine splashed down on him like a shower of blood. His nose was bent and she realized she had broken it. That was all right with her. A man who lived so violent a life as to have such hands should not have been left unscarred by it.

She spun back around, scanning again for Rouge. Velvet came toward her, cautious but smiling with a dark, erotic fervor. Charlotte had just revealed that she herself was the very thing Velvet desired.

'Oh, my God,' the woman said. 'That was so hot.'

Charlotte searched faces; most were terrified but some were intrigued, and one or two were as openly hungry as Velvet's. One guy had already turned away.

Danny Rouge.

People shied away as she crossed the vault. The bouncer tried to rise but slipped down again into the wine rack debris, moaning at the new cuts he received from broken bottles. Not all of the red on him was from wine.

Velvet was talking to her, maybe even flirting with her in the midst of all of this, but Charlotte couldn't hear her. The song of her own blood was in her ears, the music of violence and hunger that had only grown louder in the months since she had been turned. She wouldn't kill humans for their blood – not now – but the thirst for it remained, and it rushed through her in moments of imminent violence with such force that it made her want to scream, to laugh, to dance . . . to kill.

The good news was that killing didn't always make her a monster. Sometimes, it could make her a hero.

'Hello, Rouge,' she said, standing beside the booth where the vampire sat with a trio of club kids. Charlotte couldn't have described them later. They were beneath her notice.

She shifted, making sure she was directly in front of him. He stared at the table, not looking up.

'Remember me?' she asked. 'I need to ask you something.'

The vampire was not an albino, but he might as well have been. His hair was the yellow-white of cornsilk and his eyes were blue-tinted ice. Rouge had alabaster skin, but when he had freshly drunk of human blood, his cheeks became mottled with patches of pink, as if he were embarrassed. She had seen him like that, in what he called the afterglow.

Rouge lolled his head back and studied her, brow furrowed.

'If you'd come in here all quiet and meek,' he said, 'I'd have figured you wanted back in Cortez's good graces, maybe hoped I'd put in a good word. But this . . .' He gestured at the bouncer: nobody had gone to the bleeding man's aid, but he had finally managed to get to his feet and begun to stumble toward the door.

'*What are you doing?*' Sergeant Omondi said, his voice fuzzed with static, crackling in her ear. '*Don't set him off in there. Get him out of the vault, out in the open part of the club. If we try coming in through the door, we won't be able to surround—*'

'I'm not good at meek,' Charlotte said.

'So what's your deal? You just want to end it? Suicide by fang?'

'I told you. I have a question.'

'*Charlotte, listen –*' Omondi said.

She could tell Rouge was curious in spite of himself.

'You gonna ask it?'

Charlotte nodded. No more banter, now; she let him see the disgust in her face. 'Where can I find Cortez? I know he's got a place in New York, that part of the coven is here. Where's the nest?'

'That's two questions.'

Rouge shot from behind the table, his limbs a blur. His companions barely had time to scream as the two monsters came together in a flurry of blows and slashing talons. Vampire versus Shadow. Vampire versus vampire. Charlotte felt her throat flayed open as Rouge tore at her, stronger, older, more barbaric. They hit the floor, twisting and tearing, snarling and snapping.

Omondi shouted in Charlotte's ear; they were coming in. Shots rang out in the club and people screamed, all of it blending into the thumping dance beat. The people in the vault cowered and wept as Rouge and Charlotte crashed into the bar and then into a wall of wine racks, driving each other into the broken bottle necks over and over, digging at flesh and shedding blood. The pain seared her but she welcomed it.

'Stupid move, coming here,' Rouge snarled.

Stronger. Bigger.

Charlotte laughed and let her flesh shift and flow, let her bones twist and grow. She rose, towering over him, her huge head brushing the ceiling, and then she opened her mouth and let out the roar of a black bear. Rouge blinked in surprise, hesitating for a second, and she swept one huge paw down and tore off the left side of his face.

Cortez was foolish to stick to the traditions. With a little practice, a little focus, Rouge could have shifted as she did, but what was a wolf or a rat to the thousand beasts and monsters Charlotte could become?

Reeling, screaming, Rouge threw a punch, driving his talons into Charlotte's chest. Bone broke and skin tore, and she knew he was going for her heart. His fingers found it, closed over it, squeezed. Had he done so little homework on the true nature of Shadows that he thought he could kill her?

She tore his arm off and tossed it aside. Onlookers' screams reverberated around the vault, melding with the music. Omondi's voice was gone from her ear; the commlink had fallen out when she shifted. With the speed of thought she shifted back to human again, all of her wounds gone as if they had never been there.

Rouge gaped, fearful and desperate, and she knew the moment had come. Any second, he would turn to mist and slip out through the ducts. It was his only hope of escape.

He didn't see the dagger coming. She slipped it from a sheath at her back and thrust it into his gut with a wet thunk.

Confused, he stared down at the blade.

Shouts came from behind her. Heavy footfalls. The clatter of weapons being brought to bear. Sergeant Omondi shouted at her to stand aside, to get clear.

'You think that's going to . . .' Rouge began.

His eyes went wide and he took a second look at the blade. He'd been trying to mist, mid-sentence, and discovered that his one chance for escape had been taken away. The dagger had been coated with the only poison that mattered to vampires.

'Medusa,' Rouge said, voice low, eyes burning with hatred as he reached for her. 'You turncoat bitch.'

Omondi and half a dozen other TFV soldiers, some dressed for the club and others in full gear, moved in to surround him, weapons trained on him. His face and the stump of his arm had sealed up already, partway healed, but the Medusa had stopped it. Unable to shift or heal further, Rouge could be killed by a single, well-placed bullet.

Charlotte punched him, careful not to break his neck, and then she slid in close, intimate as a lover.

'Where is Cortez?'

'You know the places in Cali,' Rouge snapped. 'If he's not there, I have no idea.'

'We'll see,' Charlotte said, sure that the TFV would torture him for the truth and not caring a bit – not after what Cortez's people had done to her. 'What about New York? Where's the coven's local nest?'

Rouge hesitated.

Charlotte nodded. He knew.

She stepped back, glanced at the terrified club kids, then turned to Omondi.

'Fucker's all yours, Sergeant,' she said. 'I figure you'll get it out of him.'

Rouge snarled, searching for his courage. 'He'll kill you for this!'

Charlotte laughed darkly, then spat on him.

'Cortez killed me a long time ago.'

Philadelphia, Pennsylvania

Just past ten p.m. on the evening of the equinox, the night before Nikki's funeral, Octavian strode down the corridor of the Loews' twelfth floor with cold determination. He was unused to being summoned by anyone, and the idea that Metzger would have sent Song to fetch him instead of just walking down the hall and knocking on the door himself tonight – of all nights – made him bristle. It wasn't the sort of thing he would normally have taken as an insult. Truth be told, he didn't care enough about the opinions of others to be insulted by much. But tonight, he had too many ghosts in his head and it made him brittle.

Late this afternoon, he had used magic to make the past come alive, so that he and Allison and Kuromaku could bear witness as Cortez murdered Nikki. The vampire had been in shadow and they'd barely been able to make out his face, so Octavian couldn't be sure if this was the vampire he had met long ago, the one who claimed to be the historical Cortez. Not that it mattered. The past had no significance. Only what came next was important.

They had learned nothing of value. Allison thought that Octavian had chosen to torture himself as punishment, that he blamed himself for Nikki's death. And he would not argue. But at least they had a vague impression of Cortez's appearance, and they would know his voice if they heard it again. That was something.

Allison, Octavian, and Kuromaku had remained together for hours, discussing the best uses of their talents and those of the others Octavian believed would be willing to help. Many would be called to aid them, because the incursion in Saint-Denis would not be the last one. They needed to start considering longer-term solutions, ways to rebuild the dimensional defenses. One of those options would mean searching for the Gospel of Shadows, but that was something Octavian did not want to think about yet. He hoped there was another way to keep the horrors from slipping back into the world.

Inhuman horrors, at least. The human ones had never left.

Charlotte had gone off to New York with a TFV strike team led by Sergeant Omondi, trying to get a lead on Cortez's location. He'd been on the east coast long enough to kill Nikki, and might still be local. Kuromaku was handling calls from old friends who were arriving for the funeral. Meanwhile, Allison had begun to make arrangements for the three of them to begin their own hunt for Cortez. Whatever Charlotte learned from the TFV she would bring back to them, and then they would tear apart the loose community of rogue vampires in order to get to Cortez's coven and finally to Cortez. The killer knew Octavian would be coming; he'd ensured it by killing Nikki. There would be some kind of trap involved, but that was all right. Octavian could take care of himself, and when he couldn't, he had friends.

He arrived at the door to the hotel room that Metgzer had converted into a command center. Octavian rapped on the door and someone called an invitation from within, so he turned the handle and entered the foyer of the small suite. A Babel of voices and languages greeted him, along with the soft clatter of fingers tapping at computer keyboards.

Galleti sat on the edge of a chair, looking frustrated and displeased, and Octavian assumed she had been the one to call for him to come in. Now she looked as if she might regret it, but she only nodded in greeting. The transformed hotel room had lost all traces of its former identity. Chairs and phones and a large round table ringed with half a dozen laptops now filled it. The large, flatscreen television was on. Even with the volume muted there was no escaping the tragedy unfolding onscreen, the horror of Saint-Denis.

Metzger stood over a dark-suited woman who sat at a laptop, both of them clearly alarmed by what they were seeing on the screen.

Octavian paused in the center of the room, awaiting Metzger's attention, but the commander was engrossed in his conversation with the dark-suited woman, discussing the inability of ordinary military forces to engage a demonic incursion of this size. One by one, the soldiers and civilian aides in the room fell silent, turning toward Octavian, feeling the quiet weight of his expectations.

At last Metzger blinked, becoming aware of the strange stillness in the room, and looked up from the woman's laptop. For a moment he and Octavian only stared grimly at one another.

'You'll be happy to know your friend, Charlotte, and my strike team have turned up a location in New York connected to Cortez.'

'Is Cortez there?' Octavian asked. 'In the city?'

'We're not talking about the city. It's upstate. They're on the way now and will report back. I've got State Police tactical units standing by to back them up. If there's any sign that Cortez is there—'

'Wait,' Octavian said.

Metzger frowned. 'Excuse me?'

'Put your team in place to observe. I can be there by noon

tomorrow. Tell them to wait. If they go in and Cortez is there, he might get away. I can't risk that.'

'That's not your call,' Metzger said curtly. 'I said he was yours and I meant it. But we have no way of knowing if he's even there, and I'd say it's damned unlikely. We've got a lot of fires to put out right now. I'm not letting this one burn until you're ready to do something about it. Besides, Charlotte is with my people. They're loaded with Medusa toxin. On the off chance this guy is sitting there waiting for us, do you think she's going to let him skip? They'll bag and tag him and hold him for you. If he's there. Which logic says he's not.'

Octavian hesitated, thinking about Nikki's funeral. Thinking about what Cortez had done to her, and also what he had done to Charlotte. Anything could happen, of course. If Cortez spooked and ran before they could dose him with toxin . . .

He rolled it around in his mind, feeling eyes on him. Everyone in the room watched him, curious and wary.

'It *is* my call,' Octavian said at last. 'It's your team. Task Force Victor is yours. But if you give the order for them to go ahead and Cortez *is* there, and they lose him . . . I'll hold you responsible, Leon. You know I'm the best chance you have of getting this guy, exposing his coven and whatever his big plan is and exterminating them. You really don't think your people can do surveillance for twelve, fourteen hours, until I can be there?'

Metzger fumed for a moment. Then he cleared his throat and gestured for the woman seated at the laptop in front of him to rise.

'Go,' Metzger said, glancing up at the rest of his team. 'Give us the room, please.'

The staff seemed surprised. They were clearly performing certain vital duties, though the real battles were taking place a continent away. For Metzger to dismiss them in the midst of their work was foolish. All of that, just to save face?

'If you wanted a private chat, you could've just come to see me,' Octavian said. 'You're inconveniencing a lot of people to save yourself the trouble of walking down the hall and knocking on my door.'

Metzger waited for everyone to clear out, not speaking until, at last, the door clicked shut, leaving just the two of them and the hum of the laptops in the room.

Then the commander furrowed his brow and glared at Octavian.

'What the fuck are you still doing here?'

Octavian cocked his head and gave a little laugh, restraining himself. 'Excuse me?'

'You have my sympathies, Peter, but I'm done pretending this is anything less than a callous indulgence on your part.'

'Look, if Cortez is there and he tries to leave, the strike team will—'

Metzger threw up his hands. 'Christ, I'm not talking about Cortez! I'm talking about demonic incursions. I know you want to put Nikki to rest, but you could have postponed the funeral until this is all over. That should've been the first thing you did when I told you what was happening in France. Do you have any idea how many people have been killed? Never mind the ruin of homes and businesses and parts of French history. And you're just fucking brooding.'

Octavian shook, his skin prickling with the power that rippled through him.

'You're pissed. I get it. What are you going to do, kill me?' Metzger went on, pointing to Octavian's hands. 'Blow me through the wall? Burn a hole through me? Turn me into a goddamn toad?'

Octavian looked down at his hands, clenched and unclenched his fists, unable to draw back the dark, gold-black magic that crackled and sparked around them.

'I want to kill *Cortez*.'

Metzger threw up his hands. 'And yet here you are! Stewing in a hotel room. People are dying. Somewhere this Cortez asshole is laughing at you. We both know that's why he killed her, just to piss you off. He wanted to poke the bear. But what does he get in return? Nothing. A statue, sitting in a room. You might as well be made of stone, the middle of a fountain some-where, birds shitting on your head, for all the good you're doing the world right now.'

'The world is not my problem!' Octavian roared, roiling the air with power that cracked the television and knocked two laptops off the table, sending papers flying everywhere.

'It's still your world. The only one you've got,' Metzger said, ignoring the destruction.

'Don't tell me how to grieve, Commander. Don't you presume—'

'I didn't know your lady, but I'm betting she'd be feeling sick right about now. Probably turn over in her grave if she knew what you were letting happen in Europe.'

A chill went through Octavian and an icy numbness came over him. The magic buzzing around his fists diminished and he exhaled. How had his life come to this? Why did this weight sit so squarely upon his shoulders?

'We've been through this,' he said. 'I've put in the calls. You've got mages on site in France, people I trust, not to mention fucking armies. I'm not the only man in the world who can do something about this.'

Metzger lowered his voice. 'Maybe not, but you're the guy we need.'

Octavian shook his head and turned to leave. 'There's no funeral mass. Just a graveside blessing and a burial at half past eight tomorrow morning. I don't want anyone to die, but I won't bear the responsibility for them when you've got the French army, UN Security Forces, and Task Force Victor on site, plus two very capable sorcerers.'

'After which, you go hunting for Cortez.'

Feeling deflated, Octavian turned to face him again. 'I'm not a monster, Commander. I'm gathering my own people, Shadows and otherwise. The funeral will be over in twelve hours, probably less. The second it's done I'll send more help to Saint-Denis, and if they're not enough, and if we don't find Cortez in this nest in New York, then yes, I will put off joining the hunt for him long enough to go and try to handle the incursion myself. But it shouldn't have to come to that. You have all the tools to deal with this incursion. Do your job. The French will love you like you're Clint Eastwood. Maybe you'll get a medal.'

'It's not just France,' Metzger said.

Octavian froze in mid-turn. 'Excuse me?'

Metzger frowned. 'You didn't know? I thought Allison would have told you. There's another incursion, this time in Italy.'

'Rome?'

'Siena. The basilica there, just like in Saint-Denis,' Metzger said. 'We're sending local law enforcement to check on every cathedral and basilica in Europe and putting out warnings to the rest of the world as well.'

Something niggled at the back of Octavian's mind. 'You think it's as simple as that? We've got incursions coming through major churches, okay. But why these two? They've got to have something else in common. If it was just that they're churches, I think we'd have a hell of a lot of this happening.'

Metzger nodded. 'Of course I've got people looking into that.'

Octavian didn't reply. He narrowed his eyes, thinking, sifting through what he knew of Siena and Saint-Denis, of the basilicas there. There had to be something more. The demons they were dealing with weren't going to choose churches just to make a point. These were monstrous evils that hibernated or thrived in a thousand hells in realities parallel to this one; most of them were possessed of little more than savage intelligence. Even the smart ones weren't going to do anything for dramatic effect. They were full of hunger or hatred or both, all base desires. All they wanted was to break through. With the wakening of Navalica, they would have become aware that the human world's defenses were failing and they would have sought the weakest part of the barriers to force their way through. They—

He looked up, staring at Metzger. 'I've got it.'

'Well give it to me, then.'

'The Gospel of Shadows is lost, but I spent centuries studying it. The Vatican sorcerers who created the barriers against the supernatural, who banished those things from the world . . . what they did was like weaving, and there had to be someplace to tie the knot.'

'What the hell—'

Octavian hushed him with a wave. 'Better yet, think of them like gates. You build a fence, you always have a gate. And gates need locks. The places where the Vatican sorcerers cast their defense spells were the places where you'd find these locks. But it's been so long since anyone was paying attention to them that they're rusty. The locks. The hinges. The gates themselves. Those are going to be the weakest spots, now. And if you want to crash through, that's where you're going to try first.'

Metzger nodded, processing the information. 'You're saying the basilicas – or cathedrals or whatever – they're the places the spells were done way back when? The rusty gates?'

'Not the cathedrals,' Octavian said. 'It's the crypts.'

'What?'

'The head of Saint Catherine is buried in a crypt in Siena. The head of Saint Denis is in that basilica in France.' Octavian looked up. 'I don't remember all of them, but you find saints known to have been beheaded. Those are the Vatican sorcerers' gates. You want to figure out where the demons are going to come through next, you locate the graves of headless saints.'

9

Brattleboro, Vermont

Tori had always loved the autumnal equinox for its meditations on gratitude. Over the past century, the comparatively small earthwitch community – the true elementals, they sometimes called themselves – had co-opted bits and pieces of ritual from other pagan groups' ceremonies. But they all recognized that harvest season was a time to be grateful for what the goddess provided and for all of the blessings in one's life. At the same time, there was a melancholy air about the arrival of the dark season, an acknowledgement that every season of growing must come to an end, that every summer leads to winter, tempered by the joyful knowledge of spring's rebirth.

Bittersweet, then. Like life. Tori had seen ugliness and cruelty in her life, but had found far more joy and beauty, and she believed that was both her choice and her gift . . . to be open to receiving the beauty that her life and her world had to offer.

Taking in a deep breath of the cool September air, she exhaled with a smile and glanced around the circle at her sisters and brothers who had made the pilgrimage to be here with her and Cat tonight. Her heart ached that Keomany was not among them, but she was so happy to have Heather and Jaleesa, Vicky and Ella, and so many of the others there with them.

The move to the clearing behind Row 46 had gone well. It wasn't the perfect location, the ground not quite as aesthetically pleasing and the apple trees not quite as robust, but it would do nicely. The altar had been built from boards cut from the oldest tree at Summerfields, the cloth that covered it hand-woven by Ella, a gift at last year's celebration.

They had sung and danced and passed cups of wine around the circle, then poured the rest of the wine into the earth as a blessing. Now each of the earthwitches held up the apples they had been given when the ritual began and the small ceremonial dagger each of them had brought along. The daggers were special to each of them, etched with personal thoughts or the names of dead loved ones, handles decorated with dried husks or polished stones or twines of hair from beloved pets or children, so that they were an extension both of earthwitch and earth mother, of human and goddess.

Cat moved to the center of the circle. There were late season flowers in her hair and she wore only the sheerest, plainest white dress, which clung to her every curve in alluring fashion. Tori's heart quickened at the sight of her, and she smiled. *Look at that dress,* she thought. *And she wonders why I get horny during these things.*

She knew some pagan circles engaged in sexual rituals during these celebrations, but she'd never known earthwitches to go that far. Nudity, yes – Jaleesa was gloriously naked even now, the moonlight gleaming on her dark skin – but that was a personal choice, related to sexuality but not to sex. No one would be fucking in this circle.

At least not until later, Tori thought, almost giggling.

What is wrong with you? Focus!

She inhaled deeply. Exhaled, and a new sadness settled over her. No, she was lying to herself. This sorrow had not just arrived; she had been carrying it with her all day. The new growth in the other clearing – the secret they had kept from the eyes of passersby with a makeshift fence – gave her a hope of which she dared not speak. Surely part of it was Keomany, but until they knew precisely what it was, she would still grieve. Would the thing in the clearing, that wood sprite rooted to the soil, open its eyes and speak to them? Would it know them?

Tori knew she was meant to be focused on her gratitude and on the balance that the goddess gave the world, but she found it so difficult. Her thoughts kept slipping, her subconscious distracting her. Tonight they celebrated the equinox, recognized that they were halfway through the wheel of the year. Despite the gifts of the harvest, it was a time of endings, and the beginning of a turn toward darkness. They spoke prayers to the goddess, Gaea, the soul of the Earth, thankful for abundance and hopeful that others who were less fortunate would receive abundance of their own. They recognized the balance between light and darkness, standing precipitously in this moment when the sun and shadow were equal partners.

But Keomany was dead, and this new thing was growing in her place. What would it mean when *it* was ready to be harvested?

The sound of Cat clearing her throat made Tori blink and glance around. She'd been ruminating and had missed her cue. The prayer was done and the others were cutting their apples. With a nervous smile, trying to reassure Cat that she was all right, she pushed her dagger through the skin of the apple. The juice ran down onto her hand and the bittersweet smell filled her nostrils, and somehow that made it all right.

She exhaled again, focusing on the apple. It would be all right. Whatever was happening to Keomany, it had to be what Gaea wanted, and that would be what was for the best. She cut through the apple, evenly separating the top from the bottom and tossing the bottom half so that it rolled toward the altar. Two dozen apple halves collected around Cat's feet.

Tori held up the top half of the apple, looking at the five-pointed star pattern left behind when the core had been halved. The wind picked up and she felt a refreshing, cleansing chill. Shivering, she turned the sliced part of the apple toward the center of the circle, as did all of the gathered earthwitches, so that each of them could see the others' fruit.

'We have come to the dusk of the year, my friends,' Cat began, loudly enough so they could all hear. 'The moment of balance is upon us. Thankful for all the goddess has given us, we approach the season of long nights by offering our respect to dark mother winter, that we may – like bare branches on Gaea's tree – blossom once more in spring.'

She paused and glanced at Tori, gentle love in her eyes.

'Now, each of us will tell the goddess what she is most grateful for,' Cat went on. 'Who would like to begin?'

'I'll start,' Heather said softly.

They all turned to her. Tori smiled encouragement at her. Heather could be shy at times like this. The woman used her dagger to prise out a seed from her apple core, and as it fell to the ground at her feet, she began reciting her blessings.

'First, that I am blessed with such friends,' she said.

Behind her, the night unfurled.

White hands coalesced out of darkness, grabbed fistfuls of Heather's hair and yanked her head back. Her eyes flashed with anger and alarm, but not quite fear – Heather didn't have time for fear. The vampire darted in and sank its teeth into the pale flesh of her neck, twisted to dig in like a dog worrying a bone, and tore out her throat. Blood fountained onto the monster's face and he cocked his head back to let the spray fill his mouth for a moment before he snapped her neck and tossed her aside like a broken doll.

Only now did the screaming begin. It had happened so quickly that there'd been no time for the terror to take hold. As her sisters and some of their guests began to shriek around her, Tori could only stand, gape-mouthed, and stare at the vampire who stood proudly where Heather had been only heartbeats ago. A redheaded man, pale and freckled and long-boned, in life he must have looked kindly enough. Tonight, he wore a woman's blood like war paint, and he smiled when he saw Tori staring at him.

Smiled, and started toward her.

Tori took a step back, blinking as if waking from a trance. *No*, she thought. *No, no, no.*

Cat saw him coming and stepped into his path. She held her arms out, palms up, and started praying. Tori couldn't breathe; she felt sick. Cat had some magic, but she was no elemental. They all knew some earthcraft, but none of them had Keomany's power or skill or connection to the soul of the world.

'Not another fucking step,' Cat shouted at the vampire, all fierce bravado. To her credit, the wind began to spin around her as if a private little storm were brewing.

The vampire laughed.

And then the others appeared. A small puff of autumn mist became a towering Amazon of a woman who leaped upon a young witch from Maine. Her biker boyfriend tried to come to her rescue, grabbing hold of the vampire Amazon, but the monster barely noticed his attack. A third vampire appeared, then a fourth and fifth. Amidst the screams, some of the earthwitches broke and ran for it, including Vicky, who vanished into the moonlit orchard at a sprint with a white-haired vampire in pursuit.

Tori didn't have time to mourn for Vicky. Heather's killer had paused, watching Cat curiously, waiting for some further evidence of magic from her. When lightning did not sear down from the sky to incinerate him, he started toward her again. But Tori wasn't going to let Cat die for her . . . or die at all!

The house, she thought. Their only chance was to get out of there, to get into the house. Keomany had put wards on the entire structure, not just the doors and windows. If they could reach home, they would be safe.

Tori took a breath. Cat had always been more powerful, had a better rapport with Gaea. But growing up, she'd had more than a trace of magic herself, even before she'd become an earthwitch. It had lain mostly dormant, but she had never believed that spark had been completely gone. It had settled deep into her heart, becoming her passion for the world and for life, inspiring her love for Cat.

'Cat, run!' Tori called.

But Cat would not run. Tori knew that. The redheaded vampire slipped up to her almost like a dancer. Around the circle, its sacred blessing now soiled by the blood of innocents, their friends wept and fought and screamed. Cat pushed her hands out and the wind blew the redhead backward half a dozen feet, knocking him off balance so that he fell to his knees.

The vampire rose so quickly it seemed he'd never gone down, anger flickering in his eyes.

'Better be quick with you, I guess,' he said, the words low but clear.

Tori reached out to Gaea. With all the prayers she had ever said to the goddess she had almost never asked for anything for herself. She had been grateful, she had offered her love, she had woven small magics to help their crops grow and she had tried to lure the rain. Tonight her heart cried out to the goddess for help, and when she reached out with her soul, she felt herself touch the soul of the earth in a way she never had before. The connection filled her like a newborn's first breath, made her shudder and weep, and she fell to the ground.

Drove her fingers into the dirt.

Felt it *move*.

The earth shook and then split, opening up beneath the redheaded vampire. He fell in, and though she was twenty feet away, when Tori dragged her fingers through the soil it closed over him.

In shock, she fell backward. The connection with Gaea broke. Cat came running toward her, glancing about in fear, screaming to the rest of them to run. She reached for Tori, took her hand and hauled her up. Tori wanted to kiss her, but that was crazy. Their friends were dying. No times for kisses.

The house, she thought again. *The wards*.

Cat took her hand, and Tori counted vampires. Four. Maybe she and Cat could make it. A few others, too. Many of their friends were going to die and the thought broke parts of her, deep inside, but maybe some of them could make it. Time had slowed, but really it had only been thirty or forty seconds since Heather had been murdered. Maybe they could live.

Then she saw the mist coming out of the scar in the ground where she'd buried the redhead, saw him begin to coalesce, and she knew she'd been foolish. They were going to die.

Tori stopped. Frantic, Cat tried to pull her onward.

'Hush,' Tori said, curling a hand behind her neck. 'Kiss me.'

Cat looked startled for an instant, and then her face collapsed into the sorrow of understanding. When Tori stood on tiptoe to kiss her, Cat held her close and luxuriated in the kiss.

Furious, the redhead screamed and launched himself across the clearing toward him. The Amazon vampire started toward them as well, but the redhead shouted, warning her off.

'The dykes are mine!' he snarled.

The ground began to tremble again. Tori paused, her lips still brushing Cat's. Neither of them was doing this, and she doubted any of the others had this kind of magic, except maybe Jaleesa?

Cat screamed as the redhead grabbed a fistful of her hair and yanked her backward, twisting to hurl her to the ground, so much stronger than any human could be. Cat tried to scramble to her feet and the vampire kicked her in the chest. The sound made Tori wince; surely something had broken just now.

She cried out her lover's name as the vampire turned toward her.

'You want to try that shit again, bitch?' he sneered.

'I . . .' she started. 'I don't—'

A thick root shot from the ground and speared him through the heart. Impaled, he hung there with a ridiculous, stunned expression on his face, and he began to decay, rotting away before her eyes.

'Holy shit, Tori,' Cat said, staggering to her feet, holding onto her ribs. 'I can't believe you just—'

Tori shook her head, still wide-eyed. 'I didn't.'

The ground rumbled, and Tori knew it wasn't over.

'*Here*!' she yelled, racing toward the altar at the center of the clearing. 'If you can, gather with us!'

Jaleesa was alive, but bleeding. She ran toward them, and Ella came from the other direction. Others appeared from the orchard, fighting the urge to flee, knowing that if they were alone in the rows of apple trees the vampires would find them. It was counterintuitive to come back, but this was the trust they had in Tori and Cat, and the knowledge that they had no other chance.

Vampires leaped from their other victims, giving chase to those attempting to gather around the altar. An ugly, twisted leech laughed as he lunged, tackling Ella around the waist. Others screamed her name, and one of the guys who'd come with his wife for the equinox ran toward them, brave and foolish.

A trio of roots burst from the ground and punched through the ugly vampire, transfixing him on the spot. Others shot from the earth all around them, stabbing through the other vampires. The ground shook and the soil churned, and now Tori could see the dirt moving as thick roots snaked underneath the clearing . . . more and more of them. They thrust up from the ground, nowhere near the vampires now, and as Ella and her would-be rescuer raced back to the altar, roots shot up behind them, quickly weaving a kind of cage around the ritual's survivors.

The Amazonian vampire laughed. 'You don't think that's going to keep us out?'

A root the size of a tree trunk shot through her, obliterating the core of her torso, and she practically exploded in a cloud of ash.

The one who'd tried to kill Ella growled and turned to mist, drifting off of the spears that had impaled him and reforming beside them.

'One of those went through my heart,' the ugly leech said. 'But it's all about faith . . . all about what we believed before Cortez turned us. He wants us to sleep during the day, I can do that. But I know what this body can do, that it isn't the heart but sheer force of fucking will that holds us together. You're not going to kill me like the others.'

Another root thrust from the ground, shooting through his back – through his spine and his heart – and he roared in pain.

Maybe it wouldn't kill him, but it had certainly hurt. And the other two remaining vampires didn't look quite so confident anymore.

Tori smiled at them, terrified and sick with grief, but faking confidence as best she could.

'We can do this all night,' she said.

'What?' Cat whispered. 'What can we do? Are you doing this, 'cause I'm sure not!'

Tori shook her head, the spark of hope that had formed in her chest growing brighter.

'Not me,' she whispered. 'Don't you see?'

'See what?'

Tori took her hand and squeezed it, then nodded toward another part of the orchard, not so very far away, where a fence had been erected to shield a strange new growth from prying eyes.

'It's Keomany.'

Pollepel Island, New York

Charlotte stood on the prow of the twenty-five-foot military boat, one hand on the railing and the other clutching Sergeant Omondi's binoculars.

'This has to be a joke,' she said.

Omondi, who had given every appearance of being devoid of humor, frowned at her with what she had come to think of as Facial Expression B. Thus far he seemed not to have a C.

'What do you mean, a joke?' Omondi asked, raising his voice to be heard over the thrum of the engine and the wind and the spray of water in their faces. 'This is a perfect place for Cortez to make a nest. A coven could go for months here without discovery.'

The boat skimmed the water, thumping over the churning river at high speed. Charlotte handed the night-vision binoculars back to Omondi – she had her own night vision, born of the changes that death and Cortez had wrought on her cellular structure. And they were near enough the island now that the crumbling edifice began to come into looming focus ahead.

'It's just so fucking trite,' she called back.

Omondi looked thoughtful but did not reply. The two of them stood together on the prow as they sped north on the Hudson River, even as half a dozen other boats did the same, spread out to left and right and all of them converging on Pollopel Island. Against the indigo sky, the jagged ruin of a medieval castle seemed to stab at the night. Broken walls stood by themselves, slanted wreckage all that remained where entire wings had been. The main body of the castle had a skeletal quality, the rear of it simply gone. The windows were like dark eyes that showed only empty sky beyond. Ghosts, watching them slide along the river.

By now, the vampires would have heard them coming. They would lurk unseen in those windows, so Charlotte told herself that the shiver going through her was entirely logical. She felt as if she were being watched because she *was* being watched.

Sergeant Omondi touched his collar. 'Sharpshooters, watch the castle's airspace!' he called into his commlink.

They'd placed a single soldier on top of the small wheelhouse on each of the seven swift boats. The way the hulls were skipping off the water, Charlotte couldn't imagine that anyone would be able to manage a decent aim, but still the sharpshooters used night scopes to watch the sky above the crumbling ruin. If a bat took flight – or anything else for that matter – their job was to hit it with a Medusa-laced bullet.

Charlotte left watching the skies to the men and women with rifles. Her eyes were on the castle itself, scanning for any sign that the rotting architecture was anything other than abandoned. Nothing moved that did not seem stirred by the breeze. She wondered if the TFV soldiers sent along on this mission were nervous; surely they'd have preferred to attack during the day. But then she remembered that this was what they did, day in and day out: hunt vampires. No – *kill* vampires, like her. After that, she stopped wondering if they were afraid.

'I can't believe this place is just sitting here,' she said, mostly to hear her own voice. 'It's like a tornado picked up a chunk of some forgotten corner of Europe and dropped it down in the middle of the river.'

Omondi had already briefed her on the island, and the ominous, deteriorating pile of stones that had once been something grand. A man named Francis Bannerman had bought up surplus weapons from the US Army after the Civil War and the Spanish American War, rightly thinking there would be a market for these items later on. When the city of New York would no longer allow him to store his arsenal there, he had bought the island and spent most of the first decade of the twentieth century building the castle. According to Omondi, all of the structures on the island had been built without right angles, though it was tough to confirm that with only portions of the castle still standing after the fire that had gutted it fifty years ago.

For the first time since coming in view of the place, Charlotte tore her gaze away.

'Sergeant? What you said before about the place having no right angles? Why did Bannerman build it like that?'

Omondi gave her Expression B. 'Superstition.'

'That's not too vague. Oh, wait . . . it is.'

Expression A. Stoic and sage. 'Stories about the island being haunted go back to the seventeenth century. Local natives claimed it was inhabited by spirits. Some old legends suggest that a building without corners confuses ghosts so much that they get lost and lose any malice they might have had toward the living. Bannerman's grandson once wrote that he believed the island was inhabited by goblins who would reclaim the turrets and towers after all the people were gone, or something like that.'

Charlotte listened, staring at him, and then shook her head.

'Christ's sake,' she said.

'Does that trouble you?' Omondi said, over the wind and the engine.

She grinned. 'You mean does it creep me out? No. It's just so fucking cliché. This whole thing . . . I mean, just look at the place. It looks like the set of some Hollywood movie that they threw up and then left behind.'

Omondi found a third expression. His lip curled in amusement and he raised an eyebrow. Charlotte was proud of him.

The boat's pilot throttled down and she turned to see that they were almost at the shore, a rocky fringe of stone and dirt that ringed a tall hill of jutting stone and evergreen woods, all capped by the skeleton of the castle. It did look like nothing more than a façade, as if she could walk behind it and find that it was only two-dimensional, with two-by-fours propping it up in the back.

Now that she thought about it, she realized that the place was perfect for Cortez. His whole philosophy was to return vampires to the creatures of dread and darkness that they had been in legend and popular culture for centuries. Nightwalkers, blood-drinkers, bats flying across the moon. Cortez had embraced all of that in the same way that Hannibal had, once upon a time, but with himself as the alpha vampire. The way Charlotte had it figured, Cortez wanted to build his coven quietly, under the radar, and all around the world, so that by the time the UN found out about it, there would be too many of them to destroy easily. It seemed obvious that the one person who stood in the way of that plan was Peter Octavian. Cortez needed to take Octavian out of the equation. Charlotte assumed that killing Nikki had been phase one of that.

A shudder went through her. Her eyes fluttered closed and shards of memory stabbed at her mind and heart, images of Cortez's vampire thugs above her, beating her . . . taking her . . . raping her . . . and then Cortez himself doing so much worse.

The engine cut out and the boat coasted onto the shore, dirt and rocks scraping the hull. Charlotte opened her eyes, turned and saw Sergeant Omondi's team leaping overboard, dropping into the shallows, and starting up the shore toward the tree line. There had been no gunshots from the sharpshooters, which meant none of the vampires in the nest had tried to flee. They were either not yet aware they were under attack, or they were lurking in wait, confident and ready.

Bring it, bitches.

She smiled at Omondi, showing fang, and leaped over the side. She landed in a crouch in an inch of water, then raced forward, so swift that she quickly caught up to the frontmost of the soldiers. Sergeant Omondi would want to call her back, rein her in, but he had nothing to worry about. Charlotte wanted to know what they were going to find in that castle, but she was not about to run ahead. At her hip was a gun loaded with Medusa bullets, but she had no way of knowing how many vampires were in the nest and she wasn't interested in suicide.

If Cortez is there—

The thought nearly made her stumble. Of course he wasn't there. If he had been, surely she would have sensed him. But if he was, there were other worries than just being outnumbered. If she pulled some kind of action hero fantasy and ran in there ahead of the troops, Cortez would be much more likely to get away, and Octavian would never forgive her. She wouldn't do that. Not to him.

The commlink in her ear crackled with static. 'Charlotte!'

'I'm here, Sarge.'

'Swing west to the road. Follow the plan.'

Omondi had laid it out for her. They didn't have the numbers for a thorough search of the island – at least not until sunup. The woods surrounding Bannerman's Arsenal could be crawling with vampires. It seemed counterintuitive to approach so blatantly, without making any attempt to conceal themselves, but Sergeant Omondi believed that any vampires in the castle would already know they were coming, and Charlotte figured that to be true. The woods would be a very bad idea. In close quarters, enough vampires could slaughter the invaders in minutes, no matter how many pairs of night vision goggles and Medusa bullets they'd been issued. On the road – not much more than an overgrown path that led up to the ruin – they'd be out in the open and more likely to be seen, but it would be harder for Cortez's coven to get the drop on them and thin out the attacking forces.

Charlotte ignored his order, working her way up the steep hill, moving through the trees and over the blanket of pine needles on the ground. It was a full thirty seconds before his voice crackled in her ear again.

'Charlotte, form on me.'

'I don't think so, Sarge,' she whispered. 'If they come at you all at once, consider me your ace in the hole.'

'Be careful,' Omondi replied.

A reply began to form on her lips, something snarky, but she chose to keep silent. Omondi was a serious sort of man to begin with, but more than that, he was part of Task Force Victor. It ought to have been his job to kill her, and instead he was expressing concern for her safety. She felt a gratitude toward him that she would never speak aloud. It made her less alone than she'd been just a moment before.

Charlotte raced uphill through the trees, cognizant of the noise she made but unable to avoid it. Thin branches snapped and pine needles whispered underfoot. She could hear Omondi's team making their way up the road and she listened for sounds of an ambush. As she weaved through the woods she caught glimpses of the neglected turrets of Bannerman's Arsenal and she scanned the windows and the tops of the walls for any sign of habitation.

When she emerged from the trees at the top of the hill, standing in the shadow of the castle's ruin where the moonlight could not reach, she shivered. With its broken face and vacant windows, the castle truly did seem like a ghost. She glanced right and saw nothing that seemed out of place . . . crumbled architecture, overgrown ground, and trees. The view to the left held nothing more, save for the broken, rutted track that had once served as a road. It led up to what must have been the main entrance to the castle but was now a yawing darkness of fallen stone and wild weeds.

Sergeant Omondi and his troops came up the road moments after she'd emerged from the woods and began to spread out, quickly setting up a perimeter around the castle. Charlotte drifted toward the scorched and faded wall in front of her. She could hear Omondi giving orders over his comm and some of the replies as well; they were reporting back about where the best entry points to the castle had been found. In moments they would go in, ready to destroy every vampire they came across. One of the soldiers, a woman called Bennett, referred to them as leeches. Charlotte had heard the word many times before, but never with the weight of so much disgust. Task Force Victor weren't afraid of vampires.

They think they're *the bogeymen*, she thought. And in a way it was true; after she'd turned, Cortez had warned her about Task Force Victor the same way mothers had once warned small children not to stray far or the bogeyman would get them.

But the soldiers were wrong, too. The vampires would be wary of them, but not afraid. Bloodlust eclipsed fear, and once they got into a fight, all the vampires would be thinking about was the soldiers' blood. That was how Cortez had trained them.

This is wrong.

The thought came upon her with such certainty that she nearly shapeshifted in order to get over to Omondi faster, but she stopped herself, worried that any reminder of her being a vampire might inadvertently end with her getting another dose of Medusa, or worse. She tried to remind herself that she was more than a vampire, she was a Shadow. But with so many fingers on so many triggers, she didn't want to risk her life on such subtleties.

She ignored the soldiers who had already taken up positions around the house. Sergeant Omondi would be at the main entrance with his handpicked squad. She ran alongside the ruin. Crossing into the pool of moonlight that came through the space where the castle's front wall ought to have been, she remembered her commlink and mentally chastised herself.

'Omondi, you there?' she said.

'Go ahead, Charlotte.'

'Something's wrong,' she said. 'Hold 'em back.'

'What do you—?'

'Just hold them for a second!'

Omondi's squad swiveled around as she ran up, weapons trained on her. They'd all been briefed on her presence, all had a good look, and even in the moonlight it would've been hard for them not to recognize her red hair and pale skin. Still, she halted and put her hands up, waiting several seconds until gun barrels were lowered and a soldier waved her forward. By then Omondi had come to the front of the group.

'Report,' he said, as if she were a soldier and not an undead nineteen-year-old girl.

'There's just something off,' she said, cringing at how lame that sounded.

'You'll have to be more—'

'They'd never wait,' she said. 'Not Cortez's coven, don't you get that? If there were two or three of them, they'd have turned to bats or mist and they'd be gone. Your snipers would have taken them out or missed them entirely, but they'd be gone. If there were more than that, five or ten or twenty, they'd have come out the second they knew we were here. They're stuck on this island, hiding out, hunting when they can? You guys showing up like this would be like their moms calling them for breakfast.'

'We've killed more than that,' one of the soldiers said.

'Doesn't matter,' Charlotte argued. 'They'd have come down from the sky or through the trees, hit and run in the dark. With Medusa ammo and me along as backup, you'd have won, but they'd have come. There's no way they're just sitting in there waiting for you.'

Sergeant Omondi frowned. 'Then there's no danger in proceeding.'

Charlotte returned his frown, her own personal Expression B. 'No, no. That's what I'm saying. I *feel* them, Sarge. They were here. I can feel it under my skin. They were here and they're gone, now. Maybe they got a tip we were coming or maybe they cleared out for some other reason, but I don't think it's any of that. You hear anything moving in the woods on your way up here? A few night birds, that's it. Nothing on the ground. There had to be squirrels or something, right? So where are they?'

Impatience etched deep lines on Omondi's face.

'Step aside,' he said. 'Abandoned or not, we're here to find a vampire nest, if it was ever here to begin with.'

As Omondi gestured to his squad and they started around her, she saw the suspicion in the eyes of a couple of soldiers and realized they thought she was purposely stalling, maybe to help Cortez. Charlotte bristled, wanting to scream at them.

'This is Omondi,' he said into his commlink. 'Move in.'

Charlotte could do nothing but follow as they trooped over the fallen masonry and through the broad space where a door must once have been. One side of the ruin was washed with moonlight and the other sunken in shadow. Voices muttered in her ear, TFV soldiers following orders, entering the castle through jagged, broken walls and half-blocked doorways.

She kept silent, following Omondi closely, but they hadn't gotten very far inside the ruin when the breeze died down and she froze, inhaling deeply.

'Sergeant,' she said.

Omondi, only a few feet ahead, turned to give her a hard look. 'What now?'

'I smell blood,' Charlotte said, but it was more than just blood. Her nostrils were full of the stink of dead things.

Before he could reply, voices rang out, echoing off the bare, ruined walls around them. Weapons at the ready, Omondi's squad quickened their pace, taking care not to fall on the treacherous footing amongst the wreckage of Francis Bannerman's ambitions. The various squads had their lights out, now. With no immediate sign of attack, they swung flashlights about and called to one another as they cleared dark corners and the remnants of rooms. Bannerman's Arsenal reminded Charlotte of photos she had seen online of the Roman Coliseum, nothing but deteriorating walls open to the sky. But there were blockaded rooms and stairs to nowhere and at least one set of steps leading down into the ground, underneath the castle.

Soldiers were spread out, the lights mounted on their weapons shining as they stood guard over the rubble, as if they had just claimed new territory for Task Force Victor. Omondi's squad and one other had gathered on the far side of the vast ruin, where a rounded corner of the castle remained intact, a squat little room much like a turret, though it was nowhere near where a turret belonged.

'They were here, all right,' one of the soldiers said.

Omondi cast a glance at Charlotte but said nothing. She moved up beside him and peered between two soldiers. There were clothes strewn about the room, and some of them seemed to have been folded and stacked with a certain orderliness. She saw a few books and a great many empty bottles of wine.

Charlotte wrinkled her nose.

There were dead things in there as well. Rabbits, squirrels, birds, and something she thought must be a fox.

'This is what you smelled,' Omondi told her.

'No. It isn't.'

Charlotte turned and strode across the ruin, making her way around rubble, to the place where those stairs descended into the bowels of the castle. Half a dozen soldiers were already there, two of them starting down the stairs with their lights guiding the way.

'Let me by,' she said.

'What are you doing?' Omondi asked, and she could hear him in her ear just as well as she could through her commlink.

Charlotte turned to him, tired of being ignored.

'I know it's hard, Sergeant. I look like a nineteen-year-old girl, but I could kill you right now, before you could even aim that weapon. You're struggling between wanting to treat me like an ally or a kid and seeing me as the enemy. I don't blame you. But I'm telling you they're gone, and they left us a present. The blood I smelled – the dead things I smell, right now – it's coming from down there. Considering we have no idea what's really waiting down there, and since I'm a hell of a lot harder to kill than any of you, I'm going down ahead of you. Unless you want to give me that condescending look you've been giving me for the last few minutes again?'

Omondi furrowed his brow thoughtfully, then gestured for the other soldiers to step back.

'Lead the way, then,' he said. 'But be careful.'

Again with the concern, she thought. Omondi really was having a hard time figuring out how to feel about having a Shadow on his team. She wondered if he had worked with Allison Vigeant and, if so, whether he'd been quite so conflicted about her.

Charlotte gave Omondi a nod and went to the stairs. Moonlight lit the way, but it could not reach underground. As keen as her vision was, she did not refuse when a soldier offered her his flashlight. Shining it ahead of her, she picked her way amongst the debris and descended. Sergeant Omondi and four or five others followed her down, keeping their distance.

At the bottom of the steps was a corridor that led straight ahead, and she followed it. The stone walls and supports had held up rather well. She glanced into three rooms as she passed and found them similar to the one above, with the detritus of an abandoned vampire nest, but the blood ahead smelled fresh – perhaps only hours old.

The smell lured her to the end of the corridor, where a heavy door hung open. The smell of ancient gunpowder lingered in the air, and she realized that this must be one of the vaults where Bannerman had stored part of his arsenal. The stink of death sat heavily in the air as she stepped over the threshold into the vault and moved her flashlight beam across the room.

Charlotte counted six corpses. Four of them had been haphazardly lumped into a pile like nothing more than human rubble, just another part of the ruin. The other two had been gutted, their viscera decorating the room like party streamers. They had not even been dead long enough for the blood and stinking waste to stop dripping from their hanging intestines. Charlotte's stomach lurched and she nearly threw up. Even after all she had been through, much of her was still human enough to recoil at the sight.

'Charlotte, what've you got?' Omondi asked. All of the impatience had left his voice. There could be no denying the stench that came from the vault now.

The dead people were all dressed in some kind of worker's uniform, but she only glanced at that detail for a moment. Something else drew her eye. Her light had caught the edge of a smear of blood on the far wall. She panned the light across the wall and read the single word painted there, a haphazard afterthought. A bloody celebration.

Xibalba. She didn't recognize the word, but she wanted to make sure she was reading it correctly, so she took a step deeper into the room and felt something tug at her ankle. Tug, and snap.

Some part of her brain recognized the significance of that snap, of the wisp of string that coiled back into the shadows like a broken spider-web. In an eyeblink, she was shifting, flesh and bone turning to mist.

'Charl—' Omondi began.

And the vault exploded, buckling the ceiling above, sending a ball of raging white fire rolling up through cracks in the ground. The remaining walls of Bannerman's Arsenal were blown apart and the woods ignited with flames that began to spread.

In minutes, the fire could be seen for miles up and down the Hudson River.

The goblins, it seemed, had finally claimed all that remained of Pollepel Island.

10

September 23

Philadelphia, Pennsylvania

Octavian sat in a chair beside Nikki's open coffin, holding her hand. He knew it was absurd, clutching the cold, stiff fingers of a corpse as if he were offering comfort to the dead. Even the idea that he might draw some solace for himself from such contact was ridiculous. One glance at her face, perfectly painted and still as a wax figure, should have driven all such sentimentality from his heart. He had lived centuries in this world and many more in Hell, had seen death and sorrow in catastrophic proportions and watched loved ones die screaming. How could he fool himself into thinking it meant anything at all for him to sit here and bid farewell to a woman whose life had been extinguished days ago?

And yet . . .

'I'm alive,' he whispered, running his thumb over her knuckles, studying the lips he had once kissed and which had been sewn together by unloving hands. 'All that time I fought so hard to hang on to something inside me that I could call "human". And then I was human again. Alive. And I had you by my side, and despite everything, I thought we could live in the world the way ordinary people do. That we could just . . . breathe.'

He hung his head, angry with himself. She was gone. He was talking to nobody but himself and it made him a fool.

Only, he didn't feel like a fool.

'Now I feel like I can't breathe at all.'

He released her hand and placed it carefully the way he had found it, over her heart with the other. Her heart did not beat and her lungs did not draw air. There would be no more music from within her.

Anger and grief – the yin and yang of tragedy's aftermath – had been twined together within him ever since he had walked into her hotel room and found her. This morning, grief had come to the fore. When Commander Metzger had come to him before dawn to tell him about the explosion at Bannerman's Arsenal, his numbness had only deepened. Local police river patrol boats had been the first to respond, followed quickly by the state police and Army and UN officials and investigators. Five soldiers had survived the explosion, three of them gravely wounded, but there had been no sign of Charlotte. The lack of any trace at all suggested that she had either shifted or been totally incinerated, and he chose to believe the former. The fact that she hadn't yet reported in made him wonder if she had somehow been caught between the two, in which case it would take significant strength of will for her to reintegrate herself. Charlotte had been one of Cortez's creatures at first, which Octavian found worrisome. If she didn't believe in her own survival, then her consciousness would have scattered along with her being.

Metzger had a different interpretation of Charlotte's absence. He also figured her absence meant one of two things, and that one of those was incineration. But to Metzger, the other option was treachery; he thought it very likely that Charlotte had set them all up, leading the team to Bannerman's Arsenal for the sole purpose of getting them all killed. Octavian didn't buy it. He didn't trust easily, but he had given Charlotte his trust. She had earned it in the fight against Navalica. And he believed it would require an actress of extraordinary skill to have perpetuated the sort of deception that would have been involved.

No, Charlotte was just a girl. A kid who'd been a victim and decided she wanted to take control of her future. He hoped that she hadn't died for that ambition and that he'd see her again, in time. What Metzger might do then was a concern for another day. Even Charlotte's life or death was a worry for later.

Octavian took a deep breath and let it out, steadying himself. He looked at Nikki's waxen features again, thinking the mortician's work was a pale imitation of her true beauty. His thoughts were a jumble of guilt and recrimination and fury. That her fans still gathered in front of the hotel where she had been murdered was a good sign, because it meant they had no idea where she was going to be buried. There would be no wake, only a burial service. It would be a quiet, loving farewell of which he was certain Nikki would have approved. No hours of mourning with an open casket for people she barely knew. No church service. Just words spoken at the graveside, and a body laid gently to rest.

He told himself she would have understood the speed with which all of this had to be done. The federal government had stepped in to expedite the burial at the request of the UN. They wanted Octavian's attention refocused on what they considered more important matters than grief. The swift burial would help to guarantee a private service, but that was only one reason he had agreed. Whatever Cortez had set in motion – whatever his reasons for having killed Nikki – he was closer to achieving his goals with every passing moment. Octavian meant to find him and kill him.

Nikki would have approved of that too.

When they lowered her coffin into the ground it would not be the end of his mourning, but he would no longer feel the need to be at her side. Then there would be a reckoning.

A quick rap on the door, and it swung open. The thin, gray-haired funeral home director ducked his head in.

'Mr Octavian? I'm afraid it's time, sir. May we come in?'

Octavian stood. 'Of course.'

He wiped the dampness from his eyes and felt the static crackle of magic prickling his skin. He glanced down at his hands and saw the dark, purplish energy emanating from them – his anger made manifest without him being aware of it.

The funeral director and two of his broad-shouldered sons stood just inside the room, watching him with wide, wary eyes.

'It's all right,' Octavian assured them. He tried to dispel the power seething around his hands but only managed to diminish it. 'As you say, it's time.'

He bent and kissed Nikki's forehead, as he had so often done when they embraced. Then he kissed her lips, so softly. And then he turned away, striding past the funeral director and his sons, and out the door. He thought the old man might call him back, ask him if he was certain that he did not want to stay while the casket was sealed, but none of the funeral men said a word.

All that was left was to bury her.

Nikki's fans were cleverer and more tenacious than Octavian had believed. Somehow, the word had gotten out. The gates of the cemetery were guarded by state and local police. Octavian had thought it unnecessary, but now he was glad the cops were there. As he rode in the back of the black sedan the funeral home had provided, following the hearse that carried Nikki's body, he stared out the window at the hundreds of fans who lined the last quarter mile of the road to the cemetery's gates. He hoped the presence of armed police officers would be intimidating enough to keep the burial private.

As the funeral procession turned into the cemetery entrance and passed through the arched, wrought-iron gate, Octavian saw a pair of teenagers holding each other and crying as they watched the hearse go by. A part of him wished he could let them in. He thought Nikki might have liked that as well. But the gathering that was about to take place was not only a funeral.

It was a war council.

Through the tinted glass, the graveyard looked like another world, a dusky stone garden of tombs and markers. The stillness of the place made him catch his breath, as if time had frozen outside the confines of the car. Then he noticed the way the wind shook the branches on the trees and the illusion was broken.

The procession turned left along a narrow, rutted road that led over a rise. The hearse pulled up onto the grass on the right, nearest the gravesite that had been prepared for Nikki's interment, and Octavian's driver pulled around it, parking further along on the left. The rest of the procession – fewer than a dozen cars – followed suit. The mourners had been asked to meet at the funeral home in order to form the procession to the cemetery, but Octavian had barely paid attention to them when he had come out and climbed into the sedan. He had sat in the back behind tinted glass and waited while funeral home employees carried Nikki's casket out and loaded it into the hearse.

Now, as he exited the sedan, blinking back the brightness of the autumn morning, he had his first good look at those who had come to bid her farewell. Despite the chaos of the night before and the morning, Leon Metzger had come to pay his respects. But Octavian sought other faces, other friends and allies, and as he crossed the broken road and started across the lawn to the place where the priest stood waiting, he saw them.

Kuromaku wore a charcoal-black Victorian mourning coat, nearly knee-length. His face might as well have been carved from stone, but Octavian felt strengthened by the sight of him. He had arrived with Allison, whose gray dress was nearly as somber. Her dark sunglasses revealed as little as Kuromaku's mask of stoicism. They had wanted to be with him at the funeral home but he had refused, wanting his last farewell to be private, even from his closest friends.

Amber Morrissey seemed to have come alone, but Octavian knew that was as much an illusion as her human appearance. Thanks to her encounter with chaos magic in her hometown of Hawthorne, Amber required a glamour that made others see her the way she wished them to see her . . . as the young woman she had been before Navalica had begun to transform her into a Reaper. But since it was Octavian's glamour, he could see through it easily enough, see the thing that Amber had become. He had used sorcery to slow her transformation, but the

177

combination of his power and Navalica's had turned her into something else – something new. With her hard, burgundy skin and long hair like purple spines, she remained beautiful. Somehow even her long, vicious talons did not erase her loveliness. Neither human nor Reaper, she nevertheless had a Reaper's abilities . . . to become a wraith and sail on the wind, to become as intangible as a ghost, to reach into human beings and tear out their souls.

Octavian couldn't see him, but he knew Miles Varick had come down from New England with Amber. Like Amber, her former professor had been changed by the chaos magic Navalica had unleashed in Hawthorne. Octavian thought of him as a hungry ghost, a man turned into a vampire and then killed in the maelstrom of anarchic magic. Now he haunted his old home town, caring for the ghost of his mother, but he could drink souls and dark spirits the way a flesh and bone vampire drank blood.

'Chaos,' Miles had once said, 'is where new things are born.'

He and Amber were two very unsettling examples.

Octavian scanned faces, heartened at the sight of so many old allies, some of whom he might even call friends. Santiago had made the trip, as had two others who had fought beside Octavian and Kuromaku in the years when they had taken part in wars just to have a chance to fight for something worthy. One of them, Taweret, was a slim Egyptian who had been dragged from her dwelling on the shores of the Nile more than eight hundred years earlier and made a vampire. She had often said that her parents must have been able to see the future, for they had named her for the goddess of vengeance. The other warrior stood nearly seven feet tall, a mountain sculpted of equal parts muscle and flab. Kazimir had died in this shape and – though in time he had learned that he could have altered it

– he had chosen to maintain it. Many had called him a giant, and the Shadow warrior had embraced the idea.

Like Santiago, Taweret and Kazimir had sometimes chosen sides based on reward rather than righteousness, but in the blinding light of the modern world, they had been more cautious about their allegiances. Thanks to Octavian, they had each signed the Covenant and been none too happy about it. In truth, Octavian had not been certain they would come, but he was very pleased to see them.

There were a handful of magicians in attendance, including the German necromancer that he himself had been forced to bring back from the dead two years before, trying to find a way to return the risen Afghani war dead to their graves. That had seemed a serious crisis in those days, but the definition of 'serious' continued to change.

Octavian saw Nikki's manager and her lawyer, as well as two members of her old band who had arrived with their wives or girlfriends, and who looked very wary of the strange mourners around them. There were several faces he vaguely recognized and assumed were old friends who had learned of the burial and persuaded Allison to approve their attendance. Octavian had invited those he felt ought to be here and those he needed and had left others to Allison's discretion.

As he walked toward the grave the group of mourners parted to create a path, so that he arrived at the casket much as a bride approaches her groom at the altar. But he had come to bid her farewell, not to promise her forever.

The priest, a friend of Allison's who had come down from the New York headquarters of the American Catholic Church as a favor to her, raised his arms in a symbolic embrace.

'Ladies and gentlemen, thank you all for coming to this committal service for our sister, Nikki,' the priest began.

Octavian exhaled, relieved that he had not used her given name. She would not have wanted that. In her heart she had never been Nicole.

'The passing of a loved one is always painful, always sad, and it can create a profound emptiness within us. We must fill that empty place with our love and our memories and the knowledge that Nikki would want us to find new joy and kindness and contentment in our lives, and that she herself has gone on to find new joy and kindness, and the ultimate contentment, in the life beyond this one.'

Octavian smiled sadly, looking not at the casket but at the green veil drawn across the grave. As if he had opened a previously locked mental door, worries began to flood in. He thought of Charlotte and of the crises still raging in France and Italy, and of Cortez laughing somewhere. The priest kept talking and he vowed silently to Nikki that he would listen, that he would breathe, that he would be with her until she had been laid to rest, give her all of his attention.

The priest began to read from the Bible, holding it in one hand, even as he shook holy water from a small vial, droplets spattering the casket. A drop landed on Octavian's hand and he exhaled again, a large weight seeming to lift from him. Nikki had gone on ahead of him, but they were still connected. Once upon a time, no one could know with real certainty – no matter what faith they declared – that there were such things as Heaven and Hell, or spirits or demons or angels. But he knew firsthand, and since the Venice Jihad, years ago now, the whole world had known the truth. It amazed him how many were unwilling to accept it, but it was the truth nevertheless.

The spirit did linger on after the flesh had gone to rot.

He could not know for certain if he would meet Nikki again

in the next life, but he knew that if he could, he would seek her out. For now, that would have to be enough.

The priest gave his final blessing, inviting those who were so inclined to pray with him. As low voices joined in prayer, Octavian slipped his hand from Allison's and approached the casket. He knew he ought to have waited for the priest to finish, but the desire for some contact, a final goodbye, made him ignore protocol. He stepped up and laid his hands on the smooth metal surface. No one moved to stop him and he closed his eyes, listening to the last words of the prayer.

A low grinding noise came from not far off, the sound of stone against stone.

'What the hell—' he heard Santiago say.

The priest faltered only a few lines before the last amen.

Allison shouted his name. Octavian opened his eyes just as the first gunshots rang out. Kazimir and Taweret were already in motion, grabbing hold of humans and hurling them to the ground without worrying about being gentle. Kuromaku reached into the air at his hip and his sword appeared from nothing. The metal whisper of the blade being drawn carried, even as more gunfire punched the blue autumn sky.

'There!' Amber shouted.

Octavian spun and saw the open door of a crypt, saw the gun thrust from the darkness, bucking as it spat bullets.

Someone cried out and he saw it was the priest, who clutched at his arm and staggered to the ground beside Nikki's casket.

Nikki's casket.

Octavian heard the bestial snarl but did not recognize his own voice at first. He felt himself shaking with rage, felt the magic flowing through his bones. His skin prickled and his vision turned red, tinted by the power that poured out of him, misting from his eyes and sizzling the air around his hands.

One of the mages was painting complicated sigils in the air that would have protected them all behind a magical barrier, but Octavian was not thinking defensively. He saw his fellow warriors rushing toward the crypt and felt their fury, remembering a hundred battles he had shared with one or all of them. But this was a fight he would not share.

'Get back!' he shouted. 'Kazimir! Santiago! All of you, back off!'

Kuromaku and Allison halted, but the others kept on. Octavian raised a hand, contorted his fingers, and reached out with the power inside him. At the last moment, with a twitch of his ring finger, he altered the spell from concussive magic to defensive, throwing up a wall into which all three of them crashed, falling backward.

The light around his left hand turned a deep, emerald green and he thrust it outward. The air rippled as the spell burned through it. The entire front of the crypt blew in, the roof collapsing, the shooter crushed in a sliver of a moment.

A moment's quiet fell upon them.

'Go,' Octavian said, nodding to Allison. 'See who's stupid enough to try something like this.'

He turned to seek out the priest, thinking to heal the man. Amber ran toward him, her human guise falling away so that anyone looking at her would see her true face, her wine-dark beauty and ferocity. The hungry ghost of Miles Varick materialized behind her.

'It isn't over!' Amber shouted.

Octavian twisted round, scanning the cemetery but seeing only mourners and funeral home employees and police, out at the gate.

'What do you—'

'The ghosts,' Miles said. 'The haunters say there are—'

The thump and crack of breaking stone echoed off of grave markers and tombs as the doors of a dozen crypts were smashed open from within and bizarre figures emerged, men and women in skintight black from head to toe, with only strange lenses over their eyes to break the smooth covering. They carried handguns.

They opened fire.

Allison snarled, knocked off her feet by a bullet that struck her in the side.

'Son of a bitch!' she roared, holding her bleeding side, unable to shift. 'It's Medusa! They've got toxin!'

Octavian hit the one who'd shot her with a spell that turned him to stone. That's what Medusa had gotten him.

'Who the hell are these fucks?' Santiago yelled.

And Octavian knew. The UN were supposed to be the only ones with the Medusa toxin, but the vampires who'd gone after Charlotte had shot her with a bullet laced with the stuff. They were covered in head to toe to protect them from the sun.

'They're vampires,' he shouted back. 'Cortez sent them.'

Sent them to do this today. Not enough that he killed Nikki, he had to desecrate her funeral.

Bullets flew. Santiago shifted to mist. Kuromaku ran to protect Allison. As one of Cortez's vampires turned to shoot him, Kuromaku lopped his gun hand off at the wrist. From behind the blank black mask of his sunsuit, the vampire roared, and Kuromaku cut his head off. As the vampire fell, he began to turn to dust inside the suit. Two more came at Kuromaku and Allison, but Octavian turned them to stone, careful not to hit his allies with the same spell. Enraged, his heart thrumming in his chest, screams of fury building in his lungs, he followed that spell with pure force, hurling concussive magic that obliterated the vampire statues, turning them to a different sort of dust.

Humans screamed and warriors roared. The band members and their wives were lying on the ground, dead or just keeping their heads down. The manager crouched behind a grave marker for cover. One of the cousins had been shot and another mourner knelt beside him, muttering terrified and empty assurances.

Taweret took a bullet in the thigh and fell.

''Maku, shift!' Octavian shouted. 'I've got Allison.'

Kuromaku wouldn't want to, Octavian knew. But he did as he was asked. A moment later he coalesced behind the last line of marching vampires and began to cut them down one by one, silent and lethal. Octavian counted at least forty or fifty vampires still there.

Bannerman's Arsenal, he thought. They had abandoned the place, and this was where they'd gone, slipping into the crypts during the night and lying in wait.

Police were shouting and shooting. There were sirens. None of that would matter. The fight wouldn't last long enough for them to make a difference. Octavian wracked his brain, trying to think how he could save his friends and the other mourners, how he could destroy Cortez's creatures without hurting innocents and allies. Another vampire shot at Allison and Octavian raised a hand, froze the bullet in a tiny pocket of time, and then threw it back at the leech. It punctured the suit and the vampire fell. There would be no turning to mist to get out of here. Not for her.

He sketched at the air like one of the lesser magicians and three other vampires turned to stone.

A bullet punched through his neck, tearing flesh and severing blood vessels. Choking, grasping his throat, he felt the hot blood splashing his hands. A moment of panic ensnared him as he crumbled to the ground, pain searing him. The copper stink of his own blood filled his nostrils.

Cold with rage he clapped one hand over the entry wound. Blue light glowed so fiercely that he felt the static prickle of it at the exit wound as the flesh healed.

He rose and kept rising, floating off the ground as his body was enveloped in crackling green light. As if hurling stones, he threw concussive blasts at the vampires around him, crushing them to a pulp inside their suits and then hitting them again until the suits split open, exposing them to the sun.

And they burned.

He heard a vampire screaming and turned to see Miles Varick's ghost holding tight to a vampire, his spectral fangs sinking into the thing's throat. Miles held on, mouth pressed to the black-clad neck like a lamprey, sucking out both blood and darksoul. Nearby, a wine-purple wraith darted through the air, descending upon another vampire. Amber thrust her hand through the vampire's chest and ripped out a squirming bit of darkness that might have been its heart or the demon-soul that existed inside all of their kind.

Enough vampires might kill Amber, but they could do nothing to a ravenous, monstrous ghost who wanted only to drain their vitality from them. Other mourners were far more vulnerable.

Even as he had this thought, he heard someone chanting a spell in ancient Chaldean. Spinning, he saw a young sorceress named Holly Nevill facing half a dozen approaching vampires. She stood over an old man named Groff, who had crumbled to his knees, clutching at his heart. Bullets slowed as they approached the two; Holly was holding her own. Then the necromancer came up beside her, shouting something else, hands out in front of him, fingers into horns, thumbs touching together. The asshole was trying to take control of the vampires. They were dead, or at least had died, once, and he thought his necromancy could make him their master.

His magic disrupted Holly's defenses. The bullets came right through. At least one hit her, because she went down, but the necromancer took three or four shots to the chest and pelvis, one to the leg, and one in the temple. He went down like a crashing kite and Octavian knew there would be no bringing him back this time. His own necromancy had made it possible before, and on that occasion the necromancer hadn't had a bullet in the brain.

Holly might still be alive. The priest as well. Allison and Taweret were filled with toxin and vulnerable, and there were too many humans still to protect.

It occurred to him that he might not be able to save any of them.

'No, no, no,' he muttered, pummeling another vampire until it split like ripe fruit and burned in the sun. It felt so much better than turning them to stone.

He spun around, taking stock, counting vampires and counting allies. He needed a spell that would kill the vampires without hurting anyone else and he was coming up dry. Still, he kept fighting, moving methodically now, quickly, turning vampires to stone or ice. He saw Kuromaku slashing and killing. Saw Kazimir appear behind a vampire and do the same, grabbing hold of the leech and tugging off its head, ripping its suit open, exposing it to the sun.

Police cars roared up. Cops piled out, hiding behind their doors, guns at the ready, looking for an opening even though there was nothing they could do without the Medusa toxin. Brave or stupid, Octavian didn't know.

It was a matter of numbers now. Numbers and speed. He kept moving. Amber and Miles dropped from the sky and destroyed one at a time.

Too many.

God damn you, Cortez. Too many.

Magic burning through him, crackling all of him, he turned to another vampire, about to destroy it. The ground seemed to shift and buck beneath its feet and then a thick tree root burst from the soil and speared the vampire through the chest, piercing its heart. The vampire gave a gasp and dust came out of its mouth. It began to molder to dust inside of its sunsuit, dead. Disintegrating.

Octavian glanced around, thinking of Holly and Groff and the other two magicians he had invited here, but none of them was still standing.

The ground erupted. Voices rose in shouts, some of victory and others of fear, as the roots thrust from the soil, some twining around the vampires and dragging them down and others skewering them through the heart. Several hung impaled on roots that had thrust so high they were like grotesque trees.

In moments, it was done.

Someone else had done what Octavian could not – killed the leeches while leaving his allies untouched.

He felt the magic dissipate from him, fizzing against his skin as it burned off. He dropped a few feet to the ground, landing in a crouch. Gazing around him, he saw his friends surveying the damage and the police rushing forward to try to aid the fallen and make sure all of the vampires were dead.

Octavian frowned as he approached one of the roots that jutted from the cemetery grounds. He touched the wood, brows knitted, and then looked down at the soil beneath it. *An earth-witch*, he thought. But unless Gaea herself had stepped in, which he doubted, that made no sense. He'd only ever met one earthwitch powerful enough to do something like this.

He blinked, a hitch in his breath, and fell to his knees. He touched the blades of grass and then pushed his fingers into the loose dirt around the root. When he spoke, it was in a whisper.

'Keomany?'

11

Brattleboro, Vermont

The police cars began to roll out of Summerfields Orchard a little before ten in the morning. Cat Hein stood and watched as the line of vehicles departed – Brattleboro and State Police vehicles, as well as crime-scene folks, who had finally finished up their work. The coroner's people had been gone before the sun had risen on the first full day of autumn, taking with them the torn and broken bodies of several of her close friends, and a number of other kind and gentle folks to whom she had offered her hospitality.

She and Tori had held each other last night and cried as they waited for the police and ambulances to arrive. The EMTs had wandered the clearing with wide eyes, pale and shaken by the carnage and by their inability to save a single life. Those who had more than minor bumps and scrapes or broken bones were already dead or quickly fading by the time they had rushed through the rows of apple trees with their equipment. A burly,

189

gentle-eyed EMT threw up and then kept apologizing when he began to cry and could not stop. Several cops vanished into the trees for a while and Cat had heard retching from at least one of them, though they pretended they had only been investigating.

It had been the longest night of Cat's life and now she was just numb. She stood and watched a state police captain talking quietly with Ted Gately, the Brattleboro police chief. Her phone buzzed and she slipped it from her pants pocket to see that it was Tori calling.

'Hi, honey,' she answered.

'Why are they still here?' Tori asked, her voice brittle. Cat's chest tightened. A little part of Tori had broken last night, no matter what new magic might have come into the world, and Cat feared it would never be repaired.

'They're going,' she said. 'Though Chief Gately says he's going to post a car at the end of the drive and he wants us to stay closed for the day –'

'As if there's any way we would open for business with all the . . . the mess up here.'

'He means well, Tori. I'm a cantankerous bitch, and even I think he's a sweet old man,' Cat said, as she watched the state police captain drive off and Chief Gately lean down to the window of a Brattleboro police car to give orders to two of his men.

'I know,' Tori said, sighing. 'I do. And I'm glad they're going to stay, as long as they stay down there. Whatever happens now is for us to decide.'

There was weight and significance to her words beyond their simple meaning, but Cat could not reply the way she might have liked, for Chief Gately had just patted the roof of the patrol car to send the men on their way and was walking across the dusty parking lot toward her.

'The chief's coming over to talk,' she said. 'I'll be up in a few minutes.'

'Okay. Thank him from me, please.'

Cat said that she would and they exchanged their I-love-yous even as Cat met the chief's gaze, silently pleading for a moment's indulgence. When she had ended the call she clutched the phone in her hand instead of putting it back into her pocket, as if that would keep Tori closer to her.

'I'll have someone at the end of the drive all day and through the night,' Chief Gately said. He had wiry gray eyebrows that stuck out at crazy angles and the skin around his eyes sagged enough that she thought it must partly obscure his vision, but he still seemed a formidable man.

'Tori wants me to thank you, Chief. For everything,' Cat said. 'But are you sure that's necessary? I mean, if any of them got away, we have no reason to assume that they're going to come back.'

Chief Gately nodded with an expression of grim approval. 'No, I don't suppose they will, after what you gals did to them.' He put his hands on his hips, the leather of his gunbelt creak-ing. 'I spent sixty years or so being absolutely sure that ghosts and vampires and witches and magic were a whole lot of bunk. I guess I can file it all under things I wish I'd never learned. But I'm damn glad you ladies were able to defend yourselves. If not for that bit of hoodoo . . .'

He trailed off, obviously not knowing how to finish. They had not mentioned Keomany to the police, had claimed that the roots that had been summoned up to destroy the vampires the night before had been elemental magic wielded by the earth-witches who had gathered for the equinox. He was right about one thing, though. Without that 'hoodoo', none of them would have lived to see the dawn.

'Anyway,' the chief continued, 'you've got my direct line and the dispatch number. You call immediately if you even so much as glimpse anything out of order around here, especially after sundown. And leave the crime-scene tape up until I tell you, all right? The eggheads may want another look at something in there, although I think it's all pretty self-explanatory.'

'We won't touch it,' Cat promised. 'And thank you again.'

'What a world we live in, now,' Chief Gately said, shaking his head. He turned to walk to his car, then paused and turned toward her again. 'You know you're gonna have an inspection team out here to take statements, right? Could be UN or maybe FBI doing their grunt work. Standard procedure when vampires are concerned.'

Cat hesitated. She wished that she could have asked him not to report the incident, but she knew there was no chance of that. It would have been better if they could have handled the whole thing themselves, but the people who had been killed – her friends and guests – had families and others who loved them. It wasn't as if the survivors could have simply built a pyre in the orchard. Not in modern times.

'I understand,' she said, still biting her tongue.

She didn't want the UN involved. That meant Task Force Victor, and that meant that Octavian would find out.

Her thoughts went back to the blessed clearing with the fence around it, the one they had opted not to use, and the new growth that now thrived there. Octavian would want a say in what happened next at Summerfields, and Cat was determined to see that he didn't get it. This place belonged to her and Tori, nobody else.

Still, if Octavian had to find out, better that he find out from her.

She thanked Chief Gately and shook his hand, then watched until he had pulled out onto the road and turned toward town.

Cat turned and started walking up through the orchard again, passing the shop and barn which would remain locked up all day.

Her phone was still in her hand. Reluctantly she tapped the screen and searched her contacts for him. Octavian. Her finger hovered for a moment before she tapped the screen again. She picked up her pace as she listened to it ring.

'Cat,' Octavian said, answering. 'You were on my list to call this morning.'

She frowned. 'Why would you call, after the way we left it the last time you were here?'

'There are a lot of ugly things happening right now and I was worried that you might be in danger.'

She held her breath, the muscles tensing across her back. 'And why would that be?'

'I guess you know that Nikki's dead.'

Cat shuddered and let out a breath, cursing herself. 'Shit, yes. I'm sorry. I'm not myself or I would have—'

'It's all right. I understand. And there's more. Her funeral was this morning. During the service, we were attacked by vampires—'

'This morning? During the day? Wouldn't that make them Shadows?'

'They wore these suits, some kind of protective covering. Most of us are okay, but it wasn't anything I did. At the end, something bizarre happened.'

She listened in amazement as he told her about the roots bursting from the soil and impaling the vampires, wondering all the while if it was possible that Keomany – whatever she had become – could have extended her influence hundreds of miles away. It was difficult to conceive of, but no more so than any other explanation.

'I know Keomany's dead,' he went on, 'but I've never seen another earthwitch with power like this. Have you?'

'No,' she admitted. 'I haven't.'

'And, truth be told, it sort of . . . well, I'm not an empath, but it just *felt* like her. Does that sound crazy to you?'

While they had been talking, she had kept walking uphill through the orchard, and now she came in sight of the fence that had been built around the clearing where the new growth had sprung up, where the tree that Keomany had grown for them towered higher than all of the others.

'Peter, has it not occurred to you to wonder why I called you? I mean, you meant to call me, you said . . . but I called you, remember?'

There was a moment of silence on the phone.

'You did,' he agreed.

'Let me ask you a question. Why did those vampires come after you today? Why did they kill Nikki and then crash her funeral like this? What's the point?'

'I don't know,' he said, his voice tense. 'The only thing we can figure at this point is that Cortez killed Nikki to get to me, and if that's true, he probably engineered the attack this morning and a trap left for a friend of mine last night for the same reason.'

'And what the hell does any of that have to do with us?' Cat asked, still angry but now also afraid.

'Besides what happened with the roots this morning?' he replied. 'If he's going after people I love – my friends – he may know I have ties to Summerfields.'

'We're not friends,' Cat said quickly.

'Aren't we?' Octavian asked.

To her surprise, she realized she wasn't sure.

'We're allies at the very least,' he went on. 'Don't you think? At least that. We want the same things for the world.'

Cat paused, frowning as she stared at the wall around the clearing. One panel of the wall had been removed and she stared at that gap, awaiting whatever might emerge. She could hear Octavian breathing on the line but had nearly forgotten she was even on the phone.

'Hello?' Octavian said.

'Sorry,' she whispered, then cleared her throat. 'I'm here.'

'And?'

'And, yes, we do want the same things for the world. Sometimes I forget that. People die around you. They die because they know you, and sometimes because they know people who know you, and that just . . . it fucking sucks.'

She said this last with a hitch in her throat.

'Cat?' Octavian said, worried now. 'Did something happen?'

'You're a dangerous man, Peter. But I forget that we're on the same side. That it's a dangerous world and the fight to keep it safe belongs to all of us.'

'Cat,' he said again. 'Tell me.'

No one had come out from the fenced clearing, so she approached the opening in the wall and peeked inside. Ed Rushton was there, still pale from terror and lack of sleep, but alive and working. And Tori, of course – her beautiful Tori. But nobody else. Not unless you counted the figure that now lay on its side on the grass, curled up like a sleeping infant or a night-blooming flower, and perhaps she was a little of both. The new growth remained still. Its apple-red skin did not rise and fall with breath, nor did the vines and leaves of its hair or the bark on its arms react in any way to her arrival. It seemed inert, almost as if it were a husk now abandoned.

'Damn it, Cat, what happened?' Octavian demanded.

She looked at Tori, saw the mix of love and sorrow in her eyes, and let out a breath.

'Something terrible,' Cat said. 'But something wonderful, too.'

And she began to tell him.

Philadelphia, Pennsylvania

Allison rapped on Octavian's hotel-room door. One way or another they were checking out today, but after the debacle at the cemetery they had come back here to regroup. For her part, she felt as if she were made of lead, as if each step or motion took ten times the effort it had this morning. She had been so at home with the fluidity of her flesh that it had become second nature. No, not even that; it was simply her nature. With the Medusa toxin coursing through her system, she felt like a comet that had crashed to earth.

She didn't like that feeling at all.

'Peter?' she called, knocking again.

A low, muffled voice came from inside the room. She frowned, wondering if he had company and who it might be. Allison tried to listen more closely but the muted voice had ceased, and a moment later there came the rattle of the lock and Octavian opened the door. He seemed distracted, not meeting her gaze as he slipped his cell phone into his pocket. The voice she'd heard had been his, on the phone.

'Hey,' was all he said.

'They're all gathered,' she replied, frowning. 'Are you all right?'

Octavian laughed with something like real humor. 'I don't even know how to define that anymore. People keep dying because of me. What I'm feeling has got to be rage. Only rage burns like this. But it feels a hell of a lot like guilt.'

'What happened?'

He came out into the corridor and pulled the door shut behind him. 'You mean what *else* happened? Cortez sent a bunch of his vampires to visit Summerfields Orchard during the equinox ritual last night. A lot of people died, but it ended just like our fun at the cemetery this morning.'

Allison nodded. 'Wow, okay. Did you tell them what you said to me about Keomany? About feeling –'

'She's there,' he said, starting down the corridor ahead of her.

'Wait, what?' Allison replied, hurrying after him. She'd been on her own so long, hunted and hunter, that she was no longer used to chasing after anyone. Even when she had been human she had never liked it, but Octavian was the only person still alive that she didn't mind playing sidekick to.

He shot her a baffled look as she caught up to him.

'The other night after I left, something started growing in the field where we spread Keomany's ashes. It's like an effigy made of wood and leaves and maybe even apple, from the sound of it, but it's in the shape of Keomany.'

Allison laughed.

'That's funny?' Octavian demanded.

'I'm laughing in disbelief, not amusement,' she said. 'You're serious? And they're sure it's her?'

'No. It hasn't spoken. Hasn't even looked at them. It might be just some kind of reaction to her magic, Gaea's way of mourning Keomany's death, maybe. But they seem to feel pretty strongly that it *is* her, somehow, and that she saved their asses last night. After what happened in the cemetery this morning . . . well, I'm keeping my mind open to the possibilities.'

'Don't you want it to be Keomany?'

Octavian shook his head. 'Not in the slightest. Yeah, a selfish part of me – the part that misses her – wants her back. But she gave her life in combat; she's earned a rest. Hell, Keomany earned *Valhalla*.'

They reached the suite that had been converted into the TFV command center.

'What do you think it means?' Allison asked, thinking about the number of recent supernatural incursions into the world and wondering what it might be doing to Gaea, the soul of the Earth.

'I don't know if it means anything. But I guess we'll find out,' Octavian said, banging on the door. 'Right now, we've got other concerns.'

Corporal Galleti, the Brazilian woman who was part of Metzger's handpicked squad, opened the door and stood back to let them in. As they entered the room, Galleti eyed Allison with thinly veiled hostility and suspicion. Another day, Allison might have confronted her; it had become tiring, being painted as a renegade for her killing of the former commander of Task Force Victor when they all knew she had been entirely justified. But they were all on edge today, and Metzger's forensics guy, Barbieri, had told her there were whispers going around that Charlotte might have led their people into the trap at Bannerman's Arsenal on purpose – that she'd been working for Cortez all along. Under the circumstances, she couldn't blame them for being wary of any Shadows in their midst. And the truth was that she had felt the same suspicions about Charlotte herself. If Octavian didn't seem so certain of her allegiance, Allison would have been among those suggesting betrayal. But Octavian vouched for Charlotte, and Allison couldn't ignore that – not when he had stood by her in the past when she had been the target of similar suspicions.

A bustle of movement accompanied their arrival. As Allison and Octavian entered the suite, warriors rose to their feet, one by one. Kuromaku was first to stand, one hand on his sword, a silent indication that he pledged his sword to whatever purpose Octavian wished to assign him. The short, powerfully built Santiago did the same, followed by the gigantic Kazimir – whose hair seemed to nearly brush the ceiling – and the lovely Egyptian, Taweret. One by one, the others in the room rose as well.

Allison nodded to Amber Morrissey, to whom Octavian had introduced her in the aftermath of the carnage at the cemetery. Amber had dropped the glamour that made her look human, and Allison took a second look at the deep burgundy of her skin and those vicious talons and thought of ancient goddesses of death and destruction. The air behind Amber shimmered slightly, and Allison assumed that the ghost of Miles Varick was also among them. Two of the mages who had come to the funeral were dead and another was in the hospital with a bullet wound, but the two remaining – a pale old man named Groff, who had a bad heart, and a skittish, greasy-haired kid named Tristan – also stood.

Commander Metzger waited with his arms folded on the far side of the room, in front of the windows. This was his suite, his command center, and his body language made it clear that he asserted his authority here. But Galleti was the only other member of the TFV in the room. Allison figured it might have been just a lack of space – it was fairly cramped in there with this many people – but she believed there was more to the absence of other troops. This might be a UN operation, but these people were Octavian's new coven. They were here at his invitation and would do as he asked, so as much as it clearly went against Metzger's instincts, the commander gave no orders.

'Mr Octavian,' he said, 'you have the floor.'

Octavian nodded and surveyed the faces in the room. Allison did the same, wondering what he saw. Some of these people he had not seen in many years, and yet when he had put out the word, each of them had come running. Other than Kuromaku and herself, the Shadows among them had not even known Nikki, but they had come to her funeral. Had they sensed that more would be asked of them than to help Octavian mourn? Surely, she thought, they must have.

They gazed at him like heirs at the reading of a will, grimly expectant.

'Thank you all for coming,' Octavian said. 'Some of this you know already, so I'll be succinct. My partner – the woman I thought of as my wife – has been murdered by a vampire named Cortez. He did this, I believe, not only to hurt me but to antagonize me. Distract me. He sent the vampires that attacked the funeral this morning, and sent another group to attack an equinox ritual friends of mine were conducting in Vermont last night.'

Metzger frowned worriedly at this new information.

'There's more, and you'll all be fully briefed shortly,' Octavian went on. 'But that's just one of the troubles we're dealing with. Dimensional incursions are under way in France and Italy and the forces responding are having difficulty containing them. All of these things require my attention, but I can't be in three places at once—'

'Cortez is first,' Santiago interrupted. 'Not just because he killed your lady, but because whatever he's got cooking, it's going to boil over soon.'

'What makes you say that?' Amber asked.

Santiago shrugged. 'Pretty obvious, don't you think? He's not going to go full force on Octavian at the lady's funeral and try to take out those people in Vermont – stir up that kind of shitstorm – and then waste the distractions he's created.'

Allison nodded. Smart thinking. She decided she liked Santiago.

'Agreed,' Octavian said. 'But while I can make Cortez my first priority, I can't let these incursions go on any longer. The people over there need help. I can't be in three places at once, so I'm asking you all, now, to help me. Once upon a time, I helped found a coven that included vampires and humans. A lot of them are dead, but I've fought alongside each of you in some way over the years. I think it's time for another coven. One that isn't just about survival, but about the survival of this world. Of the human race.'

'Damn,' said the greasy kid. 'Melodramatic, don't you think?'

Octavian shot him a withering look. 'I wish it were, Tristan. I really do,' he said, then glanced around the room, looking at each face.

Allison nodded to him. 'I'm in, obviously. Just point me where you want me.'

'You're with me,' Octavian said.

Good, she thought. Cortez needed killing, and it pleased her to know she would be there with Octavian to make it happen.

The rest of them began to speak or nod their assent, and it was clear there was unanimous agreement. No one whom Octavian had summoned intended to turn their back on him now. Not on him, and not on the world – because whether Tristan thought it melodramatic or not, the peril really was global. These incursions were not just the cause of chaos and the deaths of innocents, they were eroding the walls between dimensions, eating holes right through them like rust through metal. And, like rust, the erosion would spread.

Kuromaku stood a bit taller and took a step into the center of the room.

'We are all with you, old friend,' the samurai said.

'What, you're not going to draw your sword?' Allison teased. 'Raise it up, do some kind of Three Musketeers thing?'

Kuromaku raised an eyebrow. 'I'm the only one with a sword.'

'Yeah. It would look kind of silly.'

Octavian smiled and dropped his gaze. The others looked on in surprise, maybe thinking he would be angry. But of all those in the room, Allison and Kuromaku knew him best. He might be grim at times, but he appreciated the confidence their banter implied. Confidence, and commitment. They were in this together, come what may.

'All right,' Octavian said, nodding toward the Reaper. 'Amber, I'd like you and Miles to go up to Vermont right away. We have friends and allies up there who may still be in danger, plus something is happening there that I don't understand and I would like someone up there who I can trust to tell me the truth.'

He turned to Santiago. 'Rodrigo, it means a great deal to me that you're here and I hope we have a chance to talk at length when this is over. I'd like to hear of your adventures since the last time we were together. But today, I need you to take Taweret and fly to Saint-Denis in France. There are mages on the ground already, but the troops there may need somebody harder to kill to back them up.'

Santiago nodded. 'Well, if I'm anything, it's hard to kill.' He pointed at Kuromaku. 'No cockroach jokes.'

Kuromaku gave him that same raised eyebrow and Allison smiled. Someone who didn't know better would think Kuromaku had no sense of humor at all, but it was there. Wry and sarcastic, just below the surface of that dignified air.

"Maku,' Octavian went on, 'take Kazimir, Tristan, and Mr Groff and go to Siena as quickly as Commander Metzger's people can get you there. Do what you can.' He glanced around the room. 'All of you . . . just do what you can. We've got to drive back these incursions. Somehow I've got to figure out how to reinforce the barriers the church used to keep in place, but first we put out these fires.'

'And kill Cortez,' Allison said.

'Yes,' Octavian replied, his gaze turning to ice. 'That, too.'

'If I may?' Metzger began.

'It's your room, Commander,' Octavian said.

Metzger nodded. 'Thank you, but it's not my room for much longer. We're all clearing out of here today. I've got transport ready to take you all where you need to go. Before you depart, I wanted to update you on the TFV's activities.'

Allison perked up. She could tell from his tone that he had something new.

'Miss Vigeant, are you familiar with Octavian's theory about these new incursions, that they're coming through—'

'Saints' graves, yes. Go on.'

Now Metzger looked at Octavian. 'While we waited for you, I briefed everyone else. I've got a team of UN researchers compiling a list of the burial places of saints, with a special focus on Catholic saints who were known to have been beheaded; particularly if their heads were buried separate from their bodies. There are a surprising number, and they're continuing to search.'

'Good thing I never tried to be a saint,' Santiago muttered.

'Any word on Charlotte?' Octavian asked.

Metzger's gaze turned grim. 'I'm afraid not. There's no sign she survived the explosion. You know it takes faith in her own—'

'I know what it takes,' Octavian said curtly.

'Of course you do,' Metzger replied. Then he glanced around the room. 'Octavian and Miss Vigeant are not leaving as yet, but I'd suggest the rest of you gather your things and meet Sergeant Galleti in front of the elevators in twenty minutes. Your transport is waiting.'

Sergeant Galleti, Allison thought, realizing the woman had received a battlefield promotion now that Sergeant Omondi had died. She wondered if Galleti felt glad or guilty, and if Corporal Song – wherever he'd gotten off to – was jealous.

There were murmurs and nods of agreement and one by one, the mages and vampires and other supernatural creatures in the room paused by Octavian to say goodbye and receive any other instructions he wanted to share. When Amber threw her arms around him and hugged him hard, whispering fresh condolences for the death of Nikki and what now seemed to be Charlotte's death, Allison paused to watch them. Despite her death-goddess appearance, the Reaper really was barely more than a girl. Octavian held onto her arms as he thanked her, obviously touched by her affection.

So strange, she thought. *We are such sentimental monsters*.

In the years since she had first encountered the Shadows she had often thought of a line from one of her favorite movies, *Blade Runner*. The android fugitives in the film were described as 'more human than human', and the words echoed in her mind in times such as these.

In moments, the room had emptied out until only Octavian, Metzger, and Allison remained.

'What's going on?' Octavian said.

'My question exactly,' Allison added. 'I could read it in your face. You've got something new on Cortez.'

Metzger did not smile, but his eyes lit up with purpose. 'Not quite yet, but we will. Your friend Charlotte led us to one of Cortez's people in that club in New York, a vampire named Danny Rouge. He could give us nothing on Cortez that we didn't already know, but we did manage to get another name out of him, a vampire out of New York named Holzman. We don't know for sure, but we don't think Holzman is one of Cortez's minions. This is a serious monster, an old-timer, not some punk off the street that Cortez bled and made one of his foot soldiers.'

Octavian and Allison exchanged a glance.

'I want to see him,' Octavian said. 'Now.'

'We're just about to question him,' Metzger replied. 'We were waiting for you.'

Octavian went to the door, opening it for Metzger to lead the way. Allison followed, wondering if her presence would really be necessary. When Hannibal had made her into a vampire, he had done terrible things to her – things she had done her best to forget. The word 'torture' seemed insufficient to describe the experience. In the years since, she had done horrible things when necessity required them, always with a cold knot of disgust in the pit of her stomach. But in both giving and receiving such treatment, she had learned all too well how to get the answers that she needed, especially from a vampire.

Reluctantly, she followed Octavian and Metzger down the corridor, thinking of this Holzman and wondering how old he really was, and how intimately familiar he might be with pain.

12

Saint-Denis, France

The sky above Saint-Denis roiled with dark smoke that hung thick and low, blotting out the sun and choking those still foolish or unfortunate enough to have remained behind during the evacuations. Father Laurent had a surgical mask covering his nose and mouth, a gift thrust into his hands by a passing paramedic four or five hours earlier. He rode in the passenger seat of a military vehicle whose driver seemed determined to bump over every piece of debris in their path, painfully jostling his injured arm.

'I don't like leaving,' he said. 'It feels like surrender.'

'It's only temporary,' came a voice from the back seat, the young Italian UN soldier who had been his touchstone all day. Ponticellio, that was his name. Father Laurent was having trouble remembering. He blamed it on exhaustion, though he could not help but wonder if he had hit his head at some point and forgotten it.

Father Laurent craned around in his seat and glanced back the way they'd come. Even from this angle he could see the utter destruction of Saint-Denis. The little town had become a smoking ruin. Flames still burned in certain areas, though the worst of the fires had gone out, leaving charred wreckage behind. And smoke . . . plenty of smoke.

With the sky so dark it was impossible to tell the time of day, but he thought it must only be late afternoon. Turning again in his seat, he tried to get a glimpse of the horizon, toward Paris. In the distance he could see blue-white skies and sunlight. *Safety*, he thought. *Sanctuary. But for how long?* Hundreds of people were dead and all of Saint-Denis in ruin. If they did not hold the demons here, the devastation would spread, and soon there would be thousands dead instead of hundreds.

'Is it?' he asked. 'Only temporary, I mean? Because I don't think it is temporary for Saint-Denis. All that remains of it is rubble. Half of the basilica still stands, but it will crumble soon enough.'

It felt blasphemous to say such things, but it also felt true.

The engine roared as the driver took them off the street to avoid abandoned cars that blocked their way. They drove across a wide green park in the midst of the city, accompanied by the clanking of a pair of tanks that had already blazed the trail and the growl of other vehicles participating in the final exodus. The military were abandoning the city. Another backward glance showed the dark, insect things in the air, pursuing them. Gunfire ripped the sky, cutting through smoke and tearing apart the insectoid demons.

Father Laurent closed his eyes tightly and prayed for the young woman he had last seen on the stone stairs beneath the basilica, giving birth to demons. He prayed that for her own sake she had been crushed by falling masonry so that her nightmare would be over. It made him feel nauseous and filthy to wish someone dead, even for their own sake, but he prayed for her death nevertheless. Sadly, he believed she must still live. If these things – utukki, the sorcerers had called them – were being born from her womb, then he felt sure she still lived.

He wanted to weep for her, this woman who had been condemned to Hell on Earth. He had told the soldiers and the sorcerers about her but all they had done was promise him they would do what they could. He was not even sure that Ponticello's commanding officer had believed him, though the horror in the young Turkish sorceress's eyes had told him that she believed.

So many hours had passed since then and nothing had changed. They had not stopped the demons from sowing chaos, only slowed them. Now they had another plan, and he hoped that it worked, for the sake of France and even those beyond. There was no way to know how many of these utukki would be born. Was their number infinite? Surely not, but it seemed so.

Artillery fire thumped the air behind them. Father Laurent winced and held his injured arm against his chest. Closing his eyes, he said silent prayers for the dead and for those valiant men and women who were standing against the forces of whatever fresh Hell was unleashing its monsters into the world.

Several minutes passed during which the priest kept his eyes closed. Even with the rough ride and the thunder of war and the fear of imminent attack, he might have drifted off for a bit, because the next time he was jostled enough to open his eyes, they were on the outskirts of Saint-Denis, far from the park. Smoke still filled the sky but it was a thin gray veil that the sun managed to burn through here and there.

'All right, Father,' Ponticello said, patting the headrest of his seat. 'You wanted to talk to Major Rojas, now's your chance.'

The young soldier opened the door for him and Father Laurent slid carefully out of the vehicle. The priest glanced around and saw the tanks and artillery lining up, facing back toward the center of town, though only the fires and smoke could be seen from this distance. Several demons were flying in their direction until a barrage of gunfire and a shell from the leftmost tank destroyed them.

A handful of smaller vehicles had been parked in a wide, rough circle behind the battle line and Major Rojas stood in the middle of that circle with the old Moroccan mystic and the Turkish sorceress, as well as half a dozen other men and women, officers from the French army and the UN security forces. The old Moroccan – *Chakroun, that's his name* – stood facing toward town with his hands in the air, as if he were just as formidable as the tanks in holding back the demons.

The sorceress, Beril Demirci, knelt on the ground before him, facing the same direction. She had a dagger in one hand, the blade glinting silver in a stray ray of sunlight that managed to filter through the smoke. In that pool of momentary light, Father Laurent saw her draw the blade across her palm. She tossed the blade aside as the Moroccan raised his voice, shouting at the sky. Beril held her hand above a bowl, though what other ingredients it might have contained the priest could not see from this distance.

As Father Laurent followed Ponticello over to the circle of vehicles, he saw the sorceress pick up her discarded dagger. She used it to stir the contents of the bowl, adding more of her own blood, and then she raised the bowl and poured its oddly viscous contents over the blade, coating first one side and then the other, and then pouring the balance of the mixture onto the hand that clenched the dagger.

The Turkish girl paused only a moment, glancing back at

Chakroun. Closer to them, now, Father Laurent saw that the Moroccan's flesh had been painted with wild designs, symbols and runes from some arcane faith. The priest ought to have been offended, but a man praying for deliverance in a world of magic could not afford to take offense at its practice.

The sorceress, Beril, raised the dagger over her head and plunged it into the earth as Chakroun screamed some final benediction. The blade sank deeply into the soil, a splash of light bursting forth from the point of impact – light so crimson that for a moment Father Laurent thought it a splash of blood. The soldiers and commanders standing around spoke to one another but their words were lost in the thunder of fresh artillery. Distracted, Father Laurent looked up and his breath caught in his throat.

There were not three utukki, now, but a dozen of the demons buzzing through the black smoke toward them, emerging from that cloud of fire and destruction. Thirteen of them, now – more – and Father Laurent felt his heart sink. Had they sensed the efforts of these modern mystics? Did they fear whatever magic might be unfolding here and thus were focusing their attack?

All for naught, he thought. The mystics had failed. That splash of blood-red light could do nothing to save them.

But a low thrum had begun to fill the air, growing in volume until it drowned out the Moroccan's chanting. Father Laurent glanced over and looked on in amazement as that splash of red light spread right and left and began to build upward, like a crimson-hued waterfall flowing in reverse, a fountain of churning light that built moment by moment.

Holding his breath, the priest watched as the barrier rose and spread, picking up speed until it seemed to zip itself closed. The last echoes of artillery fire still echoed in the air but the shooting had stopped. When the first of the demons emerged fully from the smoke and collided with the barrier, Father Laurent could hear the utukki's furious shriek. It faltered, tumbling from the sky, and alighted for just a moment on the other side of the barrier from where the sorcerers and officers had gathered. It rose and shook itself like a dog, its chitinous shell clacking, before it sprang into the air to attempt the attack again.

There were three of them, then five, then at least eight, all striking the barrier like bees darting against a windowpane, searching for an exit.

Father Laurent smiled. Whatever magic had been used to create this barrier, it was holding. He strode away from Ponticelli, the pain in his arm forgotten as he approached officers who were congratulating each other. He saw Major Rojas talking with Beril and Chakroun and made his way over to them.

'There you are, Father,' Beril said sweetly. 'Are you all right?'

'I should ask you the same.'

She had her hand tucked against her chest, the palm wrapped in gauze and tape.

'I'll need stitches,' she said, 'but it was worth it, wouldn't you say?' she asked, smiling and proud of herself.

How could he reply to that when he did not know what toll such magic might take on her? The ritual she had performed had required her blood and such offerings were often associated with dark magic and occult evil. And yet, no matter what danger she might have put her own soul in by indulging in such practices, she had done so for only the most noble and virtuous of reasons; surely God could not punish her for that.

'I think you've done an extraordinary job,' Father Laurent said, nodding to Chakroun as well. That, at least, was the truth.

Major Rojas had turned away, focused on the seething red barrier that had trapped the demons in the ruin they had made of Saint-Denis. The smoke from the fires had been trapped as well, and as Father Laurent watched it began to thicken, shrouding the streets and trees and buildings in a gray-black cloud. Major Rojas wore a half smile, as if she did not want to commit entirely to the relief she must have been feeling. Father Laurent thought her a very intelligent woman. The barrier was holding for now, but there was no way of knowing what new pressures might be brought to bear by the hellish forces now locked inside.

'What now, Major?' Father Laurent asked.

'Now we use our time wisely,' Major Rojas replied, turning to him. 'Mr Chakroun and Miss Demirci will consult with other mages, including Octavian if we can track him down. Caging these things is not going to be a real solution . . . not when we have to assume that more and more of them are being born in there. One way or another, we've got to put an end to that.'

Father Laurent shivered and the pain in his shoulder throbbed deeply. He stared at Major Rojas but she did not avert her gaze.

'You're going to try to kill her. The young woman afflicted by the demon, this innocent who is enduring a hell we can't even begin to imagine, being forced to give birth to these things over and over.'

Major Rojas did not lower her gaze, but she did avert her eyes for just a moment, long enough for Father Laurent to know that she felt the grim weight of the choices that lay ahead.

'You can't do that, Major,' the priest insisted.

'What choice is there?'

'How are you going to kill her?' Father Laurent asked. 'You shelled the basilica already, took down half of its stones, and obviously she still lives or there would be no more of these things. So how will you get to her?'

'Someone will have to go in.'

Father Laurent blinked and shook his head, then pointed at the shimmering barrier. 'In there?' He gestured toward Chakroun and Beril. 'These mages only just now managed to put this barrier up. Even if you could get someone inside, on their own they would be dead in minutes.'

Major Rojas nodded. 'Agreed. But Shadows could do it. They could pass right through the barrier and make it down into the basilica's sublevels without the demons even knowing they were there. If the woman can be saved, they can save her. And if she cannot, they can at least give her the mercy that will end this for her and for us all.'

'Shadows,' Father Laurent said, nodding, though a ripple of nausea passed through him. 'I see. And where are these Shadows?'

Major Rojas glanced upward, searching the late afternoon sky outside the barrier.

'On the way, Father. On the way.'

Siena, Italy

Jessica Baleeiro had found peace in Siena, at least for a little while. Across centuries of Roman and Florentine rule, the city had been largely ignored, its coffers lacking the funds to modernize. Yet in time that lack of modernity had been Siena's saving grace, as tourism began to flourish, so many wanting to get a glimpse of the well-preserved fragment of history the city represented. Its tiled roofs and gothic towers had made it a window into the past, full of charm and character.

Now, Jessica stood on a wooded Tuscan hillside and watched the past being erased. The city's signature bell tower crumbled in

213

the distance. Rain fell from a menacing gray sky, but even against the clouds the smoke demons were visible, circling the peaked roofs that remained standing, crashing through upper-story windows to ferret out those hiding in fear for their lives . . . dragging them back out through the jagged, broken glass. Screaming.

Even from here, miles away, Jess felt sure she could hear the screaming.

The rain had plastered her hair to her scalp. She used a hand to wipe the water from her face and turned away, not wanting to see anymore. For the rest of her life, she would not need any help remembering the sight of those winged harpies darting about the rooftops of Siena, all charcoal smoke and no substance. Bullets slowed but did not kill them . . . disrupted the substance of their being, or so one of the dark-suited professors working with the military had said.

Hundreds more had died since then, and the death toll would have been much higher if there had been more demons. Help, it was said, was on the way, but meanwhile the entire city had to be evacuated. That was another reason why Jess didn't want to look at the skyline any longer. Every time she saw someone else dragged from a building, the guilt hit her hard. She and Gabe were doctors; they were supposed to be helping.

We are, she told herself. *We are doing what we can, the best we can.*

As if he himself were a ghost summoned by her words, she felt him approach behind her, felt her husband's hand on her shoulder.

'You have to focus,' he said. 'I can't help other people if I think I'm abandoning you.'

Jess relaxed against him, feeling the warmth of his breath on her neck and the strength in his broad chest as he wrapped his arms – carefully, so carefully – around her.

'You're not abandoning me,' she promised. 'Just because I can't be of much help, that doesn't mean I'd deprive these people of the things that you can do for them.'

Gabe's eyes shone. 'We'll be all right,' he said.

'I know,' she lied.

He kissed his fingers and touched them to the tight splint on her left arm. She smiled to perpetuate her lie, hoping he would believe that it wasn't as painful as it truly was. The sling took pressure off of it, but she had not wanted to take a heavy dose of the painkillers the army medics had with them. There were others who would need the drugs far more than she did.

'We've got to get these people out of here,' she said.

Gabe nodded, glancing around at the makeshift camp on the hillside, overlooking Siena. There were SUVs and several transport trucks that the Italian army and the UN security forces had brought, along with three ambulances that had been commandeered from the city. Refugees were spread out, some of them with jackets over their heads to hold back the rain, though most of them just let it soak into them, numb with shock and loss. Medics helped or carried people in and out of the back of one of the ambulances for treatment. Gabe had already done more than a dozen battlefield surgeries. Given what little supplies they had available to them, she thought it a miracle that it appeared seven of those men and women would survive.

Jess had helped in Siena, when the demons had first appeared. She and Gabe had rounded people up, gotten them indoors, then hustled them from building to building, keeping out of sight of the smoke demons. Together, a group of them had stayed alive until the military had begun to show up and the evacuations had started. It had been while they were running for the back of an army transport that she'd broken her arm. A smoke demon had darted down from the sky, long talons extended, reaching for her. One of the soldiers had fired at it and another had tackled her to the ground, protecting her with his own body.

She'd broken her forearm and the pain had made her cry out so loudly that for a moment she did not hear the screams of the soldier who had saved her, as he was torn from atop her and carried off into the sky.

A shudder went through her.

'Are you all right?' Gabe asked, his brown eyes so full of love and worry.

'Just a chill from the rain,' she said. Jess had told so many lies today that one more would not hurt. She glanced over at the one tent that the army had set up. 'What's going on over there? Do they have a plan?'

'To get us out of here or to stop those things?' Gabe asked, sneering slightly as he nodded toward the broken towers of Siena and the gray, darting harpies that preyed on those left behind.

'Either one.'

As they both watched the tent, a pair of soldiers emerged. Through the veil of rain, Jess thought one of them might be an officer. Gabe had been invaluable to them. Lives had been saved because they had a surgeon with trauma experience right there with them in the midst of the crisis, but the rest of the refugees had to be moved far, far from here. *Including us,* Jess thought. If Gabe wanted to stay and continue to help, she would fight against it. She would beg if she had to. Somehow she knew that if he stayed here, he would die. They would both die. The certainty rested in the center of her chest, just above her heart.

The army had told them reinforcements were on the way and that all refugees would be evacuated to one of several nearby cities, where staging areas were being set up. The wounded would be taken to hospitals. And all of that would have offered Jess some comfort, but Gabe had shared with her things that he had overheard from the wounded he had doctored.

The smoke demons had been more solid at night. In the dark they had seemed more savage, but when dawn had broken they had become more sluggish and seemed less inclined to expand their attacks. Even now, she cast a glance toward Siena's ruined cityscape and saw that they were sticking close to the center of the city, not straying more than half a mile or so from the tower. But the day would only last so long.

'I don't want to be here when night falls,' she said.

Gabe exhaled loudly and nodded, but he said nothing about leaving.

'No more word about reinforcements?' she asked.

'Only that they're coming,' Gabe replied, his brows knitting thoughtfully. 'Colonel Neroni says they have a plan. That they're bringing . . .'

'Bringing what? Are they going to nuke the town or something?' Jess asked, having visions of mushroom clouds that made her forget to breathe.

'No, no. Nothing like that,' Gabe said. 'They're bringing in some kind of magician. A sorcerer.'

Jess blinked, shifting in such a way that the pain in her arm flared up and she winced.

'Are you kidding?'

'Not at all. Don't look so surprised, Jess. That's what they do in cases like this, don't they? Fight fire with fire? How many stories have we seen on newsfeeds in the past ten years where there were sorcerers involved?'

Jess turned and looked at the dark, haunting, awful figures circling the half-fallen tower again. As she watched, one of them dove across the street toward a darkened window, crashing through into the building. These were demons. How else to fight them than with magic? And how could she even begin to doubt that sorcery existed when she could glance out across Siena and see demons made from nothing but gray smoke?

'Does the colonel think the sorcerer can stop this?' she asked, her voice barely a whisper.

Gabe stood behind her, now, arms circled protectively around her, the two of them looking out over this place where not long ago they had been so at peace.

'You know something similar to this is happening in France,' Gabe said. 'I guess they've managed to create some kind of barrier there to trap the demons inside. They're hoping they can accomplish the same thing here.'

A spark of warmth ignited in her chest. A wall to hold them in. To buy time for the military to figure it all out, and for the refugees to make good their escape.

But then the spark went cold and a sick feeling twisted in her gut.

'What about the people still inside when the wall goes up?' she whispered. 'What about them?'

Gabe said nothing, but he didn't have to.

She knew the answer.

Philadelphia, Pennsylvania

'That's enough!' Octavian snapped.

Metzger and Allison turned to look at him, both blinking at him in surprise. They looked as if they were waking from some kind of trance, and he thought that perhaps that wasn't far from the truth. If so, it was a trance of violence and blood.

The vampire, Holzman, was seated in a hard-backed wooden chair, hands cuffed behind him and his ankles cuffed together. A third set of cuffs linked them, so that he sat with his back arched, feet bent under the chair and arms thrust down behind it, totally exposed and vulnerable. With Medusa toxin running through his system, he could do nothing to free himself. His vampiric strength was great, but these cuffs were a reinforced alloy made especially for prisoners of unnatural strength. Holzman wasn't going anywhere.

'What's the problem?' Metzger asked, eyeing Octavian warily.

Locked down onto the chair, Holzman spit a stream of blood and snot onto Metzger's trousers. The commander backed off, swearing, and Holzman bucked against the chair, testing the cuffs and the strength of the wood. Pointless, Octavian thought. He might be able to shatter the chair but he would not break the cuffs. Even if he did, Private Song stood a few feet away with an assault rifle slung over his shoulder. With the toxin in him, Holzman would die instantly if Song decided to punctuate this interrogation with bullets.

'Look at yourselves,' Octavian said, glancing from Metzger to Allison, who seemed uneasy with herself. She dropped her gaze. 'This isn't some gulag. Shouldn't we be in a concrete cell somewhere, or an abandoned warehouse? Isn't that where we do this sort of thing?'

Anger reddened Metzger's cheeks. 'Are you fucking kidding me? You're worried about the décor?'

Octavian shook his head. He glanced again around the room – an ordinary hotel room, except for the fact that they had a centuries-old vampire locked down onto a chair and had spent the better part of an hour questioning and beating him. Torturing the vampire ought to have broken a whole host of international laws, but Task Force Victor had successfully argued in front of the UN Security Council that vampires were not human and therefore not afforded any such protections.

Metzger had initially had one of his own people, a thuggish-looking Brit, doing the dirty work. The man had beaten Holzman and cut his flesh and even burned him in places. With Medusa having stolen his ability to heal himself, Holzman had bled considerably onto the plastic sheeting that the Brit had put down under the chair. After forty minutes or so, Allison had offered to take over and Metzger had sent the Brit packing, but she had not fared any better.

'Pain isn't working,' Octavian said quietly, studying the eyes of the bleeding vampire. Holzman grinned slightly, cracking the charred skin of his cheek.

Allison nodded and slid onto the bureau, the casualness of the action adding to the absurdity of the situation.

'I agree it's ridiculous,' she said. 'But what are we supposed to do? If we try deprivation or isolation or sound, not only do we need to move him to a place where that kind of thing might actually work, but it takes time.'

Metzger fumed, glancing back and forth between them, stunned and apparently furious that they were discussing their torture strategy in front of the creature from whom they were attempting to elicit information. Octavian did not smile, but he did take a certain amount of pleasure in the commander's frustration.

'We don't have that kind of time,' Octavian admitted.

Allison shrugged. 'So, we just start stabbing him until he talks or dies?'

Octavian turned to study Holzman's impassive features. Though he might not be able to heal himself, and though he had cried out in pain during his torment, he had never given any sign that he might break. At the moment, they had no idea if Holzman even knew Cortez or if he was just being difficult on principle.

'Give me the room,' Octavian said.

Metzger gaped at him. 'What?'

Octavian walked over to Holzman, staring down at the vampire, all sense of amusement leaching from him. He had been patient, had let Metzger try his own methods, but now Octavian had run out of patience.

'Give me the room, Commander,' he repeated, glancing up at Song and then Allison. 'All of you.'

Allison gave him a curious look but then she went to the door, opened it, and held it open for Metzger and Song.

'You're not going to tell me what you've got in mind?' Metzger asked.

'Answers,' Octavian replied.

Metzger hesitated a moment, then shrugged and walked out. Song followed, keeping his weapon trained on Holzman until he reached the door, then stepping out quickly and closing it behind him.

Holzman uttered a low, sandpaper laugh.

'You've really got them hopping, don't you?' the vampire said, his accent clipped and rough with the jagged edges of his Germanic lineage.

Octavian went and perched on the edge of the bureau just where Allison had been sitting moments before.

'We're going to make this quick,' Octavian said.

'You and I have met before,' Holzman said. 'You don't remember? It was many years ago. You were like me, then. A blood-drinker. A taker of life. Your blood-father, von Reinman, and I were part of the same coven, once upon a time. That would make me your uncle, in a way.'

Octavian passed his hand through the space between them and the air rippled and flowed, shimmering for just a moment with deep blue light. Holzman frowned at this display, sneered and opened his mouth to continue, only to find that no words would come out. For the moment, at least, he was mute. His expression contorted into an ugly snarl and he bucked against the chair, pulling at his cuffs.

'I'll make this quick because you've wasted enough of my time already,' Octavian said.

The hatred in Holzman's eyes warmed his heart.

'You know who I am and what I'm capable of,' Octavian went on. 'Or you think you do.'

He held out his right hand, palm up, drawing the vampire's attention to the tiny ball of sparking golden light that spun there like a miniature sun. Idly, he let that bit of magic spill back and forth between his hands as if it were some kind of prop and he a stage magician about to perform a trick.

'You know you're going to die in this room, Holzman. They can slice you up, break your bones, do whatever they like, and you'll keep silent just to spite them because you know it's over for you.'

Holzman's mouth moved, lips curling back in disdain, but still he could make no sound.

'There's only one agony I can think of that might make you beg for an ending, make you willing to tell me what I want to know just to hasten the mercy of death. I don't like to think of it, honestly. This kind of thing is really distasteful to me. But you haven't given me any choice.'

With a flourish of his hand, the golden ball vanished. Octavian slid off the bureau, studying Holzman, whose defiant glare had not wavered. The vampire expected him to remove the silencing spell now, to offer him one last chance to reveal what he knew about Cortez and his coven. But Octavian had no illusion that he could intimidate Holzman into complying with words alone.

While the vampire watched, he closed his eyes, tapping both his own memory and the reservoir of magic that he had nurtured inside himself during his centuries in Hell. There were doors in the human soul and inside the human heart that had to be unlocked to access the magic in the world. When Shadows shapeshifted, they reduced themselves to their component molecules, but in the space between molecules there existed a substance – an ether – that made up the texture of magic. It was a part of all things, but not available to all things. To touch it, to manipulate it, to master it required disciplined study, patience, passion, a natural affinity that existed from birth or the taint left behind by some profound supernatural experience. To know magic the way that Octavian knew it was to *become* magic, to be the instrument rather than the musician.

Holzman had no idea what he could do.

Octavian exhaled, opening his arms, his fingers dancing in the space between them, sketching at the air. His lips moved silently, forming words in a language so old that even the residents of Hell had no name for it. When the air began to turn gray around Octavian's hands, it did not crackle with the static he so often associated with the magical power inside of him. No, it crept. It seeped. It flowed and thinned and soon it slid like mercury away from his hands and extended a searching tendril toward Holzman's face. The vampire twisted away, attempting to escape. He tried to shout but was still mute.

'Come on, Holzman, don't squirm. One touch of this and the Medusa toxin will be gone from your system,' Octavian promised. 'You'll be able to shift again.'

The mage held out his hand as if that gray ooze were his puppet and he held its invisible string. Holzman whipped his head in the other direction, but could not elude the touch of the gray tendril. Once it made contact with his skin, it was as if a balloon full of water had burst, but instead of splashing to the floor, that gray liquid flowed horizontally, soaking Holzman's clothes and spreading across his skin, giving his flesh an ugly gray hue, the color of week-old ashes left behind in the hearth.

The vampire stopped thrashing. Despite the strange coloration on his skin, he smiled, because Octavian had been as good as his word.

Holzman shifted to mist in the blink of an eye.

Octavian put up his left hand, already glowing a bright, fiery green, and an emerald sphere seared the air around the vampire in the very same moment. The cloud of mist drifted and spun and roiled inside that sphere but the substance of the vampire Holzman could not escape.

'Don't be a fool. I told you that you would die in this room,' Octavian said. 'Your choice is only in how you die. Shift back. Now.'

Holzman did, reintegrating himself instantly. He was sitting in the chair once more, but no longer restrained. He looked gaunt and wild, his eyes a terrible scarlet, and he roared silently at Octavian, baring his fangs and lashing out at the magic that caged him with deadly talons.

'You look hungry, Holzman,' Octavian said.

The vampire shook with fury and desperation. Saliva dripped from his sneering mouth. He seemed thinner by the moment. As Holzman reached out to claw at his cage again, he faltered and slid from the chair, finding his limbs too weak to attack. For the first time, the hatred in his eyes gave way to dreadful confusion.

When he looked at Octavian again, the question in his eyes was clear.

'Now we understand each other,' Octavian said. 'I've poisoned you with time, Holzman. With entropy. The toxin's out of your system because it wore off. For me and the rest of the world around you, only a minute has passed. For you . . . *weeks*.'

Understanding blossomed into fear on the vampire's face.

'You can't possibly understand what I've lost,' Octavian went on, grief stabbing at his heart again. 'You don't know what it means to love and cherish someone. You've forgotten, if you ever knew. But it's your misfortune that those joyful human parts of me have been torn away.

'Cortez killed the woman I love. You know something, maybe not about her murder or even about his plans, though perhaps you do. But you know something I can use to get to Cortez, to find him and destroy him and his entire coven. Now, you can play coy the way you were with Commander Metzger and my friend, Allison. But I know what it's like to need the blood to live, I know what it's like when the hunger starts to eat at your insides and you feel yourself begin to wither, and it's a hell of a lot worse than the cut of any blade or the blow of any fist. A few minutes from now you will be weeping for death as if it were your mother. You tell me what I want to know, give me something I can use, and I will give you that death. Or you say nothing useful, and I will leave you here to shrivel in upon yourself until you are little more than parchment and bones, and still you will be alive. I will make sure of it. Only hours will pass for me, but for you it will be years of hunger gnawing at your soul.'

Holzman's face had crumbled into despair. Octavian took no pleasure from it, nor did he feel any guilt. This was a monster who had been offered a decade's worth of opportunities to become something more and chose to remain a monster. His fate was his own choice.

'Now,' Octavian said. 'One chance and one only.'

He passed his hand in front of him, the air wavered, and he released the vampire from the spell that had silenced him.

'Speak,' Octavian said.

'I know only rumors,' Holzman said, his voice an ancient rasp. 'Things I have heard about places where Cortez has made nests.'

'Tell me,' Octavian replied. 'And death is yours.'

13

Pollepel Island, New York

It started with the whistling of the wind, but it would be inaccurate to suggest that she had really heard the sound. Rather, she became aware of it, just as she became aware of the swaying of the pine trees and the shafts of sunlight that sliced down through the clouds without truly being able to see them. She sensed them, building a picture in her mind as if she were painting the world anew, bringing it to life on a blank canvas.

Alive, she thought.

Yet the moment it crossed her mind she realized that was not likely. She sensed the world around her more as an idea than as anything tangible. Perhaps she was not alive after all. Could it be that she existed now only as a ghost, haunting the world where others still walked and laughed and made love? Yes, she decided, it might well be that she was a ghost. But if that were true, how to explain the strange feeling she had of strength? Of invisible muscles with which she felt, oddly, that she could reach out and take hold of the trees and the sun and the wind?

Yet beneath that feeling of strength was another, more disturbing intuition. She felt as if she were diminishing with each moment, as if she had just managed to wake from a deep, dreamless sleep and if she did not hang on to wakefulness – let herself drift off again – she might vanish into that slumber forever, until nothing remained of her but the absence of dreams.

I feel . . . she thought, and then faltered. The concept of identity had shocked her, but now that it had occurred to her she knew that it was right and necessary. Who was she? She must have a name, of course, but she could not recall what it might have been. Though she did not dare to let go of the wind and the sun and the pine trees – or the deep, swift river she now realized was below her – still she knew that there were other things beyond her present awareness that she needed to discover.

No, *rediscover*. For she sensed that they were things she had lost.

Fearful of that underlying feeling that she was slipping away with every gust of wind, she forced herself to focus inward, to think and examine. Instantly she was rewarded by other flashes of awareness, and yet these were not visions of her present surroundings. They were memories. Horrible, horrible memories that made her want to scream – though she had no mouth – and filled her with pain and fury that concentrated in a burning core that might have been her heart.

Images flitted through her consciousness of cruel men grinning as they hurt her, their vacant eyes as they held her down and forced themselves on her. She could feel them still, their fists striking her ribs and breasts and face, the way the shorter one had choked her while he held her down and the way she had wept as her mind screamed for air. And she remembered the cold, calculating eyes of the other, the one who had used her and plunged his fangs into her throat and drunk from her again and again. Eyes like a leopard's. A true predator's eyes.

Cortez.

The name came to her like the whisper of the wind, there but not there, as if it were her own personal haunting. Hatred ignited inside her and those invisible muscles constricted, the burning core of her tightening, solidifying, and more memories began to rush in, along with her own name.

Charlotte knew herself, then, and her rage burned even brighter when she realized that she had remembered Cortez's name before her own.

Kill him, she thought. *I've got to kill him.*

The need for vengeance erased all other yearnings. She understood what had happened to her, now, remembered coming to Bannerman's Arsenal with Sergeant Omondi and the rest of the TFV assault group . . . remembered that chamber beneath the ruins of the castle where corpses and explosives had awaited them. The explosion seared itself upon her consciousness, even as she began to understand that she was drifting on the razor edge between life and death.

Nothing more than molecules, now, drifting apart, she had been flotsam in the maelstrom of reality since the moment of that explosion. Had she been caught in the same explosion back when she had been a part of Cortez's coven she would surely be dead, now. With no faith in their ability to exist in such a state, vampires who embraced the old ways would have drifted into nothingness, molecules spreading out until they lost all cohesion and thus all awareness. It had, she realized, nearly been her own fate.

In the instant before the explosion she had begun to shift to mist, and perhaps that had helped her. But Charlotte felt certain it was fury that had kept her from being completely obliterated. Now she stoked the flames of that rage and focused, trying to pull herself back together.

At first she felt no differently. Then, slowly . . . so slowly . . . she could feel herself stop drifting. Those invisible muscles began to knit together, the fabric of her existence rebuilding itself, using fury as its mortar.

She was Kali, now. She was vengeance.

Charlotte had been following Octavian's lead, sublimating the horrors that had been inflicted upon her. But being *this* . . . being nothing but thought and molecules . . . had freed her from the fears and doubts of the flesh, and now she understood that her claim to retribution was just as valid as the mage's.

Slowly, in the sky above the Hudson River, hate brought her back from the edge of destruction. She thought of nothing but Cortez and his effort to make vampires once more the monsters they had been before Octavian brought them into the light.

She could not wait to show him how much of a monster she could really be.

Brattleboro, Vermont

The first thing Amber Morrissey noticed while pulling her rented Ford into the parking lot of Summerfields Orchard was the yards of yellow police tape. With the gray autumn sky hanging low overhead and casting its pall upon the orchard, there was something garish about that tape, stretched from tree to tree far up on the hillside. Despite the charm of the big barn that had been converted into a store and the pumpkins and cornstalks and other autumn decorations that were on display in front of the place, not to mention the big tractor that should have been pulling children on hayrides, her eyes were drawn to that yellow tape way up on the hill for the simple reason that it did not belong. It spoke silently but all too clearly: something terrible had happened here.

She had passed a police car as she turned in. Now, as she parked and turned off her engine, she noticed movement in her rearview mirror and saw that he had gotten out of his vehicle and was approaching her.

'What does he want?' Amber said, studying her own reflection in the mirror. 'I just restored the glamour spell when we landed. It can't be slipping.' She glanced at the seat beside her. 'It's not slipping, is it?'

To others, the passenger seat would appear to be vacant, but she could see the ghost of Miles Varick clearly. Her former professor, handsome and grizzled and dead, frowned as he studied her.

'Not from what I can see,' Miles said. 'After the killings here last night, he's probably supposed to check out anyone who pulls in.'

'What, every young mother who drops by and pulls into the parking lot to turn around when she sees the place is closed?'

'You're not turning around.'

The rap on her window made Amber jump in her seat. The engine was off so it would have been easier to just open the door, but the cop was blocking her in, now, so she turned the key enough to get the electricity running through the car again and rolled down the window.

'Afternoon, officer,' Amber said brightly.

'Can I help you, ma'am?' he said.

The ghost drifted a little nearer to her, peering out the window so close that his cheek would have been almost touching hers if he could have touched her at all. The cop's gaze did not waver; he had no trace of the sight, none of the supernatural experience that would have allowed him to see Miles or see through Amber's glamour. It made her exhale.

'My name is Amber Morrissey,' she said, reminding herself that she was here on official business. 'I've been asked by the United Nations to consult with the owners about last night's events. If you want to check on that, I can give you a direct number to reach Commander Leon Metzger of Task Force Victor.'

Not quite the truth; Octavian had sent her, but Metzger would back him up.

The cop nodded slowly. 'These ladies know you're coming?' he asked, tilting his head toward the house a ways up the hill on the right, beyond the barn.

'As far as I know they do.'

He bent and looked into the back seat, then studied her face for a moment. She wondered exactly what he thought he might see that would alarm him. One twentysomething blonde in a rental car was not going to be able to continue the supernatural massacre that had taken place in the orchard last night. The daylight was fading, but it had to be clear that if she was a vampire, she had to be a Shadow, and they were supposed to be the good guys.

'You a witch like the others?' he asked.

A ripple of disgust went through her. The urge to let her glamour fall away, to show him the terror of her true face and plunge her fingers into his chest, maybe tug out a piece of his soul, was powerful.

Instead, she smiled. It was a cold smile, she knew, and enough to get him to take a wary step back.

'I'm a whole different sort of witch,' she said.

Nervously, he returned her smile and nodded as if they had shared a joke instead of a moment that would keep him up tonight.

'You go on up, if they're waiting for you,' he said, already half-turned for the walk back to his cruiser. 'Give a holler if you need anything.'

'I'll do that.'

By the time she had rolled up the window and gotten out of the car, slipping her keys into the pocket of her burgundy, hooded sweater, he was already halfway to his vehicle. As she slammed the door, Miles's ghost passed through the glass and metal and fell in beside her, the two of them heading up toward the house on the hill together.

The path to the house was not nearly so well trodden as the others in Summerfields Orchard, reserved as it was for family and friends rather than the thousands of customers who trooped up and down the rows of apple trees and through the pumpkin patch and other parts of the orchard through three seasons every year. Glancing around, Amber was surprised that they did not see a single person outside. No one worked at harvesting apples or pulling pumpkins in. The property stretched across the road they had come in on, and she realized now that they had not seen anyone on that side either – no tractors, no pickers, not a soul. The police had not just closed down the shop, they had shut the orchard completely.

Or perhaps it hadn't been the police who made that call. After their sacred ritual, a gathering of friends and those who shared their faith, had turned into a slaughter – after they had seen some of those friends hideously murdered – of course they would cease all activities on the property, out of respect if not in mourning. With all that Amber had been through, the way she had been altered, she sometimes found herself having to work to hang on to human instincts. It troubled her very deeply, but now was not the time for her to ruminate on her own problems. Not with so much grief all around her.

'I don't like the feeling of this place,' Miles said, his voice sounding like a whisper beside her ear, though she could see him gliding along half a dozen feet away. The voices of the dead always sounded like that to her, intimate and forlorn.

'I'm sure the whole aura of the place is tainted after last night.'

'Well, it's good that they're earthwitches,' Miles said. 'It may take a while, but if anyone can purify the land it would be them.'

Amber arched an eyebrow, tempted to ask what Miles knew about earthwitches. But he had been her favorite professor, once upon a time, and she'd enjoyed his lectures so much because he seemed to know something about everything.

As they approached the house, she saw someone moving past the window and a moment later the front door opened to reveal a lovely black woman with her hair in beaded rows. Amber's first thought was that she was crying, but the woman's eyes were dry and Amber realized that she had imagined it, that the sorrow that weighed on her was so powerful it cast the illusion of tears.

'You must be Amber,' the woman said, coming down the steps and holding out her hand. 'I'm Tori Osborne.'

'Nice to meet you,' Amber said, shaking her hand. 'I'm glad Peter told you we were coming. I was afraid he might not have reached you and then I'd be all awkward and . . . well, I'm glad.'

Tori gave a curious smile. '"We". That's right, he said there were two of you. Did your partner wait in the car?'

Miles Varick's ghost gave a small laugh. 'Not much of a witch.'

'No,' Amber said to Tori, pointing at the place where the ghost stood, hanging just above the ground. 'He's right here. His name is Miles Varick.'

Tori arched an eyebrow. 'Annndd . . . he's a ghost?'

'Peter didn't mention that?'

'Nope.'

Amber offered an apologetic shrug. 'It's a strange world, these days.'

The sadness in Tori had abated for a moment, but now it returned full force. 'It certainly is.'

She went back and closed the front door of her house, then started along another path that led around the side of the house and up into the orchard.

'Come on, then,' Tori said. 'You should meet Cat. And I know what you've really come to see.'

'We've come to help keep you safe,' Amber said, glancing sidelong at Miles's ghost. The phantom looked slightly offended.

Tori smiled. 'No offense, but I'm not sure what you and a ghost are going to be able to do for us if we have another vampire attack tonight.'

'You'd be surprised,' Amber said, grimly serious now.

Something in her tone must have gotten through to Tori, because the earthwitch glanced at her while they walked and seemed to be examining her anew.

'You didn't just come to see . . . well, to see Keomany?'

Amber froze on the path, staring at her.

'Did she just say—' the ghost began.

'Did you say "Keomany"?' Amber asked.

A ripple of anger passed visibly across Tori's face. 'I guess Octavian didn't tell either of us very much, did he? It's a bad habit he has. A dangerous habit. Did you know Keomany before?'

Amber nodded. She had fought the chaos goddess Navalica side by side with Keomany Shaw, and had seen her die.

'Well, then, you're going to love this,' Tori said, and then they were walking again, both of them a little faster than before.

It surprised Amber that their route took them away from the police tape instead of toward it, but Tori guided her through the orchard in a zigzag pattern of rows and trails, moving ever upward until they emerged at a broad clearing where a tall apple tree in full fruit stood at the center of a makeshift post and plywood fence, as if some animal had been penned inside. Two of the panels of that strange pen had been removed. Over the top they could see a pair of heads – a man and a woman – both turned away and gazing at something on the ground which seemed to fascinate them.

'Strange,' Miles said, his voice so familiar and intimate in her ear.

'What is?' Amber whispered, feeling like an intruder and not wanting to disturb the people inside the pen.

Tori glanced at her, mistakenly thinking that Amber must be speaking to her.

'The taint I felt when we arrived?' Miles said, his spectral brows furrowed with curiosity. 'It ends here. This clearing is just . . . it's pure, somehow. Clean.'

Tori led them over to the opening in the pen.

'We've got visitors, honey,' she said.

The two people inside the pen turned, startled from their reverie. The woman had to be Cat Hein, Tori's wife. The man was fiftyish and balding, but tall and with the powerful build of a fellow used to hard work. He clutched a baseball cap in his hands and looked on in deference, waiting for his companion to speak, which made her his boss.

The woman glanced at Tori, then recoiled in shock when she saw Amber, actually taking a step back, wide-eyed and open-mouthed.

'Holy shit!' she said.

'No fair,' Tori said. 'You can see the ghost!'

Cat took another step back, eyeing the new arrivals warily. 'Yeah, I can see the ghost. It's a ghost.' She pointed at Amber. 'But what the hell are *you*?'

The words were not spoken in disgust, but rather a combination of fear and fascination. Yet still Amber felt the kind of shame she had rarely experienced since her days of being teased in the schoolyard when Tim Hansen had told the whole sixth grade that she had stripped naked in front of him and he'd rejected her, a reversal of the truth that had nevertheless haunted her for years.

'I'm Amber,' she managed. 'Amber Morrissey.'

'Peter Octavian sent us,' Miles's ghost supplied helpfully, since unlike Tori, Cat could see him.

Tori, meanwhile, kept glancing back and forth between her wife and their guest, clearly baffled by the reaction.

'Cat, what the hell?' Tori said.

'I'm sorry,' Cat mumbled, studying Tori as if wondering why she wasn't reacting. 'Really. We've had a horrible twenty-four hours and I just . . . I knew Octavian had sent someone, but I had no idea . . .'

The woman was at a loss for words, but at least she was no longer running away.

'Why are you freaking out?' Tori asked. 'What are you . . .' She took a closer look at Amber, realization dawning. 'Wait, what do you *see*?'

'Better show her,' Miles said.

Amber and Tori were still outside that wooden pen, with Cat and the man in the baseball cap on the inside. She didn't want to frighten Tori, but Miles was right. She normally would have hesitated with the employee there, but Cat didn't seem to have any interest in hiding her reaction from him, so Amber would follow suit.

237

'Don't be afraid,' Amber said to Tori, more a plea than a warning.

She dropped the glamour, letting them all see her true countenance, the hard, burgundy skin of the Reaper, her long talons, and the hair like razor wire that swept back from her face.

'Good Christ!' said the baseball cap man, turning pale as he crossed himself.

For her part, Tori smiled in dawning awe. 'Wow,' she whispered.

Amber gave a tiny laugh. 'Now that is one reaction I did not expect.'

Tori turned to Cat. 'Maybe Peter did send us some real protection after all.'

Cat nodded slowly, taking a few steps toward the wall that separated them. It was in the midst of being dismantled and from the look of the posts it had been higher before. Now they were able to see eye to eye over the top.

'Amber, right? I meant no offense,' Cat said.

'I know,' Amber replied, though the shame still resonated inside her, mostly from memory. Her mother had once told her that people never really got over the difficult times in their lives, they just diluted them with time and experience.

'This is Ed,' Cat said, gesturing toward the baseball cap man. 'He's our foreman.'

Ed looked as if he feared she might eat his face given the opportunity. He nodded warily and raised a hand.

'Hey,' he said.

Amber smiled, then instantly regretted it. With her long, sharp teeth, her smile looked ferocious.

'Hey, Ed,' she replied.

Tori laughed quietly, apparently enjoying the peculiar awkwardness of it all.

The ghost of Miles Varick slid into the air. Amber and Cat

both watched him rise, which only seemed to confuse Tori and the foreman all the more. The ghost drifted over the top of the wall toward the huge apple tree, staring down at something that lay there on the ground, hidden from Amber's view by the wall. Yet she knew what it must be.

'She's getting stronger,' Miles whispered in that spectral voice.

Cat whipped around to stare at him. 'What are you talking about?'

'Your Miss Shaw,' the dead professor replied. 'She's growing stronger.'

'How do you know that?' Cat demanded.

The spectral face turned quizzical. 'Why, she just told me so. Can't you hear her?'

Cat turned to Amber. 'Can you hear her, too?'

Amber shook her head – she couldn't – even as Tori demanded to know what was going on. Just as she couldn't see the ghost, she couldn't hear Miles *or* Keomany. While Cat quickly explained, Amber at last moved around the wall and entered the clearing. Her breath caught in her throat when she saw the extraordinary figure lying prone on the ground, roots thrust into the soil. Her thoughts went to wood nymphs and other folkloric forest sprites and spirits, but Keomany Shaw was so much more. The dead earthwitch had been reborn as some kind of avatar for Gaea, a thing of wood and leaf and even fruit, and yet somehow – to someone who had known her – she was still recognizably Keomany, as if someone had constructed this beautiful growth as a living memorial to her.

'What's she saying?' Amber asked, which caused Cat and Tori's conversation to halt abruptly.

'Yeah,' Tori said, searching the air for a spirit she would never see. 'What *is* she saying?'

They all turned to look at the beautiful, impossible figure of wood and bark and leaf that lay curled upon the ground, a garden shaped like a woman.

The ghost of Miles Varick drifted downward until he appeared to alight on the grass beside the new body that Gaea had grown for Keomany. The spirit smiled kindly down upon the elemental, then looked up at Cat and Tori, though he had to know that Tori could not hear him.

'She wants you to know that it's really her, that she's here with you, alive and aware,' Miles said, his voice like the whisper of the wind. 'And that she loves you all. She's weak, now, because there are terrible things happening to the earth just now . . . to Gaea.'

'What can we do—' Cat began.

Miles held up a hand, listening to something that might have been Keomany's own ghost or the elements themselves.

'She says you shouldn't worry for her or for yourselves. She can protect you as long as you are here. And she doesn't want you to fear for Gaea, either. "The goddess is getting angry," she asks me to tell you. The goddess is getting angry, and Keomany is getting stronger.'

Oriyur, Tamil Nadu, India

The building in Oriyur looked nothing like a church. But nothing in the tiny village of Oriyur looked like much of anything. No one visited the village except for traders and the occasional Christian pilgrim seeking the burial place of Saint John de Brito, the Portuguese missionary who had traveled the whole area in the late seventeenth century, spreading the word of his God.

The pilgrims came in pursuit of legend more than fact. Elsewhere there were schools named after him, but here one could find only the place where his execution was said to have taken place. And perhaps the deed had been done on that very spot. As to the disposition of the missionary's remains, however, there were many opinions. Some said that his body had been returned to Lisbon, to the halls of his fathers, and others that it had been buried in Calcutta. Locals insisted that Saint John de Brito had been buried right there in Oriyur, and many still blessed his name.

But the small, crumbling shop with its stone foundation received very little attention. No one still drawing breath in this world remembered that the stone foundation had once been a church, under construction at the time of the saint's execution. No one knew of the space beneath the stones, the chamber there and the stone box within it, or that the box contained the severed head of the martyred missionary.

It was said that on the day of his murder, the nearby sand dunes had turned red with blood. Nobody knew it, but that was a bit of melodrama, an apocryphal tale.

When the ground shook and the little shop collapsed and the stone box in the basement of the forgotten church began to disgorge massive, lumbering creatures made of brightly burning cinders and the bones of the damned, that ancient fiction became reality.

That night, the dunes were red indeed.

Philadelphia, Pennsylvania

Octavian sat in silence in the back of the sedan as it crawled through late afternoon traffic, the sky beginning to bleed daylight in small increments. Evening was still quite a way off, but the hour of long shadows had arrived and the slant of the light turned the world to phantoms.

'You know this could be nothing,' Allison said, her words clipped and blunt. She had been a reporter in a previous life and whenever he forgot that fact, this tone would appear to remind him.

'I know.'

He stared at the back of the driver's head. The man did not glance back, nor did Corporal Song, who sat in the front passenger seat and stared straight out through the windshield. Song was either intimidated by them or still pissed about the way they had pushed him around earlier; probably a little of both. Octavian didn't like him, but neither did he blame the man. Song was a soldier, and pretty soon they might be in the midst of combat, side by side. Octavian figured it would do them all good to remember that.

'I mean, he would've said anything—' Allison went on.

Octavian shot her a dark look. 'He said what he knew. You were in the room and you doubt that? Under the circumstances I have no doubt that he believed what he told us, and that he told us all he had to tell us. I was satisfied of that . . .'

The rest of that sentence hung in the air unspoken, but they both heard it.

. . . before I let him die.

Allison glanced out the window for a moment before nodding. 'I agree. But Task Force Victor have been all through the places where Cortez and his coven were supposed to have nests in California and they're all abandoned. Why are we assuming this one in Seattle will be any different?'

'We're not,' Octavian replied, staring at the back of the driver's head again. 'But it's all we've got.'

Allison fell silent, then, and he understood why. He knew that she must be feeling just as useless as he was, that she had become a creature of action, that in the midst of crisis, idle time made her want to crawl out of her skin. That was, in fact, the sole reason that they were on the way to the airport right now; Octavian could not stand to be in his twelfth-floor hotel room a moment longer. After today he hoped never to return to that hotel. Hoped never to come back to Philadelphia. There would only be pain here for him from this day forward.

In the front, Song shifted in his seat and frowned, putting a hand to his right ear to cut out the ambient noise of the car engine and the city rolling by around them.

'This is Song. Come again, Commander?' The Chinese soldier listened for a moment. 'Thank you, sir. I'll pass that on.'

'What's going on?' Allison asked.

Song turned to look over the seat at them. 'We sent a team to sit on the location, monitor activity—'

'You were supposed to wait for us,' Octavian reminded him.

'They weren't going in, just observing,' Song said. 'But there's nothing to observe. The building there used to be a music company – offices, a pressing facility for CDs, even studio space, apparently – but there's no music there now. No building, either.'

'No building,' Octavian repeated.

'It burned down,' Song explained. 'Within the past week. They're contacting the Seattle police and fire departments, and of course they will sift the remains of the building.'

'You won't find anything useful,' Octavian said, thinking hard about Cortez's strategy. So many of his nests had already been abandoned. He had blown up Bannerman's Arsenal and now burned down this place in Seattle. Where had they all gone?

'We have to try,' Song replied.

'If you add all of these supposed nests up . . .' Allison said.

'That's a lot of vampires,' Octavian finished for her. 'I was just thinking the same thing. They're going somewhere, which means Cortez has some kind of plan that we haven't stumbled upon yet. All of this stuff he's doing to divert my attention is just that . . . diversion. He's trying to keep me away from wherever his real plan is going to go into action.'

Realization sparked in Allison's eyes. 'And where has he kept you away from so far?'

Octavian nodded. 'Europe. All of this – Nikki's murder included – has kept me from responding to these incursions in person, the way I normally would have.'

Song had been too polite to intrude up till now, but he scoffed at this.

'I'm sorry,' the soldier said, 'but you are jumping to some very large conclusions. I will admit it seems like this Cortez is antagonizing you with a purpose and that the abandonment of his nests hints at some larger ambition, but there has been nothing to even suggest a connection to the incursions in Europe. We know what has caused them. You dismantled the magical hierarchy keeping our world's defenses in place, and the appearance of the chaos goddess you fought in Massachusetts let the demons of a thousand Hells know there might be a way through. This isn't Cortez's doing, Mr Octavian. It's yours.'

Octavian smiled thinly. There were times he wished he still had fangs to show, and this was one of them. He hoped that the glint in his eyes would be enough to warn Song to hold his tongue.

'Octavian didn't give birth to these demons, you imbecile,' Allison said. 'And he didn't ring the damn dinner bell. To insinuate—'

'Stop,' Octavian said, holding up a hand and glancing at her. 'Thank you, but stop.' He looked at Song. 'Nikki's in the grave now, Corporal. And we have no solid leads on where to find Cortez. I could spend the next year hunting him, or more. The next hundred years, if he decided to make it really difficult. So while I'm waiting for something helpful to turn up, I'm going to do what Commander Metzger has wanted me to do all along. We're already headed to the airport. Call ahead and tell them to put a little more gas in the tank. We're headed to Europe. Italy first, and then France.'

He glanced at Allison, who nodded to confirm that she intended to accompany him, though he'd had no doubt at all.

They sat silently together, these old friends, as Song used his commlink to radio their intentions ahead. After a minute or so, with the traffic now flowing around them and a view of planes taking off and landing in the distance as they approached the airport, it was clear that Song's conversation had shifted. He wasn't doing the asking anymore, but the answering. Apparently Commander Metzger was back on the line. He had gone ahead of them by more than an hour to make sure that all would be in readiness by the time they arrived and it sounded as if he were giving Song difficulty over their decision. Octavian didn't understand that. The commander had been hoping he would go to Europe to deal with these demons since the first incursion began.

'What is the problem?' he asked angrily.

They had slowed to a stop in front of a massive chain link fence with a guard shack in view. Now the gate rolled open and the driver sped the sedan through the opening. Seconds later they were on the tarmac.

'You might want to hear it from Commander Metzger,' Song replied.

'Hear what?' Allison demanded before Octavian could get out the same words.

The sedan rolled to a stop. Song glanced back over the seat at them.

'Maybe you'd better hear it from him,' the soldier said.

As Allison started to argue, Octavian popped open his door and climbed out, tall limbs unfolding from the rear seat. A small jet stood parked nearby, in the shadow of a wing of the airport. Lights blinked on the plane and on the runway. Soon the day would turn gray and the gray would slide into night, and then the lights would be brighter, calling travelers home to safety. But safety was hard to come by these days.

Commander Metzger stood waiting for them by a second sedan, which was parked much nearer to the jet. A small coterie of soldiers had gathered nearby, including Sergeant Galleti. There were travel bags and weapons cases on the ground behind them and as Octavian and Allison approached, Metzger made a whirling gesture with his finger, the wings-up, let's-take-off command that anyone could recognize. Galleti and the others grabbed their bags and picked up weapons cases and marched toward the jet. Its stairs had already been lowered and in the twilight its interior was fading from gray to black shadow.

'You've changed destinations, I hear?' Metzger said.

'Seems like the right thing to do,' Octavian replied. 'If that barrier's still holding in France, we'll go to Siena first.'

'They're both covered,' Metzger said. 'You've already got people helping us in Saint-Denis with more on the way, and the team you're sending to Siena left hours ago.'

Octavian cocked his head, confused. 'You've been trying to get me to go—'

'There's a third breach,' Metzger cut in.

'Oh, shit,' Allison whispered.

'The middle of nowhere in India,' Metzger went on. 'Our people generated that list of saints who were beheaded. This location, as remote as it is, drew a hit on that list. Saint John somebody. Portuguese missionary.'

Octavian exhaled. 'All right. India it is.'

The driver of their car set down the rucksacks they'd packed. There weren't any weapons for them; neither of them needed a gun, though Octavian wouldn't have minded one loaded with Medusa toxin-laced bullets.

'I'm staying,' Allison said.

Octavian looked at her, startled. She'd always gone her own way, but this . . .

'I spent a few years as a bloodhound for Task Force Victor, Peter,' she said. 'I want to head out to California and sniff around, see if I can pick up Cortez's trail. If you need me, you can always call.'

Octavian hesitated. 'You know I'm not abandoning her.'

They both understood to whom he referred.

'I know. And you have other responsibilities. Go do what needs doing. That's always been what you've been best at. Let me keep trying to run this bastard down, and when I've got him up a tree, I'll keep him there for you.'

Octavian barely heard the words. His attention had strayed to a dark shape in the sky, a crow that descended toward them. He frowned as he watched its unwavering path. Beyond it, an airplane lifted off a runway, but his gaze remained locked on the crow.

Allison said his name, wary and curious, and in his peripheral vision he saw her turn and also begin tracking the crow's descent. Metzger and Song did likewise, and Song unholstered his gun, taking an instant bead on the crow, whose path was now certain.

'Don't,' Octavian said, gesturing at Song, and a sphere of bright blue light appeared around the hand holding his gun. He would not be able to pull the trigger now.

'Is this an attack?' Metzger asked, backing up a step or two and glancing worriedly at Octavian and the magic he'd used to stop Song from firing.

'Well, it's not a bird,' Allison muttered.

Octavian frowned. No, it wasn't a bird, but neither was it an attack. Though dusk had arrived, if Cortez was the stickler for tradition – for the vampire as monster – he would never have allowed one of his people to slip in as a crow. It would be a bat, the image that had been rendered absurd by a thousand parodies.

'Be wary,' he said, taking a step forward. He felt the static of magic between his fingers, felt it running through his bones, ready for anything.

In the gathering darkness, the black bird seemed almost to vanish . . . and then it ignited in a ball of flames. Fire seared the night, roaring brighter, and Octavian lifted a hand to protect his eyes. The growing blaze touched the tarmac, climbing higher, smoke rising. Song swore loudly, angry at Octavian, wanting access to his weapon. Metzger barked a warning, hoping that the mage knew what he was doing. But Allison only stepped up beside him and watched as the fire began to sculpt itself into a human silhouette.

A woman on fire.

The flames diminished and then drew inward, as if pulled back into the very flesh of the figure who now stood where the fire had been.

Octavian smiled. 'Hello, Charlotte.'

'Holy shit,' Metzger said under his breath.

Charlotte stood before them, head bowed as if she feared to meet their eyes. Her copper red hair hung down in front of her face, hiding those ocean blue eyes, and she seemed to hesitate. Octavian had been inside the worst asylums of eras past, and for just a moment she reminded him of the wary patients he had seen there, wandering the halls and talking in empty corners.

'You just left me,' she whispered, lifting her gaze at last. Those blue eyes were like ice.

Allison stepped forward. 'The explosion . . . we figured you were killed.'

Charlotte shook her head regretfully. 'No faith.'

Octavian thought she would smile, then, teasing them for not believing in her. But there wasn't a trace of jest in her expression or her tone. He felt tempted to embrace her, but she radiated anger. The girl did not want anyone trying to make her feel better.

'I thought you might have survived,' he admitted. 'But I wasn't sure how long it would take you to pull yourself together and we've got a whole world falling apart. I'm sorry, Charlotte, but we needed to stay focused.'

Again she seemed to lose herself, gazing off into some haunted middle distance. Then she blinked and nodded.

'I'm good,' she said. 'Your lady's dead and the planet's going to shit and you've been next to useless, sitting around like your hate might kill Cortez by remote control while I go out with a couple dozen guys who get vaporized around me.'

'Charlotte –' Allison began.

'While *I* get vaporized,' the redhead went on, blue eyes wandering as she looked at anything except for Octavian. And then she froze, staring at him. 'I get it, Peter. Priorities. You're a warrior. Every battle is fucking triage, right? You fight to win and fight to live and everything else is a luxury.'

'If I had known what would happen—' Octavian said.

Charlotte gave a throaty, humorless laugh that made it clear she had been broken and put back together slightly wrong.

'I'll get over it,' she said. 'I have no illusions as to who's the good guy and who's the bad guy in all this shit. You're not the one who killed me. Not the one who raped me. Not the one who blew me to fucking smithereens. So let's get down to business, shall we?'

Octavian glanced at Allison, then at Metzger and Song. They all looked as profoundly worried about the girl as he felt, but he suspected they were more concerned with what she might do next than they were about what would become of her. Somehow, after all that she had been through at Cortez's hands and the transition from human to vampire to Shadow, she had managed to keep her head together. But this latest horror had been too much for her, as it would have been for almost anyone.

Her grin made him shiver.

'We've lost Cortez's trail for the moment,' Octavian said. 'Allison is going out to California to try to track him. I'm headed to India to deal with the latest incursion.'

'I don't think you are,' Charlotte said. 'See, I was down in the basement of that damn armory. Cortez had left us a welcome present, a whole big pile of dead folks and a ton of explosives. But right before the blast, I saw something . . . something written on the wall in blood. It was like an artist's signature on a painting. *Xibalba*.'

She spelled it for them.

'Does that mean something to you?' Allison asked.

Charlotte narrowed her eyes. 'Never did before, but you can be sure I won't forget it.'

Octavian glanced at Song, who had regained control of his hand and his gun, which dangled at his side. He and Metzger both seemed baffled, though the commander did seem to be thinking hard on the question.

'What about you, Peter?' Charlotte asked. 'You know all this stuff. It's all stored away in your brain, isn't it? A whole world's occult bullshit, going back thousands of years.'

'The place of fear,' Octavian said, earning surprised looks from Allison and the two TFV men. 'That's more or less how it translates.'

'If you say so,' Metzger said. 'But what does it mean?'

Octavian searched Charlotte's eyes and realized that she understood, that she had sought out the significance of that word before she had tracked him down here tonight. He nodded to her, then bent and picked up his bag and started toward the airplane.

'Let's go,' he said. 'You too, Charlotte.'

'Oh, I wouldn't miss it,' she said, striding after him.

Allison fell into step beside Octavian, gripping her rucksack in one hand. Metzger barked an order at Song and then hurried to catch up.

'What does it mean, Octavian?' Metzger asked, trying to put his authority behind the question.

As they hustled toward the plane, Octavian didn't look back at him.

'It means we're going to Guatemala.'

14

Airborne

Allison liked that they were all in the same compartment. She had been on too many planes where the troops were treated like cattle, herded into an ugly, narrow space and strapped in for the duration, while the officers flew in relative comfort in a forward compartment. This jet had an aisle down the middle and a row of seats on either side – not your typical military transport by any standard. She liked Metzger's style.

Still, the TFV soldiers had filled the plane from the back, leaving the seats closest to the cockpit for their officers. Sergeant Galleti had taken a spot in the third row, forcing Song to retreat amongst the other subordinates. That left Allison, Octavian, Metzger and Charlotte filling the front four seats. Allison had taken the second row on purpose so that she would be adjacent to Charlotte, and though she tried not to stare at her, she kept aware of the girl in her peripheral vision. Her tattoos were still there and she still had the face of a nineteen-year-old – hell, she always would – but all the fun had been burned out of her.

As far as Allison was concerned, that made her dangerous.

Charlotte had experienced things that would have broken most people and come out the other side. But this . . . Allison could see just from the ice in her eyes that this had turned the girl's heart to stone.

'All right,' Metzger said, emerging from the cockpit and clicking the door shut behind him. 'The pilot has her instructions. We're headed for Guatemala.' He slid into his seat and began to buckle his belt. 'Now, you want to tell us why?'

'Thank the Mayans,' Octavian said.

'What do the Mayans have to do with any of this?' Allison asked.

'Probably nothing. But Xibalba . . . that's not an accident. Maybe it's just what Cortez calls his coven, and if so we're going to waste a lot of gas on this trip. But I'm betting there's more to it than that.'

'It's just a word,' Metzger said, turning to look at Allison, behind him.

'No,' Charlotte said, her eyes haunted and grim. 'Cortez wasn't counting on anyone surviving that explosion. He wasn't counting on me being there.'

'How can we be sure?' Allison asked. 'He knows I used to track for Task Force Victor. He had to have realized I might be there, and he couldn't be sure that blast would kill me.'

Octavian nodded. 'Point taken. But I'm banking that he figured anyone who got close enough – deep enough into that basement – to see that word up close was going to be killed. If this is some kind of ruse, it feels like there are too many variables. More likely that after murdering all of the people in that basement, he painted that word on the wall in celebration or as some kind of declaration.'

'Punctuation,' Metzger said.

'That was the feeling I had,' Charlotte said.

'So we take it as a given for now,' Allison said. 'To which I still say, "what the hell do the Mayans have to do with anything?"'

'Xibalba is the Mayan underworld. All their dark gods . . . their death gods . . . lived there. According to legend, there was a physical entrance to the underworld, an actual door or gateway of some kind, in what is now Guatemala, near a city called Cobán. It's locked, of course, barred to keep the demons on the other side.'

Charlotte gave a small grunt that might have been a laugh. 'Or it's supposed to be.'

Octavian glanced back at her. 'You found the story, I assume? The legend about the last time the door to Xibalba was opened?'

Charlotte nodded.

Allison shuddered, a tremor of dread passing through her. 'This sounds like the same kinds of breaches that are happening now.'

Octavian gave her the lopsided smile that she had always found charming. Tonight, she found it unsettling as hell.

'Doesn't it, though?' he said. 'Go on, Charlotte. Tell them.'

Metzger and Allison both turned to study Charlotte more closely. The vampire girl still wore a grim expression, but now she focused those deep ocean blue eyes on Allison.

'One of the Maya death gods was called Mam,' she said, her voice husky, and drifting as though she spoke from distant memory. 'Or maybe they were all called that. From what I read, the word meant "grandfather", and the people used it out of respect. When the door came open, only one man managed to stand against them, a holy man called Brother Simon, though I'm sure it was originally something else.'

'Early Catholics called him a saint,' Octavian said.

'They stopped?' Allison asked, cocking her head.

'Short version?' Charlotte said. 'Brother Simon got the door to Xibalba closed. Guy had some serious mojo, like Octavian. But the story says that one of the death gods, Mam . . . he was holding the door open. Brother Simon defeated him by doing something crazy. Somehow he merged with Mam, almost like inviting possession. Death god and holy man became one. The door closed and he/she/it sealed it up tightly. End of story.'

'Only it's not the end of the story,' Octavian continued. 'When the Catholics rose to prominence and they were trying to bring pagans into the fold, they co-opted pagan symbols and saints all over the world, like Saint Brigid in Ireland. Here, they made Brother Simon into Saint Simon . . . at least for a while. The problem was that the people did not want to forget his real origins. They not only worshipped the man he had been, but the thing he became afterward.'

Charlotte glanced out the darkened window. 'They called him Maximón, this weird fucking god-man hybrid. For a long time, the Mayans worshipped it as a god on earth. And then it went mad and started eating them and tried to re-open the door to the underworld, and they killed it . . . this thing the Christians called Saint Simon . . . and they cut off its head.'

Allison blinked, feeling as if she were awakening from a dream. She looked at Metzger but he seemed unphased, still in the grip of the story, so she turned to Octavian and saw the glimmer of dark knowledge in his eyes.

'Oh, shit,' she said. 'No, no, this guy is not that clever. Please tell me that Cortez does not seriously have that kind of power.'

'What?' Commander Metzger demanded. 'What are you talking about?'

'For Christ's sake,' a voice piped up behind them, 'spit it out!'

Allison turned to see Sergeant Galleti in the third row, leaning out of her seat and listening with rapt attention. Beyond her, many other faces peered over the tops of their seats or around into the aisle. They had all gotten too loud. The entire team was listening now. But perhaps that was for the best.

'This thing, Maximón, was considered a saint among its people,' Allison explained. 'Don't you get it? Even the Catholics called it Saint Simon—'

'They excised all of that from the records later,' Octavian added. 'Put Maximón's face in the place of Judas's in all of the images of Judas Iscariot that you'll find in Guatemala. Look for yourself and you'll see it. They tried to make the people look at him as a demon instead of a saint.'

'But the locals thought of him as a saint. And he was beheaded,' Allison said to Metzger. 'And they buried his head right on top of the door to Xibalba.'

'No,' Metzger said. 'You're not suggesting that Cortez is tied to the breaches we've had in Europe and India? All based on one word painted in blood in some basement?'

Octavian gave him a grim look, arching an eyebrow. 'Leon, listen to yourself. You know it fits. It all fits.'

'No, it doesn't,' Sergeant Galleti put in, leaning further from her seat. 'With all due respect, if the magical defenses on this reality were put into place by Vatican sorcerers, and they used the graves of decapitated saints as the focus points, basically the gates where they could put in a key and lock it shut, then this doesn't make sense at all. Xibalba predates all of that. This story predates all of that. And you just said the church doesn't recognize this Brother Simon as a real saint.'

'I thought about that,' Octavian said. 'And you're right. This gate to Xibalba predates all of that. Brother Simon the holy man, before he became Maximón the demon-saint – he was a sorcerer, and he sacrificed himself to close and lock that gate. He did it with magic. Now, let me ask you a question: do you think the Vatican sorcerers invented all of the magic in the Gospel of Shadows? Some of it came from the Nazarene, we know that. But not all. They collected it from around the world.'

Allison exhaled. The hum of the plane seemed to vibrate in her heart.

'This was the beginning,' she said. 'They based the spells they used to seal off the world on the magic Simon used to close the door to Xibalba.'

Octavian touched the tip of his nose with a finger. 'There you go.'

Metzger swore again, shaking his head. 'So all of this . . . the other breaches . . .'

'Could be accidental or coincidental,' Octavian admitted. 'After what happened in Massachusetts, it's possible. But it feels more likely to me that he's engineered it all somehow. He wanted us busy elsewhere.'

Allison stared at Octavian. 'He wanted *you* anywhere but South America.'

'So he could open the door to Xibalba,' Charlotte rasped.

'Just throw the doors open and let all the demons in?' Metzger said. 'I don't understand. Cortez is a vampire, I know, but if what he wants is to prey on humans and be the prince of darkness or something, how is that goal served by letting a bunch of ancient Mayan death gods back into our reality?'

But Allison had no trouble understanding. It was all very clear to her now.

'Maybe he doesn't just want to befriend the death gods,' she said.

Charlotte nodded. 'Maybe he wants to be one.'

Octavian turned away from them, sliding back against his seat. 'Why not?' he said. 'After all, it worked for Brother Simon.'

Brattleboro, Vermont

Now that night had fallen, the air had turned cold. Tori snuggled up against Cat on the sofa, thinking that one of them should get up and turn on the heat. Even a fire wouldn't be out of the question, not in Vermont in late September. But as Cat stroked her hair and kissed her forehead, she knew that neither of them had any intention of getting up off of that sofa. At least not yet.

Across the living room, Amber Morrissey stood in the open doorway that led to the dining room and leaned against the wall, her cell phone pressed to her ear, a troubled expression on her face.

'So, even now you see her as she really is?' Tori whispered.

'Yes,' Cat replied.

'It's sort of beautiful, isn't it? That dark purple like black grapes.'

'Like wine,' Cat said.

'Beautiful.'

Cat looked at her. 'But terrible, too.'

'And that,' Tori agreed, turning from her wife to study Amber again, searching the air around her. 'You see the ghost, too?'

Cat shook her head. 'No. I don't think he's here right now. I think he went back out to the clearing to try to talk to Keomany some more.'

Tori stiffened. She didn't like the idea of the ghost out there having conversations with Keomany that none of them could

hear. Yes, Amber vouched for the ghost of Miles Varick, and
Octavian vouched for Amber, but that left the question of whether
or not Tori trusted Octavian. Cat certainly did not, but Tori had
always believed that the mage was a benevolent man, that he
meant well no matter how often things went to hell around him.
But could one blame firefighters for the blazes they extinguished,
or the people caught in the conflagration? Of course not.

She ought to have been celebrating the idea that Keomany
had been reborn. She would never be the same woman, never
be human again, but she existed now as some kind of avatar of
Gaea. Most earthwitches would be envious of such a pure,
direct connection to the goddess and of the power that came
along with it. Tori just missed her friend, knowing that nothing
would ever be the same.

But she was dead, Tori thought, *and now she's alive. It's a
blessing*.

As she pondered that, she began at last to believe it.

Amber finished her call and turned to them, slipping her
phone into her pocket.

'That was Peter,' she said, coming back into the living room
and perching on the edge of the armchair. 'He's in the air, flying
to Guatemala—'

'What's in Guatemala?' Cat asked.

'Answers, or so he thinks,' Amber replied. She slid down
into the chair wearing a contemplative frown on the face she
allowed the world to see. 'It sounds like these breaches in
Europe aren't a coincidence. Apparently there's one in India,
now, too. But they're all part of a coordinated attack.'

A shiver ran through Tori. 'You're saying these demons are
working together?'

'I didn't get that impression, no,' Amber said. 'More like
bombs all timed to go off at the same time.'

'So who's the bomber?' Cat asked.

'The vampire who killed Nikki.'

Tori felt the dread in her belly tighten into knots. She burrowed even closer to Cat, though she knew that her wife could not protect her from the kind of darkness Amber was talking about. They would fight side by side if they had to fight, but evil on this level was so far beyond their small magicks.

'What can we do?' Cat asked.

Tori looked at her, surprised. 'Us?'

Cat kissed her temple. 'Yes, us. Can't you feel the question?'

'The question?' Amber repeated.

'The one you're about to ask,' Cat said. 'It's just hanging in the air. And I can see it in your eyes. What is it?'

'Gaea needs your help,' Amber said.

Cat laughed softly. 'So now Peter Octavian is going to tell us what Gaea needs?'

Amber cocked her head, studying them both. 'I'm guessing he doesn't need to tell you. These breaches are ripping Gaea apart. Each one is like a wound, right? How many do you think it will take to do irrevocable damage? This is the whole world on the line.'

'With Octavian, it always is,' Cat said dubiously.

Tori took a deep breath and extricated herself from the comfort and safety of her wife's embrace. She sat up, turning to face Cat.

'Then it's a damn good thing he's around, isn't it?'

Cat met her gaze for several long seconds and then nodded slowly. 'I guess it is,' she said, glancing at Amber. 'What does he need us to do?'

'Talk to Keomany,' Amber said.

'How?' Tori asked. 'Your ghost is the only one who can talk to her.'

'Miles is the only one who can hear her, at least right now,' Amber replied. 'But Keomany is a direct line to Gaea now and we don't yet even know the full extent of her abilities. She's something brand new in the world, at least as far as Octavian knows, and she's still in the process of becoming whatever it is that she's going to be. The way Miles tells it, talking to her is like having a conversation with someone who's only half awake.'

'And you want us to help you wake her up,' Cat said.

Amber fixed them both with a grim look. 'If Octavian's right, what's happening now will start a chain reaction that will tear the soul of this world apart. To me, that's all metaphysical bullshit. But for you . . . he's talking about your goddess. And my guess is that whatever this thing is that Keomany's becoming, if Gaea is torn apart, Keomany will die right along with her. And maybe all the rest of us, too.'

Tori shivered, wishing more than ever for a fire in the hearth. She was tempted to burrow up against her wife again, but there was no hiding from this. Instead, she turned and took Cat's hand.

'Let's go,' she said, getting up from the couch and trying to pull Cat up beside her.

Cat resisted, giving her a pained look. 'Octavian got Keomany killed once already.'

'No, he didn't. Chaos killed her while she and Peter were busy trying to save the world *again*. You may not like him—'

'I know, I know,' Cat said, reluctantly getting up from the sofa. She turned to Amber. 'We'll do whatever needs doing.'

Tori smiled. 'Just don't ask Cat to like him.'

*

261

Saint-Denis, France

*In her dream, Beril Demirci is a little girl again. She sits on a
flat shelf of rock overhanging a river, breaking the heads off of
daisies and tossing them into the rushing water to watch them
swept away. While picking flowers in the nearby field she found
some violets as well, but she loves the vivid purple of their
petals and does not want to throw them. And yet . . . when the
last of her daisies has floated downriver, she picks up one of the
violets, breathing in its lovely scent. Then she breaks off the
stem and tosses the flower into the water.*

*As it rushes away, regret washes over her and she reaches
out for it. The broken, beautiful violet rises from the water, gliding back toward her outstretched hand . . .*

And she wakes.

Frowning, troubled even in her sleep, Beril grumbled as she
forced her eyes open, taking in her surroundings. She lay on
her side on a cot, facing the featureless drape at the rear of a
tent. Somewhere beyond the tent she heard the crackle of radio
static and the mutter of voices and then, far off, someone
sobbing with grief. After the casual joy of her dream, she felt
her heart begin to ache, yearning for a return to the sweet innocence of slumber.

Something poked her hard in the back.

She cried out, twisting around and scrambling off the edge
of the cot, heart hammering in her chest, thinking of demons.
But the two figures that stood over the cot were not monsters
and they were not evil, just a pair of serious men wearing iden-
tically impatient expressions. Considering that Father Laurent

was decades younger than Chakroun and a kind-hearted man, it seemed strange that the priest and the ancient Moroccan conjuror could look so alike.

'What the hell is wrong with you?' Beril demanded. 'I was sleeping!'

'Yes,' Chakroun agreed. 'And we have been trying to wake you.'

In his hand he held a rough-hewn walking stick, which she now recognized as the offending instrument. She had the urge to poke him back, but let it pass.

'What could be so . . .' she began, before realization struck. 'Wait, are the Shadows here?'

Father Laurent looked dismayed. 'Not yet. But Monsieur Chakroun—'

'I believe I have a way for us to slip a small group through the barrier without dropping it entirely,' the ancient mystic said.

Beril rubbed her eyes, climbing to her feet. She had fallen asleep in her clothes but still felt somehow exposed and vulnerable, the men having come upon her while she was dozing. Her thoughts were still caught in the sticky webbing of sleep, but she forced herself to make sense of what they were saying. She and Chakroun had managed to create a barrier around all of Saint-Denis, trapping the utukki demons inside, but the barrier would not hold forever and the utukki continued to multiply inside that magical sphere. According to Father Laurent they were being born from the womb of a human woman who lay in the basement of the ruined cathedral, not far from the single creature that had infected her with its spore and thus fathered them all. Killing woman and demon would end this incursion, but if someone was going to go down there to try to kill the demon, they had all agreed to try to save the woman it had attacked.

'We were going to wait for the Shadows to come,' she said. 'Surely one of them has a better chance of getting inside the basilica than any ordinary person?'

'True,' Father Laurent said. 'But hours pass and then hours more, and we are promised that they are on the way and they do not come.'

'And the demons propagate,' Chakroun said. 'And the woman suffers.'

A sound startled them, the clearing of a throat, and all three of them turned to see that Sergeant Ponticello had entered the large, military tent. Behind him, silhouetted in the opening, stood a short, muscular, bald man with a goatee, his arms and neck covered in occult tattoos. A tall, slender woman waited beyond him.

'Visitors,' Sergeant Ponticello said.

Beril studied them. 'Are you—?'

The tattooed man took a step deeper into the tent, and now Beril could see the beautiful female behind him.

'My name is Santiago. This is Taweret,' the tattooed man – the Shadow – said, gesturing toward his companion. Then his eyes narrowed with grim purpose.

'Tell us about this woman.'

Siena, Italy

Just after four in the morning, chaos erupted out of relative calm. Most of the refugees from Siena had been loaded onto trucks and transported to a safer distance. Jessica Baleeiro tried to think of what the next city was but her mind had gone blank.

We shouldn't have stayed, she thought. *Why did we stay?*

But she knew the answer. Jess and her husband, Gabe, had

stayed behind because they were doctors and, God help them, doctors were not supposed to run when there were people who might die without them. The last of those with minor injuries had been taken away just before two a.m., but there were three wounded who were still waiting for evac, all of them soldiers who had sustained their injuries after night had fallen and the smoke demons had returned to their full ferocity. They needed to be medflighted out and the officer in charge kept telling Gabe and Jess that a helicopter would arrive just as soon as the barrier had been stabilized.

Just thinking about it in such a mundane way, like the white-haired old Sicilian man they'd brought in was going to build a brick and mortar wall instead of some kind of magical shield that would trap the demons in the city . . . it made the world feel soft and uncertain beneath her feet.

Now she glanced at the old Sicilian and wondered what would become of him.

'Jess, come on!' Gabe shouted. 'We've got to go!'

He took her by the elbow of her uninjured arm and tried to rush her toward the transport truck that waited. Soldiers were running for it, leaping on board, while others climbed into smaller vehicles or piled on top of the two tanks that stood ominously still about fifty yards away. Engines roared and orders were shouted in Italian. The lieutenant who had been so appreciative of Gabe's work on his wounded comrades – and had joined Gabe in urging Jess to evacuate with the others because her injured arm meant she could not help care for them – came racing over, gesturing frantically to them.

Jessica shook loose of her husband, sending pain lancing through her arm and shoulder. She turned and looked back at the sorcerer, whose name she had never learned. From here she could see his lined, leathery face and his bulbous nose.

He looked more like a fisherman than a sorcerer, but there could be no mistaking that the barrier that shimmered and crackled between them and the city came from his fingertips. It did not extend from his hands so much as it responded to them, as if the wall were made of music and he its maestro. When he moved his hands it bulged and billowed and when he gestured to a place where the shield seemed to be breaking down it glowed again with its full force, lighting the darkness.

But it was crumbling, that shield. The fisherman-sorcerer had been standing there all night. Exhaustion burned at Jessica's eyes and weighed on her bones, but she could not begin to imagine how badly drained the old Sicilian must be. Now, after many hours of keeping the horrors back and buying the military forces the time to do what they needed to do for the evacuees, he was faltering. Cracks appeared in the barrier, thin spots that seemed to wear through until holes opened, and he had to reinforce those thin places.

In the amber light from the old man's magic, even from this distance, she thought she could see tears on his wrinkled face.

'Jess!' Gabe shouted, grabbing hold of her again.

She turned to stare at him and the lieutenant. 'What about *him*?'

Gabe hesitated. He understood, of course, and she knew that the idea of leaving the poor old man to his fate must be gnawing at his heart the way it did at her own. But he was ready to go – ready to run – and somehow she couldn't make her feet move. She knew there was nothing they could do, but that only paralyzed her more.

'Signora, please!' the lieutenant cried. 'We must retreat!'

Jess searched her husband's eyes. Over the engines and the shouting, she could hear her own heartbeat.

'What about our patients?' she asked. 'The helicopter never came.'

'They've been loaded onto a truck,' he told her, even though he had told her the same thing several times already.

It was an answer, but not to the question she was really asking. She knew they were on the truck, just as well as she knew that all three of them were going to die on that truck. Gabe and Jess could have gone with them on a chopper, kept them stable on the way to a hospital, and there would have been medical supplies on the helicopter. But in the back of a truck, with no idea how long it would be before they reached a hospital, all three men were as good as dead. The simple fact that Gabe hadn't been asked to go with them in their transport was a silent and grim acknowledgement of their fate. They might be dead already.

She felt numb. Shaking her head, she looked back again at the old Sicilian and felt a tight knot of nausea in her gut. When she tasted salt on her lips, she realized that she was crying.

Gabe took her chin in his hand and tilted her head back so that he could gaze into her eyes.

'I know,' he said. 'But please, my love. I can't watch you die.'

'I don't want to die.'

'Then we must *go*.'

The lieutenant swore in his native tongue and Jess turned to see him backing away from them, staring at the barrier. She and Gabe both turned to see it beginning to fail on a large scale, holes appearing and spreading while the remaining parts of the wall dimmed and hissed. The old sorcerer staggered, thrusting his hands into the air, patching the holes as best he could, but it was useless.

The tanks started to move out and the trucks followed suit. The lieutenant shouted at them, then turned and ran.

'We're going!' Gabe said, grabbing her arm again and dragging her along behind him.

Jess let herself be pulled along in the wake of their fear, but she remained somehow numb. Her feet moved beneath her and she found herself running – they were all running, after the last of the trucks, at the back of which soldiers screamed at them to hurry, to jump, to live – but all she could think about was that she did not know the old sorcerer's name. If she had known his name she could have called to him, let him know that he wasn't alone, that someone would mourn for him when he was gone.

They were at the back of the truck, running after it as it kept rolling toward the narrow road into the hills. Most of the Italian and UN forces had already pulled back to a safer distance, created a new perimeter while the sorcerer did his job. But the shield had never stabilized and now it was falling and she wondered if they had pulled back because they had expected this to happen. Expected the old man with his big, Santa Claus nose to do his best and then just die.

The lieutenant jumped into the truck, helped up by other soldiers, and then turned to reach for Gabe and Jess. Her husband tried to urge her forward, to get her onto the truck before him, but a noise like the world sighing came from behind her and she turned to discover that it was the sound of magic failing. What remained of the barrier crackled one final time and then turned to nothing but wisps of glowing smoke.

The demons came through as if born from that smoke, screaming in the voice of Hell, beating their wings and darting through the air, talons bared. The first one descended upon the old sorcerer, talons raking his face, ripping right down to the bone. He screamed as a second fell upon him, the smoky thing like some nightmare bird of prey. It plunged a fist into his chest and tore out a dark, glistening mess that could only be his heart, and his scream ended . . . but it would linger forever in her mind, waiting for her every time she closed her eyes.

'Go, Jess!' Gabe cried. 'Move it!'

He swore in Portuguese, calling for the Italian soldiers to grab her. Somehow she had kept running, stayed on her feet, and now she turned to look at the truck only a couple of yards ahead, rolling slowly enough for them to jump on. The lieutenant reached for her again. Gabe had one hand on her arm and the other on the small of her back and she knew that he was about to try to physically hurl her up into the truck bed.

'Jump, love,' he said. 'Ju—'

She felt him brace his hand against her back, ready to push, and then it was gone. The other hand gripped her arm, digging painfully into her flesh, and she cried out as she turned. Gabe pulled at her, no longer hurrying her ahead but now clutching at her, drawing her upward.

Jess stared up into her husband's terrified eyes and saw the smoke demon above him. The harpy had him by the throat, its other arm wrapped around him from behind, clawing at his chest as it lifted him into the air.

The truck rolled away as she screamed, crying as she reached for him with her injured arm, blinding pain shooting through her. But she grabbed him by the wrist of his outstretched hand and held on. The smoke demon pulled and Jess pulled back and Gabe dug his fingers into her arm until she began to lift off the ground along with him.

His eyes went wide as he realized what he was doing. She saw the moment of his decision and the bottomless sorrow in his gaze just before he let go of his grip on her. Shrieking in anguish and pain, she tried to hang on by her injured arm, to be an anchor for him, to keep him with her, but her fingers would not obey. Her grip slid from his wrist and she fell three feet to sprawl on the road.

Scrambling to her feet, she screamed her husband's name, thinking not of all the memories they had made together but all of the years without him that now stretched before her, so cold and empty. Gabe did not scream for her. It might have been that the thing had already killed him as it rose higher into the sky, but Jess watched them go, breath hitching in her chest, the icy numbness of denial spreading through her, killing even her pain. This could not be happening. She and Gabe had a life. They had love.

Screams from behind her made Jessica turn. The transport truck was under attack by several of the smoke demons, the harpy-things dragging soldiers from the vehicle or slaughtering them in place.

She heard wings flapping above her and she looked up. Death had come for her and it was nothing but mist, a cloud of charcoal smoke in the shape of a monster. The demon had eyes the color of butterscotch. In her numbness, that was all she could think. *Butterscotch.*

It dove toward her and she froze, waiting, watching it come.

The bird that slashed across its path might have been a hawk or a falcon – she wasn't sure of the difference. It flew at the ground as if it meant to dash itself to death against the road, and then it changed. The air rippled and a figure took shape there as if a human being had been poured into creation, built from nothing in an instant.

A man stood before her, tall and dark-haired, his Asian features severe. He glanced at her for a single heartbeat, then reached to his hip and drew a long Japanese sword from thin air, with a flourish worthy of a stage illusionist. The demon attacked, clawing at him without even realizing that he had already cleaved it in half with his sword. The twin halves of the demon fell to the road, but they were made of some insubstantial, infernal mist that immediately began to draw and flow together again.

The swordsman – the Shadow, for that was what he was, she realized – stabbed it in the heart and then brought the blade down to split its head in two. The thing turned to viscous liquid, black tar, and splattered the road. An eyeblink later that tar began to evaporate, smoke rising from the ground like a fire had just been put out.

Something moved to her left and Jess twisted away from it, thinking another of the demons had come for her. But the creature that stood above her was a man, not a thing of smoke and death. He was, in fact, one of the biggest men she had ever seen, a literal giant, and he threw his head back and shouted at the demons darting across the sky in a language that might have been Greek.

Two of them swept down to attack him and the giant grinned, revealing fangs, and then his flesh rippled and fur sprouted and he transformed into the biggest bear she had ever seen. Like the Japanese swordsman, he was also a Shadow.

'Come,' a voice said.

She tore her gaze from the bear grappling with the demons and saw that the swordsman had appeared just beside her. He offered his hand, intending to pull her up, but her numbness shattered and she began to sob with grief, thinking of Gabe reaching for her . . . of the look in his eyes just before he let go.

'Come,' the voice said, softly now, in her ear.

He took her arm and helped her up, taking note of the way she held her injured arm.

'My name is Kuromaku,' he said. 'Stay with me.'

'What's the point?' she said, glancing up at the harpies

circling above them, trying not to hear the sounds of screaming soldiers or see the giant bear tearing into the smoke demons nearby. 'The barrier's down. You're too late.'

'No,' Kuromaku said, finding and holding her gaze with his own. 'There is another barrier. We brought mages with us, two of them, and they have created a new wall where the military has made their camp.'

She stared at him, trying to take it all in.

'The new perimeter,' she said. 'There's a wall there?'

'Yes.'

'But that means that we're . . .'

Kuromaku arched an eyebrow. 'Yes. It means the barrier is up and we are on the wrong side. My friend and I came to aid you all,' he said, gesturing around him. 'To protect you as you retreated to the new wall. I am sorry we did not arrive sooner.'

'You're too late,' Jess said, gazing up into the night sky – now turning from black to indigo, just the barest hint of the coming dawn.

'Not for you,' Kuromaku said.

Jess looked at the place in the sky where she had last seen her husband.

'Too late.'

Then the giant was beside them, no longer a bear, and the Shadows were hurrying her toward the army transport, where soldiers kept shooting at smoky things their bullets could not seem to touch. But the Shadows and their weapons could kill the monsters, and Jess knew that if they were very lucky, some of the soldiers might be saved. And she knew, also, that if they were wounded they would need her help. Despite her own injury, despite the grief that had gutted her, leaving only a hollow core, she would do all she could.

She was a doctor.

15

Lanquin, Guatemala

As seemed to be true wherever the faithful gathered, there was a small church in Cobán with a legend surrounding it. El Calvario church had been founded upon a hillside, in a place where a hunter had seen a pair of jaguars resting in the sun on one day, and an image of Christ the next. Tour guides never attempted to explain the connection between jungle cats and the son of God, nor did they give much credence to the legend that Saint Simon had been buried in the foundations of the church. Their disbelief could not alter the truth, however. The grave existed and would never be discovered until the church was torn down.

But the head of Maximón had not been buried with his body.

Less than an hour's drive away, a mile outside the small village of Lanquin, there lay another remote tourist destination, an extensive system of limestone caves that had never been properly explored. Lights were strung along a half mile or so of the main cave and visitors braved the guano-slicked surfaces every day during welcome hours, but there were signs everywhere that warned spelunkers not to go far on their own, as no maps had ever been made of the system's furthest and deepest reaches.

Had local authorities ever been bold enough to attempt it, they would have found that the vast underground hollows went far longer and deeper than anyone imagined, and that the furthest and deepest of them ended abruptly in a wall that geologists would have at first mistaken for hardened volcanic lava due to the way the stone seemed to have flowed in to close off a segment of tunnel that lay deeper still.

At the base of that strange wall lay a small cairn of three black stones, each etched with symbols whose meaning had been lost with the death of the last Mayan sorcerer centuries before. Beneath that cairn lay a flat, unremarkable stone obelisk, the lid of a stone box that had been sunken into the floor of the dead-ended cave. And beneath the obelisk lay the severed head of the demon monk the locals had first called Brother Simon and later Maximón.

A river flowed out from the main Lanquin cave entrance, creating a place of beauty and serenity that drew tourists even beyond those who wished to explore the subterranean mystery. On this night, the sun had set shortly after six p.m. and now, several hours later, the only people in the vicinity were a group of eight British university students who had set up a trio of tents in the camping area not far from the river and the cave mouth.

Two of the students were in their tent making love while the other five sat around a small fire they had built to heat their coffee. They talked of the beauty of Guatemala and argued over whether it was possible to be homesick while also being tempted to stay forever. Of them all, only Meg heard the sound that issued from the mouth of the cave and carried over the burble of the river onto the wind.

'What is it?' one of the others asked when she frowned and turned toward the water.

'Not sure,' Meg replied. 'An animal, y'think?'

Screaming, she thought. *Something is screaming.*

But the screams did not come from an animal. They rose from beneath the obelisk lid of a stone box set into the floor of the furthest, deepest part of the cave . . . from the severed head of Maximón. The caves began to tremble and the black rock atop the cairn slid to the stone floor.

The strange wall blocking the tunnel began to bubble and then to drip, and soon the rock started to flow like molten lava, melting and spreading along the cave floor. With a hiss, an opening appeared at the top of the wall, growing quickly wider. Air rushed through from the cave into the darkness beyond, but only for a moment before the depths behind the melting wall seemed to exhale a sulfurous steam.

The caves quaked and the earth groaned.

Above ground, the British campers fled, clutching at one another. Meg called back to her mates, the two who had been making love inside their tent.

When the entire cave system cracked open, releasing a blast of heat and the steam of an underground river evaporating, the entire campsite tumbled down into the rocky maw. Like the jagged mouth of the planet itself, the huge break in the earth went on for miles, but Meg could only stare at the spot where her two closest friends had been swallowed up by the stretching, roaring fissure.

The unexplored depths of the Languin Caves had been laid open to the sky.

She could only watch as gigantic, impossible things began to emerge from the stink and steam and stone.

Meg fell to her knees in prayer, though whether she prayed to her own God to protect her or to these ancient, terrible gods to spare her, even she could not be certain.

Airborne

Octavian stared out the window of the airplane into the night, its blue-black hue a shade of darkness only found above the clouds. After a moment, he turned to Commander Metzger.

'You're sure about this? The legend says the entrance to Xibalba is in Cobán.'

Metzger still clutched his phone. He'd received a call moments before and now he held the object out as if it were evidence.

'I'm only telling you the reports that are coming in,' Metzger said. He glanced at Allison and Charlotte, then back at Sergeant Galleti. 'Twenty-seven minutes ago – more like thirty, now – massive seismic activity was recorded in the Alta Verapaz region of Guatemala. An earthquake, yes, but impossibly local- ized, very much like what happened in Saint-Denis.'

Octavian nodded. 'All right. So it's not Cobán. Where did you say—'

'A place called Languin,' Metzger replied. 'There's an unmapped cave system that draws tourists to the area. I'm told it's only an hour or so from Cobán.'

'It does make sense,' Allison said. 'You said yourself that the entrance to Xibalba was supposed to be underground.'

Octavian took a deep breath and turned to look at the people on the plane – two Shadows and a handful of soldiers who spent most of their time hunting vampires. If there were demons pouring out of a hole in the ground, they'd be as good as dead unless he could take the brunt of the battle upon himself. It would take hours for the local military to get troops to such a remote location, and even longer for any UN forces to arrive. The UN security forces were already stretched thin, and Octavian realized that Cortez had been counting on that as well. This unseen enemy, unknown to him until so recently, had been planning for a very long time, but Octavian still did not understand the end game. Did Cortez really think he could make himself some kind of modern death god?

'I knew there would be a breach,' he said, addressing everyone on the small plane. 'But I'd hoped we had figured out what Cortez had in mind in time to get here before it happened. Well, now it's happening. We're going to land as close as possible to the location of these caves and then we'll be right in the thick of it. We will be the First Responders here. I guess I don't have to tell you all how ridiculously outnumbered we're going to be.'

He let that sink in for a moment and then he looked at Metzger.

'Some of us have been here before,' Octavian said. 'Not literally here, but in situations as large and as grave as this one. Allison and I, and to a lesser extent, Charlotte—'

'We've all been here before,' Commander Metzger said.

Octavian frowned and studied the faces of the soldiers who sat silent and grim.

'You were there for the Tatterdemalion, Commander. I'll give you that one. But for the rest of you, unless you were also in that battle, or in Salzburg when Liam Mulkerrin came back, you can't know what you're walking into. I won't ask you to stay back, because I know that's not what good soldiers do. But

I will ask you to fight smart, to rely on Allison, Charlotte and myself, to use us well. The three of us will be very difficult to kill.'

He let the second half of that sentence go unsaid, knowing they would all hear it regardless. They were fragile. Mortal. Ordinary.

'I insisted on finding Cortez before I worried about these breaches,' he went on. 'I never figured the two could possibly be connected.'

'Nobody did,' Charlotte said, more tenderly than Octavian believed he deserved.

He tipped a slight nod toward her in silent thanks, and went on.

'It's my belief that Cortez is here somewhere. He wasn't at Bannerman's Arsenal or in Seattle and we can assume he wasn't in Saint-Denis or Siena or Oriyur, either. But if our theories about Maximón are right – and I think they are – then whatever's going on here has been his purpose all along. I don't know him—'

'I do,' Charlotte said, her eyes dull and reptilian. 'He's a cunning, ruthless son of a bitch. And he's proud. If whatever he's doing is coming to a head, he wouldn't miss it.'

'I'm counting on it,' Octavian said. 'You keep your eyes open. You spot any vampires you think might be giving orders, you give me a shout out on your comm unit. I will take him out.'

Commander Metzger sat up straighter. 'We talked about this. If you kill him before we can find out what he was planning—'

'Then he can't finish whatever he's starting,' Allison put in.

Octavian dropped his gaze, logic fighting his hunger for vengeance. At last he nodded.

'The commander is right,' he said, glancing at Allison and then at Charlotte.

'Peter—' Charlotte began, a warning in her voice. He didn't blame her. After all Cortez had done to her, she had as much reason to want him dead as Octavian himself.

'If he's set something in motion that only he knows how to stop, we'll have to hold off killing him until the crisis has passed,' Metzger said.

'And then he dies?' Charlotte asked, fixing her gaze on Octavian rather the commander.

'Screaming,' Octavian promised.

Charlotte said nothing, but the hard edge of her gaze said that she would hold him to that.

'How much longer?' Allison asked, breaking the moment.

Sergeant Galleti asked the same question, this time on her comm.

'Less than thirty minutes to touch down,' she said. 'They're just confirming that there's room enough on the road for us to land.'

'On the road?' Allison asked.

Octavian felt the plane begin to bank and descend, and as it did – and they moved closer to Cortez – he let the grief and fury that he had held in abeyance begin to flow back into his heart.

The flesh of his hands prickled with the dark, murderous magic that simmered inside him.

Almost time, Nikki, he thought. *Almost time.*

*

Cobán, Guatemala

Charlotte felt herself caught in the current of fate, as if it were a deep river carrying her over rocks and hurtling her downstream without any hope of her making it to shore. She knew that was foolishness; at any moment she could step back from this and simply walk away, not engage in any further conflict. She could leave war and vengeance to Octavian. But when the explosion at Bannerman's Arsenal had scattered her atoms and she had spent so long drawing her consciousness back together again, she had also surrendered herself to destiny. She had no experience with war, but she knew how to fight and how to reach deep into her heart to muster the strength to go on.

Her heart felt like cold black stone in her chest, now. And yet the hollowness she felt was an illusion, for she was not entirely devoid of emotion. Hate remained, as did – if she allowed herself to admit it – just the tiniest sliver of hope. If she survived this crisis and saw Cortez dead by her own hand, or by Octavian's if fate decreed it must be so, then perhaps she would find a spark of light still remaining in her, and a way to live without the revulsion and rage that now ate at her.

'You all right?' Allison asked.

Charlotte flinched, startled from her reverie. She glanced at the other woman – the other Shadow – and gave a small shrug.

'What does that even mean?' she asked.

Allison frowned. 'What it always means. Is there something wrong?'

Charlotte arched an eyebrow. 'I appreciate the concern. Really, I do. But are you fucking kidding?'

For a moment Allison looked worried, but then she gave a small laugh. 'Yeah, I guess it's a pretty stupid question. Just do me a favor?'

'What's that?'

'Whatever you've got stewing inside you, keep it reined in,' Allison said. 'When the fighting starts, we've got to be able to rely on you. Peter's put his faith in you. Try not to be so distracted by whatever's haunting you that you get somebody killed.'

Charlotte's first instinct was to utter some kind of cutting reply, but she thought better of it. Allison's eyes revealed her tenderness and understanding and Charlotte knew her words were genuine.

'Don't worry, okay?' she asked. 'I'm focused, that's all.'

Allison nodded and the two Shadows fell silent. Not far off, Octavian and Metzger were talking while Sergeant Galleti seemed to be having difficulty with her comm unit. They were on the tarmac at Cobán Airport and they were not alone. Metzger had been in touch with the Guatemalan government moments before they had taken off from Philadelphia and though they had been just over four hours in the air, there had been four companies of Guatemalan soldiers awaiting them when they landed. There were Jeeps and other rough terrain vehicles, as well as four army helicopters which stood black and silent on the broken tarmac.

Considering the condition of the airport, Charlotte liked the idea of helicopters. They could take off and land without having to roll down the rutted runway. Metzger's pilot had done his best but their landing in Guatemala had been rough and frightening. At one point the plane had shaken so badly that Charlotte thought the landing gear might be about to tear right off of the undercarriage. They'd made it without that kind of damage, but she wasn't sure how easy it would be for the plane to take off again.

Instead, she was about to have yet another helicopter ride. A few days ago she had never been on a helicopter, but suddenly climbing into one of the machines felt almost ordinary.

'Uh-oh,' Allison said. 'This doesn't look good.'

Charlotte glanced up just in time to see Octavian and Metzger glaring at each other, practically nose to nose. They were arguing about something, but kept their voices low. Whatever Octavian had to say, he finished saying it and spun on his heel, marching over to Charlotte and Allison.

'Let's get aboard a chopper,' he said.

'What's wrong?' Allison asked.

At first, Charlotte thought he wouldn't answer. He strode grimly toward the nearest of the black, unmarked helicopters and she and Allison followed him, wearing equally grave expressions. But when he had slid open the door in the side of the helicopter and stepped back to let them board before him, he shook his head in frustration and glanced at them.

'I wanted him to let us go in alone,' he said.

Charlotte's mouth hung open. 'Why the hell would we want to do that?'

'We wouldn't want to,' Octavian said, gesturing at the soldiers who were even now responding to barked commands from their superiors, racing to their vehicles and to the other three helicopters. 'But these guys are cannon fodder and there are more on the way. For the moment, we should have the element of surprise. I'd go in by myself if—'

'Not gonna happen,' Allison snapped.

'If not for that,' Octavian said, his anger abating for the first time. 'But if the three of us go in quickly and quietly, I could cast the spell to erect the same kind of barrier they're using at the other incursion sites and get whatever's coming through the breach contained. A lot of these guys wouldn't need to die.'

'Why wouldn't Metzger agree to that?' Allison asked.

Octavian gave her a hard look. 'He wants Cortez. If I throw up that barrier and Cortez is there, odds are he's going to be on the inside. It's not a solution, just a temporary measure.'

'I get it,' Charlotte said, feeling her heart darken again. 'And I agree. We don't need a temporary solution. We need to get Cortez and kill him. If he's really running the show it'll all fall apart and we'll worry about picking up the pieces after he's dead.'

'And if we don't find him right away?' Octavian said, turning his ire upon her. 'If we don't find him by sunrise? Or tomorrow? Or the next day? How many men and women will die because we wanted Cortez dead more than we wanted them alive?'

'That's not fair—' Charlotte began.

'Charlotte,' Allison put in, 'nobody wants Cortez dead more than Peter.'

The pit of Charlotte's stomach turned to ice and she glared at Allison.

'He raped me. Killed me. Nearly killed me again,' she said.

Allison reached for her hand but Charlotte pulled back as if scalded.

'I've been there,' Allison said. 'Exactly where you are. Tortured. All of it, thanks to Hannibal.'

'Hannibal's dead, right?' Charlotte asked.

Allison nodded.

'Well Cortez is still walking around.'

Octavian had fallen silent, but now she saw that he was looking around the tarmac at the soldiers rushing into action and he had a darkly thoughtful look in his eyes. Abruptly he climbed into the back of the chopper and turned to face them from within.

'Move it,' he said. 'Quickly. And turn your commlinks off.'

Allison and Charlotte were aboard in seconds and Octavian slid the door closed. The helicopter pilots had all been sitting in the cockpits of their aircraft waiting for orders, so he greeted them but said nothing more.

Octavian rapped the ceiling twice. 'Take us up!'

The pilot gave him a dubious look, which didn't go away when Octavian repeated the order in Spanish. Allison darted forward between the seats, her flesh rippling and fur bursting through her skin as she shapeshifted into a tiger. Showing the pilot her teeth, she gave a low growl, more menacing than a roar because it was laden with purpose.

'Take us up,' Octavian repeated.

Rigid with fear, the pilot complied, watching the tiger out of the corner of his eye. The radio crackled and voices cut through, first with inquiries and then with angry shouting, but the presence of the tiger caused him to ignore anything but Allison's jaws and growled threats. Octavian told him their destination and then they were on their way, Allison remaining up front with the man, just in case his fear eased up enough to cause him to do something foolish.

'What changed your mind?' Charlotte asked as they sped through the night sky, the whump of the rotors loud and brutal.

Octavian glanced at her and then at the Allison-tiger in the front. 'I realized there was a way to keep the troops safe and still go after Cortez now instead of trapping him inside a barrier.'

'How?' Charlotte asked.

His eyes were narrowed, but she felt sure she saw golden sparks dancing across them.

'Simple enough,' he said. 'When I put up the barrier . . . we'll be inside.'

*

Lanquin, Guatemala

Allison thought Octavian's plan more than insane – it was suicidal. Or it would have been, had any of them been ordinary. Even with his magic and their shapeshifting, she thought it was still foolish, the kind of risk only a lunatic would take. But she didn't share these observations with him. After all, it hadn't been her partner that Cortez had murdered. And if Octavian was going to trap himself behind a wall with a bunch of demons and an open gate to Hell, then she was going to be there to back him up.

I guess that makes me a lunatic, too, she thought. But the knowledge didn't change her mind.

Fortunately for her, Octavian's plan began to unravel moments before they reached their destination. New voices had crackled to life on the helicopter's radio. The pilot continued to glance at her in fear and she had begun to grow very comfortable with the shape of a tiger, with the muscles corded across her back and the feel of her lip curling back to reveal her teeth when she growled at him.

Then she noticed that the sound of the helicopter's rotors had changed. They had an echo, now, or a parallel. Shifting at the speed of thought, she transformed into her usual guise and turned in the seat to glance out the window. Octavian caught her eye and must have seen the alarm there, because he turned as well.

'We have company,' Allison said, spotting a pair of helicopters that were buzzing after them, quickly gaining. She glanced at the pilot. 'Our friend here must have been taking his time.'

'Maybe you're not as terrifying as you think,' Octavian said.

'He wet himself,' she replied. 'I'm pretty terrifying.'

In truth, she felt badly about the pilot wetting his pants. The poor guy would carry that humiliation his whole life.

'What now?' Charlotte asked.

'Doesn't matter,' Octavian replied. 'We're here.'

Allison twisted around again and peered out the windshield. He was right. What had been the Lanquin caves was now a deep canyon, a scar on the flesh of the world. It had to go on for at least a mile, but they were descending and with only the moonlight she could not get a good view of what awaited them.

Then the lights began to go on, huge banks of them popping on at once as generators fired up.

'What the fuck?' Charlotte said, scrambling to the side window.

Long trucks were illuminated, lining the narrow way that led off of the main road, along with a dozen military transports and two enormous artillery guns on flatbeds.

'The army's been busy,' Octavian said.

'They couldn't have beaten us here,' Charlotte muttered.

'They didn't. These are reinforcements, coming from elsewhere, and they've just rolled up,' Allison said. She turned to look at Octavian. 'Our timing sucks.'

But by then he wasn't looking at her. He had slid over to peer out the port window.

'He's down there,' Octavian said.

Allison looked as well, but how he could see a single vampire amidst the horrors rising from the newly splintered earth she had no idea. The caves were a chasm and in the light, monsters were rising. Some had already emerged, massive devil-bat creatures larger than any winged animal known to man. They swept in and out of the field of illumination, casting long and jagged shadows. Huge serpents swayed in the depths as if summoned by music, and she saw one slither out of the gash in the earth and vanish into the shadows.

But other things were rising from that chasm as well. She could see huge shapes moving in the constant play of shadow and light. At first their size made it impossible for her to accept what it was she saw, but then she realized that these enormous shapes were the heads of giants, just beginning to emerge as if being born from the womb of some ancient Hell. One head gleamed in the light, the yellow of long-buried bone, and the other was adorned with a forest of sprawling antlers.

'Oh, my God,' Allison whispered, and though they were words she had not spoken in a very long time, she meant them as a kind of prayer.

'They're not your gods,' Octavian said, as if he'd never indicated that Cortez might be below.

And how could he have known such a thing with all of the horrors at play down there?

Yet even as Allison wondered, the helicopter banked slightly left and she saw what he had seen. Not far from the chasm, whose fetid odors now began to invade the interior of the chopper, she spotted a large gathering of small figures that might have been human beings if she didn't know better. Dozens of them – perhaps more than a hundred – had arranged themselves in three concentric circles with a single figure at the center. As the chopper dropped lower she saw the gleam of light on their flesh and realized that the vampires, what remained of Cortez's enormous coven, were all naked and in motion, engaged in a strange, shuffling dance.

A ritual.

And look what they have summoned, she thought.

With a flash and a ripple of color, something huge burst from the trench, escaping the reach of the army's lights almost immediately. Octavian swore under his breath. While Charlotte was asking what he'd seen, Allison watched it spear upward through the darkness. Moonlight and the glow from below glinted off of its undulating body as the huge thing slithered through the air in a serpentine ribbon, trailing feathers of gold and green and red. It arced toward them, and Allison cried out for the pilot to bank left, but it didn't matter. The thing veered off, driving straight into the windscreen of the nearest of the choppers behind them. It coiled around the craft, rotors snapping off as they struck unyielding flesh, and then together the helicopter and the feathered serpent plummeted to the ground.

'What the fuck was that?' Charlotte demanded.

'My signal to get the hell out of here,' the pilot said in heavily accented English. Nobody called him on his facility with the language; they were too preoccupied with not dying.

'Not yet,' Octavian said. 'Get us lower.'

The pilot scoffed. 'Or what, you kill me? I die if I stay.'

The chopper continued veering left for another moment and then straightened its course, heading due south, away from the trench and the evils issuing from it. Octavian started arguing with the pilot but Allison's focus was elsewhere. She craned her neck to see behind them and to the right, where three of the devil-bats – horned, leathery things with fifteen-foot wingspans – were attacking the sides and front of another chopper, staying well away from its rotors.

'What about Metzger and Galleti and the others?' she asked. 'They've got to be on one of those. Maybe the one that just went down.'

Charlotte stared at her. 'Why do you care? I mean, after all Task Force Victor did to you?'

Allison would have explained to her, would have said that Leon Metzger was a good man and that his unit was doing important work, that he didn't deserve to die because he had followed orders and kept Allison on the TFV's most wanted list. But then the chopper already on the ground exploded and the blast shook them, even this far away.

'The second one's going down,' Octavian said, his voice cold and grim.

'Shit,' Allison whispered.

They watched quietly as the helicopter under siege by devil-bats lost altitude. One of the creatures had laid itself across the windshield, and the other must have gotten in the way of the rotors after all, because they were tangled with strands of its slippery viscera. They still spun, but slowly, and as Allison watched it descend she prayed that some of those aboard would survive the landing.

What then? she wondered. *What would become of them on the ground?*

'Tell the last chopper to land or turn back!' Octavian snapped. Then he reached up and grasped Allison's arm, tugging her toward the rear of the chopper. 'Come on. Enough of this.'

He grabbed the latch and hauled it back, then dragged the port gunnery door open. The chopper swayed with the change in air pressure and the pilot shouted at him, but Octavian was past listening. Allison understood. They'd passed the point of no return a long, long time ago.

'Go!' Octavian shouted.

Charlotte needed no further urging. She leaped out of the helicopter, shapeshifting as she hit the open air and began to plummet. Allison expected an eagle or hawk but instead the girl became a sparrow, perhaps thinking herself small enough to reach the ground unnoticed.

Octavian took two running steps and dived, his hands seem-ing to ignite with emerald flame as he did. A shimmering disc of magic took shape beneath him and a moment later he was standing atop it, lowering himself to the ground as if riding an elevator to the ground floor. Allison turned to mist and drifted after them, spun away in the wake of the helicopter for a short time before she could descend swiftly to the ground, where they could all greet the horrors close up.

As she restored her flesh, she heard chanting, the voices of dozens of vampires raised in either worship or incantation. *Or both*, she thought with a shiver. Shrieks of devil-bats joined the chanting and the sound of retreating helicopters, but above the cacophony she heard her name and turned to see Charlotte running toward her, red hair flying in the breeze.

'The second chopper didn't explode,' Charlotte said, coming to a halt and immediately gesturing back the way she'd come. 'If there are survivors, they're not going to last long without help.'

Allison started rushing back in that direction with her. They hurried across sharp grass and past copses of trees.

'I don't get it,' Allison said. 'You were the one who didn't think I should care what '—'

'Medusa!' Charlotte said, shooting her a sidelong glance as they ran. 'In vampires alone we're outnumbered about fifty to one. If any of Metzger's people were on that chopper, their guns are loaded with Medusa bullets. We need those guns, need the toxin.'

Shouts came from up ahead, punctuated by gunshots that echoed through the night. The wreckage of the helicopter loomed and Allison heard rending metal and breaking glass as the pair of devil-bats that had survived their encounter with the machine continued to beat and tear at it to try to get to the human meat at its core.

'You think they have enough bullets to even the odds? Did you see the size of Cortez's coven?' Allison asked.

Charlotte replied but over the chaotic noises around them, Allison didn't hear the words.

'What's that?' she shouted, racing toward the helicopter and its attackers. She glanced at Charlotte, saw the outline of the girl's tattoos gleaming in the moonlight and the grim set of her jaw.

'I said, as long as Cortez dies before me, I don't care about the odds.'

'That's a cheerful thought.'

Charlotte scowled. 'It is to me.'

16

Lanquin, Guatemala

Allison and Charlotte raced toward the downed helicopter. One of the devil-bats crouched on the nose of the craft, shoving its snout through the shattered windshield, forcing its head deeper despite the jagged glass in the frame that dug into its pelt. One wing was torn and bleeding. Gunshots came from inside the chopper and the devil-bat's body jerked as bullets struck it in the head, but it only slowed a moment before redoubling its efforts.

The second one crashed into the side of the downed helicopter, then scrabbled with its claws at the door. The windows had to be broken but the opening was not large enough for it to do more than bite at it, trying to tear the metal. More gunshots punched into this one and it darted backward, then launched itself over the top of the wreckage to the other side, trying the same tactic there.

The one on the helicopter's nose screeched in triumph and screams rose as it dragged a soldier out through the broken windshield. It chewed him several times and then tossed its head back, trying to slide the man down its gullet.

Allison said nothing. The horror of the scene demanded the respect of silence.

'Fucker,' Charlotte growled as she dropped to the ground, transforming into a huge Bengal tiger, which bounded forward.

Tiger-Charlotte leaped atop the wreckage and kept going, jaws wide as she rocketed at the devil-bat's chest. Claws tore its flesh and she lunged for its throat. The devil-bat twisted, gouging the tiger with one of its horns and knocking her away. It bit the soldier in half and quickly swallowed as it crawled after the tiger, awkward on its broken wing.

Amateur, Allison thought.

Between one footfall and the next, she spread her arms and they became wings, growing and spreading wide as she took to the air, molecules reassembling and gathering others as she transformed from a woman to a devil-bat half as large again as the wounded thing dragging itself after Charlotte.

The tiger staggered to its feet, shuddering as Charlotte repaired her injury. Allison wondered what the hell Octavian had been thinking by bringing her into this battle. To one who could disassemble and reassemble herself from one shape to another, a wound was just another form and healing was no more difficult than shapeshifting. It should have been nearly instantaneous.

Charlotte turned, yellow tiger eyes flashing, ready to lunge at her attacker's throat. She never had a chance to leap. Allison attacked the creature, using her own talons to rake its chest and tear its wings. It screeched until she silenced it with a single dart at its throat, and then she turned toward Charlotte, just in time to see the tiger take to the air and transform again, mimicking Allison's own strategy.

The dead devil-bat twitched and bled at Allison's feet as Charlotte flew at the other one, which had continued to attack the wrecked chopper. The two creatures collided, falling to the ground in a shrieking mass of claws and wings and darting jaws, but at least the soldiers on the chopper were safe for a moment.

Allison alighted, molecules pouring into her human form again as she rushed over to the chopper, even as Sergeant Galleti kicked open the pilot's door and dropped to the ground. The Italian woman spotted her and a look of gratitude spread across her features.

'Help me,' Galleti said.

Allison reached her just in time to help a wounded soldier climb out of the wreckage, and others followed. There were six survivors, all Task Force Victor, and the last of them was Leon Metzger. Screeches and chanting continued, but the nearest commotion ceased and Charlotte came walking around the front of the downed chopper, apparently having killed the other devil-bat.

But there were others, Allison knew. A single upward glanced showed her well over a dozen, and she suspected there would be even more.

'Thanks for your help,' Metzger said, as Charlotte walked over to join them.

Allison studied the man a moment and then nodded. 'You're welcome,' she said. The past and its grudges seemed impossibly far away from them now.

Metzger had a gash on his face and his limp suggested he had torn something in his left leg, but he barely seemed to notice either. Galleti and the two others who had suffered only contusions and lacerations climbed back into the wreckage and started bringing out whatever weapons they could find.

'Where's Octavian?' he asked.

Allison frowned. She had barely had time to wonder what had become of Peter, but she knew that he must be all right. With all the sorcery at his disposal, she figured Octavian might well be the hardest person in the world to kill.

'I'm sure he's—'

The ground rumbled and she nearly lost her footing. A loud hiss filled the air, a static that built to a buzz, and as she looked around for the source she saw the wall of crackling blue light shimmer into being.

'Son of a bitch,' Metzger said, spinning around to watch as the walls went up all around them, perhaps a mile or so away in each direction.

They were practically at the epicenter of the sizzling magical barrier.

'I guess he's still alive,' Charlotte said.

'*Affanculo!*' Galleti barked. 'What is he doing, the idiot? He's trapped us inside with them!'

'Forget it,' Allison said, turning to Metzger. 'We've got one move here. If Cortez is pulling the strings, then we kill him. I'm guessing the Guatemalan troops we saw with all the trucks and the lights and the tanks don't have Medusa toxin, so you six are coming with me and Charlotte and we're going after Cortez.'

Metzger had a heart of stone, ice in his veins, and a soul made of leather, but even he laughed at this.

'You're out of your mind! Take a look around you!' he shouted, throwing out his arm like a ringmaster at Hell's own circus.

Devil-bats circled above, having spotted them. Allison saw them and knew the others had as well. The serpents would be crawling from the trench now and at least one of them would doubtless find them soon. And across the grassy, tree-spotted landscape, where the bright banks of lights had turned night into day, she could see the heads of the same two giants as they climbed from the gash in the flesh of the world, slowly, as if not quite awake. One of them had huge antlers and from the side its face looked like an open wound. These, she felt sure, were the death gods of the Mayans, the ones that Brother Simon had died to drive back to Xibalba . . . and one of whom he had subsequently become, at least halfway. A demi-god. An evil Hercules.

She had no doubt that Cortez wanted the same honor.

'I'm not blind,' she said, her voice carrying despite the chanting of Cortez's coven several hundred yards away, beyond a stand of trees.

'So you see that?' Metzger said, pointing to the antlered god, whose head alone was taller than the trees.

Allison sneered at him. 'Leon. Do your fucking job.'

Whatever panic had clutched at his heart, her words were like a slap in the face. He flinched, then blinked and looked around at his soldiers, who were watching him and whose lives were in his hands. Whose blood, most likely, would be *on* his hands. She saw the understanding dawn in his eyes, the knowledge that even if Octavian lowered the wall they were unlikely to escape this alive, which meant fulfilling their objective was the only possible goal.

'Sergeant Galleti,' he said, 'have you retrieved all of the weapons and ammunition from the chopper?'

Allison looked at Galleti, who raised her chin, nostrils flaring as she did her best to contain her fear. She carried two pistols and had a pair of automatic weapons slung over her shoulders. The others were all armed with multiple guns as well.

'Yes, Commander!' she snapped.

The others all stood at attention, save for the soldier who lay unconscious at their feet.

'Then we're moving out,' Metzger said. 'Fast as we can. The quicker we move, the better chance we have of reaching the vampires before the things from the breach can take us all out. And everybody watch the sky.'

He turned to Allison, who nodded.

'What about Creaghan?' Galleti asked, looking down at the unconscious soldier, whose head wound was caked with blood. The side of his skull had a dent in it that made Allison wonder how he was even still breathing.

'I'll carry him,' Charlotte said.

'What?' Metzger said.

The soldiers all stared at her, some in relief but others in suspicion, no doubt worried that she'd try to drink the dying man's blood.

'He isn't going to make it,' Allison said, hating the hard edge in her voice. 'One look and you can see that.'

'I know that,' Charlotte replied, then turned to meet Metzger's gaze. 'But you're not going to let us leave him behind as long as he's still breathing and we need to go.'

The commander looked reluctant, but then a devil-bat flew low above them and two of his soldiers fired at it, driving it away for the moment, and he knew they had no choice.

'Be careful with him,' Metzger said.

Charlotte ignored him, crouching to heft Creaghan easily off the ground. To a Shadow, the man weighed little more than an infant.

'Don't waste bullets that have the toxin,' she said. 'Don't fire at the things unless they're right on top of us. We're going to need every bit of ammo you have.'

Then they were running across open ground toward the line of trees that were all that separated them from Cortez's entire coven, the chanting growing louder as they ran. Allison felt a strange calm coming over her. She thought back on all of the people she had loved and who had loved her . . . all of the loves that she had lost. And yet she did not feel alone. Octavian was here, somewhere. And Kuromaku still lived, halfway across the world. They knew her as she was, not as she had been once upon a time. They had known her when Will Cody still lived and when he had loved her.

If there was a chance she might die before the sun rose, then it helped to know there were those who truly *knew* her. Knowing them helped her to know herself. Even if she died alone, she would not die lonely. That was something.

Charlotte ran at her side, the soldier, Creaghan, in her arms. The other TFV soldiers followed behind, with Galleti and the limping Metzger taking up the rear. As they ran, the tanks began shelling the trench, firing at ancient Mayan death gods so huge that even a direct hit would likely seem little more than the annoyance of a gnat.

In a gap between shelling, with the echoes of warfare rolling across the grass, Allison thought she heard something else there as well. In her mind she saw the serpents crawling from the trench.

'Watch your back,' she told Charlotte.

The girl did not reply, her grim gaze looking only forward, as if she could see Cortez through the trees and amongst so many other vampires.

Twice the soldiers fired skyward at a devil-bat that flew too low, but the things veered off without attacking, at least for now.

Then they had reached the trees, and Allison paused in the

midst of that cover to let Metzger and the other survivors of his unit catch up. One by one, they straggled in amongst the trees, staring at Charlotte for some reason. Allison waited on Metzger, watching him limp as she listened to the chants of the vampires, which were much louder now, and she knew the commander would have to stay here, taking cover in the trees. If he couldn't run, he couldn't stay with them.

But when Metzger joined her, he did not even glance her way. Like the others, his attention was on Charlotte. Frowning, Allison turned toward her. For a moment she did not understand, and then she saw the way that Creaghan lay in Charlotte's arms, his limbs hanging lifeless, his head lolled to one side.

'Put him down,' Metzger said.

Charlotte winced. Despite the hard edge she'd acquired, his tone had hurt her. She set Creaghan down beneath a tree and took a step back.

Galleti was kinder than her commander. The Italian woman put a hand on Charlotte's shoulder and whispered her gratitude. Charlotte nodded and then retreated to stand beside Allison as the soldiers shared a moment of silence. When Metzger turned he had a defiant glint in his eyes that made Allison realize there would be no leaving the commander behind.

'We'll bury him when this is done,' Metzger said, though it was clear he thought they'd all be dead before they could manage it. Dead and left to rot, just like Creaghan.

Again, Allison heard a rustling noise out in the grass behind them. She went to the edge of the tree line, peering back the way they'd come, and then jumped back a bit when she saw the serpent sliding by, perhaps thirty yards away. If it noticed them, or cared to kill or eat them, it gave no sign.

'They're far from the worst things trapped in here with us,' a voice whispered beside her.

Allison spun, baring her fangs before she realized she knew that voice. Octavian stood beside her, his face streaked with some dark substance but otherwise none the worse for wear. She thought it must be blood, perhaps from a devil-bat, but it seemed unimportant in that moment.

'Where the hell were you?' she asked.

His eyebrows went up. 'The beach. Where do you—'

Charlotte practically tackled him, throwing her arms around him and holding him tightly. Allison watched in surprise, wondering for just a moment if the young vampire had feelings for him. Then Charlotte backed away and punched Octavian in the arm, and Allison realized the girl did have an attachment to him, but it wasn't a romantic one. At the age of nineteen, she'd been dragged into a world of horrors, with no one to look after her, no figure of strength for her to turn to when life took an ugly turn. Somehow Octavian had become a kind of father figure to the girl.

Metzger and the other soldiers had finished saying goodbye to their dead comrade, and now they approached with grim and expectant faces.

'You've locked us in here,' Metzger said. 'You might as well have killed us all.'

Octavian pulled away from Charlotte and took a step forward to face him. Sparks danced in his eyes and along his arms to his fingertips, and Allison realized that they had been there all along, only fainter and barely noticeable. Flickers of gold and coppery red swirled around his hands.

'You'll recall I wanted to come alone,' Octavian said firmly. 'Even stole a helicopter to make it happen. Now here we are, Commander, and we all share the same goal.'

Metzger glanced at Sergeant Galleti, who turned away to hide her frustration and fear.

'True enough,' the commander said. 'But I'll tell you this much, Peter. You'd better have a plan.'

Octavian cocked his head a bit, staring at the commander.

'A plan,' he said, as if musing on it.

'Peter?' Allison asked. 'You do have some kind of plan, yes? Something other than just yelling "charge"?'

Octavian gave her his familiar, lopsided grin. 'Well, there is something I've been thinking about since before we left Philadelphia, but I wouldn't call it a plan.'

Charlotte gazed at him, mouth set in a tight line. Her hard exterior had crumbled for a second when he had rejoined them, but now it had begun to return.

'It's more like a prayer,' Octavian said.

With that he turned away from them and knelt on the soft ground beneath the trees. The magic crackling around his hands grew brighter, the gold and copper sizzling the air as it expanded. Allison and the others watched, first in wonder and then in surprise and consternation as he thrust his hands into the ground, the magic around his fingers allowing them to spear the earth, digging deeply into the soil.

He spoke so softly that Allison doubted anyone else was close enough to hear him.

'Come on, Keomany,' he said. 'I hope you're paying attention.'

Bratteleboro, Vermont

Deeply asleep and dreaming of her mother, Tori felt herself being shaken. Her head swayed on her pillow and her eyelids fluttered as she returned to consciousness. She groaned, reaching up to wipe at her mouth and cheek even before she recognized that the single voice in the room was addressing her.

'. . . up,' she heard. 'Tori, please wake up.'

Blearily, she turned in the darkness of her bedroom to see that Amber Morrissey knelt on the edge of her bed. Amber reached over her and started to shake Cat and for a moment Tori thought she might still be dreaming, because Amber didn't seem to notice that she'd woken up.

'What's wrong?' Tori breathed.

Amber recoiled, pulling away quickly, as if she had given up on waking Tori and was now startled to have accomplished it.

'Oh, God, listen,' Amber said, so anxious and ordinary that it was hard to accept that her features were an illusion, that beneath the glamour she was a beautiful monster. 'Something's going on. You've got to get up, both of you.'

Tori frowned but dragged herself up to a sitting position. She felt exhausted and fragile and just wanted to hide in her bed, but the world was in crisis and Tori and Cat had become inextricably linked to it through Keomany and the events of the past couple of days. And through Gaea, of course. They would do anything for their goddess.

She reached out and shook Cat. Tori sometimes had trouble sleeping, but Cat slept as if she had an off switch and she'd been powered down for the night. It would take more than a gentle nudge, so she shook harder.

'Wake up!' Tori said. 'We've got trouble.'

Cat began to mumble and her eyes slitted open, none too happy.

'We do, right?' Tori asked, looking at Amber. 'Have trouble?'

'That's just it, I don't know,' Amber said. 'We're not under attack or anything, but something's happening with Keomany.'

'I'm up,' Cat said, tired but awake now. She looked from Tori to Amber and back, then threw back the covers. 'Talk while I find pants.'

She didn't have to go far; the jeans she'd shucked off were in a neat pile on the floor beside the bed. Cat grabbed them and began stepping into them, even as Tori rose and grabbed the thin, pink-striped cotton robe that always hung behind the bedroom door. Sockless, she slipped her feet into the slim boots she wore while working. They were moving quickly now, but Tori still didn't know why.

'That's it?' she asked. 'You don't have anything more than "something's happening"?'

'Miles is talking to her,' Amber said, and for just a moment her face seemed to flicker, as though her glamour was slipping and the wine-dark, terrible beauty of her true visage might emerge. She was clearly troubled.

'And?' Cat said, irritated and unsympathetic. She pulled a sweatshirt on over the threadbare Mickey Mouse t-shirt she'd worn to bed, then grabbed a pair of old sneakers and didn't bother to lace them up.

'Well, he *was*,' Amber went on. 'But now he says it's like she's talking to someone else. She's babbling about healing wounds and about being a harbinger of rebirth. That's like a messenger, right?'

Tori glanced at Cat. 'Something like that.'

Cat led the way out the bedroom door and down the stairs. Amber had left the front door open, the autumn air gusting through the screen. They pushed out into the night and let the screen door slam behind them, hurrying into the orchard with the unfailing direction of those to whom it was home. It had rained and the ground was wet. Amber kept pace with them, though Tori knew she could have flown ahead, and in a handful of minutes they were racing toward the enclosure in the clearing where they had left Keomany to continue to grow and become . . . whatever she was becoming.

Tori dashed into the clearing with her beaded hair jangling and Cat right behind her. She ran to the opening in the enclosure. The rain had stopped and the clouds had begun to break up, letting through pools of moonlight. The thing that stood in one of those patches of silvery light looked at first like some exotic scarecrow.

'She's . . .' Cat began, coming to a halt beside Tori, who had barely realized that she stood frozen in place.

'Keomany?' Tori ventured, frowning as she studied the figure before them.

Though she had been lying on the ground before, rooted to the soil, this strange manifestation of Keomany now stood, but she did not lift her head to look at them. If she had eyes, she did not meet their gaze. The vines of her hair hung before her face and cast dark shadows that hid her features.

'Hey,' Cat said, taking two steps toward Keomany. 'It's us. Are you . . . are you in there?'

Tori turned back to Amber, who hadn't come any further than the opening in the enclosure. 'Was she like this before?'

'No,' Amber said. 'This is new.'

Nodding, Tori moved closer to Keomany, but warily. The creature – her friend – had not so much as twitched since they had arrived. Her first thought, that it was some kind of scarecrow, seemed unsettlingly accurate as she drew nearer and saw that Keomany's new body seemed to have withered since just a few hours before. Her new skin looked dried and her hair wilted, and an awful, hollow feeling touched her.

'There's something else,' Amber said, voice tinged with worry.

Tori turned to her again. 'What is it?'

'Miles,' Amber replied. 'He's not here.'

'The ghost is gone?' Tori asked.

'Goddess,' Cat whispered.

Tori turned around just in time to see Cat's fingers brush Keomany's cheek, which cracked like dried parchment with a puff of dust. The scarecrow's head sagged in that direction, then cracked under its own weight and fell to the ground with a dry thump.

With a gasp, Tori jumped back, staring at the shattered head. It reminded her of a long-abandoned wasp's nest, split and broken and dried out.

'Miles isn't the only one who's not here,' Cat said, looking up at Tori.

'Is she dead?' Tori asked. 'It doesn't make any sense—'

'Not dead,' Amber said, crouching at the scarecrow's feet now and poking around in the grass, revealing the thick roots that went deep into the ground. 'Just gone, I think. And wherever she went, it looks like Miles went with her.'

Languin, Guatemala

The trees seemed to stand guard over them as Octavian stood to face his allies. The magic around his fists diminished but still a frisson of static danced around his fingers and raced up his arms, and he could feel the same electric crackle in his eyes. The magic simmered inside him, almost as if it had some awareness of its own and knew that combat was mere moments away.

'Commander,' he said, turning to Metzger and his small cadre of TFV soldiers. 'You need to arm Charlotte and Allison.' He pointed at Sergeant Galleti, who was still draped with guns, including a pair of assault rifles. 'With those. They need as much Medusa ammunition as you can give them and the most firepower behind those bullets.'

'What're you planning?' Metzger said. He glanced at the dirt that remained on Octavian's hands and then at the place where the mage had been kneeling only moments before. 'What the hell was all of that? I'm not some amateur at this, Peter. If you've got some strategy, share it with me. Let me help.'

Octavian glanced at Allison and then Charlotte before turning his focus back to Metzger. He pointed at the place just to the east of their position, where the giant Mayan death gods were still emerging from the trench.

'With all due respect, Leon, you've killed a lot of vampires but you've never faced anything like those,' Octavian said. 'This situation we find ourselves in now . . . in this, you are an amateur.'

'Now hold on—' Metzger began, bristling at this embarrassment in front of his soldiers.

'If I had half a dozen more Shadows, I might feel good about our chances of killing resurrected gods,' Octavian went on. 'But this is it. Us. I trust your people to be able to protect themselves if those devil-bats come at them, and not to let the serpents eat them, at least as long as you still have bullets to defend yourselves with. But that's a game of attrition and you know it. What your people do best is kill vampires, so that's what we're going to do. It's not pretty, and it's not any kind of strategy. But you need to arm the hell out of the only Shadows we've got and send them in there with the element of surprise and a shitload of Medusa toxin. Take away the ability of Cortez's people to shapeshift, and you and your people can kill them easily.'

Metzger scowled and looked away. 'You can't be . . .' He rubbed at his eyes. 'You're serious? This is your plan? There have to be over a hundred vampires over there. There's no way two of your Shadows are going to be able to hit them all with toxin.'

'I can improve their aim,' Octavian said, watching as the magic misting from his eyes and dancing around his fingers turned a vivid cerulean blue. 'And with luck, I can take down the ones they don't get to put a bullet into.'

'Still . . .' Sergeant Galleti said.

Metzger exhaled, nodding heavily. He held up a hand to Galleti.

'All right,' the commander said. 'We don't have a lot of options. I just hope you're right and that when Cortez is dead, these breaches slow and you can seal them up again.'

'So do I,' Octavian said, brushing the dirt from his hands, magic crackling around them.

Looking at Galleti and the other TFV soldiers, he almost told them that things might not be as grim as they seemed, that he had an ace in the hole. But he wanted them to fight for their lives, without relying on magic to save them. He thought that Keomany had heard him, but he couldn't be sure she had, or if she would be able to do anything to help. All he knew was that every one of these breaches was like an open wound in the soul of the earth, and it had to be tearing Gaea apart.

She heard me, he thought. *I felt her listening.*

And yet thus far the trees were only the trees, the ground only the ground. The best he could do was to follow his plan. No matter what else happened tonight, Cortez must die.

'All right,' Allison said, stepping over to Galleti and reaching out for a weapon. 'Let's do this, before something crawls out of that pit and eats us.'

17

September 24

Languin, Guatemala

Despite all she had been through with him in the scant days since they had met, Charlotte did not know Peter Octavian well. She understood that he was a warrior and a man of honor, but that for a time in his life he had killed the way that vampires killed. She knew that some epiphany had made him seek a different path, and that though he was no longer a Shadow, he was a powerful magician, or sorcerer, or mage, or whatever the hell word people felt like using this week. Charlotte had seen Octavian in action, and when he combined his magic with his determination and skill as a warrior, he was a fearsome sight. Yet she was still just beginning to understand that he had more subtle magicks at his command as well.

Silent and swift, she set out from the cover of the trees toward the rings of chanting vampires with Allison on her left and Octavian on her right. Somehow, they managed to make her feel safe, even though she was far from it. Charlotte knew a little about Allison's background, enough to know that she had been a Shadow for a time measurable in years but not in centuries. She wondered if Allison could still remember her first kiss or the sound of her mother's laughter, if she could still recall the way her heart had quickened at a compliment or the excitement on the day that school let out for summer. For Charlotte, such memories were fresh and vivid. Her high school graduation had been a little over a year before and, despite all that she had seen and done in the intervening time – despite what she was – she still held on to a cherished fragment of her innocence, locked inside her like a rose under glass. She held a secret hope, one she barely admitted to herself, that she could preserve that fragment forever.

Could Octavian remember his mother's laughter? She thought not. And yet he had made himself a good man, and that gave her hope for her own future.

If you have a future, she thought.

'This is—' she began.

Octavian put a finger to his lips to shush her, as they ran across the open field. And he was right – nervous talking for the sake of talking was a bad idea right now – but she couldn't imagine the vampires could hear her over their own chanting and the thunder of the shelling from the tanks that had been caught inside the wall Octavian had put up.

And according to Octavian, Cortez and his coven wouldn't be able to see them, either. Charlotte reminded herself that they were not invisible, although if she understood correctly the end result of the spell Octavian had cast would be the same. As long as they moved steadily and did not meet the gaze of any of the vampires, they would pass unnoticed amongst the coven until they drew attention to themselves. Since shooting people with bullets tended to draw attention, the first shot she fired would effectively break the spell, but by then she'd be right in the center of the circle.

Only yards from Cortez.

She reminded herself that she had promised to leave Cortez's fate to Octavian and kept moving in broad, quick strides, never quite running but never slowing. In moments Charlotte, Allison, and Octavian passed through the outermost circle of vampires. Charlotte had to battle the temptation to look at their faces, to see if they had noticed the intrusion, but she didn't want to be the cause of breaking the spell too soon. Octavian had gone to the trouble of working his subtler magicks, and she wasn't going to blow it.

He had worked a second spell as well, one he had alluded to with Commander Metzger. Back in the trees, just before they'd set out, he'd had everyone – Shadow and human alike – lay out all of their ammunition on the ground and he had cast a spell upon every last bullet, ensuring that each would find its target. She and Allison had assault rifles filled with Medusa-laced bullets that were guaranteed to hit what they were aimed at. But now that she was walking amongst the vampires – passing through a second circle – she wondered how much help that would be. She heard their chanting in a language she did not recognize and she tried to count the feet to her right and left as she rushed past. Extrapolating, she realized there really were over a hundred vampires, and probably closer to one hundred and fifty.

A ripple of revulsion passed through Charlotte as she slid between two vampires in the second ring. They stank like offal, and she wondered where they had been sleeping during the daylight hours. One of them moved, raising his arms as an extension of his chanting, and she had to dart aside to avoid him touching her.

Reflexively, she glanced back at him and caught herself just before their eyes would have met. In that small glimpse, however, she saw that he was smeared in blood and human viscera and fluids, and she knew where the rank stench had come from. Though it now looked like a disaster site, this had been a tourist area. Anyone who had been here when the earth tore open had been slaughtered by Cortez's followers, their innards used as some filthy element of this ritual. Anyone who had come in response, people who had rushed here to help, had likely suffered the same fate.

Hate calmed her. Fury burned inside her, an engine to power her onward.

The ground trembled with the movements of the giant death gods. She glanced over to see that the antlered one now towered higher than the trees she had left behind. Even at that height, only the upper half of its body had emerged from the trench. It put its hands on the edges of the broken earth on either side of the crevice and tried to pull itself free, but for the first time Charlotte realized that it was stuck. Both of these enormous ancient beings were forcing themselves slowly from their own world into this one as if tearing free of a caul from their mother's womb.

Oh my God, she thought, staring at the impossibility of it all. *What am I doing here?*

As they passed through the third ring, almost at the center of the circle of vampires, she thought of her mother again, but suddenly Charlotte could not recall her face. Panicked, she tried to summon the memory of her mother's laughter, which had been so simple for her just moments before and now seemed impossible. The memory seemed just out of reach and she needed to hold on to it tighter than ever.

The world seemed to go still for a moment. The tanks had stopped firing and the chanting reached a pause. Even the wind dropped for a second. Only the last ring remained, perhaps twenty vampires in a tight circle, with a lone figure at the center who could only be Cortez. She would know him on sight, but even with the army lights glaring, the circle around him cast their shadows upon him.

The moment of stillness threw Charlotte off, and she hesitated. Stopped moving, just for a moment.

A moment was enough.

'Who the hell are you?' a vampire snarled, and she felt his hand clamp onto her bicep.

Nearby, she heard Allison swear, glanced over and saw Octavian catch her eye. She thought he would be angry but he only gave her a tiny, almost imperceptible nod and raised his hands, magic blazing and sparking around them in icy blue fire.

The world had held its breath. Now it seemed to shatter.

She twisted, tore her arm loose, raised her assault rifle and pulled the trigger. Bullets punched into vampire flesh as she ran amongst them. Arrogance and confusion combined were their worst enemies. They had not anticipated an attack from within and as she kept moving she saw the same expressions over and over – hunger followed by amusement at the idea of being shot, and then the horror etched in their faces as they realized the Medusa toxin was coursing through their blood.

Someone grabbed her hair and she tore free, darted and fell and rolled and popped up again. A huge vampire woman caught her by the shoulder, talons growing long, tearing her flesh, and

Charlotte turned and fired a bullet into her face . . . waited a second and fired again, killing her on the spot. She didn't want to waste Medusa, but if they took her down before she had hit as many as possible with the toxin then it changed the odds for everyone.

Shouts arose. The last of the chanting died as gunfire echoed. She heard Allison's gun barking off to her left, making its way around the circles. Lights flashed as Octavian tore through clusters of vampires and the air crackled with his power, seared by magic.

Somewhere not far off a familiar voice cried out and more gunfire erupted and she knew that Metzger, Galleti, and the others had arrived and were trying to kill as many of the Medusa-afflicted as possible.

And all the while, all she could think was *don't shift, don't shift, don't shift* – because none of them had been certain what might happen if she and Allison shapeshifted with their guns loaded with Medusa toxin. If she went to mist, she might never be able to shift back.

Abruptly, there was space around her.

Charlotte spun, aiming her weapon all around her, looking for targets. In the splashes of light from Octavian's magic, she saw that most of the figures that loomed around her were made of stone . . . the mage's own version of Medusa.

Half a dozen vampires were closing on her. Lifting the gun with a speed only her species possessed, she shot each one. Then, with Metzger's people too far away and the vampires too close, she shot them again.

Whipping around, on guard, she realized that she had made it to the center of the now-shattered circle. A pair of naked human corpses lay on the earth, wrists and ankles staked to the ground, torsos flayed open. From their faces she took them to be twins, one male and one female, perhaps fifteen years of age.

Beyond them stood Cortez, clad in black trousers and a simple white cotton shirt now drenched in blood.

With his sad eyes and wispy, pointed goatee and the black hair he wore at shoulder-length, he looked more like a poet than a monster. But that sad face lived in her nightmares with all the pain and humiliation she had ever felt. She switched her weapon over to continuous fire.

Cortez scowled at her in disgust. 'Prodigal. *You*, I did not expect. But perhaps I'll have use for you yet.'

Any other day she might have mustered up an insult or a profanity. Instead, she took aim and pulled the trigger, spraying a dozen bullets at his face and chest.

With a gesture, Cortez threw up a shield of purple-black light. When the bullets struck it, they melted in mid-air and dripped to the ground.

Charlotte stared, hope fading.

Cortez was a mage, like Octavian. She had never seen a hint of it before, never seen him do the slightest bit of magic, but there it was. Gunfire still punctured the darkness so she knew that Allison and some of Metzger's people were still alive, and so were some of the coven. But none of that mattered.

The only thing that mattered now was which mage was more powerful.

As if summoned from the ether by her thoughts, Octavian stepped out from behind the stone figure of a dead vampire, hands still burning with flame that had turned a rich, coppery gold.

'Hernan Cortez,' Octavian said. 'I thought you were dead.'

Cortez turned to face him, smiling. 'Aren't we all?'

*

Octavian burned with the magic inside him, felt it searing through his bones, eager to be unleashed. The sorcery within him had a clearer connection to his heart than to his mind, and the urge to incinerate Cortez on the spot nearly overwhelmed him. But he had seen the coven master use magic to shield himself from Charlotte's bullets – more than that, he could feel the dark magic seething inside Cortez, coiled and ready to strike – and he knew he had to be wary.

Hands at his sides, fingers splayed like a gunslinger at high noon, he moved two steps nearer to Cortez, careful not to stray too far from the nearest of the vampires he had turned to stone. They were statues now, frozen in death, but they could provide cover.

'Peter?' Charlotte said, her weapon still in her hands.

He ignored her, hoping his silence was message enough. They had passed the point where her presence could be helpful. More than anything he wanted her to go, to just take cover, but he feared what might happen if he gave Cortez any reason to think that her fate mattered to him.

'It's over, Cortez,' Octavian said.

'Is it?' the vampire mused.

Octavian could feel the magic charging the air between them. The ground began to crackle, grass to stick straight up as if electrified, and little particles of earth swirled, small stones floating off of the ground, vibrating.

Gunshots ripped the night sky, but fewer than before. Allison and the TFV soldiers were still fighting. The Medusa toxin and the element of surprise had given them a chance and they were making good on it. Devil-bats wheeled and darted overhead, but they seemed unwilling to come too close to Cortez. The ground rumbled and a terrible miasma of stink began to roil across the ground, rolling off of the death gods. Octavian saw a serpent coiled around the upper arm of the second of the gods, while black birds roosted on the antlers of the giant who had climbed three quarters of the way out of the breach.

Hell was breaking through into his world, but none of it seemed important to him now. The only thing that mattered was the cruelty of the creature in front of him. He heard shuffling over his right shoulder and knew that Charlotte had not gone far. She had taken cover behind one of the stone vampires.

'There's just one thing I . . .' Octavian began, and then faltered. He trembled with his hatred. Even speaking to Cortez made him feel sick. 'All of this . . . everything you did to distract me from your plans . . . killing Nikki, the breaches in Europe and India . . . If you wanted to keep me away, you'd have been better off doing nothing. Had you done nothing, odds are I wouldn't be standing here right now.'

The smile Cortez had been wearing slid away, leaving a malevolent intelligence that glittered in his eyes. When he sneered, his fangs glistened in the moonlight.

'Call it a roll of the dice,' Cortez growled. 'As for killing your mate . . . that was mostly for pleasure. If you'd heard the way she screamed—'

Octavian raised a hand, cold murder in his heart. Scarlet light sliced a broad arc across the darkness, aimed for Cortez's mid-section.

'Quiet,' he said, though what he really meant was, *Die*.

Cortez held up both hands and a sickly yellow light flashed around them, cleaving that scarlet arc in two so that it passed on either side of him, leaving him unharmed. He snarled, fangs bared, and sketched at the air with contorted fingers, drawing into existence a pair of silver silhouettes, like the ghosts of wolves, apparitions that dove through the air, jaws wide with silent hunger.

Octavian shook his head in disdain as he waved them away, the silver running like liquid mercury and vanishing as it touched the ground. He still had questions, things he did not understand, but he could live without knowing the answers. He required only one thing of Cortez.

Memories of his imprisonment in Hell seared his mind. Images flashed inside him of the abominations he had seen there, of the magicks he had studied and the torture he had endured as he learned, only to rise up and make demons scream. As powerful as he was, Octavian had locked those memories deeply within him, but now they came surging back, right alongside images of Nikki, lying dead in her hotel bed.

A single word burst forth from his lips, in a language never before spoken in the human world. He thrust his hands out and the magic that flowed from him had no color or form, none of the static most spells gave off. The lines that traced the air from his fingers to Cortez's flesh were like rips in reality, glimpses into a darkness this world had never known. Using such magic, Octavian had clawed at the skin of creation. Dangerous sorcery, but he would risk anything to put Cortez down.

The vampire screamed as those rips shot through him, and Octavian saw it as justice. He had opened breaches in the flesh of the world and now Cortez had been speared through by other dimensions. For a moment he hung on the air, impaled by slender fingers of another reality, and then they vanished and he collapsed to the ground.

The sky erupted with the sound of the tanks shelling the outside of the wall Octavian had erected around the breach. The ground trembled and he realized that his barrier must have wavered for a moment when he had attacked Cortez, giving the army hope that they could break through. But for their own safety he would not allow that.

'You think you understand magic,' Octavian spat, striding toward Cortez. The vampire looked pitiful, with his dark, mournful eyes and his sculpted goatee. 'Did you really think you could resurrect these ancient gods and they would make you one of them? That somehow you'd be king of the world?'

Cortez stared down at the holes in his chest and gut. They were knitting closed, but far more slowly than any ordinary wound. Octavian felt sure that the vampire would try to shapeshift and escape. Charlotte had not been able to shoot him with the Medusa-laced bullets, but Octavian would not allow Cortez to elude him.

But instead of trying to turn to mist the vampire looked up at Octavian, weak and disoriented but with a kind of lunatic pride in his eyes.

'I have no dreams of my own,' he whispered, and his voice seemed different. Somehow familiar. 'I'm a servant, not a king.'

Octavian froze, cocking his head to one side. He stood above Cortez, ready to kill him . . . ready to draw on the most ancient of magicks to do so . . . but the words made him hesitate. *Don't do it*, he thought. *Don't give him time to scheme*. But if Cortez was speaking the truth, if he was only a servant . . .

'Who do you serve?' Octavian demanded.

Cortez dragged himself up to his hands and knees, a wounded dog.

'The one king,' the vampire said, and a ripple of rancid orange light flowed from his hands across the grass beneath Octavian's feet.

Octavian jumped aside, but the spell did him no harm.

Cortez started to rise. 'The King of Hell.'

A rustling came behind him but Octavian turned too late.

Powerful hands clamped on his arms and shoulders and he tried to pull away. In the distant glow of military spotlights he saw the rigid gray faces of two vampires he had turned to stone, somehow reanimated by Cortez's magic. They held him tightly, stronger by far than he was, but Octavian struggled only a moment. Emerald light sparked and swirled around his fists and misted around his eyes. He needed no spoken words to turn them to rubble.

Still, in that instant he wondered. In a handful of days Cortez had gone from an unknown enemy to a renegade vampire to a lunatic with delusions of Hellish grandeur, but now to discover that he was a mage? Where had he learned such magic? It had taken Octavian a thousand years in Hell. Cortez might not be his equal, but he had skill and power.

Someone called his name and Octavian turned to see Commander Metzger stumble into the circle of stone vampires, helping Sergeant Galleti along beside him. Galleti clutched at her abdomen, and blood dripped from her hands. Both soldiers took in the scene before them and their eyes widened. As one, they separated and began to raise their weapons, turning them toward Cortez.

'Now, Prodigal,' Cortez spat, face etched in pain from the holes in his torso, where moonlight still shone through.

The words sank in just as Octavian released the concussive spell that had been building in him. The animated stone vampires shattered and crumbled to the ground even as he turned toward Charlotte. He saw her copper-red hair and those ice blue eyes glinting in the distant glow of the spotlights and the pale shine of the moon, saw the intricate design of her tattoos beneath torn clothing, and saw the way she raised the assault rifle in her hands and turned the barrel toward him . . .

Her body jerked like a marionette. Her eyes were wide.

'It isn't . . .' she said, unable to finish. She didn't need to. He understood.

Either now, or long ago, Cortez had made her his puppet.

The coven master grinned. 'Fire.'

'No!' Charlotte screamed, but her finger tightened on the trigger.

Octavian threw up a shield to defend himself and the bullets that struck it became smoke. But he heard the wet thump as they struck human flesh and the cry of pain and spun just in time to see Metzger stagger backward, his chest torn up by close range gunfire. Galleti had caught only one bullet, but it had passed through her neck and now she clutched at her throat, trying to stop the gushing blood, her torn-open abdomen all but forgotten.

He turned away even as Galleti dropped, moments from death. Charlotte screamed in sorrow and fury and she tried to fight her own body as she took aim at Octavian again. With a gesture and a muttered word he turned the gun to molten slag in her hands. Burning and melting, it fell from her grip.

Again he spun on Cortez, intent upon pushing him back into some parallel dimension piece by piece.

'*Who* sent you?' he screamed. 'Who is the King of Hell?'

Magic coursed through Octavian, straining to be unleashed, and at first he had assumed the tremors to be coming from within him. But then the ground shifted and roots thrust up from the soil, spawning vines that slithered toward Cortez.

Keomany, Octavian thought, distracted for a moment. *At last.*

Then he saw that Cortez had not noticed the roots and vines. The coven master no longer seemed interested even in defending himself, smiling as he tilted his head back to gaze at a part of the night sky beyond and high above Octavian.

A terrible moan filled the air, like the sky itself had a malevolent voice.

A dozen feet away, Charlotte screamed for him to run.

Octavian turned, a pit of dread in his gut as he realized that the trembling he'd felt had not come from inside him, but from the footfalls of a giant.

The resurrected, antlered death god towered so high above him that its head was beyond the reach of the army spotlights. But its eyes burned a hellish crimson as it bent down toward him, a huge, gnarled hand reaching for him. Viscous fluid dripped from its open, jagged maw and the slits in its face through which it breathed.

Octavian gaped at it. 'You have got to be fucking kidding me.'

He unleashed the magic that had been building within him in a single burst of concussive power straight at its hand and the death god snarled and clenched its fist, proving that he'd caused it pain.

But its other hand closed around him, ripping him from the ground like a child plucking a flower from her mother's garden.

Octavian cried out as it began to crush him. As he felt himself lifted higher into the darkness above the reach of the army's lights, the mad god tilted him enough that he could see Cortez down below.

Even from that height, he could see the vampire begin to applaud.

*

Siena, Italy

Kuromaku stood on the back of the military transport as the smoke demons pierced the air with their harpy's scream and bent their wings to make another diving attack upon the survivors who were attempting to retreat to the barrier that Octavian's surrogate mages had thrown up around Siena. On a tank forty feet away, the gigantic Kazimir stood like some mad king, shouting at the sky. The smoke demons would come again and Kuromaku would hack them apart with his katana. Kazimir would grab and break and rend them with his bare hands . . . or else his hands would pass right through them as if they were nothing more than mist. Either way the creatures would fall or drift away and then slowly coalesce and rise into the air once more. They weren't defeating the enemy, only buying time for the survivors to get to the magical barrier and, hopefully, slip through to the other side – and that was if the mages could maintain a doorway without letting the whole wall come down, setting the smoke things free.

Kuromaku only knew the warrior's way, but this was not a war he could win. Two Shadows and a handful of soldiers? They would be lucky just to get out of Siena alive, and the barriers that had been erected here and in France – and that must by now have gone up in India – were a temporary solution. The breaches would continue to worsen and widen if they weren't sealed. He knew Peter Octavian well enough to know that his old friend must have been confident that he could manage the task eventually, but meanwhile, Kuromaku felt useless.

If his sword could not kill his enemies, what was its purpose?

'There!' Kazimir shouted.

Kuromaku turned to see two of the winged things diving toward his transport. Several wounded soldiers lay in the back, seen to by Jessica Baleeiro, the doctor they had rescued but whose husband had been taken by the harpies. The smoke creatures plummeted from the sky, taloned hands extended hungrily, drawn to the men who were already bleeding – already dying.

No bullets flew, no gunshots pierced the early morning sky. The soldiers took cover as best they could in the open back of the transport. Some held on tightly to the framework of the truck's flatbed while others aimed their weapons, perhaps intending a final, useless attempt to defend themselves. Dr Baleeiro bent low over one of her patients, twisting toward Kuromaku with a worried look in her eyes.

She needn't have worried.

Kuromaku took two running steps, dancing over the prone forms of the wounded, and launched himself into the air. The katana whickered through the air, glinting with morning light as it hacked through the two smoke demons. He landed beside the doctor, turned and cut them again, then a third time, so that pieces of them spilled away into the air like a dispersing cloud of insects.

Something had changed. He had felt it in the resistance against his sword. And now as he watched the remains of the demons pulled away and swirled onto the wind, he realized that these two were not coalescing again. They were not rebuilding themselves.

Kazimir roared with delight and Kuromaku glanced over to see him rending one of the smoke demons to pieces, tearing off a wing even as he bent its head too far for it to survive. The giant was killing the thing.

'That's new,' Jessica Baleeiro said, standing beside him, hanging on to the framework in the rear of the truck.

'I don't understand,' Kuromaku said.

'I do,' she replied. 'I noticed it yesterday. They're more solid while the sun is out. Sluggish, too. If this means you can kill them . . .'

Kuromaku nodded slowly. 'It does. But there are only two of us, and hundreds of them, with more coming. There is no way that we can kill them all.'

'But this helps, right?' the doctor asked. 'We'll reach the wall?'

Kuromaku had no time to reply. He heard the horrid screech of the harpies again and turned, bringing his katana up. Three of the smoke demons were bearing down on them, jagged wings bent, charcoal flesh less transparent in the daylight. The truck bumped and swayed over rutted earth but he kept his footing, watching their descent, seeing every facet of his attack in his mind before he began to move.

'Stay down,' he said.

The katana felt warm with the memories of all of the battles they had fought together over the centuries. He flexed his fingers on the handle.

The ground shook beneath the truck. Dr Baleeiro grunted and tumbled on top of one of her patients, who cried out in pain. One of the soldiers swore loudly and gunfire stitched the morning light. Kuromaku had a moment to mentally curse the transport's driver, and then he realized that the shaking had not ceased. The ground beneath them had bucked and now continued to tremble.

'Holy shit!' Dr Baleeiro said, pointing.

Kazimir called out for him to look, but Kuromaku did not need the instruction. He stared in fascination as the earth itself erupted, rock and soil driving upward toward the three smoke demons and colliding with them . . . flowing over them . . . enveloping them and dragging them back down into the ground.

'What is it?' Dr Baleeiro called.

Kuromaku stared as huge roots the width of mature trees shot from the ground, spiked skyward to coil around other smoke demons and dragged them down as well . . . down beneath the earth. Where the demons were pulled underground, the soil glowed with a shimmering silver light, as though they were not being buried in the dirt so much as removed from the world.

And put where? he wondered.

'Are the mages doing this?' the doctor shouted at him. 'The ones who came with you?'

Kuromaku could not be certain, but he doubted that very much. This was something else. Something more.

Saint-Denis, France

The sun had risen but the barrier that kept the insect-like utukki demons trapped in the ruin of Saint-Denis also held in much of the smoke from the fires and devastation. Air passed through, but not without some resistance from the tense magic of the wall, and so the smoke filtered slowly. Inside the protective dome, what remained of Saint-Denis lay in shadow created by the smog of its destruction.

Santiago and Taweret had moved through the barrier as mist. There had been a trick to it, a slow persistence required, but they had managed the task and then drifted side by side through the air above the fallen roofs and broken steeples of Saint-Denis. Utukki crashed through the tiny windows of top-story garrets and burrowed into wine cellars in search of survivors.

As they floated swiftly across the city, Santiago heard the occasional scream as the demons found someone who had remained hidden until then. He had no muscles to flinch, but his consciousness recoiled at those screams as he imagined men and women or even children who had evaded the monsters so long that they might have believed themselves to be safe. But none of them would be safe until he and Taweret put an end to this.

Through the smoky haze, they drifted toward the Basilica of Saint-Denis. Most of the western façade had collapsed, eclipsing any chance of entrance through the front doors. But they didn't need to worry about the rubble, for this corner of the basilica had shattered so completely that the church below lay open to the elements and to intrusion from the air.

Something shifted in the rubble as Santiago descended through the jutting, broken beams and inside the pile of debris that had once been the city's most beautiful structure. With a thought, he rebuilt himself from mist to man, feeling the comfortable weight of flesh and bone. As malleable as it might be, he preferred the solidity. Santiago would never have admitted it, but the ephemeral nature of shifting to mist frightened him. The lack of substance made him feel like nothing, as if he weren't even real, and such thoughts were far more terrifying than demons.

Taweret appeared beside him, sculpted from mist and then flesh.

'This way,' she said, striding elegantly across the debris, as confident of each step as a dancer on a stage.

Santiago turned in a full circle, taking in the wreckage of the basilica. Columns jutted from piles of rubble and partial walls still stood, bearing the ornamentation and iconography that represented the wealth and faith of the reborn church. If the woman they were seeking really still lived – the woman this

Father Laurent said had been touched by the father of all of these utukki – that was its own sort of miracle.

Off to the left the rubble shifted again, but Taweret was already headed in that direction. She had noticed it as well. Now, as Santiago followed her, he saw a strange formation ahead, where the debris seemed to have been piled up around a wide hole like the mouth of an anthill. It was here that the rustling noise had come from.

'Taweret,' he said, attempting to warn her.

The demon wriggled from the hole. As it slipped free it turned on Taweret, a high, chittering noise coming from somewhere inside the creature. The utukki took flight, darting at Taweret, who caught it mid-flight and drove a fist through the hard shell over its chest, rooting around in search of delicate organs. The thing struggled for several seconds and then went limp, hanging from her arm, dead and leaking rank-smelling ichor.

Taweret glanced at him. 'Down?'

'Down,' Santiago confirmed.

Taweret did not hesitate. She lay on her belly on the debris anthill and slid headfirst down the gullet of the thing, into what could only be the utukki's birthing room. Santiago did not blame her; the idea of descending feet first into the hole without knowing what awaited him below was not a pleasant one, but he wasn't sure coming face to face with one of the utukki in such close confines would be much better.

She won't, he thought, suddenly sure of it. They were being born into the world, but there's an interval. He recalled Father Laurent had said something about it. They had a few minutes before the next one was born and he wanted to take full advantage of that.

Santiago swore silently as he lay on the edge of that anthill on his belly, then reached down inside the jagged gullet of the thing and dragged himself in. He might have tumbled straight down but he had the strength to keep himself from plummeting, and his clothes caught and tore on sharp edges of fallen stone and glass and shattered wood. As he moved deeper, the walls of the hole were slick with a viscous, putrid substance he could only imagine must be some kind of demonic afterbirth, and he lost his grip and slid the rest of the way.

Tucking his head up, he tumbled out of the hole onto the filthy stone of an ancient stairwell, where Taweret crouched in the gap between debris and steps, waiting for him. The edges of her lips crinkled in what might have been amusement at his oafishness, but he took no offense, certain he had looked foolish. Now he scrambled to his feet, glanced around quickly, and started down the stairs. She turned and had begun leading the way, grateful that lights of some sort still burned up ahead, either candles or oil lamps, deep in the cellar below. Shadows could see much better in the dark than humans, instinctively altering the composition of their eyes to adjust for anything but total darkness, but he was still glad of the light.

'Do you hear it?' Taweret asked.

Santiago frowned. He'd been so preoccupied with his own thoughts that he hadn't been paying enough attention. Now he heard the slow, ragged breathing that came from further down the stairs and the low moan of pain that interrupted it. A quiet laugh followed the pain, a sound of madness and surrender.

He shifted to see past Taweret, even as she continued down the steps, and he could see the young woman splayed in the stairwell. Her belly gleamed in the lamplight, distended and lined with blue veins. Her legs were wide open, thrust so wide she looked as if she had been split by a warrior's axe. Blood slicked her thighs and, holding his breath a moment, Santiago could hear the slow drip of it running down the steps. He had no idea why she was still alive.

Until he heard the shifting and the scraping even further below and looked past Taweret to see the massive demon lolling there at the bottom of the stairs. Its eyes gazed up at her in some kind of infernal adoration, and suddenly Santiago knew the woman remained alive because the demon wished it, because she was its host, mother to its children.

Taweret took a step beyond the woman.

'Stop,' Santiago said curtly.

She turned to him, frowning; Taweret did not take kindly to instructions.

'If it kills us both, who will release her?' he asked, gesturing to the helpless, damned madonna on the stairs.

Taweret seemed to look at the ruined woman for the first time. She stared a moment at the slick, bloody wound the woman's vagina had become and she shuddered, turning slowly away. Santiago noticed that the woman's belly had grown. As he watched, it bulged further and something squirmed inside. The woman seemed barely conscious, but with the demon-child moving within her, she opened her eyes wider and let out the most pitiful noise. Had her throat not been raw from days of this, it might have been a scream.

'What's your name?' Santiago asked, kneeling beside her.

'I don't want to know her name,' Taweret said, her accent thick. 'Do what must be done. Release her.'

'Someone should remember her name.'

'*Kill* her, Santiago. Kill her before she has to suffer the birth of another of those nightmares, or get out of my way.'

Santiago knew Taweret was right, and it was not as if he had ever hesitated to take a human life in the past, when the moment called for murder. It just troubled him that she might die without anyone ever knowing who it was who had suffered here.

Then her head lolled to the side and she looked at him with eyes that might have been pleading or might have been empty, evidence of a mind hollowed out and driven mad by torment.

A quick snap and it would be done. After that, they would try to kill the demon father. He only wished they had been able to bring the mages with them to try to take this curse from the woman, but they would likely never have made it all the way to the basilica alive.

'I'm sorry,' he said, reaching for her throat.

The world shifted. The stairs cracked and buckled and thrust upward, throwing Santiago and Taweret against the wall. The damned madonna rolled to one side and slumped and slid down half a dozen steps, much closer to the demon that waited in the crypt below.

'What is—?' Santiago managed, before the ground surged and bucked and split again.

Pieces of broken masonry rained down overhead. A chunk struck his shoulder, breaking bone that he reknitted instantly. He heard a terrible, ragged, wheezing scream and looked down to see that a massive piece of stone and mortar had crushed the woman's legs. More than ever, mercy demanded that he take her life, but even as he started downward, Taweret staggered in front of him.

'I'll do it,' she said, leaping the distance and alighting right beside the broken woman.

The demon moved, lurching to its feet and then practically gliding up the stairs toward Taweret.

Santiago shouted for her to defend herself, but he needn't have bothered. Before Taweret could even turn, the ground shook again and thick roots burst up through the shattered steps, wrapped around the demon and began to haul it down into a hole that appeared in the stairwell. For a moment he thought the steps had fallen away into some kind of abyss, but then he saw the way the darkness down in that hole shimmered and flexed and flowed, and he knew that it was not a hole at all.

It was a portal.

The twisting roots thrust the demon down into that portal as if feeding it into the ravenous maw of another world.

Languin, Guatemala

Octavian turned the antlered god's eyes to stone. It started with pain, as his ribs began to crack in its grip. The death god raised him up, a hundred feet off the ground, and studied him with the cruel purpose of a dark-eyed child bent on tearing the wings off of insects. Octavian couldn't breathe and he felt a couple of ribs give way, and as the pain roared through him the magic erupted from him like a scream. One of his arms was pinned beside him but the other remained free and he lifted his hand and a bolt of vivid light lanced from his fingers. He gave no conscious thought to the spell but some unconscious part of him chose, and as the antlered god jerked backward, trying to twist his face away from the attack, that emerald lightning struck its eyes.

The death god's eyes went dry and dark for a moment, then solidified to cracked gray stone. Its head drooped, dragged down by the new weight of its eyes, and it used its free hand to reach up and scrape at its eyes like an animal, perhaps thinking something had obscured its vision instead of taken it away completely.

It froze, chest heaving with grunts of anger and confusion, nostrils flaring. Short of breath, black spots in his vision from oxygen deprivation, Octavian tried to muster up another attack. His thoughts whirled, searching for any spell that might work on a demon such as this. Attack magic – some simple concussive blow – would do nothing. Monsters this ancient and powerful were not as affected by simple magicks so he needed something else. But his thoughts raced and focus eluded him. The black spots were not just on his eyes but in his mind. Pain burned in his chest and back and he could hear his own internal voice screaming in his head and he knew any second the antlered god would put two and two together and realize that the tiny, fragile thing in its grasp was the one who had made it blind.

It started to tighten its grip.

'Peter, strike now!' a voice cried.

His vision fading, he looked up to see Allison; she dropped through the air, shifting from falcon to female overhead, and lunged at the death god's throat. Moonlight glinted off of the long talons that her hands had become, just before she landed and thrust them like daggers through its flesh and began to slice and tear.

Its grip loosened a fraction, giving Octavian room for a single breath. In that instant he thought of Hell and the most primal of the magicks he had learned there, in its deepest pits. Dragging his other arm free, he clapped his hands together and held them out in front of him, as if he might dive upward out of the antlered god's grip.

The magic that surged through him seared his bones and he screamed as it built into a raging ball of silver-black energy around his joined hands. It felt as if he were tethered somewhere, like some umbilical still connected him to Hell, and the maelstrom of infernal power that roiled there came flooding up through him. For the second time that night he spoke a language known only to the first beasts of Hell.

The death god reached its free hand to drag Allison from its neck, but she hung on, ripping open a long flap of flesh. Thick, dark ichor spilled from the wound. The god clenched its fist in reflex and Octavian felt his broken ribs stabbing him deep inside. Grinding his jaws together he managed to grunt the final syllables of that spell and a shaft of silver-black light erupted from his joined hands. That light lasted only a moment before it vanished, revealing a gash in the flesh of reality, a rip that showed a glimpse of another dimension beyond.

That bolt of nothing punched a hole through the death god's cheek, up through its head and out the top of its skull, right between the antlers. Octavian's arms dropped and he had a moment to see the rip in the world healing, reality flowing back into the breach, and then the death god began to collapse. He saw Allison leap into the air and shift back into a falcon even as the god's hand fell open, releasing him.

Octavian did not flail as he plummeted toward the ground. He breathed evenly, forcing away panic and pain, and contorted his fingers to summon a sphere of emerald light. His fall slowed gently and then ceased completely, and he found himself hanging a dozen feet above the circle of vampires he had turned to stone, cradled delicately in the grasp of his own magic.

The stone vampires woke something in his mind.

Cortez! he thought, heart flooding with hatred.

Exhaling, he summoned a healing magic that bathed his body in a golden mist, and as he descended to the ground he could feel his ribs knitting back together. A pleasant heat replaced his pain. When he alighted, he was himself again and he spun around in search of Cortez, watching the shadows around the vampire statues.

'You bastard!' Octavian snarled. 'Where are you?'

The flap of wings made him twist around, ready to burn a vampire bat from the night sky, but it was not Cortez attacking. The falcon cried out and spread its wings, its flesh expanding and reconfiguring, and Allison landed on her feet beside him.

'Over there,' she said, indicating a statue to their right.

He gave her a small nod and felt the strength of the bond between them. They had never been lovers but she might well be the best friend he still had in the world. Along with Kuro-maku, she was the closest thing he had to family.

Side by side, they stormed across the field in the brightness of the army's lighting array. A horrible screeching came from above and Octavian glanced up to see a devil-bat swooping toward them. Before he could even defend himself, the ground shook and a thick vine thrust from the earth, whipped into the sky to coil around the monster, and dragged it down into a shimmering patch of darkness, which closed up again the moment the devil-bat had been fed into it.

The ground continued to shake and Octavian glanced back to see vines wrapping around the corpse of the antlered god and drawing it down into a shimmering hole in the ground. A root shot skyward, twined around a giant serpent, which flailed as the root twisted more tightly and then dragged it back down.

'What the hell is going on here?' Allison demanded as they raced around the stone vampire.

Octavian did not need to reply. The answer waited for them amongst the cracked stone vampires. Allison staggered to a halt.

'Holy shit,' she muttered. And then a small laugh bubbled up from within her. 'Keomany?'

Three people stood in the clearing ahead of them, dark silhouettes against the brightness of the army's lights. Charlotte's copper-red hair gleamed. Her clothing was torn and ragged but she had passed the point of caring. Cortez did not so much as stand but hang erect, propped into an upright position by the vines and roots that bound him and wound around him. The holes that Octavian had shot through him had not yet healed, as if pieces of him had been shunted into a parallel reality. Octavian thought that might be precisely what had happened.

Keomany stood with them, a woman of leaf and husk and thorn, unsettling and yet strangely beautiful. As Octavian and Allison raced up toward them, Keomany turned and he saw the pale, translucent phantom that hovered behind her.

'Is that a—' Allison began.

'Ghost, yes,' Octavian replied.

Then they were all together. Once upon a time Charlotte would have hurled herself at Octavian in celebration of their survival. Now she only glanced at him with haunted eyes and turned back toward Cortez as though she thought he might somehow still be manipulating them all.

The ground rumbled and roots tore devil-bats from the air. Several hundred yards away, a forest of vines and roots seemed to be overrunning the huge chasm in the ground, sewing the breach together as if it were a torn seam. The ground itself appeared to surge and flow, and it all seemed to require no more effort from Keomany than maintaining the magical shield around their perimeter did from Octavian.

He stood before the elemental, the earthwitch reborn as something new and perfect, ignoring Cortez. Octavian stared into her eyes. They were not human eyes and yet he felt sure he could see her essence there.

'It's really you,' he said.

Her smile managed to be both beautiful and grotesque. 'It's me,' she said, and her voice was like the wind scuttling autumn leaves across the grass.

'I told her what we're facing,' Charlotte announced, still staring at Cortez.

Octavian studied Cortez, this vampire who had been his secret enemy for so long. Then he turned and reached out to Charlotte, touched her arm and found her skin ice cold.

'What are you waiting for?' he asked.

Charlotte blinked and turned to stare at him in confusion. 'Say that again?'

'Why haven't you already killed him?' Octavian said.

Trembling with emotion she tried desperately to hide, Charlotte glanced at Allison as if the other Shadow might come to her aid.

'You?' Charlotte said, pulling away from Octavian's touch. 'We were waiting for you. He killed Nikki.'

'Nikki was my friend,' Keomany said, as if this fact had been lost to her and now bubbled up from the depths of her memory.

Octavian glanced at Cortez. With Medusa toxin coursing through him, there would be no escape for him, but he did not plead for his life. He hung there, glaring with bitter hatred and a tinge of madness in his eyes, and listened to them speak of his execution with imperious disdain. Octavian believed his presence tainted the very air around them, that he was a stain on the world that needed to be removed. The desire to burn him, to eviscerate him, to break his bones and make him suffer, made Octavian's hands twitch and a familiar, brutal magic swirl around his fingers.

He turned to Charlotte. 'I loved her. In my heart, at least, she was my wife.'

Charlotte gazed at him, sharing his pain. 'I know.'

'But Nikki's pain is not my pain. What he did to her was done to her, and she is dead. But you're still alive, Charlotte, and I want you to be able to live, now. If destroying Cortez will help you do that . . .'

Her grim expression cracked and he saw the pain and heartbreak of the teenage girl she had been showing through the hard veneer she had adopted.

Another devil-bat screamed across the sky above them only to be dragged from the air by whipping vines and pulled into a portal in the earth, which vanished after swallowing the monstrosity. The ground still shook, but there were fewer and fewer of the demons from the breach.

The ghost of Miles Varick drifted toward him, manifesting more fully. If not for the bright lights, he would have looked almost solid.

'That's not the only reason we waited for you,' the specter said.

Octavian glanced at Keomany.

The elemental nodded. 'Miles reached into the vampire—'

'He what?' Allison asked.

Octavian glanced at her. 'I explained this to you. The darksoul in vampires, the part of you that's demon . . . he can rip it out.'

'He eats it,' Charlotte said, her tone almost a warning to Allison.

Allison swore softly, glancing at Miles warily now.

'It's not any different from you drinking human blood,' the ghost said, his phantom figure fading slightly.

'Enough,' Octavian said, turning to the ghost. 'What made you stop?'

Miles drifted nearer to Cortez. Octavian saw the ghost run out his spectral tongue and lick his lips. He pushed his hand through Cortez's chest, the ghostly substance of him passing harmlessly through flesh and bone, and tugged out a fistful of squirming, oily black mist.

Cortez roared in pain, or perhaps it was anguish.

The ghost turned to look at the rest of them, focusing on Octavian. 'There's more than one of him.'

'More than one darksoul?' Allison asked.

'Yes,' Miles replied. 'One is his, but the other is an intruder.'

'How is that even—' Charlotte began.

'Would you like to see it?' the ghost asked.

Octavian took a step closer, staring at Cortez. 'Absolutely.'

Thrusting both hands into their captive vampire, the ghost of Miles Varick seemed to be twisting and tearing at something inside him. Cortez screamed again as Miles drew out one hand, forcing the separation of Cortez's darksoul and the intruder, the parasite that had taken up residence there.

Octavian stood riveted by the sight. He had only ever seen a vampire darksoul up close once before, and it had been his own. The thousand years in Hell had aged him to the point where he had retreated inside a strange cocoon, within which he underwent a process no other Shadow had ever undergone, his flesh separating itself from the two external forces that had so deeply altered him. The sliver of divine spirit that had been inside him had ascended into some kind of Heaven and the demonic part of him – the darksoul – had plotted against him and been destroyed.

Now that Miles dragged the darksoul out of Cortez, the last thing Octavian expected was to recognize it.

'No way,' Allison breathed.

Keomany turned to stare at her, then seemed to notice the look on Octavian's face.

339

'You know this creature?' she asked.

Charlotte spoke, asking what was going on, but Octavian barely heard anything his companions said. As far as he knew, he had been the first Shadow to be imprisoned in Hell for so long, the first to undergo the metamorphosis which divided the three elements of a vampire's existence into individual entities. But he knew of at least one other Shadow who had been lost in Hell . . . who had been a part of the effort to rescue Octavian from the inferno and had been lost there and, out of necessity, left behind with The Gospel of Shadows.

'Lazarus,' Octavian whispered.

'No *fucking* way,' Allison said.

The darksoul hissed and lunged at Octavian, twisting its insubstantial form in the grip of Miles Varick's ghost. It snapped and hissed again, lashing out with long, mistlike claws. The ghost grabbed the darksoul by its wrist, opened his mouth impossibly, inhumanly wide, and bit the hand off halfway up the forearm.

Opening its mouth in a silent scream, the darksoul turned its hate-filled glare upon Octavian. Savage as it was, there was intelligence there, and it was consumed with hatred. Behind the ghost and the darksoul, Cortez still hung from the vines and roots that held him up, but he dangled there now like a broken marionette, moaning softly.

'What . . .' Octavian began, but he went silent as he recognized the foolishness of any question that might follow.

Lazarus had sacrificed himself for Octavian, traded his own freedom to return Octavian from damnation for the good of humanity and Shadows alike. He had been in Hell now even longer than Octavian had been. Of course he had undergone the same metamorphosis. But if the darksoul was here, where was the divine part of Lazarus . . . and where the human?

Was the flesh and blood man trapped in Hell? The question horrified Octavian more than any other he had ever considered. As a Shadow he had barely survived there. As a man . . .

No. He must be dead.

'Is Lazarus still alive?' he asked, knowing it was impossible. Praying it was impossible.

The darksoul began to laugh, twisting and lunging to escape the grasp of the ghost. It snapped its jaws like a mindless beast, but Octavian knew that it was not mindless. If it did not speak, it *chose* not to speak.

'I don't understand,' Charlotte said. 'Was this thing inside of Cortez all the time, pulling the strings?'

'I was thinking the same thing,' Allison replied. 'Did Cortez kill Nikki, or was it this . . . whatever we want to call it?'

Octavian remained silent. He turned to study Keomany, looking at the smooth red apple-skin that created the illusion of flesh on some parts of her body, though her arms were little more than tightly woven leaves and branches and husks that looked like corded muscle over bone, but with the skin stripped away. Keomany stood inhumanly still, swaying slightly in the breeze.

'What do you—' he began.

The elemental turned her face away from him and he frowned. The ground still trembled and the vines and roots still shot from the ground in the distance, pulling demons down into shimmering patches of earth that could only be doorways into a parallel realm. Gaea had brought Keomany back to life as her harbinger, her avatar, and perhaps her warrior, and Keomany had begun to rid the world of the monstrous evils that did not belong here, pushing them out of this reality entirely, perhaps back to where they had begun. Through Keomany, Gaea had begun to heal and cleanse the world by force.

But part of Keomany was still just the woman from Vermont who sold handmade candies at her confectionery shop, Sweet Somethings. Part of her remained human, and Octavian felt sure it was that part of her that could not meet his eyes.

'Keomany, look at me,' he said.

Gazing into the distance, toward the banks of lights the Guatemalan army had brought in, she behaved as if he had not spoken at all. Frustrated, Octavian looked back at Miles's ghost and the darksoul that squirmed in its grasp. Beyond them, Cortez looked sickly and barely conscious, as if at any moment his body might collapse in upon itself. He seemed hollow, now.

Charlotte stepped nearer to the ghost and the squirming darksoul. Confusion etched on her face and pain in her eyes, she studied the thing's slim, sinister features. It flowed like black silk, but Octavian knew that face and it belonged to Lazarus.

'Was it Cortez who killed me?' Charlotte demanded, her voice cracking. 'Who raped me and tortured me? Or was it *you*?'

The darksoul only smiled.

'It's not going to tell you anything,' Allison said. 'And how can we threaten it? What can we possibly do to it?'

Octavian narrowed his eyes in thought, then turned to look at Miles. The ghost wore a thin, empty smile that had a tinge of madness and a sort of furious hunger with which Octavian was all too familiar. The ghost studied the lunging, struggling darksoul with predator's eyes, but he would not act as long as Octavian needed the thing alive.

Bitter fury roiled inside Octavian. He had wanted to avenge Nikki, and Charlotte had sought her own vengeance, but now they no longer knew how to define that vengeance. Kill Cortez? Destroy the darksoul?

He glanced at Charlotte, again saw the pain in her eyes, and knew there was a simple answer: do both.

'Miles,' Octavian said, turning to the ghost. 'Are you hungry?'

The ghost quivered with anticipation, but there was a trace of self-loathing in his eyes.

'Always,' he replied.

'It's yours.'

Miles Varick's ghost did not ask for elaboration. Opening its jaws wide, the hungry specter darted forward and tore a chunk out of Lazarus's darksoul. It did not cry out as the ghost ripped it apart, feeding itself shreds of silken darkness, but Octavian saw the panic in its eyes, and then nothing.

'What the hell is this?' Allison shouted.

Charlotte cried out for the hungry ghost to stop, but it was over in seconds. For her part, Keomany did not even glance up. She still would not meet Octavian's gaze.

'Peter, what the fuck?' Allison snapped. 'We need to know—'

'What?' he interrupted. 'How it got inside Cortez? Why it was there? Whether it was controlling Cortez? You saw its eyes, Allison. You know as well as I do that we weren't going to get any of those answers. Here's what we know: Cortez, or that damned parasite, was taking orders from someone else that he referred to as the King of Hell. At the end of the day, that's who we want. That's where we get our revenge, not to mention putting a stop to all of these incursions, because it sounds like whoever this self-proclaimed king is, he's got a lot worse planned than what we've seen so far.'

'And how do we find all of that out?' Charlotte demanded with a snarl that bared her fangs.

Octavian pointed at Cortez, still suspended upright by the

vines Keomany had summoned. The vampire was blinking and glancing around groggily, as though waking up from some enchanted slumber.

'We ask him, see if any of that information is in his head,' Octavian said, before turning to Charlotte. 'And then you kill him.'

Charlotte and Allison exchanged a look, and then Charlotte smiled.

'I can get behind that.'

Octavian nodded and started toward Cortez, but as he did he heard a whisper beside him and turned toward Keomany. He frowned, certain she had spoken, but still she did not so much as glance at him. Her words had been barely audible.

'Keomany, did you say something?'

Slowly, with a dry rustle, she turned her inhuman gaze upon him. For the first time he saw emotion on that strange face, in the pinch between her brows and the narrowing of her eyes and the disturbed wrinkling in her smooth apple skin.

Octavian shuddered, unsettled by her regard.

'I said "I'm sorry",' she rasped.

He frowned, not understanding, even though he felt the ground shaking beneath his feet. Even though he'd noticed that the last of the devil-bats seemed to be gone, and the serpents as well.

Then a thick root thrust up from the earth beneath Cortez and twined around the vampire, joining the other roots and vines that had held him upright. The ground beneath him shimmered and Octavian saw a distant blackness there, as if the soil had become a window into nothing.

'No!' Charlotte screamed, and she dove for Cortez with her arms outstretched, even as the roots began to drag him down through that portal and out of their world.

Allison grabbed her, wrapped her arms around Charlotte and held her there so that she would not tumble into whatever limbo lay beyond that shimmering nothing. Octavian had taken a single step forward before he had brought himself up short, knowing that there was no chance. He could only watch as Cortez was dragged down by the twining, tugging roots, and as the shimmering dissipated and the vines and roots withdrew, leaving only solid ground.

Octavian turned and grabbed Keomany, dragging her toward him, forcing her to look at him. Magic surged inside him, crackling and misting and rolling off of him in waves.

'What the *fuck* are you doing?' he demanded.

This time she did not look away. 'What must be done.'

Saint-Denis, France

The stairs cracked beneath Santiago, the stone shifting. A chunk of masonry crashed down a few steps higher. Anger flared inside of him. He would not be killed by falling stones or quaking earth, but he and Taweret had come to stop more utukki from being born and he refused to fail.

Down below in the cellar crypt, the hole that had appeared in the floor had vanished. There were cracks but the shimmering portal into which the demon father had been drawn had disappeared. Roots whipped about, sliding on the stone floor even as they began to withdraw into the cracked floor.

'What is this?' Taweret called to him over the groan and rumble of the earth. 'Something the mages have done?'

Santiago didn't know the answer and had no time to consider it. A huge slab of stone crashed down from the ceiling at the bottom of the steps and the tremors showed no signs of ceasing. The woman on the stairs cried out, her belly distended, another utukki only moments from birth. He'd thought the removal of the demon father might stop more from being born, but her screams told him otherwise. Without the mages, there was only one way to end this and he could not count on falling masonry to do the job. Before she was buried here, Santiago had to save her from her own, personal Hell, and to save her, he had to kill her.

He knelt by her, stone cracking beneath his knees. Once, he felt sure, she had been beautiful. Now she was pale and sweating and dirty and her eyes rolled back to show bloodshot white as she wept and moaned.

'I'm sorry,' he said.

The stairs shook and with a loud crack, split open wider. The roots shot up through them and wound themselves around the girl, even as the edges of the crack began to shimmer and a silver-black sheen filled the gap like some kind of liquid mirror.

'No!' he shouted, reaching out to grab hold of her arm as the vines pulled her down inside that portal.

Santiago thought of her spending an eternity in some other world, some other Hell, giving birth to utukki forever. He couldn't let her meet that fate alive and he tried to hold her back, hauling on her arm, reaching down to hook a hand beneath her other arm. Then one of the vines wrapped around his wrist and tugged. He fought it, tried to tear himself away, but beneath him the step cracked again and another portal began to shimmer into existence. Thick vines shot up, snaking around his waist and throat and yanking downward.

He tried to shapeshift, but his body would not respond to his thoughts. Something in the touch of those vines, some poison bit of magic, had confused his mind. Panicked, he turned toward Taweret just in time to see her dragged down through a third portal.

'No!' Santiago roared, until the vines choked off his words.

His fingers scraped smooth stone, searching for something to hold onto, and then he felt himself falling.

He could see the silver-black edges of the portal diminishing above him, and then that limbo darkness swallowed him up.

Siena, Italy

Dr Jessica Baleeiro watched Kuromaku's hand vanish into the earth. At the last moment, he dropped his katana and tried to find purchase on the rutted ground, but another root twisted around his arm and yanked it backward, and then he was simply gone. The shimmering darkness that had opened up beneath him faded as if it had been nothing more than a mirage, but what Jess had seen had been no illusion. The samurai had been taken, not just dragged into the ground but, if her glimpse into that strange pool had been any indication, out of this reality entirely.

The gigantic Shadow – Kazimir – had also been taken, and now she fell to her knees and looked out over the smoking ruin that had been made of the road and the hill and of the city of Siena in the distance. No more dark shapes darted across the sky. The smoke demons were gone, leaving death and destruction in their wake.

Stillness reigned.

The breach had been sealed. The demons had been removed.

And so had the vampires.

*

Languin, Guatemala

Octavian held Keomany's wrists, thorns drawing blood from his palms and fingers. Charlotte cried out as roots thrust up from the ground and dragged her down into a shimmering pool of mirror-smooth blackness that reflected the moonlight. Allison fought, tearing free of whipping vines, and tried to run for it, beginning to shapeshift into a falcon . . . to take flight. Other roots thrust high, blocking her path. One impaled her and she screeched in pain even as the roots cocooned around her.

Shouting, Octavian released Keomany and turned, magic boiling around his hands. Pale blue light churned around his fists and lanced outward, slicing through vines and roots, trying to set Allison and Charlotte free.

One of them struck him from behind, a dagger-sharp root that punched through his left side. Staggering forward, the pain distracted him for mere seconds, but they were enough. As he bled and fell to his knees, the roots encircled him tightly, holding him down. No portal opened beneath him but once again he felt his ribs constricting, bones snapping. With a cry of rage he unleashed a burning magic that scorched the roots to ash.

Freed but injured, with no time to waste on healing himself, he turned to do the same for his friends . . . just in time to see Allison's face looking up at him, her eyes pleading as she vanished inside that mirrored portal, just before it closed. Of Charlotte, there was no sign at all.

Octavian rounded on Keomany, letting that destructive magic blaze around his fists and leak from his eyes.

'Make it stop!' he roared at her, the magic radiating out of him. 'Bring them back!'

Keomany had become something inhuman, yet he could still see the emotion that tore at her. Those bizarre plant eyes were full of sorrow.

'I can't,' she said. 'I'm sorry, Peter, but this is what Gaea wants. Only earth magic from now on. Nothing from Hell, or any other dimension.'

Octavian reached out a hand and the magic flowed out of him, wrapping as tightly around Keomany as the roots had twined around him moments before. With a thought he lifted her from the ground, hearing the crinkle and snap as bits of her broke inside.

'Refuse her!' he shouted, mind a maelstrom of unwelcome thoughts of his friends suffering the torments of one Hell or another. 'Bring them back or I swear to you—'

'I'm sorry,' Keomany said . . . and then she went limp, the light going out of her eyes.

Only then did Octavian see the long roots that trailed beneath her, connecting Keomany's body to the earth . . . to Gaea.

'No!' he shouted, shooting a lance of green light from his left hand, snapping those roots and severing her connection to the soil.

Too late.

The figure he held aloft with crackling magic had become little more than an effigy, a dry husk devoid of any trace of her consciousness. The way it hung in the air, withered and stiff, he knew that Keomany had fled that body and returned to the earth.

When he dropped his hands and let the husk fall to the ground, it cracked open and emitted a puff of dust, dry and papery and dead.

Octavian stood alone, bathed in the brightness of the army's lights. He heard the wind in the trees not far away and only then realized that the rest of the noise had died away. The ground had ceased its trembling, the tanks had stopped their shelling, there were no screeches overheard from devil-bats . . . because there were no more of them. All of the things that had emerged from the breach had been forced from this reality, with only the collapsed crevice that had once been the Languin Caves as evidence they had ever been there at all, a scar on Gaea's perfect flesh.

Alone.

Raging and grieving and confused, he thought of Allison and Charlotte and then his thoughts strayed further afield, wondering what had become of Kuromaku and Santiago and the others and knowing – deep in his heart – the startling truth. They must also be gone. All of his friends, nearly all of those left in the world who cared about him at all, were no longer *in* the world.

'Peter?'

Octavian spun, magic springing to his fingertips, ready to kill. But the voice belonged to one already dead.

The ghost of Miles Varick manifested a few feet away, pale and translucent, barely visible in the bright lights, like the ghost of a ghost.

'We should go home,' Miles said.

Octavian stared at him, heart breaking. Nikki was dead and his friends were all gone. Cortez was gone, as well, and he imagined Gaea had put a stop to the incursions in Europe and India just as she had done here. The hunt and the battle had both come to an abrupt end, but he felt frozen, unsure in which direction he ought to take his first step.

'Peter—' the ghost said again.

Octavian nodded. 'I agree,' he said, turning toward the dead man. 'I'm just not sure there's anywhere left for me to call "home".'

EPILOGUE

September 26

Brattleboro, Vermont

The sun shone brightly but the crisp autumn air brought a chill with every gust of wind. Children raced across the field toward the tractor that pulled the hayrides through Summerfields Orchard, laughing and bumping each other, all trying to be the first one on board. The smell of cider donuts baking filled the air, along with the rich, earthy aroma of crops ready for the harvest. Girls from the high school were face-painting to raise money for new cheerleader uniforms. On a small stage, a trio of scruffy twentysomething boys played folk music that came straight from their hearts.

Tori Osborne felt like crying inside.

People laughed and the tractor rumbled and a little girl cried, upset because her parents wouldn't buy the pumpkin she wanted. Tori walked past them all, waved to Jenny and Tom, who were working at the outside window where people were lined up to pay for their apples. She glanced over at the picnic area to her right, where families were spread out, enjoying the day. Just a handful of days until October arrived and they would have to start decorating for the haunted hayride, and Tom and Jenny would be out with Ed building the hay maze.

She wasn't in the mood for ghosts and goblins, but Cat had insisted that they had to give the customers what they wanted. If their seasonal regulars couldn't get what they wanted at Summerfields, they would go and become regulars somewhere else. Tori had tried to argue that the country – the world – had had their fill of the supernatural, but Cat felt strongly that people would find comfort in the make-believe haunts and frights, that they would want to go on pretending that there wasn't any real reason to be afraid of the dark, even though they all knew the truth.

'Hey, Tori!' called Becca Farley, a regular who'd dabbled in earthcraft but lost interest after a time.

Tori put on her best smile and waved back, trying to look busy and purposeful so Becca wouldn't take offense that she kept walking, turning left toward the entrance to the store. Customers sat on the stone wall in front, sipping coffee and guarding their purchases, in no hurry to lug their pumpkins and bags of apples and bottles of maple syrup across the street to the field that the orchard used as a parking lot.

She walked into the store, passing through the big double barn doors, and instantly she felt better. Exhaling, she took in her surroundings, and knew this was where she belonged. The two registers dinged and clanked off to her left, while to the right, down a short ramp, the cider donuts were being baked fresh and served up hot, almost faster than the bakers could get them out of the oil and sprinkle them with sugar and cinnamon.

Fruits and vegetables and homemade chicken pot pies and harvest-time arts and crafts and Halloween decorations were on display, and selling well.

They had reopened yesterday, a Friday, two days after Keomany had vanished from the orchard, leaving only a husk behind. Since that time, Tori had stayed shut up inside her house while Cat had come down here to the store to take charge of every aspect of the business. The orchard had loyal and hardworking employees, and Tori and Cat both knew how lucky they were, but in these past days it had been made clearer to them than ever. People had died here – not in the store, but on the property – but their employees had not only shown up for work, they had actively campaigned in town, letting friends and strangers know that Summerfields had endured a tragedy but was reopening for business and that its owners needed the community's support.

Tori looked around the inside of the store and felt herself genuinely smiling for the first time in days. They had needed the support, and they had gotten it. While she had sat in bed and watched CNN reporting from the sites of all four breaches, tallying the dead and interviewing mages, her wife and their friends and employees had gotten on with the business of life. While self-defined experts had blathered about demons and parallel realities and vanishing vampires and pondered whether or not the world was safer now or in more danger than ever, apples ripened and pumpkins fattened, and people came to buy them.

All over the world the dust settled and life went on, but in the aftermath of all that had happened during the equinox and afterward, Tori had felt as if she had been frozen in ice. Then, last night, Cat had snuggled up beside her in bed and told her to take her time, promised that she would take care of everything until Tori felt up to rejoining the rest of the world, and Tori had felt the ice melting.

This morning, things had felt different. Still, she had taken things slowly, but now – with the lunch hour approaching – she knew she was ready to dive back in. Questions still nagged her and the absence of friends haunted her, but she owed it to the living, herself included, to get on with her life.

Many voices and smiles greeted her as she walked through the store, searching for some way to be helpful. She made mental notes about some of the baked goods and an order she'd have to place with the woman who made the funny little holiday wall signs that sold so well, and then she turned and saw Amber Morrissey unpacking a crate of lettuce and putting it on display.

'Good morning,' Amber said.

'Hey,' Tori said, a bit shyly.

Amber had been staying with them, but even though the young woman had been in her house, they had barely spoken in that time. Cat had been playing hostess, and it was a role for which she was ill-suited.

'Listen,' Tori went on, 'I just want to thank you for sticking around and helping out.'

Amber gave a little nod, sad in spite of her smile. 'Happy to do it.'

The rest of it went unsaid, but just as Tori did not need to see Amber's true face to know it was hiding under there, she didn't need to hear the words to know they were there, just waiting. Amber wanted to go home to Massachusetts, but she had come to Brattleboro with the ghost of Miles Varick, her friend, and though she'd had no communication from him these past few days, she was hesitant to leave without him.

But she would, soon enough. Time would pass and it would seem awkward for her to be waiting, and she would go home.

Or perhaps not, Tori realized abruptly. Perhaps she would rather be where there were people who knew what she was and were not afraid of her. Though, if Tori were honest, she was a little afraid.

Tori started to move further into the store, but she paused when she saw the empty display case at the back with the sign still hanging above it that read *Sweet Somethings*. The chocolates had mostly been sold and others had been packed away and refrigerated. It was Keomany's little shop inside the larger store.

'What are you going to do about the space?' Amber asked.

'I don't know,' Tori replied. 'Whatever we do, I don't think it'll be candy. It would feel wrong. Disloyal.'

'I don't think Keomany would—'

Tori frowned. 'It isn't about what Keomany would think. It's about how Cat and I would—'

Almost as if summoned by the speaking of her name, Cat came rushing in, moving through the store at a pace just short of a run. A ponytailed soccer mom jumped out of her way and swore under her breath, but Cat did not even slow to apologize.

'Tori,' Cat said. 'Outside, now. You too, Amber.'

Cat took Tori's hand and led the way, weaving back through the displays without any apparent concern for the stares of staff and customers alike. Amber followed, asking questions every step, but Tori said nothing. She just followed her wife, knowing the look in her eyes all too intimately. Cat Hein was angry and afraid in equal measure, and the only thing that made her feel that way was the unknown. She didn't know what was going to happen next.

Together, the three women stormed out of the old, converted barn. Outside, Tori thought the scene seemed unchanged. A man on his cell phone was arguing with someone in a hushed voice, but other than that, all she saw were people drinking coffee and eating cider donuts and gathering up their purchases to head back to their cars.

Then Amber breathed a single word. 'Miles.'

Tori glanced up, even as Amber ran past her to meet a man almost no one else could see. An obese man with a walrus mustache wiped sugary fingers on his faded Harley Davidson t-shirt and turned to say something to a gray-haired woman beside him, and that was when Tori saw Peter Octavian striding toward them from a rental car he'd left parked in the road.

Octavian caught her eye but did not smile. He had lines on his face she had never seen before and was in desperate need of a shave. His sweater and jeans were both gray and rumpled.

'Where the hell have you been?' Cat said as he approached.

The people around them became spectators, and they watched as Octavian ignored her. He focused instead on Tori.

'Is she here?' Octavian asked, his voice grim and clipped.

For a moment, Tori was distracted by the sight of Amber standing beneath a tree by the road, chatting happily to thin air.

'Is—' she began.

'Keomany,' Octavian said, eyes alight with purpose. 'Is she *here*?'

'What? No.'

'We thought she was with you,' Cat said, standing beside and almost between them.

Octavian exhaled, deflating a little, and when he raised his eyes again Tori saw the pain in his gaze.

'She took them,' he said. 'All of them. Evil sons of bitches like Cortez and my friends, too, like there was no difference between one and the next.'

'The vampires,' Cat said.

'*Shadows*,' Octavian corrected. 'Kuromaku, Allison, and the others . . . they were Shadows. My people. My friends, and she put them in one Hell or another. They could be dead right now, or suffering, and I don't know how to reach them, how to get them back. So you tell me, right now . . .'

He turned to look at Cat, indigo light spilling from his eyes like flames.

'Where is she?'

Cat swallowed. 'We don't—'

'Don't lie to me!' Octavian shouted, raising his voice for the first time.

Birds burst from the trees and all of the voices around them fell silent. Tori blinked and looked around in horror to see that everyone had frozen in place, as if Octavian had stopped time for everyone except himself, Tori, Cat, and Amber, who now stared at him worriedly, whispering to a ghost.

'What did you do?' Tori asked, raising her own voice now.

'They'll be fine,' Octavian said. 'But I want the truth, Tori.'

'You've got it!' she snapped. 'Keomany never came back here. I know you don't trust Cat, but I've never given you reason not to trust me. I'm sorry about your friends, but that's got nothing to do with us. Keomany isn't here!'

He turned away, hanging his head, then looked up at the sky as if searching for answers.

'I don't know where else to look,' he said.

Grief radiated from the man. Tori reached out for him, but Cat caught her hand and pushed it back down by her side. Octavian did not see.

'What are you going to do?' Tori asked.

Octavian frowned thoughtfully. 'Only one thing *to* do. They're my friends. Wherever Keomany stranded them, I'm going after them.'

'But if she's really closed all of the breaches, sealed the world off from other . . . dimensions, or whatever,' Cat said, 'how are you going to get through?'

'There's a way,' Octavian said. 'There's got to be a way.'

Without another word, he turned and left them, striding back through the motionless crowd.

'Hold on,' Amber said as Octavian passed. 'Miles and I want to help. We'll come with you. Just let me get my bag.'

But Octavian walked by as if she, too, were a ghost. He climbed into the car he'd left at the roadside and slammed the door. The instant the engine growled to life, the paralysis broke around Tori and Cat and all of the customers were moving and talking again, some of them staring at the place Octavian had been, then glancing around as if he had simply vanished.

In a way, Tori thought, that was precisely what he had done.

She stood hand in hand with her wife and watched Octavian drive away, road dust swirling up behind the car as it went over a rise and disappeared. Amber stood silently with the ghost, staring after him, as if they thought Octavian might come back for them, but the car did not reappear.

Tori noticed that the trees that lined the road had seemed to bend slightly, as if they too were watching Octavian drive away, and were now upright again.

Just the wind, she told herself.

But the morning had brought only a light breeze, barely enough to loosen the autumn leaves from their branches. Frowning, she studied the trees again, but they did not move at all.

Just the wind, she thought again.

'You all right?' Cat asked.

'Yeah,' she said. 'I think I am.'

Tori turned to stare up into the branches of the nearest oak. Wondering.